the

Silent

Woman

the $\int$ilent Woman

a novel

SUSAN DODD

WILLIAM MORROW   75 YEARS OF PUBLISHING
An Imprint of HarperCollins*Publishers*

This is a work of fiction. Names, characters, places, and incidents either are the products of the author's imagination or are used fictitiously.

HarperCollins books may be purchased for educational, business, or sales promotional use. For information please write: Special Markets Department, HarperCollins Publishers Inc., 10 East 53rd Street, New York, NY 10022.

FIRST EDITION

Designed by Kelly S. Too

Printed on acid-free paper

Library of Congress Cataloging-in-Publication Data

Dodd, Susan M.
    The silent woman : a novel / Susan Dodd.—1st ed.
        p. cm.
    ISBN 0-688-17000-5
        1. Kokoschka, Oskar, 1886– —Fiction. 2. Dresden (Germany)—Fiction.
    3. Artists—Fiction. I. Title.

PS3554.O318 S55 2001
813'.54—dc21   00-067571

01 02 03 04 05   QW   10 9 8 7 6 5 4 3 2 1

For Gael Mooney, the painter

Satin and velvet, voile and silk: She led me to textile altars, taught me to worship lambent deities. Concealed in display, displayed in conspicuous concealment. By sunlight she draped herself in the wannest of pallors. She emerged after nightfall swathed in fever. I was driven to delirium by the heat and the hues and the nap of her.

I put on her skin.
I slept in her coat.
I never slept.
Almi my beautiful eye.

the

ilent

Woman

Prologue, 1914

Her summerhouse, displacing a grove of ancient trees, seized a spring-green meadow below a scallop of mountains. Semmering, though no great distance from Vienna, lay in another world. Crowing roosters nagged away darkness. The water tasted of iron.

The great composer had left his widow . . . far from *wealthy,* she bravely allowed, but well-fixed, yes. *Comfortable.*

Oskar Kokoschka could not imagine being comfortable anywhere Gustav Mahler's spirit loitered. But Alma Mahler, seven years older than Oskar, was terribly worldly and not easily cowed.

"This little house will be *ours.* Only ours." Alma nibbled her lover's paint-dappled fingers, licked a trace of gold dust from the pad of his thumb. "Our own little haven," she said.

Oskar imagined a cottage, perhaps three rooms, each so small that all day long he'd find himself gently bumping against her soft white shoulders.

The house was completed in late spring. Das Landhaus, Alma called it. Its eight rooms were high-ceilinged and broad. Plenty of room for the Maestro's looming shadow. From the day Oskar and Alma moved in, there was not the least ambiguity as to whom the villa, solely and in perpetuity, belonged. Although allotted a shelf in her wardrobe, he kept most of his things in a portmanteau just under the foot of the bed.

Semmering's vistas were wide and green and curvaceous. Alma rarely went outdoors. So fair a complexion . . . she lived in dread, she said, of the sun. She kept the tall windows closed for reasons varied and pressing: heat and chill, dampness and dust and privacy. Throughout that spring and summer, her pearly pallor shuttered, Alma ignored the looming slopes and devoted herself to the minutiae of decoration. The setting she contrived for herself was a concoction of leaves and flowers. Jeweled petals. Embroidered vines. The divan covered with velvet moss, the drapes a lichenous brocade. Her bower.

Oskar had hoped he might thrive in this new climate. Two years now he'd been with Alma, but ever a guest. Wary of overstaying his welcome, he lived on his toes. He'd painted too little, suffered too much. Her passion fed on torment.

And Vienna kept coming between them. The doors of her home on the Elisabethenstrasse opened too readily. Their happiest times had been traveling, the Dolomites and Naples, Holland and the Alps. But travel was, in every respect, costly. An artist needed to light somewhere, Oskar said. And love could sink deep roots in Semmering's rich earth. Well-grounded beside her, his gifts could fully bloom.

The idyll proved perishable. By the end of their first summer there Almi seemed always bent on urging him away: errands, obligations, needs. *Her needs.* She must rededicate herself to music, to poetry, to art . . . was it not sinful to waste one's gifts? The more prodigious the talents, the greater the offense to heaven.

But how was she to think, let alone *create,* Oskar hovering about with his hangdog expression, his hungry mouth? Another *child*! Worse than her little Gucki. Yet . . .

Love him? *Mein Gott,* she *adored* him!

Which was precisely the difficulty, of course. If only he could manage to occupy himself elsewhere for a day or two . . . for a single *afternoon,* there might be enough of her left to jot down the notes of *das Lied* that had been teasing her since early spring, waking her before dawn. Surely a man who truly *cared* for her would have noticed the lavender shadows about her eyes?

But then how to expect such alertness from someone who'd scarcely noticed a *war*? Franz Ferdinand assassinated in June . . . the calamity seemed by July to have slipped Oskar's mind. Quite oblivious, evidently, to a world falling apart. *Ein Mann, ein Mensch,* would be putting his affairs in order, making arrangements to join an honorable regiment . . . while *he* stood in a trance in the verdant drawing room, staring up at his half-finished fresco above the fireplace . . .

Was he *listening?*

The sweet white meat of her licked by flame and rising to be consumed by heaven, while in an inferno of serpents below he . . .

Hell was to live *without fire.* How, Oskar wondered, had it come to be thought the other way around? Did the error originate with Dante? Some prophet's poor sense of direction, perhaps?

On mild early-autumn days, Oskar stared at his tortured likeness writhing above the mantel, and his teeth chattered with hell's chill.

THE FIRST COLD OCTOBER MORNING, AFTER AN ESPECIALLY STINGING EX-change, Oskar did as Alma asked: he left. Let her face the first frost without him.

She watched him go without a kiss or tender word.

Reaching the road, Oskar forbade himself a backward glance. Keeping his eyes straight ahead, he pictured a crater behind him where the house had stood, a deep gash in the red earth surrounded by stumps of shattered trees.

For months his mother had been pestering him to return to Vienna. When Oskar finally got there, however, her welcome was tepid. Like Alma, Romana Kokoschka had much else on her mind. Her younger son, Bohuslav, had recently been conscripted, assigned to a battleship in the Adriatic. From the night of his bloody birth the boy was star-crossed. Now to his mother's dark Gypsy gaze he appeared doomed.

Oh, but wasn't she glad to have her Oskar home! Rousing herself, Romana shifted the weight of her fabulous terrors onto her eldest son's slumped shoulders. She whispered of fevers, of burial at sea. Soon she was cooking Oskar's favorite dishes, fretting over the cost of their ingredients while exacting a fluster of vows:

An immediate stop to the scandalous relationship with this shameless widow, too old for him anyway (not that she supposed he gave the least thought to providing grandchildren, carrying on his father's name! And did he really think shaving his head made him look *older?* A schoolboy with ringworm, more likely!) and dishonoring the great Maestro's mem-ory, the corpse still lukewarm . . . a stable, *respectable* livelihood before the entire family starved . . . and the safekeeping of his baby brother, he must do *something* (he knew so many important people) because if anything happened to her Bohuslav . . . not that she was suggesting Oskar himself should go off to fight . . . he must not even *think* of such a thing, because if any harm should come to *him* . . .

Ach, he had such fine silky hair.

Was he listening?

His second morning in Vienna, Oskar went to the railway station to arrange his return to Semmering. He knew if he went back too soon, Almi would still be angry. But if he stayed away much longer, he would die.

Slow, raucous lines blocked the ticket agents' windows. Oskar stood waiting patiently, wrapped in the memory of Almi's soft white arms and legs, breathing in the pollen of her bright hair. The world, all cold shoulders and sharp elbows, shouts and rank breath, pressed up against him. Pushing back, he folded himself deeper and tighter inside his adamant dream.

He could not get a seat on a train until the following day. The ticket's price was more than he could afford, its class better than he needed.

Given another day to endure in Vienna, Oskar thought he might pay a call on Adolf Loos. The architect, a friend and something of a patron, would understand the urgency of coming up with a little something to tide the family over before Oskar left. A small farewell supper this evening might even be proposed . . . Romana's heavy dishes, while bland, were hard to digest.

Daydreaming, Oskar wandered deeper inside the station. Beyond the waiting area, on a grid of greasy track beneath a sooty iron dome, an eastbound train was preparing to depart. All around him, swathed in steam, uniformed figures detached themselves from loving clutches. Girls wept and babies wailed. Beside stiff-backed fathers with downslanted eyes, mothers pieced together heroic smiles.

It was true, Oskar realized, he'd scarcely noticed the war. Now here it was staring him in the face. He tried to retreat to his dreamworld, but as often happened, Alma would not have him. *Ein Mann, ein Mensch,* would . . .

Oskar's orphaned attention sidled up to a pathetic little passion play nearby: a soldier bidding his wife farewell. The man, obviously drunk, looked too old to fight. His filthy breeches and disheveled tunic mocked the Empire. With elaborate buffoonery, the fellow bowed and bawled and blew kisses. His wife's smile was crimped. Her hollow cheeks looked blue in the depot's smirchy light.

Then the man, as if yanked taut by wires, came to a sudden standstill. Tears began to leak from the leathery corners of his eyes. "*Ach,* Irma," he said, stretching out his hands to her.

The woman threw back her head and filled the black iron bowl overhead with keening.

Oskar tried to turn away but found he could not. His eyes transfigured the soldier into a drawing. Oskar stared, stricken, at the charcoaled skull. His brother's gullibility abashed its grimace. His mother's terrors blackened its sockets and clefts.

Superstition was Oskar's birthright. It was not hard for him to believe that throwing himself into the war could keep Bohuslav alive, keep Romana's heart from breaking.

But neither his brother's life nor his mother's heart lured Oskar toward battle. Could he have risked his own life for those who loved him without reservation? He doubted it. Yet he was quite prepared to die for a woman whose love, if love at all, was only a whim, and occasional.

She is right, he thought. I am not a man.

Loos had, as usual, come through in fine fashion: a little celebratory supper for Oskar, a little nest egg for his mother; with letters of introduction to several high-ranking officers in the illustrious Fifteenth Imperial-Royal Regiment of Dragoons, a few little strings were pulled. "If you insist on going off to war," the architect said, "you must go in high style."

Soon it would all be arranged.

Oskar returned to Semmering in feverish high spirits. No doubt Almi was still furious with him for leaving. But her hot scoldings burned less than the hard freeze of her disdain. In any case, hearing of his imminent enlistment in the Empire's most prestigious cavalry regiment, she would soon be covering her lover's face with kisses.

Finding the mud-spattered motorcar parked beside the house was a most unpleasant surprise. Kammerer again!

The biologist's shiny suits reeked of formaldehyde; his beady beetle-browed gaze probed everything. He'd come barging in all summer with his murky glass tanks and scum-slick specimens. Soiling candlelit linen with his revolting dinner conversation, endless learned babble about mealworms and mantids.

Kammerer had an unfortunate tendency to repeat himself. On at least four occasions he'd described how the female praying mantis, in the afterglow of mating, ate the male. "I wish you could see it." He'd garnished each account with an insinuating wink in Oskar's direction. "A most cautionary spectacle, my boy!"

The biologist was particularly taken, that season, with the midwife toad. He was engaged in experiments involving the injection of India ink in its nuptial pads . . . something about altering its mating habits. Kammerer lectured obsessively on the species, as if to obscure the true genus of his obsession: his hostess.

"The female has merely to lay the eggs. Then it is all up to her . . . consort." Kammerer daintily patted his flabby lips with a damask napkin. "The poor fellow must then hop around dragging them from his hindquarters."

"How fascinating," said Alma without discernible irony.

"If not terribly appetizing," Oskar said.

"On the contrary." The biologist's eyes rolled down the slope of Alma's bosom. "The eggs are quite lovely. Like golden caviar." The wet tip of his brick-colored tongue flicked his mustache. A crumb vanished into his mouth.

How was it Alma, so easily irked with her lover, could show endless forbearance for such a tedious parasite?

"He is a brilliant scientist," she told Oskar. "We should be *honored* to contribute to his work."

"We contribute to his paunch," Oskar said. The man had an insatiable appetite, particularly for sweets. He chewed with his mouth open and smacked his lips. "Not to mention his erotic fantasies."

Alma managed to look both skeptical and delighted.

"He's waiting for you to devour me, you know." Laughing softly, Oskar traced her lower lip with a paint-flecked fingertip.

Alma smiled.

A blue forefinger slipped through the lapels of her pink dressing gown and found her nipple.

"He dreams of limping through life up to his knees in your 'golden caviar.' "

She pushed Oskar's hand away. He was *jealous*? Of Paul Kammerer? Alma adored it when Oskar was jealous, but really, my darling . . .

Besides, the professor was, as everyone knew, *married*.

"You might remind *him* of that inconvenient fact!"

She pretended not to hear him.

Now, apart from a flurry of letters (addressed solely to Alma, of course, as if Oskar were not even there), Professor Kammerer had been blessedly absent from Semmering for a month. The university term had begun, causing Oskar to hope the biologist's amorous attentions were back where they belonged, with reptiles or something.

Now Kammerer had returned like some persistent plague . . . surely Alma couldn't have known he'd be coming?

The front door was bolted. Well, a sensible precaution for a solitary woman in the country . . . and who, after all, had left her there alone?

It appeared, however, that Alma was not alone.

Oskar knocked, then waited several moments. To call out would be undignified. He knocked again, bruising his knuckles. He *lived* here. Why had he never been given a key?

After a few minutes, Oskar walked around the side of the house to the garden. Warm weather had returned while he was gone, whipping the late lilies into a frenzy. No one had watered them. No one was there.

Perhaps they'd gone off for a walk. Kammerer had a knack for coaxing Almi out into the sunlight. And ever since he'd made Gucki an aquarium, the child showed an unfortunate enthusiasm for helping the biologist lure his slimy little prisoners into captivity.

Ah, but Gucki was spending the week in Vienna with her grandparents, wasn't she? The Molls would then deposit her at a boarding school in Lucerne.

What, Oskar wondered, had become of the village lad Alma had hired to look after the garden?

The french doors at the back of the drawing room were unlatched. How like her precautions to be random! Oskar stepped inside, pausing on the threshold to listen. Outside birds sang in the thinning trees. Within the house, all was quiet.

Shutting the door behind him, Oskar turned and surveyed the room. Yes, her bower, he thought. Her lair. Ravenous palms and ferns lurked in the corners. The watered-silk walls looked jaded.

The room had a peculiar odor, not strong, but unpleasant. Closing his eyes, Oskar pictured a stagnant pond, the underside of a rotting log slick with leeches. When he opened his eyes again, he had the sickening sensation that the floor was moving under his feet.

Six large glass cubes lay on the floor across the room, near the windows. Kammerer's tanks. Light falling through the shutters lashed the greenish, cloudy glass. Five of the tanks had tipped over, and looked empty. The sixth remained upright. Behind its murky facade, frantic shadows seemed to leap up and lick its rim like small dark flames.

How could he have imagined quiet? The house was astir with small sounds, furtive and frenzied.

Oskar stepped toward the tanks. Something soft twitched under the thin sole of his boot. He looked down. Watery red streaks bled out from his toe. The red looked heinous among the formal gold and green and ivory elaborations of the patterned rug.

He could not bring himself to lift his foot to see what his boot had crushed. Oskar heard a deep groan somewhere deep inside the house. Then he became aware of a rhythmic creaking. He raised his eyes to the ceiling. The creaking grew faster. Shuddering, Oskar wrenched his gaze back down and looked at the floor.

All around him the carpet pulsated and writhed.

Tiny claws skittered under his trouser cuff, tearing at his shin.

His skin prickled. He could not move. "Almi?" His voice was tremulous and thin.

The claws dragged something up his leg, something cold and slick and wet as a well's innards.

The creaking quickened.

The claws mounted his knee and moved inward, claiming his thigh.

Oskar's hands covered his groin.

The carpet danced and slithered. The ceiling creaked and moaned.

Through the coarse weft of his woolen trousers, the collop of warm flesh felt pulpy and frangible in his cupped hand.

Ein Mann, ein Mensch, would . . .

Behind him, in the nearly finished fresco above the ornate mantel, a figure roped in bright snakes threw back its head and wailed.

Falling to his knees among the mating toads, Oskar vomited on the carpet's bruised petals and twisted vines.

1

He arrived empty-handed. A refugee. Dispossessed. The war went on without him. The war would never end.

He was tall, but stooped, and thin. His pale quicksilver eyes were set deep in tarnished sockets. He shaved his head, now and then, like a convict.

A sanatorium had first drawn him to Dresden. Its exceptional costliness attested, he thought, to its curative powers. But Oskar's sojourn in Dr. Teuscher's airy rooms (and cramped closets) in the Weisser Hirsch district had remedied little, apart from opening a few doors.

Still, Dresden in 1916 had been less crippled by war than Berlin, less mendacious than Vienna. Worse spots for a young artist to set up camp . . . a climate salutary for his prospects, if not for his health. New alliances were formed, more doors flung open. A position, soon enough, was promised.

Oskar Kokoschka was not without friends.

THE SPRING OF 1918: WAR, EPIDEMIC, STARVATION. FOOD RATIONING, HOStility from as far away as China, and Klimt as cold in his grave as Mata Hari. The world, like Oskar's heart, lay in ruins. The monarchy was finished. Who was going to *take charge* when things settled down?

Oskar's teaching duties at Dresden's art academy would not commence for several months. "Give yourself time to . . . habituate." His
host, Hans Posse, was the most considerate of men. "My friend, you
have been through a great deal."

Oskar was, for a moment, at a loss. It was not unusual that a war, a
near-fatal head wound, the assault of deadly gases upon lung and nerve,
should slip his mind. He simply wondered how Dr. Posse could detect
a broken heart.

The two men paused in their stroll on the edge of a pond. It was early
May. The trees' new leaves looked carved of jade. A fat speckled duck
skidded past on absinthe water. Six ducklings paddled in her wake, frantic to keep up. Hans Posse smiled. The mother scarcely seemed to notice the stir behind her. Neither did Oskar. The older man touched the
young painter's elbow. The two men resumed walking, skirting the
pond's rim of wracked stone.

A widower of fifty-six, Posse was Director of the Gemäldegalerie,
Dresden's haughty art museum. Not only had he been instrumental in
arranging Oskar's appointment as a professor at the Kunstakademie, he
had offered as well room and board in his own home. Indeed, he had
virtually insisted.

"Until your salary begins, I'd hardly expect . . ." Posse delicately
looked off into the distance, where the upper edge of the Zwinger's Wall
Pavilion made a fanciful doodle against a faded blue sky. "I began as a
painter myself. Did you know that? Never mind. It's best forgotten."
The Direktor smiled. "I remember the struggle, though, to make ends
meet. If the figure we discussed is too much . . ."

Oskar, had he been paying attention, might have laughed. *Too much?*
The home whose ornately carved doors were being thrown open to him
was a Baroque paradise, one of eight villas stretched out on sunny lawns
surrounding the Zwinger Palace. The figure Dr. Posse had, when
pressed, proposed for weekly room and board might buy a bun and coffee in Berlin.

And even less in Stockholm, where Oskar had squandered most of
his mustering-out monies the previous year. The principal beneficiary
had been a widowed baroness, a woman with refined tastes, a profligate
bosom, and marriage uppermost on her mind. A marvelous woman,
Karin. If only she hadn't demanded the whole heart Oskar no longer
possessed. Certainly she had helped to restore him in the aftermath of

his hideous sojourn in Uppsala, Professor Baranyi's harrowing and futile treatments there. Shell shock seemed an affliction more persistent than most. Hardly surprising that it resisted Baranyi's mad methods: the spinning chair, the weights that were supposed to coax the brain into salutary spasms. Good God! No wonder shell shock's symptoms had seemed, for a time, more pervious to the Baroness's tender ministrations. Now Oskar's small cache of savings was gone, frittered away on rare orchids, rich meals and heady wines that had, in the end, neither satiated the famished Baroness nor restored his own appetites.

So Dresden, this smug little woodcut of a city, was to be his sanctuary and his penance. Never mind that his cell appeared more regal than monastic. Oskar calculated its nominal charge as Posse's discreet nod to a struggling artist's pride. His benefactor was a man of true civility. And not without experience.

OSKAR KOKOSCHKA WAS BEING ADDED TO A MÉNAGE SEVERELY DIMINished. Frau Posse had died some years earlier of pernicious anemia, leaving no children for the consolation and care of her spouse. Her older sister, who had promptly stepped in to keep house for the widower, had recently departed, a look of bitter disappointment about her. Hans Posse was further burdened by the care of his ancient father, a retired army general whose wandering mind did not for a moment relax his exacting standards. Now the two Posse men, one bereft, the other bedridden and incontinent, were left to fend for themselves.

A young maid had been imported without fuss from the country. "A slight little thing," Posse observed. "But you'll find our Hulda's willingness robust. Saxon, you know." He smiled. "I've every intention of hiring a housekeeper. The girl will need supervision. Still, one is reluctant . . . a household's equilibrium is an impish thing."

Posse quickly glanced away. Oskar watched a dull red flush rise from his host's thin neck to his sharp cheekbones.

"I hope my own weight won't—"

"These stuffy rooms will be set right by your vitality," Posse said. "But you may find our small *Haushalt* disheveled. Things have grown shabby with my dawdling." He winced. "It can be difficult, dislodging a woman once she's taken charge of a house."

Herr Direktor's tenor was ironic, the leeriness behind it seemed utterly grave. So amiable a man likely knew the idle exhaustion of trying to please a woman. Only natural, Oskar thought, preferring truant housekeeping to domestic tyranny.

"I myself relish a life without . . . undue interference," Oskar said. "I take no exception to dust and irregular hours."

Hans Posse plucked at a loose thread on his moleskin jacket. A chipped button dropped to the shaggy lawn at his feet. He and Oskar both smiled.

"Perhaps I should hire a man for the gardens," Posse mused. "Let things indoors drift along for a time . . ."

"Not being a man of property, I can't presume to advise you." Oskar stooped to retrieve the button and dropped it into his host's hand. "Still, it sounds a sensible economy, investing in perennial flowerings, the constancy of trees."

"The girl will see us properly fed, at least. I can promise that much."

Dr. Posse studied the horn button in the palm of his hand. "What useful purpose . . ." he murmured. "On a sleeve?" He passed the button back to Oskar, who, with an extravagant arch of arm, tossed it into the brambled border of the woods.

Relic of some stag, the artist thought, trimmed or slaughtered for the sake of fashion. Returned now to its given ground. He and Hans Posse were both, for the moment, smiling.

HE HAD BARELY STOPPED THINKING OF HIMSELF AS A BOY WHEN SHE'D come along to unman him. A stripling, green and easily bent. She howled and battered about him like a gale. Had he not been thinking like a lad, he'd never have jumped into the war as if it were a game, never have imagined battle as the means of burnishing him. Fleshing him out.

Oskar had not yet begun to recognize the enemy. After all, he was an artist, a *prodigy*. He had trusted imagination as his most loyal and powerful ally.

While *she* . . . oh, his Almi had negotiated a pact with passion! Unimaginable passion in league with lies and unscrupulous selfishness. A *man* would never have capitulated. Oskar, all pliancy and innocence, had ceded his very soul to her. She occupied him. He yielded everything.

Alma's betrayal with Kammerer—a *dalliance,* she said—had left Oskar too distraught to notice Gropius. Her penitent tears were gorgeous. They glittered like diamonds on her cheeks. Then there was Oskar's enlistment to arouse her. She sent him off in a daze of exhaustion.

By the time Oskar was mortally wounded, Alma was already carrying the architect's child . . . was married before he could leave the hospital at Brünn.

Three years gone by, nearly three years, and still Oskar's traitorous imagination refuses to disclose how, still in her possession, he can go on living without her. Sometimes he suspects captivity to the past may be his saving grace. His sense of the present is clouded, his regard for the future dim. Alma took what remained of his life when she abandoned him, leaving only the litter of a used-up past. These dry morsels keep Oskar alive. He chews and sucks on them, grinding his teeth when he sleeps.

Perhaps in Dresden he will sleep better.

Oskar almost never sleeps.

TWO YEARS EARLIER, HE HAD FIRST LIMPED INTO THE CITY, CRADLING HIS wounds and dragging the war behind him. The largesse of Dresden's culture, its order and scale and hospitality, had struck him as the perfect climate for convalescence. Oskar believed he had stumbled upon paradise.

Now that he's come to inhabit it, however, Dresden does not appeal to him. There is something provincial about the city, a self-consciousness that betrays itself by leaving too little to chance. Obligatory gardens bloom everywhere, stunted, ruly, and pale. The architectural muddle of Renaissance and Baroque seems a particularly infelicitous miscegenation. A dowager wearing too much jewelry to deflect attention from a shabby frock.

The city's name, Dr. Posse has mentioned, derives from an ancient Slavic dialect: "people of the forest." Little sign now of simple folk along this sinuous stretch of the Elbe. Centuries of despotic bishops and warmongering emperors had seen to that. Each hill within sight is crested with a castle, each castle ringed with a moat. Remaining swatches of woodland have been tamed into public service—*parks,* the very idea! As if Nature were mere human invention. The Grosser Garten tarted up with trains going nowhere and a palace nobody lived in . . .

Ditches, scooped out by charlatans, posing as lakes . . .

The so-called zoo an impoundment of gorgeous exotics wasting away in exile, and all for the amusement of spoiled children . . .

No, the city does not appeal to him. Dresden's one great virtue is its being neither Vienna nor Berlin. Irritably, Oskar investigates its avenues, looking down his nose at its monuments. Even its back alleys are tidy. Such oppressive neatness makes him want to weep.

Shunning the overcivilized avenues, Oskar eventually begins to etch his own path along the river's edge. There, for an hour each morning and evening, he can forget his whereabouts, indulge in the luxury of imagining himself somewhere else.

Dresden, his sanctuary and his penance . . .

The Elbe, swollen with spring's rains, has an unbecoming mossy look. Oskar, merging with trees' shadows, entwined in brush, spies on the river. Almost against his will, he finds himself studying the bickering views of Dresden that float on its swardy surface. The river blunts razored rooflines and cusped turrets. It cuts the city down to size for him, deflates its pretensions, loosens its stays.

Bit by bit, Oskar's mind's eye begins to assemble its own city, a benign landscape he might be pleased to occupy . . . should he ever awake from the nightmare he presently inhabits.

A GREEN BOTTLE, ITS NECK SHATTERED, LEANED AT A ROGUISH ANGLE against the churchyard's chinky stone wall. Dresden is growing slipshod, the Direktor thought.

Hans Posse had always adored the city's tidy disposition, its anomalous harmony a bargain struck between order and frivolity. The Empire lay now in shards. Dresden denied, after centuries, its status as Residenzstadt. Already the sumptuous structures that had for centuries housed a court were beginning to look ridiculous. The unfortunate war would soon be over, the only possible victory for Germans the grace with which they acclimated to defeat. The new regime had to come. Posse accepted all that. Yet how he dreaded the muss and tumult he knew must accompany it.

Thank God his father, *der General,* was no longer likely to notice the Visigoths milling ever nearer the city's gates. The monarchy's demise was one of a number of things best kept from the old man. How easily so brittle a heart might break.

The emancipation of dissonance. Posse had stumbled across the phrase just recently, but where? Something about music . . . yes, this iconoclastic Viennese composer Schoenberg with his so-called *Manual of Harmony.* Fresh upstart taking on the obstreperous business of shattering a tonal system that had been sufficient to Beethoven's purposes . . .

Well, the results were said to be interesting, if one cared to believe Berlin. Shock was rarely without interest, of course. And despite his early abdication of the creative life, a life lived among artists had certainly softened Posse's sympathies to art's inevitable little assaults on the sacred. Still, something in his heart wished to object, to claim that setting loose the forces of dissonance was a lesser feat than containing clamor . . .

Ach, I am petrifying, Herr Direktor thought. Amazing the indictment should less bother than please him. Any day now he would be an elder, his full majority forestalled only by the stubborn pump of the old heart upstairs. *Mein Vater.* Thank Gott for the restless pacings of young Kokoschka, another of cacophony's champions, guarding the lower floors from complacency. It was good to have him in the house.

HE WAS NOT WITHOUT FRIENDS.

Fräulein Käthe Richter, of course, had preferred to think they could be more . . . sweet Katja, with her improvident blood and lavish heart. Oskar hadn't liked to say no to her. Nor *had* he, not at first, though knowing he should.

Odd and downright vexing, finding himself demoted now back to chum. Sometimes Oskar's hands forgot, drawn toward a taut nipple's press to the thin silk of her mannish shirt when he merely meant to help his friend on with her coat. But Katja didn't mind. No, she rather liked it when Oskar's abstemiousness escaped him. Alone with him, she'd pose and pout and tweak. Her hands, under half-moon café tables, often strayed toward his lap. In company, however, she'd relish ignoring him at every chance. Her citrine eyes would shower their sparks on other men.

This week it was poor Ernst smoldering with her attention, decorous Ernst who in two months' time was due, at last, to marry the money and position his future hinged on. Without substantial backing, one could hardly take up the enterprise of publishing fine-art books. Käthe seemed bent on the sabotage of respectability.

"You are misbehaving," Oskar told her. "Rather outrageously, even for you."

His brief appearance in the role of stern and sensible uncle drew peals of laughter. Acting was Käthe Richter's craft, not his. She threw back her head as if spotlights hovered to brighten her eyes, a balcony to applaud her levity. Conversation was suspended midsentence at several nearby tables. His Katja knew how to capture an audience.

"Darling," she said, "you're jealous."

Her low-cut Gypsy blouse was the color of emeralds. She leaned toward him, calculating to the centimeter his view of her bosom's upper scarp.

Pale and firm as ivory, Alma's monumental breast . . .

Käthe's bosom, small and soft, seemed in a perpetual flush. Oskar's hands yearned to reach across the table, scoop Katja's breasts from their green satin hammock. Closing his eyes, he saw how they'd spill out onto the tablecloth. Settling slowly beside a plate of iced cakes, they would quiver like blancmange.

"Jealous? Perhaps I am." How could he keep from smiling? "But our Ernst's are the prospects your little *Liebschaft* hazards, not mine."

The slope of her smile steepened with delight.

"You might try at least to *look* abashed."

"Really?" Katja leaned farther across the table. "Would an abject expression suit me, do you think?"

"Probably not." Oskar pinched a shred of coconut from a powder puff of pastry. *Unverbesserlich,* his friend . . . incorrigible.

"Ernst needs to learn how to loosen his cravat," Katja said. "I'm helping him."

"Ernst needs to button himself into the vest of propriety," said Oskar. "Though I can think of several other gentlemen of our acquaintance who might benefit from your lessons in . . . dishabille."

"Let me borrow one of those drawing pencils of yours," Käthe said. "I must jot down your list, check it against my own."

They both laughed. Then Katja, sighing, leaned back in her chair. "You will come to the opening with me, won't you?"

Oskar was staring across the café at a woman in a gold velvet hat. The hat resembled one Almi had worn in Italy. Her face a priceless pearl in the bonnet's ornate setting. This Dresden hausfrau, florid and coarse, in such a hat . . . how dare she?

"Ernst is hoping I'll ask *him,* of course," Katja said.

"I'm sorry?" said Oskar.

"To escort me." His chum was losing patience with him. "These extraordinary doll-like figures . . . does this sound the least bit familiar, Oskar? I've been telling you for weeks now about this woman from Stuttgart."

"I'm sure the exhibit will be . . . captivating." The woman in the hat had faded eyes. Her cheeks looked pinched and doughy. "I'm simply not fit company," Oskar said.

"True enough." Katja waited for him to look at her. "All the more reason for you to be grateful . . . how many women could endure you?"

"What is her name?" Oskar asked absently.

Katja turned around, craning her neck. "That woman in the dreadful hat?"

"The artist . . . a Stuttgart dollmaker, you said?"

"Only because . . . whatever else might one call her? Papa says we must try to make her sound respectable. They're terribly erotic, these creations of hers. We don't want to keep decent people away."

"If it's *decent* people you're recruiting . . ."

Käthe smiled. "And, for a bit of variety, *you.*"

"I can't give my word," Oskar said.

"As if it meant anything these days." She plucked a candied cherry from a macaroon's peak and popped it into her mouth. "You'll try?"

"You'd be better off without me," Oskar said.

"Mama's dressmaker is making me a jacket for the opening, a little bolero sort of thing. Red linen." Käthe smacked her lips. "I am delectable in red, Ernst says."

"Perhaps you'll sit for me," Oskar replied absently. "A red bolero . . ." His eyes grew hazy.

He would not, for the foreseeable future, paint.

Across the noisy café the dough-faced woman noticed him staring. She slanted her face away. The hat was nothing like Almi's, nothing at all.

"But darling, I nearly forgot!" Katja sounded breathless again. "What was I thinking of?"

"I dare not imagine," Oskar said.

"Don't be mean. You'll find this delicious."

Looking into her eyes, Oskar slowly ran the tip of his tongue around his lips. *An incomparable instrument, his tongue.* He wondered if Katja recalled telling him that. "Give me a taste, then," he said. "Don't tantalize."

"Can I help it?" Katja laughed. "But listen. This Fräulein Moos—"

"Fräulein who?"

"The dollmaker," Katja said. "She of the gloriously lurid fantasies? Someone told Papa—I can't swear it is true—that she once made gowns for your late beloved."

Oskar's smile turned brittle. "For—?"

Katja nodded. "The legendary Alma," she said.

"You are not amusing."

"Not at the moment, no." Katja's voice turned cool.

Oskar's was cooler. "Spiteful lies are hardly the means to my attention," he said.

"I don't know," said Katja. "Frau Mahler . . . excuse me, Frau *Gropius,* isn't it? Your seraphic Alma seems to have done rather well with lies, where your dubious attention is concerned."

"We'd best end this discussion." Oskar pushed back his chair.

Katja reached out and touched his sleeve. "It isn't a joke," she said. "Someone reported it to Papa."

"Almi's dressmaker." A sheen of sweat broke out on Oskar's chalky forehead.

"A rumor," Katja said. "But I knew it would interest you."

She should not have mentioned it. Oskar looked truly ill. She doubted there was anything to it, at any rate. What use could a Viennese lady of fashion have had for a Stuttgart seamstress?

Käthe Richter reached over and blotted Oskar's brow with her napkin. "Never mind, *Liebchen,*" she said.

Oskar looked at her with dazed and wounded eyes. He hardly seemed to remember her.

Katja now felt reasonably certain, however, that the opening at her father's gallery the following week would not slip Oskar's mind.

DOLLS? HARDLY THE PROPER TERM FOR SOMETHING SO . . . PROFANE. THE figures were unsettling. They were altogether astonishing.

Oskar had come to the opening early, intending to excuse himself be-

fore too many others arrived. Now, hours later, he lingere
gallery's smallest room. It was nearly an hour past the app
time. In the front gallery, Herr Richter and two young a
tidying up after departing guests, collecting champagne flu..., gathering
nosegays of soiled napkins. Oskar wondered if anyone realized he was
still there.

Attendance at the opening had been sparse. The cusp of summer was
not art's best season, Herr Richter allowed. Those with deep pockets
were already packing for the mountains, draping their heirloom furniture with bedsheets.

Even Katja was absent. A fortuitous late-spring cold had sequestered
her at home. Oskar muttered a blasphemous Deo gratias for his friend's
weak chest. A roomful of delicate and gorgeous obscenity, all wrought
by hands that had perhaps taken measure of Alma's flesh . . . encountering this intimacy in the presence of a few strangers had been excruciating. Doing so before eyes that saw into him as Katja's did . . . well, that
would have been unendurable.

The figures, formed of wax, shone gold. They might, for their glow,
have been lit from within. Even the largest were no bigger than the ca-
puchin monkeys caged in the Grosser Garten. Nor, the disposition of
their limbs suggested, would they prove less limber or lewd.

Oskar wanted nothing so much as to be alone with them, these two
dozen or so miniature females. He knew them as both offspring and the
utter fulfillment of basest desire. From within his soul's deepest ambush,
what Oskar spotted in the stunted sybarites was himself.

But how could she know . . . who *was* this Fräulein Moos? And
where on earth was she?

Dolls, sculptures, totems . . . no word in any language Oskar knew
could name or describe the figures displayed before him. Still, it seemed
essential to call them *something,* even if the chosen term never traveled
beyond his own mind. Icons, perhaps? The figures did suggest a sacred
derivation, the intention of a worship both formal and arcane. But using
a religious reference to summon up these profane . . . oh, what name to
give? Some manner of his soul's address for these improbably lifelike
creatures with whom his deepest being was already engaged in passionate discourse . . . with whom he was, to tell the truth, altogether fiercely
in love.

Ikone might invoke sacrilege. What esoteric religion's art would ountenance splay-legged goddesses with jeweled labia? Deities lent flesh were bound to make awful trouble—what was mythology, after all, if not the ages' proof of that?

Oskar studied the figures. I will not speak of them, he decided. What need? But of course there was. Great need. His head roared with cries and songs, all he had to say of them. What might the artist herself have called them? He was desperate to know.

He settled, finally, on *Fetisch*. Less risky to imply magic and superstition, surely, than to swipe vocabulary from even the most dubious heaven. Fetish would have to do.

One figure in particular held Oskar in thrall. All sense of time and place deserted him as he studied her. She was the least naked of the group, most of her body covered by a sort of surplice. The lace garment, heavily beaded, disguised her opulent contours, yet amply suggested them. A thorny vine of rose gold snaked out through the lace where the pubis would be. It seemed to be growing toward him, bent on entwining him. Just as the two enameled and jeweled rosebuds crowning her breasts appeared about to burst with the heat of his enraptured gaze. Her lips were parted, revealing the head of a serpent where her tongue should have been. The serpent had sapphire eyes.

She knew Alma. That was confirmed for him now. The woman from Stuttgart knew Alma intimately. Oskar's breath raced. Blood drummed in his ears. How could something inanimate produce such salacious energy? Simply to look upon the miniature women, unmoving inside their stodgy cabinets of mahogany and glass, seemed both to contaminate and to sate him. He was frantic to learn their secret. Even his Almi . . .

Never had Oskar looked upon such prurience.

Never had he been so helplessly seduced.

The room filled with the scent of her. Oskar sank down into it, smothered, lost . . .

Almi, my beautiful eye.

IT WAS SHE—NEVER MIND THE FALSENESS OF HER TONGUE—WHO HAD tutored him in true grief. Years later, in a world shrunken and shattered, as Oskar tosses on a hard and narrow borrowed bed, she yet provides accompaniment to his fitful sleep. Remembered lies, melodious and pitch-perfect, rouse him, the prelude to dawn.

She was still growing into widowhood when they first met. It was a misty mid-April evening, Vienna cold-shouldering her way through the usual springtime snit. Oskar, more or less cornered, had accepted an invitation to dine at the home of the artist Carl Moll.

Moll's spacious house in the fashionable Hohe Warte district was laughably bourgeois. Oskar kept feeling the corners of his mouth twitch as the drawing room's prizes, both artistic and social, were flaunted before him.

Moll's portrayal of the Bohemian was . . . strenuous. The man put too fine a point on his eccentricities, favoring paint-daubed cravats and striped waistcoats ill-suited to his banker's demeanor. Moll tended to smudge the line between politics and art. Still, his artistic enthusiasms had been known to pry open purses, his own and those of well-fixed friends. Carl Moll had a good many friends.

Anyway, the patron Moll was vastly superior to the painter he claimed to be. His art was proficient, derivative and dull. I must have been hungry when the invitation was extended, Oskar thought. What else could have possessed me to accept?

Oskar was largely motivated at the time by hunger. The year was 1912. He had just turned twenty-six. A little old, perhaps, to keep playing the enfant terrible. But how to give up a role so suitable, so cozy? Besides, Egon Schiele, the Expressionist painter with whom he shared the part, was already thirty, wasn't he? And in jail at the moment, for his . . . fondness for children. What was Vienna to do for a whipping boy now?

Oskar, for once, was simply in the right place at the right time. It was the harshest of winters. The guardians of Viennese culture, complaining of chilblains and seeking new sport that would not be too arduous, set their cold collective heart on teaching cheeky Kokoschka a lesson.

He'd hoped his lecture ("On the Consciousness of Visions"—even its billing somewhat tongue-in-cheek) might cause a little commotion. Vienna needed a bonfire to warm up January. So he'd simply struck a match. Now, in a cold spring, Oskar's dismissal from the Schwarzwald School appeared imminent. He stood accused of creating "noisy demonstrations" at the Academic Society of Literature and Music. If indeed he'd done any such thing, were thanks not due? The least variation in Vienna's triple-time monotony should have been welcome, he thought.

He wished he could recall just what he'd said to raise such a fuss. That art's purpose is the revelation of private visions, that the same

visions tend to recur in varied form throughout the artist's lifetime . . .
what threat to civilization in that? There was, of course, the audience,
a field richly sown with friends . . . was their rambunctiousness *his*
fault?

A few stiff boards had taken exception to the poster, naturally. His
self-portrait, a death's-head pointing to a wound in its side, was nothing
new. Karl Kraus's fledgling magazine, *Der Sturm,* had already used a
slightly different version in Berlin. But Berlin's irony was, it seemed, Vienna's blasphemy . . . Oskar supposed he should have expected as much.

Twenty-six years old and already celebrated in Berlin, Munich—all
over Germany, in fact. Not to mention considerable notice in Budapest
and what passed, in stodgy Switzerland, for an art world . . .

Meanwhile, in his native territory, a hand-to-mouth subsistence . . .
borrowed time and charity suppers. Still, the role of outcast rather became him, Oskar liked to think.

Moll was, at heart, a bluff and good-natured soul. He'd simply dined
out too long on his ties to Klimt and the Secession, didn't know when to
take the hint, change the subject. Klimt's precious gold-leafed elegance
had begun to look more like the jeweler's profitable craft than true art.
Yet here was old Carl Moll, second-rate painter and first-rate bore, posturing in what he took for a libertine vanguard. The prospect of an
evening with him and his pretentious, homely wife had started Oskar
yawning at noon.

He'd forgotten, however—Oskar's usual disinclination for sorting
out the social connections so vital in Vienna—the single exotic bloom on
Carl Moll's hybrid family tree: his stepdaughter, Alma, was Gustav
Mahler's widow. So young at thirty-two for such a role, and a legendary
beauty in the bargain, to hear Vienna's verdict. The lady in question was
a local product, of course.

The Maestro had died the previous May, his heart holding out just
long enough to bring him back home from an ill-advised (if highly paid)
sabbatical in America. The Metropolitan's tedious machinations had
taken their toll. But the New York Philharmonic, Vienna claimed, was
Mahler's final undoing. Keeping possession of the podium while the
Americans brutalized Schumann's *Manfred* had shattered the Maestro's
heart beyond repair.

There were also, of course, those who insisted the great man's demise
had more to do with a passionate young wife than with New York's gasp-

ing oboes and quavering strings. Such tales naturally grew like morels in the Vienna Woods.

ONE LOOK AT THE YOUTHFUL WIDOW'S SENSUAL AND HAUGHTY FACE SET Oskar speculating that Vienna's roving gossip circus might, for once, have staked its tent on truth. Such accidents were possible, if rare. The woman did look a grave risk for the faint-of-heart.

She made an incomparably charming widow, Frau Mahler. Black suited her. As did histrionics. The grand scale of her performance of mourning might, in memory of a lesser man, have seemed unconvincing, even uncouth. But the stern and noble profile behind her was the Maestro's. One could envision a benign smile bestowed from on high upon the widow's stylized grief. To imagine a smile cracking Mahler's face was somehow easier, now that he was dead.

Oskar, no stranger to staged drama, appreciated the brash artfulness in Alma Mahler's pose. A corona of gaslight rays from a serpentine brass chandelier haloed her head. A fan of peacock feathers, anchored in a majolica urn, preened with mythic nuance at her back. I shall paint her as Juno, Oskar thought, then quickly discarded the notion. The widow Mahler was Aphrodite. Any other goddess would be absurd.

Draped black velvet made much of her bosom, daring to bare incomparably white shoulders. Her mouth had, for the required period of mourning, renounced smiles. Nothing, however, could shroud the gaiety native to her blue eyes. Staring, Oskar struggled to name the hue of her hair, previously encountered only in a paint tube . . . *Titian,* yes. Had he once dismissed the shade as too rich for nature's practical palette?

What Oskar grasped above all, however, this first instant in her presence, was Alma Mahler's genius for proportion. It was said of her that when standing beside the Maestro, she had known how to diminish her own rather imposing frame, increasing the puny conductor's stature in a way that flattered them both.

Now, in Anna and Carl Moll's overwrought drawing room, the widow displayed herself in a perfect ratio of pathos and pluck. The plumpness of the hassock whose edge she occupied lent a becoming touch of frailty. The red brocade upholstery, its skirt of gold silk fringe, turned tawdry and tarnished against her widow's weeds. Alma Mahler, in the face of loss and tastelessness, bore up bravely. Oskar sensed in her the true artist's ruthlessness in exploiting contrast.

Frau Moll presented him to her daughter as if enacting a sacred rite. Was he expected to kneel? Shocking, Oskar thought, that so graceless a creature as the bovine Frau Moll could have given birth to perfection . . . but then hadn't Aphrodite sprung, fully formed, from Jupiter's brow? (Or was it Athena? Love, wisdom . . . Oskar wondered if he would ever learn to keep the two straight.)

"Herr Kokoschka?" Alma Schindler Mahler was offering her hand.

Oskar took it. Her hand was dainty and pale. Against it, his own was a village lad's, coarse and ungainly and red. I shall, in my way, suit her, he thought.

Anna Moll, having swiftly dispensed with obligatory florid reference to the late Maestro, proceeded to extol her daughter's own singular gifts. "Zemlinsky's prize pupil," Frau Moll was saying. "Hardly more than a child, yet her touch on the keyboard . . . well, we didn't need a Zemlinsky to tell us our roof sheltered a prodigy!"

The widow Mahler's chilly hand seemed disinclined to remove itself from his. Oskar began to tremble. He wondered if she sensed it.

"And already she has composed . . . how many, *Liebchen*? At least fifty lieder by now, I should think . . ."

It was said that the gnomelike Zemlinsky—Schoenberg's teacher and something of a genius, or so Brahms had thought—had been driven to madness by protracted exposure to Alma's beauty. Only fifteen, yet . . .

"I sense the gift for composition, yes." Oskar's gaze briefly risked Alma's ice-blue eyes. She stared back at him. He shivered and glanced away.

"Our darling shan't play this evening . . . pity. But she mustn't, of course." Frau Moll smelled of camphor. "Still in mourning, it would not be—"

Oskar envisioned the older woman caught in a frenzy of moths. "I understand," he murmured.

"Herr Oskar Kokoschka," Alma said. "I've heard tales of you. Quite wonderfully scandalous tales. How can it have taken so long for us to meet?"

"The fates have been punishing me," Oskar said.

"Myself as well, it seems."

Anna Moll, her husband, the motley of guests all vanished. Air that seconds before had smelled of wine and spiced meats was scented now with gardenias. Beyond a latticed window, soft rain began to fall.

"You must have misbehaved quite . . . energetically? To earn such disfavor."

"Mere exuberance." Oskar lowered his gaze modestly. "Youth's usual excess." A temptation of jet beads crept into the cleft between her breasts.

"Am I, too, to be penalized for your excesses?" Alma Mahler sounded hopeful.

"How should I forgive myself?" Oskar asked.

"You need only confess." She patted a place on the hassock beside her. "I am here to absolve you."

Oskar sank down next to her. The hassock sighed. After a moment he permitted his eyes the deep look they craved, into hers.

"Tell me everything," Alma whispered.

Smiling bravely, Oskar fell through the ice.

Alma's perfect face, in a rare departure from mourning's strict code, hinted at a smile all its own.

THE EXHIBIT REMAINED AT THE RICHTER GALLERY FOR TWO WEEKS. IT WAS hardly a *succès d'estime*. It wasn't even the *succès de scandale* it ought to have been. Dresden's attentions were elsewhere. In bondage with the monkeys, perhaps. Summer had arrived. Banal Dresden was busy coaxing Holland bulbs to bloom in ornate window boxes . . . gilding lilies . . . painting tin soldiers . . .

The war went on without him.

Day after day, Oskar was helplessly drawn back to the gallery on the Hauptstrasse. Katja's father, a spruce gent with waxed mustaches and Italian boots so lustrous and supple they would figure in Oskar's dreams for several years, never failed to greet him effusively. Herr Richter saw, in the Viennese painter's constant attendance at a failed exhibition, garden-variety infatuation, nothing more.

Though it would not behoove his bohemian standing to admit it, Georg Richter wished to hell his daughter would give up this acting business, marry, settle down. Maybe then the girl wouldn't be so nervous, so often ill. Young Kokoschka was making a name for himself . . . he supposed Käthe could do worse. (*Had done,* actually, hadn't she?

Several times.) One of these days his daughter was going to wake up looking closer to thirty than twenty, no longer a commodity on the marriage market . . .

Not that Herr Richter would have put it that way. Would it seem high-handed, he wondered, to offer the timid painter a hint? Mooning around a deserted gallery . . . surely a spitfire like Käthe required hotter pursuit. A gentle shove in the right direction might not hurt. A self-respecting bohemian parent didn't like to meddle in his child's affairs. But his daughter's suitor clearly needed coaching.

The exhibit seemed, by its second week, to have been forgotten by everybody but Kokoschka. Trying to work up nerve to approach me, Herr Richter thought. So nervous you'd think he was still a boy. Never mind the bald head.

Oskar would emerge from the gallery's back room, having spent an hour or more with Fräulein Moos's lecherous little ladies. The painter's already haunted-looking eyes would wear a dark glaze. He'd run up against some bloodthirsty Cossacks in Volhynia, or some such godforsaken pinprick on a map of the Russian front. Shot in the head, supposedly. And gassed as well, Käthe claimed.

Georg Richter suspected the war was much overrated, as adventures go. Wars always were. Oskar Kokoschka might be a hero. Certainly a casualty, anyway, shellshocked, a bit befuddled. But then how dissimilar, really, were the symptoms of a good gassing and falling in love? A mercy, in any event, to ease the poor fellow off the miserable hook of thwarted desire. Each day his narrow face looked a little more like Christ's in Gethsemane.

Late Monday afternoon, waiting for Oskar to depart so he could close up shop and go home, Herr Richter interrupted his own small talk. "Was there something you wanted to ask me, sir?" The paternal twinkle in his eye was meant to smooth the way.

Oskar Kokoschka, however, looked as if he'd been slapped. His tight-lipped mouth opened slightly, then closed again. His long furrowed cheeks were morbidly pale.

"Perhaps I am mistaken," Richter said. "I thought—"

"Not mistaken," Oskar mumbled. "I was merely—"

"'Merely'?" Georg Richter smiled. "It is a minor matter, then, you wish to bring up?"

Oskar, turning even paler, shook his head. Richter looked for a scar but could not find one.

"Would it help to know I am not without sympathy for your cause?"

The intended reassurance seemed to addle him further. "Where *is* she?" he whispered. "Is she expected? Why in God's sweet name is she not here?"

He is not sound, Georg Richter thought. He laid a calming hand on Oskar's shoulder. "It is only, as I told you, a spring cold."

"A cold?"

"Nothing more. She is nearly recovered."

The confusion on Oskar's face sharpened into outrage. "You are speaking of Katja."

Richter's hand drew back. "Of course." He should not have allowed Heinrich to leave early. Not that his puny assistant would be much defense against a madman's rampage. Still, it was clearly imprudent, remaining alone in a place open to the public . . . especially with a display of work whose obvious intent was to challenge convention, to inflame passions, to—

Oskar, his eyes tightly closed, reached up to cap his stubbled skull with both hands. As if the wound he'd suffered had torn his head asunder, leaving him to live in fear of his thoughts flying out, escaping him.

"My dear boy—"

Oskar groaned softly.

Richter drew back, moving closer to the door to his private office. The door was heavy and had a lock, if only he could—

Oskar's eyes snapped open, a sudden cool and tranquil silver blue. "I was inquiring of the artist," he said. "I had merely hoped for the privilege of meeting her."

"The artist?"

"Fräulein Moos." Oskar's face was icy.

"It is my understanding that the lady prefers . . . to avoid attention," Herr Richter said.

Oskar's shout of laughter made him flinch. *He is not sound . . .*

"She is shy," Herr Richter said.

"Oh, yes, one senses her reticence." Oskar could not seem to stop laughing. "Such modesty. You must give me an address then . . . in Stuttgart, isn't it? I shall convey my compliments in a letter."

Oskar wiped tears from the corners of his eyes with his thumbs. Then his hands returned to the crown of his head.

"Are you perhaps . . . not well, Herr Kokoschka?"

The ungainly red hands dropped slowly. Oskar stared at Herr Richter. His eyes had turned a guileless, uncomplicated blue. "I have been half-mad with worry," he said. "Dear Käthe. Might I call on her tomorrow, do you think?"

"Perhaps another day or two . . . for rest . . ." Herr Richter removed a key ring from his vest pocket and dangled it rather ostentatiously. Was he never going to leave? Would Käthe never cease befriending lunatics? Must every half-decent painter in Europe be so damnably *odd*?

"Stuttgart," Oskar whispered. "If I might trouble you for that address?"

"No trouble." Georg Richter managed to enter his office without turning his back on Oskar Kokoschka. "No trouble at all."

Hermine Moos's address materialized on the back of a torn envelope, scribbled in an unsteady hand. *Her* hand?

Accepting the envelope, Oskar's own hand trembled.

The envelope fell to the floor.

Stooping to retrieve it, Oskar saw its front was blank and lacked a stamp. The handwriting must have been Richter's.

The gallery owner watched Oskar's back as, without so much as a *danke,* he wandered out into the spring dusk. He moved like a sleepwalker. Käthe must have been correct about the gassing.

Herr Richter wished Oskar Kokoschka would buckle down, get back to painting . . . get over the damnable war and forget about writing those incomprehensible plays Käthe and her friends at the Albert Theater were so taken with.

Oh, yes, he was supposed to be a writer, too, one of the avant-garde's momentary darlings. Käthe had performed in one of Kokoschka's plays last year. Not that Richter or his wife had glimpsed their daughter's lovely face, despite their front-row seats. For some reason the actors all wore masks. The audience was small but noisy. The fact that no one really understood the play only seemed to heighten the enthusiasm. Original, they said. Daring, they said. *Dada,* they said, sounding like infants.

Well, one didn't necessarily have to comprehend Kokoschka's talents to see that he had them. He hardly looked a good prospect, though, to be leading Eurydice out of darkness, particularly not a Eurydice who happened to be one's precious daughter.

It had perhaps been incautious, so readily furnishing Fräulein Moos's address. Georg Richter hoped Oskar would not start making a nuisance of himself in Stuttgart. On the other hand, better the dollmaker be rattled at a remove by the odd painter's attentions, than his own gullible child. Even a bohemian must protect his little girl.

HE WOULD WRITE TO HER.

The skin—my desire to experience its many textures is reckless. Yet I swear to you my ruffian urges will be tamed the instant the object of need lies within reach. Rowdy fingers gone meek with denial's quell . . .

I dream of her skin, and the pads of my fingertips soften as I sleep. My cuticles are silken threads. Each morning I wake to pare my nails, pumice away the least roughness . . .

For a time I cannot paint, must not. Shall I, as dream draws nigh, risk harsh solvents? My gift is hers. Only hers. I must not . . .

He would keep from her nothing.

Calluses soften and vanish as I sleep. I cannot . . .

I awake weeping.

He would, on paper, display to her his every desire.

My only vision is that which you, my accomplice, shall create for me.

Even from a distance, she would succumb to his helplessness. This Fräulein Moos would be the angel borne to earth to resuscitate his heart.

She would, by all that was holy, restore his sight to him. His soul. His Almi.

2

An embroidered edge of starched linen sliced across the old man's neck. His emaciated body vanished under the bedclothes. Looking from the doorway, Oskar saw decapitation, nested in a superfluity of pillows.

"Papa?" Dr. Posse bent over the bed's high edge. *"Vater."*

Hans Posse was nearing sixty, Oskar supposed, nearly twice his own age. From the time of their first meeting over a game of cards at the home of a mutual friend, the museum director had struck Oskar as the most self-possessed of men. He radiated calm reason, and warmth. Oskar envisioned Posse in a nimbus of a color he'd only recently identified. Not unlike mauve, yet rosier, a bit darker . . . a watercolor wash delicately dusted with charcoal. Souls, particularly those of great purity, tended to bleed colors. Not everyone was equipped to discern them, of course.

Oskar had first seen the inscrutable hue he came to identify with Hans Posse on his early-evening walks along the Elbe. His mind often dallied with the pleasant task of naming this subtle shade dusk cast upon the river's dimming gloss. So far his three languages had all failed him, the hue remained nameless. Sleep without dreams would be such a color, Oskar thought, a peace scarcely to be imagined. He had envied his host, a man who, though harried, appeared never to have been haunted.

Now, however, witnessing the Direktor's gaze upon his dying father,

Oskar saw, distraught and lost, the face of the fatherless boy Hans Posse must soon become. Frantic and directionless, an urchin darted out from a dark thicket taken for safety and cowered in the light on Posse's face.

Poised on the threshold of the airless sickroom, Oskar gripped the doorjamb with both hands. *There are no guides,* he thought. And: *I have no business here.*

Dr. Posse dipped a handkerchief into the water glass on the marble-topped commode beside the bed. He touched the cloth to the corners of his father's half-open mouth. The old man's lips looked dusty. Oskar caught the scent of death gathering between them, preparing to be expelled in one terrible final gust.

"Papa, we have a guest." Dr. Posse's voice was a brittle parody of delight.

"Nein." Under the bedding the old man's skeleton stiffened. "No." His son flinched.

"Absolutely not." The old man's pale stare was fixed on the figure in the doorway, the bare skull and bony shoulders.

Oskar, cold fingers tight on the jamb, closed his eyes. *He thinks I have come for him.* Shame scalded his face. *He mistakes me for death.*

When Oskar opened his eyes, the old man was still staring at him.

"Verzeihung," Oskar and Hans Posse both said at once. Forgive me.

The General's laughter sounded like bone splintering.

A sickly yellow light seeped into the room, weak sunshine simmering away morning's fog. The old man's eyes, caustic and bleached, plumbed Oskar into transparency.

HAIR THICK AND DARK, BUT NOT BLACK, NOT QUITE. HULDA, THE HIRED girl, is seventeen. The reddish cast to her hair is easy to miss, except in sunlight. Under the sun her hair catches fire.

Hulda's hair, though her orthodox stepmother often threatened it, has never been cut. The girl's head must, at the very least, be shrouded. Her father's new wife insisted on that. Although furnishing no explanation, she did provide the scarf. Its coarse wool was the soiled oily color of boiled dandelion greens. When the scarf slipped from Hulda's head, *die Stiefmutter* cursed her. *Unnütz,* this new mother called her. Vain.

Hulda's hair, here in Dresden, is no longer the cause of argument. The artists and wealthy patrons who come to take Sunday-afternoon coffee in Dr. Posse's indulgent drawing room love to argue. Controversy arouses them. Love affairs and theories of art, the outcome of war and revolution, the fate of the Habsburgs and the implications of Klimt's demise are all subject to debate. Who, in such an enlightened and tipsy assembly of freethinkers, skeptics, and negligents, would dream of suggesting a girl cover her hair?

Each morning, as Hulda weaves her hair into the thick braid she wrests into a figure eight, she remembers the oily green scarf she has not been able to discard. It waits, balled up in the bottom of the potato bin in the pantry, in case it is ever called for.

A shard of old mirror is affixed to the wall in the room off the pantry where Hulda sleeps. When she looks into the sharp sail-shaped slice of glass, the room's one small window peers over her shoulder. Fine mornings show Hulda how her hair catches fire. *Unnütz.* She pins the tortured twist of braid to the back of her skull, her scalp there scored and scabbed by her fierce way with hairpins. She remembers the scarf in the potato bin. She thinks of Emil, the dead soldier she loved when she was still a child and had no inkling of her father's interest in taking a new wife.

Emil had wanted to make love to Hulda before he left for The Front. Where was that, she asked, The Front? Emil did not know. He said only that many days would be required for the journey. It was of the utmost importance to have a good pair of boots.

It was Emil's desire—unthinkable!—to make love to Hulda. They would marry, he said, as soon as he returned. Soldiers are handsomely paid, Emil said.

His hand was large and rough. His touch, uncertain, was gentle as a child's. Hulda, tucking her chin into her neck like a bird, saw Emil's hand shaping itself to her small breast. Skittish and urgent as a child's first prayer, Emil's hand. His lips quivered. His eyes were full of belief. They would marry in springtime, roast lamb and dancing beneath a huppah of blossoms. "I am already yours, Hulda. Be mine."

Did she answer him? What might she have said? Hulda recalls only that the girl she was then had nudged the boy's hand from her breast. She allowed him instead to unpin her hair. Emil had wrapped his face in Hulda's hair. A few months later—where?—Emil's head was crushed under a caisson when he slipped from the back of a casualty cart.

War, war . . . it is nearly over, it is suddenly everywhere again in Dr. Posse's formerly sedate household. Hulda hears things falling, breaking. She knows the guest hears them, too. Hulda hears the guest moan at night. His agonies braid themselves into her dreams. In Hulda's dreams Emil's head, crushed and eyeless, is bandaged in her smoldering hair.

Shells explode in the guest's bruised eyes, blinding him once and for all. He moans, some word that sounds like *alle* perhaps, finished . . .

Or was it *allein,* alone?

Upstairs, in the breathless room at the top of the house, the old man is dying. *Allein.* Sometimes he shouts out orders in his sleep. The house explodes in the dead of night with muffled groans and screams.

In the morning, trapped in a jagged piece of glass, Hulda stabs three hairpins into the back of her skull. Then she stands for a moment very still. Her work-worn hands hang at her sides. She imagines the scarf, a soft greenish fist in the potato bin. It must already be moldering there in the damp dark. Soon nothing will be left of it.

Hulda's arms rise up like wings. The wings fold back. Her blunt fingers push underneath the tight braid at the back of her head. Her fingers come away stained red.

Unnütz. Vain.

Emil.

Hulda.

The war has disposed of them all.

"FORTUITOUS," HANS POSSE WAS SAYING, "OUR MEETING AT DR. NEU-berger's . . . then so soon again at the Felsenberg." He made two tidy cuts in a boiled potato and lifted a small, neat wedge to his mouth. "Here you will have more privacy. And truth be told, I am glad of company." He chewed deliberately. He swallowed hard. "Things being what they are . . . upstairs."

Oskar steered the tines of his fork through a pool of gravy. "The good fortune is mine." The delicate swirl he created instantly began to fade. He continued to stare at his plate after his small ruckus was gone.

"My father was—"

The door to the kitchen opened. Oskar saw in the gap a slice of pastry-white face, an eye dark as a Bing cherry. The smells of strong coffee and cinnamon leached into the dining room.

"I wish you'd known him." Hans Posse winced. "Before. He had an exceptional mind."

The door slowly closed. The eye was gone. Oskar wondered if he'd imagined it.

Posse pinched salt from a silver-and-cobalt cellar and rubbed it absently between thumb and forefinger. His hands were remarkably refined, smooth and fine-boned. Almost, Oskar thought, like a woman's.

"I sit with him, when I can, in late afternoon. He's often asleep. Sometimes I'll stare at that face for an hour or more without spotting a clue to the man he was."

The salt sifted down, white grains vanishing into the white damask tablecloth.

"Life is an endless sequence of them, isn't it? Disappearances." Oskar sounded as if he were talking to himself. Speculating. "Yes, mostly that," he murmured.

"Hardly endless." Posse smiled. "But mostly that, yes. I suppose it is so."

Oskar continued to study the still life of uneaten food on his plate. Everything was brown. For contrast one would have to exploit texture.

"Forgive me," Hans Posse said gently. "I should try to be more cheerful, when you—"

"I found war reassuring, actually. There's a kind of permanence . . ." Oskar offered his host an off-kilter smile. "When you are in its midst, war shows not the least inclination to disappear like most things do."

Posse's gray eyes filled with compassion. "And now?" he asked.

"Now all the more." Oskar laughed softly. "It does not disappear. But I should have painted it then," he said. "From inside. I should at least have tried."

Hans Posse reached across the table and laid a putty-colored hand on his guest's frayed cuff. "You'll begin to recover here," he said. "Rest and companionship . . . some regularity to your days . . ."

Oskar was staring at him with an astonished expression. "Do you think that's what I want?" he asked. "To recover?"

Posse waited, saying nothing.

The kitchen door sidled open again.

Posse withdrew his hand.

Oskar's eyes took measure of the quoin of light around the doorway, the dark chip of eye.

"Shall I paint him?" he asked.

"I beg your pardon?"

The frame of light around the door narrowed but remained. The eye was just a slit. Oskar stared into it. The eye, a spark in it, stared back.

"Before he disappears altogether," Oskar said. "Your father."

Your art, dear Fräulein, like the master magician's, must reside entirely in the unseen effect.

Do I ask of you the impossible? Only, if so, because my survival rests upon it—your Zauberkraft. I swear the catch of my eye on a single stitch would mean my very soul's unraveling. Conceal your sorcery or consign this supplicant to wretchedness without end.

Believe me, please, when I confide: Not mere lost love, but life itself I beg you to restore. I call myself an artist—ein Künstler, Fräulein! I am a young man, yet already my name is known in Vienna, in Munich and Berlin. Now to my shame I discover I cannot enter the creative act except by way of woman. And how, apart from such acts, am I to subsist? Do you wonder at my despair, the true poverty of my nature having been now so proven?

As you ply your craft upon our fickle darling, please know that the life your fingers resurrect is that of

Your grateful OK

THE SERVANT GIRL HAD ACQUIRED THE HABIT OF INVISIBILITY. HE HAD EN-countered her, of course. They had been properly introduced. But he had not seen her.

It was not until his third or fourth morning in the Posse household that Oskar's gaze happened fully upon her. Hilda, was it? Helga? Her opaque eyes hinted at obliteration. *The color of my own disappearance,* Oskar thought.

When forced out into the open, the girl kept her eyes, for the most part, lowered. Or at least decently askance. Oskar sat at the breakfast table alone. Dr. Posse was above, looking in on his father, who had passed a difficult night.

"What is your name?" He should remember. He did not care what her name might be. He merely hoped to force the girl to look at him with those clandestine eyes.

But Oskar's smallest hopes these days seemed hell-bent on proving their allegiance to futility.

"Hulda." The girl studied the butter dish.

Ah yes, Hulda. His father had briefly kept a milk cow by that name when Oskar was a boy. The family had eaten the beast once it became obvious she would never give as good as she got.

"Hulda," Oskar said, "may I inquire as to the color of your eyes?"

The question did not seem to unsettle her. The girl simply lowered her face another notch and mumbled something that sounded like *Dunst,* haze.

"Perfect," said Oskar.

The girl, her hands shrouded in a soiled tea towel, turned toward the kitchen.

"Wait."

She froze.

"Turn around," Oskar said. "If you would."

She seemed, without moving, to bend.

"You know who I am?" His voice was neutral.

"Herr Direktor's guest."

"But I meant—"

"I know nothing more, Captain."

"We must decide what you shall call me." Oskar laughed softly. "Not *Captain,* please."

"Whatever you wish, sir."

Oskar thought for a moment. *"Opfer,"* he said.

She did then, at last, look at him. Her eyes were not in the least like haze. She must have meant something else. Hulda's eyes were the deep, freighted brown of the velvet hangings over Alma's bed.

"Herr Opfer," the girl whispered. *Mr. Casualty.* He thought that was what she said.

"Why do you look at me so?" Oskar smiled. "You look as if you are afraid."

A shudder seemed to grab the girl by the scruff of the neck. Her shoulders tried to shake it off.

Oskar stopped smiling. "Surely you don't fear me?" His voice was mild.

"How am I to know, sir?" the girl replied.

Eyes the color of the molasses cakes his mother, Romana, used to bake on Oskar's birthdays . . .

. . . the color of Gypsy music.

. . . the color of the Maestro's shadow.

It seemed a long time before Oskar could bring himself to look again into Hulda's eyes. Her eyes were, he thought, the precise shade of obliteration.

Your work, I regret to report, was poorly displayed. The exhibit was not well attended. Still, I knew the moment I stepped into the gallery's cramped lesser room that I had found my means to salvation. Through you, Fräulein, through you alone might my love be remanded.

You say you have not known her, you never met. I do not believe you.

There can be between us no secrecy. Nor room in you, esteemed friend, for falsity or trepidation. Your hands must possess the daring to form themselves to the very shape of desire. Indulge yourself, I beg you, in pleasure's every dimension. Yet do not in passion neglect proportion: the head's weight to the neck's slender forbearance, the extravagant incline of breast to the rump's rich declivity. The ruin of such celestial ratios would be my heart's undoing.

It is a matter of particular urgency to me that you grasp without stinting the lunar curvature of belly, re-creating it in a way made for touch, as well as gaze. I confess my every waking dream resides in fingers that crave the juncture where fat and sinew connect to bone . . . that slight protuberance of hip cage, the clavicle's tender dip . . .

IF THE GIRL KEPT HIS HEAD PROPERLY RAISED WITH THE THREE EIDERdown pillows he was forever having to remind her of, the old man was able to see his favorite view of the city: a delicious slice of sky garnished with the tenderest portion of the Hofkirche's sweet steeple.

There were, even now, days when Augustus Posse's gut remembered all too well the appetite that had accompanied him to Dresden. A fresh and lusty lad from a village no longer in existence, and hunger his greatest talent. Dresden. The old girl had not only fed him, she'd spread her thighs for him. *Mein Gott,* how the juice had run! Was he supposed to have forgotten its sweetness simply because he was old?

He knew what they were saying downstairs, keeping their voices low, his own graying boy and that hollow-eyed, war-stunned painter he'd taken in. The doctor no doubt confirmed it on his weekly calls. Even the runt of a servant girl, with her swan's neck and slaughtered gaze, spread the news in her uncouth little prayers: The old man was bound soon to die.

Well might he. But wouldn't they be amazed, amazed and a little disgusted, if they knew how a whiff of this old slattern of a city yet made his mouth water?

The General was still smiling as the girl, staggering under the weight of his dinner tray, nudged the door open with her hip. Caught with a randy gleam in his eye, good.

The food on the tray—tepid broth, dry toast, stewed fruit, weak tea—weighed next to nothing. No doubt she'd dismiss his smile as senility. Her scrawny young arms were trembling as she lowered the lacquered bed tray over what had been a nicely begun erection. The freight of all that porcelain and silver wasted on him.

What was left of the old man's appetite died as he watched the girl cross the room to close the one open window, draw the drapes.

"Leave it be," he said, but too late. His voice in recent months had lost all authority.

Still, the girl was respectful. "The light is near gone, sir. The evening air brings a chill." She kept her eyes lowered.

Pleurisy, the old man's friend . . .

"I would welcome it," he muttered.

Augustus Posse knew, before she replied—*Bitte*—and slipped into the corridor, that she hadn't heard him.

It was his favorite time, dusk. Each day the girl stole it from him. She thought nothing of it.

Her footsteps descended to the lower floor without sound. There was something foreign about her. Something subversive. She wore stout boots. From time to time he glimpsed them over the flat horizon of the mattress. Still, the old man imagined her feet in threadbare cloth slippers, leaving no impression in the pile of the thick Turkey runner that carpeted the stairs.

Our beauty must, I think, be formed of many layers . . .

An altogether too obvious tenet, perhaps, in light of the female nature we are attempting to duplicate? I am, I assure you, possessed of an intelligence more subtle than our correspondence might imply. I parade the

specificity of my desires simply to foster their fulfillment. Forgive me,
then, Fräulein, if I seem to blazon the flagrant . . .
    Her flagrancy . . . would that, together, your genius and my passion
could replicate that!

A THOUSAND DAYS AND MORE SINCE HE HAS SEEN HER. FEASTED ON THE
sight of her flesh. She, the heat and aroma of her, married now to another. *His.* No matter. His own heart's shattering the foregone conclu-
sion Oskar has always somehow sensed it must be. Skull scored by a
bullet. War. Blood spattered by savage hands like paint on a torn foreign
canvas . . . not even my horse, in the end, my own, though God knows
I paid for the beast, leaving my old mother hungry. War . . . the costs . . .
    Exorbitance.
    My miscalculation, Oskar thinks, believing passions like Alma's could
not be overspent. Tutored in her extravagance, he had nearly managed
to forget his mother's strict lessons in scrimping and disappointment.
    But his Almi knew nothing of rigor, she lacked staying power. The
Maestro had seen to that, bleeding his bride dry of the juices his last
days, his last works had required . . . the dire *thirst* of parched genius. It
was tempting to imagine Mahler in hell . . .
    If only one had never heard the celestial music.
    One day I may hear it in some distant concert hall, Oskar thinks. I
shall perch on a spindly gilt chair in Paris or Prague, or sink slowly into
the gaudy plush before some second-class American orchestra . . . when
suddenly there they'll be, raining down on me from within his gorgeous
damnable last symphony: the last drops of love, the love that should
rightfully have been mine . . . mine and Almi's.
    I shall be an old man myself.
    The earth by then may blanket her bosom.
    Or perhaps death's kindness shall bring us together again . . . may my
withered hands be granted this: to spread a quilt of roses over my love's
final rest.
    Oskar's eyes fill with tears. But her imagined death does not devas-
tate as desertion has. Dying, his beautiful love—
    No, he is finished with extravagance, done with hope. Alma, mother
of another man's child, is forever gone. The outcome Oskar wishes now
is modest: that someday, decades from now, the remains of his lost

dream of love might find their way back to him, a sweet aftertaste to the Maestro's bitter final music.

But even this, Oskar supposes, may be asking too much.

"HULDA."

She tried to look up.

"Hulda?"

Her eyes would not consent to be lifted.

"Professor Kokoschka will be moving into the summerhouse."

The girl, recalling the skeins of spiderwebs her broom had recently exiled from the rafters, shuddered. No place for a guest, the summerhouse. Surely witches lived there, or had done until her unlucky broom drove them out.

They would be back eventually. And punishment likely due the one who . . .

"Hulda." The master's voice was patient. Dr. Posse was always patient with her. Always kind. "Perhaps you could show him the way? Help him with his things?"

If only she could have raised her eyes to the level of the Captain's face, Hulda would later think, she might have made safe passage. Precious little in that long, sad, wounded face of his for a girl to love. She ought not have let so fanciful a thing as witches distract her from the true danger before her . . .

She ought to have looked straight at him.

But Hulda's gaze, an indocile thing, refused its reach.

Such bashfulness is hardly becoming, her father's new wife had told her. *You look like an oaf, Hulda, staring down at the floor that way.*

Had her father, hearing this, laughed? Hulda sometimes remembers moments that never happened.

Dr. Posse was waiting. The Captain, too.

Ever so slightly, the girl cast up her chin. The faintest flutter captured her eyelids.

"Child, are you unwell?"

You look like an oaf . . .

"I am well, sir," Hulda whispered. "Quite well."

The Professor's hands were overlarge and raw-looking. His nails appeared gnawed, perhaps torn.

"Please." Hulda's hapless gaze fell into his unlikely large red hands. He will take away my name, she thought. She wanted to bolt from the dining room, dodge through the kitchen into her own little cubicle behind the pantry. *He will take away my name and give me a new one.* From the fragment of glass on the wall above her washbasin a stranger's face would stare back. *He will force upon me a new name.*

A voice inside her keened for the lost last glimpse of someone she would never again be.

Hulda.

"Please, sir," she said. "If you will follow me?"

"Danke." He did not sound like a professor. His voice was too frail for certainty. Would a professor of the academy not be expected to know a great deal with the stoutest certainty?

Once more Hulda tried to look into his face. Impossible. *Are you unwell?* Too late. Her eyes were already lost, lost to the unseemly all-wrong hands.

"Bitte." She raised her voice above the keening. "This way."

His hands were a laborer's hands. His knuckles were roughened, his fingertips split. She felt him close at her back. She imagined his rough red hands reaching for her, his feet trampling the distance between them.

. . . a new name. And I will not understand.

The beloved face beckons, but eludes . . . how my Almi loves the chase. Am I absorbed with play? I fear it must sound so. Yet I am, like yourself, engaged with the arduous. I am hardly such a naïf, mein Fräulein, as to suppose the natural appearance might be attained without artifice.

It may surprise you to learn I have taken up a cuisine of sorts. Far from painting, yes, but art of a kind. It should certainly astonish my dear mother and sisters to learn of my sudden interest in the secrets of cookery! Whatever arcane pleasures they imagine for me here in Dresden, I doubt their rashest dreams could picture me these past few evenings, stirring in my nicked saucepan dainty concoctions of powder and fruit juice, gold dust and wax.

The small coal stove in my garden room provides heat just temperate enough for my delicate undertaking. I find myself oddly content.

Despite the stymieing of verisimilitude, mine proves an instructive and plucky endeavor. I even, now and then, succumb to bouts of hope . . .

If ever again I am able to paint, must portraiture not profit from this dabbling with the palette of human complexion?

No ordinary complexion, my darling's, of course . . . you must remem-

ber. Only a face dipped in nectar and slowly dried in spring's first sun might approximate . . . surely you recall?

But let me tether fancy, if I may, to some useful instruction:

It is a truth of human anatomy that the body's tenderest parts incline toward the skeleton, as tendrils of new shoots grow toward the sun. These parts—delta of thigh and navel, elbow's inner curve, list of lower leg and spine's downmost slope—demand in our darling a plushy gleam, as if snippets of velvet were appliquéd there, where succulence resides. A faint dusting of saffron comes near . . .

The oils of certain nuts suggest the delicious lingering of skin shadows . . . in cleavages, in sockets . . .

Color's secret, I am coming to see, is its essential need to be squandered. But daintily, Fräulein. Squandered ever so daintily.

THE GIRL'S EYES ARE SET RATHER TOO FAR APART. OSKAR IMAGINES SHE CAN see everything, always, from two different angles. He himself is trying to learn to see likewise. An artist must. Might she be able to help him?

Hulda's eyes are brown. Eyes the color of:

. . . the velvet hangings that swoop low and heavy from the bed where Alma slept her youth away with . . .

. . . the cigars she persists in keeping in the humidor beside the Maestro's favorite chair.

. . . the sheared beaver muff that concealed her ice-white hands as she walked with him, with Oskar, through Venezia's fog-draped labyrinths on evenings too cold for April, too . . .

What more had he desired, after all? Merely that his hands be allowed to keep possession of Almi's.

She denied him.

The churches' innards were moist and cold-blooded. Trapped in cadaverous spaces, Oskar had gazed into the miraculous beating hearts of Titian's masterpieces, Tintoretto's, and seen himself for a feeble, bloodless thing. Oblivion nipped at his heels. I should wizen into nothingness, he thought, without Almi's hands to move my blood.

OH, HE HAD SEEN THROUGH IT FROM THE START, THE ELABORATE SHAM OF her widow's grieving. Had even admired it. A passionate creature like

Almi, still young . . . was the rest of her life to be wasted worshiping on her knees, those pearly plump dimpled knees, before a shrine to a petrified icon of culture?

The night he first met her, when near dawn he at last fell asleep, Oskar dreamed the Maestro back to life for the sole purpose of slaying him. And he had nearly done so, with sword and considerable style, when a rooster's crow woke him. In the dark around Oskar, Mahler still breathed.

Over the course of the next several years Oskar would, in his dreams, slay Gustav Mahler countless times in countless ways. He would strangle and gut and behead and castrate the composer. Each time he would wake in a lather, yanked from the dream before the Maestro gave up his last breath.

His failure to kill Gustav Mahler was something Oskar came, in time, to accept, an unalterable tenet of his inner life.

Mahler, disturbed (according to Almi) by his inability to satisfy his wife, had once consulted Dr. Freud.

Freud (according to Vienna's grapevine) had forced the composer to travel all the way to Leiden for the privilege of taking a stroll with him.

Oskar pictured them, two aging men in black frock coats, pacing between banks of yellow tulips, Mahler's crippled libido limping along behind them like an elderly lapdog.

Oskar had not yet decided whether to regard Sigmund Freud as prophet or quack. Either way, some of the man's notions were quite amusing. Doubtless they'd meet one of these days, he and Freud. Vienna's true intelligentsia could fit comfortably into one good-size parlor. One soon ran out of the stuff of fresh impressions.

Oskar looked forward to the inevitable encounter with Dr. Freud. My murderous dreams may entertain him, he thought.

A digression? Once Almi appeared, Oskar's thoughts were prone to scatter. A mind too easily captivated by its own giddiness . . . no wonder she'd found him, at times, so terribly young.

As in time Oskar came to see, below the dewy skin and gleaming hair and resilient flesh of her, a core of ancient sorrow in Alma Mahler.

Almi's authentic sorrow, unlike her widow's grieving, did not make a spectacle of itself. Oskar sensed in it, in fact, a desperate need to hide.

When, given the right occasion, she wept for Mahler, Alma's tears poised like tiny diamonds spiked on her lashes. Her cheek yielded nothing of its impeccable pallor. She grieved for her late husband *beautifully*.

The first time Oskar glimpsed this other sorrow in Alma, though, the primordial one, he recognized the urgency of her need to keep it to herself.

Oskar did not grasp the nature of this sorrow. Had no idea of its cause. But he did gauge its force. Alma's clandestine grief had the power to steal her beauty.

THEIR AFFAIR WAS NEW. ONLY THREE EVENINGS EARLIER OSKAR HAD FIRST been granted the privileges of the Mahlers' marital bed. Then followed two torturous evenings of being largely overlooked while his beloved's attentions were squandered on the pointless others with whom she displayed a sudden and inexplicable need to crowd her parlor.

Oskar sulked in a window seat, in a tizzy of desire. He'd been unable to eat or sleep. The taste of her was still on his tongue. She ignored him, and worse—she was *cordial* to him. She offered him coffee and cake.

After two nights of her ruinous hospitality, starved and stunned, Oskar committed the faux pas of paying a morning call on Alma.

He'd intended to present himself properly, of course. He had not entirely lost his senses.

On his way up the front walk to her door, however, Oskar spotted Alma in the garden that ran along the east side of the house. Haloed by a misty light, she occupied a stone bench. Her head was bent. Her spine was a curve of distress.

The morning was warm and moist. Her simple white lawn frock (a wrapper, perhaps?) should have been sufficient suggestion that she neither wished nor intended to be seen.

Her taste was on his tongue.

She ran down the back of his throat, a sweet liquefaction.

Oskar swallowed hard.

Holding his breath, he leaped over a privet hedge, landing in a tripod squat just shy of the pointed toes of her white calfskin house slippers.

From the brick pathway to the house, he'd seen her only from the back. He would not have imagined her hands covering her face, nor the broken angle of her proud neck.

And nothing, of course, could have prepared him for the face disclosed to him when, at the sound of her name, Alma looked up. Her hands dropped heavily to her lap. She seemed not to recognize him. He hardly recognized her.

Alma's face looked as if it had been repeatedly slapped. Her bisque complexion was defaced, a crude debacle of violet and red. Her eyes lay in bruised sockets, their lids swollen and raw. Her lips appeared parted by force. Her whole exquisite face was streaked with a random glaze of spit and tears.

Oskar shifted from his ungainly half-crouch to his knees. "Almi."

He had not bothered, last night, to hide his petulance from her. He had acted, he saw now, worse than a spoiled boy. But how could he have imagined the extravagance of her distress?

"My sweet darling," Oskar said.

How could tears continue to flow from eyes so frozen?

Oskar, too, began to weep. "My love, say you forgive me."

"You have no right to be here." Her voice was distant and dull. "I do not want you here."

Little as he knew at that moment, Oskar understood that Alma would in such fashion often break his heart. This was only the first time. The years to come would require him to get used to it.

"You mustn't send me away," he said. "That is the one thing you must never do, Almi."

She seemed not to hear him.

He sat on the ground at her feet. The earth was damp with rain. He was wearing his best trousers. Alma would not look at him. After a while Oskar considered it might be best if he stopped looking at her. She needed privacy in which to compose herself. He offered this by the barest turn of his head. She gave no sign that she noticed. He hoped she did not. He did not wish to give a mistaken impression of spite.

In time Alma stopped crying. The late morning that had appeared to be brightening as Oskar arrived on the Elisabethenstrasse was again dimming. When it began to rain, Alma rose from the stone bench and, without bestowing a word or a glance, entered the house.

Oskar, insensible to the rain, sat in the garden for a long while. She would surely return. Would show some pity.

She would do no such thing, of course.

About Alma Mahler, Oskar still, on that morning, had everything to learn.

HILARIOUS, ACTUALLY, OSKAR'S JEJUNE ASSUMPTION THAT HE COULD CAUSE a sorrow so sumptuous.

Nor did the Maestro's ghost hold such sway over Alma's heart. No indeed.

It would take Oskar many months to discover the true source of Almi's secret grief: The loss of her first child left them both, the Maestro and himself, forgotten in the mud.

It was common knowledge, the death five years earlier of the Mahlers' small eldest daughter, Maria. Diphtheria.

(Already five years? As stingy a snippet of time as the girl had been granted on earth.)

Mahler's *Kindertotenlieder* had been composed not upon the occasion of his own child's death, but in what would soon seem dreadful prescience of it. His music had nonetheless immortalized the little girl he'd called Putzi. She lived on in the songs' plaintiveness.

Among other things. Also keeping little Maria Mahler alive were her mother's unpredictable bouts of grief every few months. Grief that turned a beautiful woman ugly, that terrified her young lover and plunged her surviving child into awful nightmares.

Oskar was to learn from Alma many things. One of the first and most durable of these was a complex equation involving the subtraction from beauty of grief and love.

DEEPLY AS SHE GRIEVED FOR HER DEAD DAUGHTER, ALMA WAS NOT, WHEN it came to her living child, an especially devoted mother. Her attentions to her younger daughter, named Anna after her maternal grandmother, were ungainly and sporadic. In an expansive mood she spoiled the child outrageously, dressing, undressing, rearranging and embellishing and fussing over her as if she were a doll.

But Alma was also capable of forgetting altogether the child's existence. During parties Oskar would spot little Anna drowsing, ignored, in a corner as midnight drew near. Her topknot would be listing, her nightdress dingy. Oskar began taking it upon himself to look after her. Carrying the child to bed, weaving a little tale for her perhaps, or hearing her prayers, assigned him a specific role in Alma's complex social evenings.

Maria, the first child, had emerged from the womb bottom first. Mahler had taken an instant shine to her. His Putzi clearly took after him, he claimed, showing straightaway a cheeky disdain for the world.

But the Maestro may have had an even softer spot for his more demure second child. The pet name he gave her, Gucki, referred to the soft peeping sounds she made in lieu of crying. Loath to disturb him, Mahler crowed, considerate even as an infant, respectful of her father's work.

It made for a nice little family legend. But Oskar suspected Gucki had instinctively grasped her place in a household already oversubscribed with *Sturm und Drang*.

She was a stolid little thing, Gucki, with chunky legs and a touching downturn of mouth. Her small face looked overburdened by the elaborate coiffure Alma inflicted upon it in duplication of her own. Gucki could, it seemed, bear almost anything without making the least fuss.

Oskar was not much drawn to children. They simply failed to engage him. Gucki's tenuous perch on the periphery of her mother's notice, however, her quiet resignation to being overlooked, laid claim to Oskar's heart. And the little girl's company was a comfort when he, too, found himself fallen outside Alma's fickle ken.

Gucki's birth, her mother often mentioned in the child's presence, had been a dreadful ordeal. For weeks before the delivery Alma was confined to bed. Long and dreary weeks, alone of course. The Maestro was not about to be distracted by his wife's natural discomforts when he himself was struggling with a recalcitrant Sixth Symphony and an even more recalcitrant case of composer's block . . . poor Gustav! What would a genius know of chapped nipples? A summer's seclusion at Maiernigg nicely suited his purposes. If his wife happened to find her confinement lonely, it would be over soon enough. While his own labor . . .

Alma's laugh was indulgent and brave. "Our little peeper was a troublesome package, weren't you, *Liebchen*? And plain as a turnip." The aftermath of her pinch was a scarlet mark on her daughter's cheek, shaped very nearly like a kiss.

Gucki was hardly a year old when her sister died, and only six at the death of the father who adored her. When Oskar landed in the child's life she had just turned seven, the age deemed, by the Catholic faith Mahler had adopted in the last decade of his life, the age of reason. Oskar found the notion capricious at best. A hypothesis he was willing to test out, however, in his relations with Alma's young daughter. Heaven knew a touch of reason could do no harm in Gucki's unpredictable universe.

Was that what accounted for the little girl's devotion? Oskar's singular willingness to traffic in reason with her? He hoped not. Reason was hardly his strong suit. Nor was it a quality he prized in others. If *he* was to be her sole acquaintance with stability, little Anna Mahler was bound for a life of furor and quake.

Still, Oskar was pleased to see to it, on occasion, that despite her mother's entertaining, Gucki got a good night's sleep. He could slip her a nutritious snack when regular meals fell by the wayside. He'd have liked to dismantle the elaborate pouf of hair that weighed down Gucki's head, too. perhaps replace it with a pair of simple pigtails. His sister Berta had taught him years ago how to make plaits. He'd practiced this craft on the wispy tail of a swaybacked mare his father had received in payment for some bit of work he wouldn't discuss. Like many entertainments in the Kokoschka ménage, the mare hadn't lasted very long.

Gucki was a pretty child. Braids would have suited her round sober face, offered a clear vantage point on her eerily wise eyes. Unfair to display her in the glare of her mother's brilliant beauty. Beside Alma her daughter, at seven, resembled the sort of dour matron the Viennese bourgeoisie turned out like cookies.

But Almi would never have stood for interference, of course, not when it came to principles of style. It was simple prudence to go about the business of befriending Gucki surreptitiously. Oskar slipped the child apples and bedtime stories and reasonable answers to her timid questions when he had them. He kept his hands off her hair.

> *Have I spoken to you, esteemed friend, of horsehair? Forgive me if, like a tedious crone, I should repeat my small preoccupations. Do relentless notions of our magnificent undertaking deprive you as well of sleep, deny you nourishment, companionship, all essential forms of human sustenance until you fear . . .*
>
> *But what matter? We concur, do we not, that the techniques of layering and piecing together are the key? All implemented with, of course, the lightest hand. Experiments indicate a construction of horsehair might serve for the figure's innermost layer. You must find an old horsehair sofa. (A chair would be inadequate . . . a settee? Perhaps.) Procure something that can be quickly and reasonably purchased, dismantled with ease. It must immediately be disinfected, of course!*
>
> *Once the crude armature of horsehair is complete (no doubt an atrocity—I am thankful I shall not have to look upon it, risking its lasting hold*

on memory), the time shall come to address the buttocks and breasts. Goose down, in the most minuscule bundles . . . accruing more and ever more lightly. Your cupped hands will not hesitate to announce, I trust, when the sublime heft and curve have been attained. May your palm overflow with life and beauty!

THE GIRL WAS SO DOCILE AS TO APPEAR ALMOST SULLEN. SLIGHT, YET HEAVY on her feet. Prone to bungle. Quiet mornings in the Posse home exploded as its trappings fell prey to the careen of dust cloth and broom. Had the late Frau lived, it would likely have been in a perpetual state of disgruntlement.

Hans Posse, however, seemed unperturbed. A slight cringe now and then, a comic roll of eye, were his only reactions. Oskar suspected his host of secret relief. Frau Posse had surrendered to her flawed blood several years earlier. Her profuse legacy of domestic ornament, an oppression of hand-painted china and handblown glass, seemed merely to harp upon her absence.

Ornament und Verbrechen . . . decoration and crime. Clutter muddied up clear colors, blurred clean lines . . . there was a kind of savage depravity in it, Adolf Loos had written. Tattoos were the criminal's art. What other sort would be moved to deface one's own hide?

Alma was a great one for landscapes of fuss. Sometimes Oskar's eye, scanning her rooms, had failed to distinguish his beloved's form from the camouflage of needlepoint and tapestry and marble, of porcelain and silver and crystal, arranged about her. How, he wondered, would the homely, spindle-legged architect be adapting? One heard increasing talk of Walter Gropius these days, his exacting choreography for design's pas de deux with machine. Asceticism was bound, in a chaotic age, to have a certain appeal . . .

Oskar imagined Almi embroidering red Chinese dragons on her husband's stern black cravats, befogging the window glass of his famously austere structures with lace . . .

The stinting Herr Gropius may send her packing back to me one of these days.

Oskar, trying to laugh, felt his chest split with pain. Late yesterday, wandering aimlessly into the kitchen, he'd come upon the girl with a cleaver raised over her shoulder. He remembered the skimping mortal snap of perfect aim and force, hewing the capon's breastbone.

The girl, for all her ineptitude, showed astonishing deftness in the kitchen. The unassailable Frau Posse herself would have been forced to concede it. Perhaps Hulda felt more at ease, or was simply less distracted, in the one room the late Frau's appetite for froufrou had not consumed. A gift for cookery was the natural birthright, pure and common, Hans Posse claimed, of one derived of good Saxon stock.

Hulda had been raised in the country outside Görlitz, daughter of a farmer and sometime butcher, or some such. A neighboring family here in Dresden with a girl from the same region had recruited Hulda for the Posse household several months earlier, when Frau Posse's elderly maiden sister, who had supervised her sister's illness and the running of her home, had announced her belated intent to return to Pirna, repository of her girlhood memories.

"Not a vast distance." Hans Posse's smile was enigmatic. "Yet our Trudl is sufficiently . . . removed," he said.

The Direktor's sister-in-law had reveled, Oskar gathered, in maintaining a shrine of ornament to her sister's memory. Regrettably, however, Fräulein Trudl was rather too fastidious to master the kitchen arts. The Direktor hinted—in the kindest possible way, of course—that it was his guest's good fortune to have missed his sister-in-law's perfunctory lukewarm meals.

Our Hulda, on the other hand . . . *ach!* Such potato pancakes, dainty golden antimacassars crisped at the edges . . .

No hint of kinship to the fare on which Oskar had been raised. Romana's *Reibekuchen* were pale mittens, soggy with lard and reeking of onion. His mother's Wiener schnitzel (not that the family often indulged in costly meats) might have found better use resoling boots.

"Our little Hulda," the Direktor gloated, "could coax savor from a grasshopper's haunch."

His grateful boarder could hardly dissent.

Not to say he had much appetite. Oskar ate just enough to appear mannerly, before slipping back out to the summerhouse lair where, unobserved, he could freely pine.

The hollows in his cheeks steepened. His eyes' deep-sunk sockets went dark. The bow-shaped upper lip, denying its sensuality, thinned and straightened until his teeth made a display of themselves. Several times, catching sight of his grimace in the vestibule looking glass, Oskar fancied a likeness to his early portrait of Father Hirsch. Perhaps he ought to cultivate a mustache? Could anything hope to grow on so dead a face?

THE BUTCHER HAD BEEN LESS THAN SCRUPULOUS. THE REMAINING BRISTLES were stubborn. *Ungenießbar,* the girl thought. *Unfit.*

The oxtail, half its ideal size, barely filled her palm. When it was clean, Hulda laid it gingerly in the bottom of the pot. So puny. She hoped the meat hadn't come from some creature too diseased or maimed to reach maturity.

A pathetic creature at best, an ox. She remembered one her father had slaughtered for neighbors when she was a child: a scabby nose wide as a butter plate, rosettes of yellow mucus at the corners of its eyes. Ach, why recall the beast now? Only a pot of soup she's making . . . just a little something to help the professor's guest regain strength.

He put her in mind of that ox, the poor Captain. Dumb with grief, as if already dying but not yet aware of it.

Hulda had always wondered if some dumb beasts weren't grateful to die. Some of the older, weaker ones put up remarkably little fuss. Her father, of course, insisted slaughter was painless. A properly sharpened blade was purest mercy, he'd say. "Besides," he liked to tell his daughter, "the moment they're upside down they think they're already dead."

He'd laugh at his own joke then, a dark hollow laugh like a struck iron kettle. Hulda's mother had not cared for such talk, not that she'd have dared reprimand her husband. She'd find some reason to touch her daughter, smoothing her hair or straightening a collar. When Hermann Meyer mumbled a blessing over the bread, he'd still be smiling. His wife and child would keep their eyes lowered.

Hulda pestered God to find her father work in the vineyards, like Otto and Frieda's father. What stained the edges of Herr Koeppel's nails wasn't blood. Just the sweet sharp juice of grapes, something one could bear to imagine while chewing dumplings . . . nothing that would close your throat, keep you from swallowing, tempt your mother to go away . . .

Had her mother been grateful to die?

She fled to the Creator's arms, Hulda's grandmother told her. The child pictured hairy forearms thrown wide in a terrifying embrace.

Then, scarcely a month gone by, hadn't the old woman followed her daughter into the dark? *It was her time,* Hermann Meyer said, his eyes greedy on the flat edge of light where his village ended. Where another life began.

He was thankful his wife had left no sisters to obligate him. There were in the vicinity several widows, capable and not entirely unattractive. Hulda was old enough to start pulling her weight. Was it not a father's duty to find for her a proper tutor in womancraft? Any day now the girl might find herself bleeding between the legs like a slit rabbit. A woman would be required to explain. He'd best not dawdle in making his choice . . .

It was, as it happened, Frieda's mother who explained the blood, who taught the girl to fold and fasten the rag to hold it. Frau Koeppel also intended to show Hulda how to bake bread. Unfortunately, with all she had to do, they never made it past the first lesson (the blessing) to the second (yeast). Hulda, in Dresden, discovers she can say the blessing in her sleep. *Baruch atah Adonai* . . . The foreign words elude her the moment she is awake. Yeast she learned on her own. It has never given her a moment's trouble.

A neighbor too distracted, a mother too ill, a grandmother too old, a stepmother too mean . . . no one had taught her. Cooking was just something the girl seemed to know.

When the oxtail was well browned on one side, she turned it over. Grease spattered up over the lip of the pan. A spot on her wrist felt like a sizzling match head pressed into her skin.

Hulda smiled.

The Direktor's guest was peaked and poorly. The soup would enrich his blood.

Hulda raised her wrist to her mouth and licked the grease from her skin. Her tongue contented itself with imagined sweetness.

3

———

"Without motherhood I should never have discovered my true nature."
The refrain became a kind of lullaby Almi would, in a mood of tender
self-regard, sing to Oskar. She adored hearing herself say it, he could
tell.

Precious, such nights, and rare . . . Gucki fast asleep upon her
flounced bed in the narrow room allotted her at the end of the hall . . .
servants retired, guests departed . . . and Oskar, at long last allowed to
lie in the arms of his tormentor and muse, his beloved, his Almi.

Awed and jittery, he lay under the same tobacco-brown velvet
canopy that had sheltered the Maestro's insomnia. Mahler had never
slept in this house, of course. Never even seen the place, as far as anyone knew. Alma had moved into the house a year after his death. That
didn't prevent the Maestro's seeping from the plaster, winking in gilt
cornices. No cry of passion could stifle the sound of his dogged breathing in the dark.

"It tears a woman open." Alma lay on her side, her lush body curved
around Oskar. A heap of lace pillows banked her. "It is transcendent,
mystical . . . how could a mere man understand?" She shifted lan-
guorously, tipping her breast toward Oskar. She smoothed the new
down on his scalp. "A storm unleashed in body and soul."

Down the hall a child's whimper alarmed the darkness.

Oskar, startled by the sound, pulled his gaze from Alma's to glance toward the hall. The bedroom door, naturally, was closed.

Alma grasped Oskar's jaw, sharp nails indenting his skin. She pulled his mouth to her nipple.

Rose madder, Almi's nipples . . . sweet and grainy as marzipan. Sometimes when she knew he was watching at her dressing-room door, she would rub perfumed oil on them. Her babies had left her breasts an agony of tenderness, she said.

"The body is no longer one's own," Alma murmured. "It knows only giving. It has no other need."

On the far side of the house, Gucki moaned, then cried out softly. *Mama.*

Behind a drape of brown velvet the Maestro wheezed.

"Almi?" Oskar whispered. "Don't you hear?"

Alma summoned his mouth back to her breast. "Ssh," she said.

Rosewater and sweet almond paste mingled on his tongue.

It was only Gucki, after all, having one of her dreadful little dreams.

THE MORNING SKY WAS FAT WITH GREASY-LOOKING CLOUDS. OSKAR SAT AT his empty desk in the summerhouse and picked a splinter from a nipple-shaped drawer pull. His host had apologized repeatedly for the shabby furnishings. The summerhouse was hardly used, Hans Posse had explained, apart from storage.

Oskar felt quite at home among discarded goods. He was learning to cherish his self-pity. Its exorbitance was Almi's love-token: she had cultivated a hardy strain of self-indulgence in him.

A trimmed-down sheet of linen-textured drawing paper lay before him, beside it a glass inkwell and a pen with a rusting point. So had they sat for a quarter hour now, idle, useless. Oskar could not begin to imagine a selection and pattern of words to tell his sister how little he had to offer. She always asked for, *expected,* so pitiably little, poor Berta. Which only increased her brother's desire to smooth the way for her. Her modest wedding expenses, freighted with the security required for a naval officer determined to marry during active service—ten thousand kronen!—had nearly sunk him. Why couldn't she have fallen in love with a civilian? Oskar was still paying off the debt.

Berta wasn't asking for herself, though. She never was. Oskar read through a page and a half of apology before he got to the heart of the matter: There was not enough. Even with Berta and her husband crowding into her parents' home, even with Emil's pay, which might or might not materialize from one week to the next. It seemed the Austro-Hungarian Navy had better use for its monies than the trifling salaries of officers given the honor of conducting its legal affairs. Last week Emil had come home with a pay envelope holding nothing but expressions of Imperial gratitude . . .

Oskar's monthly draft was keeping them alive, yes, and how grateful they were! But Papa was getting old, Mama was getting forgetful . . . and food, *mein Gott,* you'd think Vienna's bread was crusted with pearls! She hoped and prayed it was not so in Dresden, which she imagined a smaller and kinder place, though she'd never been there. She was sorry and ashamed, for she knew he was still far from well. And with all he must have on his mind—a professor! They were all so proud, even Papa. *Especially* Papa. But just a little more, if Oskar possibly could . . . Berta really did not like to ask.

Well, he *could,* he supposed, yes . . . a little bit more would not have been impossible, now that he had the contract with Cassirer. Except for one thing: He would need to begin painting.

Unless, of course, he had a backlog of works to sell . . . the gallery owner was a reasonable man, quite fond of Oskar actually, and there did seem to be some demand. Even for early work, since Westheim's kindly praise in *Das Kunstblatt* last year. And the Dada show in Zurich, of course.

Just now he was unable to work, true. But for years he had been so prolific . . . indeed, he had been the object of some rather mean-spirited envy among his friends. Then those thirty-eight months when his life was buffeted by the turmoil of Almi . . . even then his daily devotions to art had not failed. Love was a distraction, yes. But *passion* . . . living in Alma's atmosphere, deprived of oxygen, he'd painted like what he was: a man wrapped in flames.

Now, for the first time, Oskar found himself taking account of those years' worth of work. Work that, like his soul, had vanished into Alma's grasp. The paintings and drawings and sketches . . . the seven swanskin fans he'd made for her—why, those alone . . . now with his name acquiring a certain gloss, who knew what prices such fancies might fetch?

Oskar slapped the desktop. The inkwell shivered. The sheet of paper edged away. Oskar shut his eyes, picturing the habitual heap of soiled nightclothes tossed in the back of Alma's lacquered wardrobe. A few meters of lace trim stripped from them—Alma would hardly have noticed the lack. His sister would have wept for joy.

Oskar felt his eyes begin to swim, then quickly blinked the tears away. This weakness for melodrama—a onetime consort of the Widow Mahler was bound to have it. A flicker of a smile appeared, then faded . . . *Frau Gropius,* he corrected himself. Alma had not been solicited for donations to the trousseau. He had known better. He had managed on his own. Even from the front, even with an officer's absurd expenses, he'd always managed to send something home. Whatever his failings now, he would not fail his family.

"My darling sister," he wrote. Then he paused to study the effect of his strokes on the page. His handwriting looked rickety. Berta would notice. His mother would be alarmed. Oskar folded the sheet of paper and tucked it inside the back cover of a sketchbook.

For a moment, he sat very still, collecting himself. He'd hardly been in Dresden a week . . . well, all right, two weeks then . . . two weeks and a few days. Surely they would understand at home if he needed time to get settled.

His salary from the Academy, Oskar calculated, would barely cover the cost of supplies and his weekly debt of bed and board. Then his contract, of course . . . but twenty-five hundred marks per month was starting to look less magnanimous than it had at first seemed. Who knew what a mark would amount to, once the war was played out?

Oskar tried not to think of the sum soon due Fräulein Moos. Nor of the fine clothing his heart was set on for his Silent Woman, the luxurious underthings already ordered from France. Only the French truly understood lingerie, Almi said. His income simply must increase. Substantially. Would it be brash to ask Herr Direktor's aid? Hans Posse daily waltzed among Dresden's wealthy. Surely opportunities for private tutoring . . .

Oskar reached into his pocket and pulled out his watch. Barely eleven . . . another two hours before the midday meal. This peckish feeling, its touch of dizziness, assailed him daily around this time. It might be prudent to ask for a cup of tea or broth in his rooms at midmorning. It should really, in the end, save trouble. Another invalid to carry trays for was the last thing the girl needed. Were he not so shy of funds, he could offer her a little something, a deposit on discretion. But he must not seem to find Dr. Posse's hospitality inadequate, nor tamper with domestic routines. After all, his tenure in the house was set apart by only the slightest of sums from pure charity. It would not do to appear demanding.

Oskar rose from the desk and crossed to the french windows that had seduced him into choosing the drafty old summerhouse for his quarters. Warm tapestried rooms under the eaves were offered, of course. But just down the hall from the sickroom, a certain scent . . . yes, there was that. And the old man's assumption (not incorrect, not entirely) of Oskar's chumminess with death.

Beyond the streaked panes, the morning was visibly warming. In the distance, streamers of mist trailed from the hem of the woods. Oskar turned toward the house. His eye studiously avoided the birdbath, prissy and aslant, in the center of the small courtyard whose otherwise natural, somewhat slovenly appearance soothed his eye. Clearly the flowers and shrubs had long been allowed to run amok. No more mention had been made of a gardener. What once had been tame now called to mind Rousseau's stiff jungles, Gauguin's overrated Edens.

How, in a world so full of beauty, do you keep finding ugliness to paint? Almi had teased him when first they met. A scant month was enough to strip the veneer of good humor from the argument. *Die Windsbraut,* his bride of the wind . . . he had quaked and bent in the chill gusts of her reproval. *I paint* you, *he had told her. How much of beauty can one eye absorb before its light blinds?* Had she pestered the Maestro for waltzes to make her gay? And what of poor Gropius . . . was she now forcing his fine abstemious hand to whatnots and filigree?

On such a beautiful morning, a painter should be outdoors painting . . . if only he did not ache so . . . *why on earth should I miss her?*

He looked absently at his watch, then felt a prickling of excitement. Gold, for goodness' sake, filling the palm of his hand. The links of the chain were heavy. Its face was a pearly maze, finely wrought. Engraved on the case his initials were intertwined, *OK* become one fanciful curvature. But there was deceit in the letters' embrace. Their purpose was not to identify but to claim him. Oskar liked to pretend, daydreaming, that

Almi had given him the watch. But in fact it had been Karin's gift. The *K* was her initial, not his.

I shall sell it, Oskar thought. I'll have to. Thinking of Karin made him melancholy anyway, and he was hardly apt to forget her. He wondered if he still had the scarred old steel-case watch of his student days. Its face was spattered with paint, he seemed to recall, and its winding stem was bent. Likely here somewhere, in one of the boxes or bags he had yet to unpack.

Karin would never know . . .

Karin would understand.

Almi would never forgive him.

At least he wouldn't have to write Loos to bail him out again . . .

The knock on the summerhouse door was so timid that Oskar first mistook it for some random sound—the plod of a passing drayhorse, a woodpecker's distant zeal. Another tap turned him from the ruined garden. *"Ja?"*

The girl entered without invitation. Her eyes studied him with concern. They really weren't, those eyes of hers, such an extraordinary color. It was merely their lack of calculation, Oskar realized, that made them disquieting.

"Was wünschen Sie?" He managed to sound distracted. What is it you want? Her stare made him curt.

The girl set down a covered porcelain cup on the corner of his desk. *"Dort ist es."* She smiled. There it is, as if he had sent for something.

He lifted the lid. Steam rose from the cup. The bouillon was the hue of mahogany. A thin slice of lemon drifted upon a surface richly dotted with fat.

Oskar looked at the girl, his lips slightly parted. "Oxblood?" He recalled a Berlin masquerade, his only concession to costume an ox bone still dripping fresh blood, from which he had sipped now and then. How young he must have been, craving that sort of attention, believing in an art whose first obligation was simply to make the bourgeoisie queasy.

"Oxtail." The girl's gaze remained downcast. *"Nahrhaft."* She sounded as if it were a secret she was confiding. "Nourishing." For a dreadful instant, Oskar felt he might weep.

"Danke," he whispered.

She nodded. "It is nothing."

"Vielen Dank," Oskar said. *"Vielen Dank, Reserl."*

She looked up, her eyes pained. "My name is Hulda, sir."

"This must change." Oskar studied her. He thought of the disowned cow. "The name does not suit you. Not the least bit."

"It does not suit *you*. Is that what you mean?"

She looked taken aback by her own impudence.

Oskar laughed. "Perhaps you are right," he said.

She started to go, then turned back. "Why would you choose that name?" she asked. "Reserl."

"Must I have a reason?"

She did not seem to grasp the art of teasing. Indeed, she seemed to lack humor entirely.

"I do not always have reasons." He was not teasing now. "Not that I know of."

"My name," the girl said. "What is it to you?"

"A just and weighty question," said Oskar. "Do you suppose I might be given a day or two to dwell on it?"

For a moment her eyes seemed to lighten, tempting him to imagine a smile he had never seen. But her expression remained grave. "As you wish, sir," she said.

"Reserl." He was filled with belated remorse, even shame. "Hulda," he said. By the time he reached out to detain her, she was gone.

For a long time Oskar stood before the french doors, gazing out upon the hausfrau's spoiled garden, his watch ticking in his pocket, the soup cup warming his cupped white hands.

My most salutary discovery, to date, is the spectrum of rose tints, from faintest flush to profoundest blush. Can you guess?

Mix water with a good red wine. The earthly simplicity of it! Yet what I hand you is the key to the stoutest door yet to bar us. This tint will vivify every sensitive area of a woman's body, from mons veneris to foot's sole. Imagine!

Apply color at first sparingly, dear overseer of my heart's most finical wants . . . your hands are massaging the flow of blood beneath the skin— the flow of life! Belly and breast, calf and cheek, even the delicate blossom of nostril will bloom from the stimulation . . . as you work, you must believe this.

You understand, of course, no instrument may be used, save your

hands? (Unless of course your tongue cannot refuse . . .) Need I specify
that only the tenderest human touch will do?
    How I envy you, Fräulein, your sacred task!

THE GIRL OWNS, IT APPEARS, THREE DRESSES. ONE IS BLUE. TWO ARE
green, one slightly more faded than the other. All three are otherwise
identical. Reserl's dresses are high-necked, loose and shapeless. They
button down the back. When Reserl's hands are idle, her knuckles vanish under the frayed edges of her dresses' long sleeves.

There is on her body no hair . . . none, anywhere, but for the dark
thick fall of it from her head that, at liberty, tickles the small of her back.
Reserl's hair looks, from a distance, like a cape. A dark (yet not quite
black) velvet cape.

Oskar can imagine Reserl attired in such a garment, though surely
she herself cannot. The girl's imagination, though commodious, does
not incline toward luxury. Reserl is only a girl, seventeen. What Reserl
can imagine of a future halts frivolity in its tracks.

There is no hair on Reserl's body. How can Oskar be so certain of
that? From time to time it befalls him to know things he would just as
soon not. Sudden certainties, captious and adamant, waylay him. Oskar
knows that when he finally holds her, Reserl will—like the grotesque
stand-in he must procure for love—feel nothing.

Oskar lowers his head into his folded arms and closes his eyes in a pan-
tomime of infinite weariness. The chipped walnut desktop is warm with afternoon sun. Nearby the sky is already exploding. He remembers a young
Ukrainian woman bathing him in a makeshift field hospital near the front.

He'd just been wounded. His condition was grave. "You cannot be
moved," someone had said. Who? He could not see.

Cannot be moved? A curiously damning indictment. The words,
whispered close to his ear, were pronounced with a kind of tenderness.

The gray-eyed Ukrainian woman said nothing. Nor did Oskar. He
spoke (with a facility many admired) three languages. Surely they could
have found something, he and this gray-eyed woman, to say to each
other? Some nicety? Some common word?

War had taken his tongue prisoner. Hers, too, perhaps?

The woman had bathed first his face, his head. She had not shied
away from the wound in his skull. Her touch was gentle. Yet her hands,

wringing out the rough cloth over a wooden bucket on the floor beside his pallet, betrayed some acquaintance with force.

Her hands, containing their power, moved slowly down his body, water cooling as they advanced. When the cloth's stroking reached his waist, Oskar's breaths began to crowd together. He imagined Alma's chilled white fingers lowering the sacking that passed for his bedsheet. He saw how her eyes would smolder, turn smutty in the lowered light. Such appetite, his Almi, as she consumed him! He felt the heat of her swollen tongue, the intaglio of her teeth on his flesh, and he waited for the Ukrainian woman's touch just there where . . .

She was bathing his feet. She spent a particularly long and strenuous time washing between his toes. I am expected to die, Oskar thought. This woman to whom I cannot speak is preparing me for burial.

He drifted toward something like sleep. Her cloth was making rough passage up his legs. Oskar, his eyes closed, imagined her polishing his ankles. He saw his shinbones and kneecaps brought to a fine gloss.

Her touch, reaching his thighs, turned light. The woman might be a dream. He was wounded. He knew that. *He could not be moved.* Where was he? Many of the wounded died, in the end, of fevers.

And so Oskar told himself that the Ukrainian woman was a fever-dream when, returning at last to the center of him, her warm wet fingers set about restoring what Alma's hunger had devoured.

Even in summer, his Almi's fine hands were like ice.

His breath quickened. The gray-eyed woman waited. Finally, he moaned. Another moment passed before her fingers released his wet flesh. She remained kneeling on the floor beside him until his breathing slowed and he opened his eyes.

He had not, until then, taken in the whole of her.

He saw, as she disappeared through a rough-hewn doorway, that she was scarcely more than a girl.

He did not know where he was. *He could not be moved.* But the blood moved faster inside him. His skull, for the first time, felt the full force of its pain.

Now, newly dead and safe here in Dresden, Oskar knows that in time he will hold the girl. Just as he had known, as the gray-eyed woman left him that day, that he would not die. Not then. He had wept at his blood's announcement. Thinking of Reserl's hairless body, the inevitability of his hands upon it, Oskar feels he should weep again. But where would the tears come from? *He cannot be moved.*

Although we are, in fleshly terms, strangers, you and I, it is as a lover I must speak to you now. I pray that I, in the interest of our mutual masterpiece, may do so without offense . . .

I have heretofore supplied you with the most meticulous of measurements and specifications. Do you, despite your sympathy, find my precision in these matters tyrannical, oppressive?

Let me assure you that, my apparent mania for detail notwithstanding, not for an instant do I forget you are an artiste, dear Fräulein. An artificer . . . indeed, a sorceress. Why otherwise should I have engaged your gifts for this enterprise on whose success my entire life and being depend?

It is acknowledgment of the wizardry I require of you that emboldens me to speak to you as, now, I must:

When you have studied the sketches I send, when you have calculated to the smallest fraction each divine measurement, I bid you go, as last resort and first authority, to your own body. For your efforts must, in the end, be guided by your own hand's explorations. Plunder all the softness and heat you, as a woman, possess. For only those can transmit to your conversant fingers what must ultimately defy measure. Our aim is no less than transubstantiation, that metastasis of matter into spirit that is art.

I beg your indulgence for discourse many would condemn. Were I not myself an artist, I should hardly dare raise such private subjects with you. Since first encountering your remarkable work in Herr Richter's gallery, however, I have recognized in you one who shares my sacred and profane knowledge: That the true work of art must ultimately partake of our deepest wantonness.

Submit to this knowledge, my friend and accomplice.

Tantalize the gods with your boldness.

You possess the means to bribe the fates.

Ransom, I beg you, this captive soul!

OK

THE GIRL'S YOUNG HIDE, ALREADY WIND-TOUGHENED, IS SPRINKLED WITH freckles and moles. Perspiring, the dip in her upper lip collects dewdrops. A mossy scent wafts from her clothes.

Oskar recalls tales of lost travelers saved from freezing by animal body heat, wild creatures briefly tamed by human distress. He imagines sleeping in a hayloft, the girl curled around him, smelling of damp earth.

Would she feel nothing?

A birthmark the color of tea slaps the inside of her wrist. Oskar stares at this mark as the girl sets meals on the table, whisks soiled plates from view. Oskar stares and stares and now and then nearly catches sight of . . . something written there, written inside Reserl's wrist.

Letters? Numbers? He can't quite make it out. Sometimes the birthmark lightens, flushes. It no longer resembles a tea stain, then, so much as the shadow of a blow . . . the aftermath of a rough clasp. Oskar imagines someone grabbing Reserl, dragging her somewhere she is desperate not to go . . .

No birthmark then, but a scar?

When the inside of Reserl's wrist reddens, Oskar sees the madness of his imaginings . . . nothing is written on that tender mistreated curve he so wants to touch, just there, letting his fingers confirm what his eyes can well see: No message, just the merest suggestion of force, of pain . . .

Where were they trying to take you? he longs to ask her.

In the part of his mind that feels like memory, Oskar hears Reserl's cries. The cause of her punishment is unknown, she tells him. They tell her nothing. The voice he hears in the dream feels like memory. He knows it is only an echo of the voice that has been taken from her.

In silence Reserl clears the tea things from the corner of Oskar's desk. "Will there be anything else?" she asks softly.

The teapot is a poor attempt at chinoiserie, its lid suggesting a coolie hat, its ear-shaped handle aping bamboo. *Plunder.* Junk. The girl handles it like a precious object. Were Oskar her master he would order her to smash the dreadful thing, so that it needn't lord it over either of them ever again. *Müll.*

She sweeps the corner of his desk with a damask napkin. With the motion of her hand the cuff of her blue smock turns back. The skin inside her wrist is the harsh color of a dowager's rouge. Something is written there. Numbers. He is sure of it.

"Thank you," he says. "Nothing else."

Out in the hallway, the girl smiles and nods. *"Mein Herr,"* she whispers. Master.

The door between them has already clicked closed.

Her right wrist? Her left? Afterward he can never remember. But he is sure he glimpsed something written there.

DIE SCHWEIGSAME FRAU . . . HIS SILENT WOMAN SHALL DWARF HER.

Narrow hips, demitasse breasts, an impossibly slender neck . . . a neck this world is bound to snap.

Soap-reddened hands like something he has, over and over, already painted, painted into immortality. One day he would no longer be able to help himself. He would paint her.

He has made a vow he will not . . . he will never defile her purity. Not in that way, he swears . . .

Defile her? Nakedness would dignify her. Oskar hates to admit it, but he has learned this one thing from Egon Schiele, the plagiarist.

The critics always seemed to be mentioning them in the same breath these days: *Schiele and Kokoschka, Schiele and Kokoschka* . . . when it ought at the very least to be the other way around! For years Egon has been helping himself to Oskar's gifts, nourishing his own puny talent with generous swipes from another's cupboard. Were it otherwise, how many would even know Schiele's name? Except in Vienna, of course, where a scandal has eternal life. Years since the painter was arrested and their native hive is still abuzz with it. Yes, Schiele has made a name for himself, all right.

Well, the Viennese with their heavy cream and the critics with their heavy jowls and the patrons with their heavy purses . . . none of them hard to hoodwink. But what of Schiele? Could he himself think Oskar wouldn't notice his pilfering? So only fair, Oskar thought, to snatch a little tidbit from brother Egon . . .

The delicious urchins Schiele was always after, the unsavory preoccupation that landed him in jail . . . perversity notwithstanding, the painter's instinct was true: Those urchins of his had to be stripped to be worth painting. Clothing must be mastered. Children let their garments impose upon them.

She is scarcely more than a child, Reserl. Nakedness would dignify her.

Perhaps he could paint just her hands. Reserl's hands: shirred with days in hot water, ruddy as Siena stone. They wring the life from pullets, scrub scum from cooking pots.

Alma's hands, too often idle, were utterly white and, even in summer, icy.

Plump as peonies, Alma's hands . . . closing his eyes, he sees them: a collar the color of death wreathing Reserl's chalky neck.

Vienna: The premature announcement of his death had sent her to his studio within the hour. Had he given her a key? He cannot recall. She may have tampered with the lock. It was her way to break and enter. Frau Gropius.

Paint the girl without touching her? He could hardly expect that of himself. But only her hands . . . if he . . .

Almi was the subject of each picture she laid claim to. Only those. What interest might she have had in the others?

Her hideous clothing was what debased the girl. He would husk her to purity. He would wrap her gritty fingers around a boar-bristle brush. He would not permit her to stop brushing until the ends of her hair spit sparks and burst into flame.

The pictures were more or less an afterthought. It was the letters that sped her to the morbid atelier. Letters *she* had written . . . surely that made them hers?

He does not need her nakedness for corroboration. There is no hair on Reserl's body. He knows this. Only upon her head, hair that, paroled from its austere braid, would rush and tumble down her back, a dark spill. An avalanche.

She *would* have mourned him, of course. Sooner or later Almi would have got around to that. There had, for a time, been much between them. For her he had gone to war, the officer's sky-colored tunic the costume of manhood. Weeks before he left, he saw himself, impeccably tailored, returning, returning to toss a blazing bouquet of heroic deeds at her feet. If only the architect had not been there to comfort her, so that her attention had been diverted from the pain of her lover's absence . . . if only Oskar had been more watchful, had not allowed the absurd little dalliance with Kammerer to distract him from the real danger, from . . .

There is no hair on her body. None, anywhere.

There was luxurious fur on her, his Almi, in the most unexpected places. Once he began to master the fine art of stroking her, she purred. She purred for him like a cat.

The girl's nipples will be small and hard and brown, coffee candies forever melting on the tongue.

He does not begrudge her the pictures. Their beauty is her belonging, of course.

He feels a curious pleasure when she looks directly into his eyes. It is the girl's one power, the withholding of a glance. He suspects she knows this. She looks at him but rarely, and never for long.

The letters are what he regrets. He would not, no matter how many times they pronounced him dead, have parted with her letters. Ever.

When her hair became a river of flame, he would kneel before her. His head would sink into the oasis of her thighs.

She purred like a cat. Her hands were always icy.

Were he to defile this child with his hunger for touch, her fingers should prove warm, nourishing as broth.

He shall not, for the foreseeable future, paint. How could he?

The war goes on without him. It will never be over, the war.

He cannot be moved.

4

Der General: He looks, outfitted in an ancient skin, like a lizard. His eyes are hooded. His cheeks are draped. He lies in a pool of sunlight, pretending to drowse. He is wrapped in scales. *Die Eidechse.* General Lizard.

Hans Posse will not be lunching at home today. An important patron is paying a long-fostered visit to the museum. One of the portrait galleries will be closed to the public, a sumptuous luncheon laid within sight of Heinrich the Pious and his overdressed bride.

Oskar has gone several times to view the much-vaunted portrait. Enjoying a meal within its view is inconceivable. Surely the Elder Cranach's lumbering symbolism would spoil the appetite. The patron, however, a lifelong romantic and recent newlywed, has a soft spot for the fussy painting. He also has a reputed weakness for French cuisine. A menu commencing with vichyssoise and concluding with marrons glacés is planned. Appropriate wines. The Direktor hopes to create an atmosphere favorable to discussing acquisitions. A superb Canaletto is about to come on the market in Rome.

Oskar, who finds rich food disagreeable, was relieved to learn the favor his host meant to ask of him would not require his presence at luncheon.

"If you could just look in now and then," Hans Posse said.

Der General. Die Eidechse. "Of course," said Oskar. "A chance to get acquainted."

"He doesn't exactly . . . converse. Please don't think him rude if—"

A tactful lift of Oskar's hand let the Direktor off the hook. The subject of his father obviously pained him.

"If it's a question of . . . physical comfort? The girl, of course, sees to such needs."

"Of course." Oskar pictured Reserl's strong hands grasping the General's shoulders, overturning him, kneading salve into a bony haunch.

"He will be looked after," Oskar said.

Hans Posse's frayed face worked into a taut smile. "It is such a great help," he said. "Having you here."

Her fingers, puckered and rosy, would smell of eucalyptus . . . at their tips the fine-grained coarseness of a cat's tongue . . .

"You must not worry," Oskar said.

HE HAD EVERY INTENTION OF PAYING A CALL TO THE GENERAL SHORTLY after his host's departure for the museum. Once Dr. Posse was gone, however, Oskar was undermined by lethargy. He could barely imagine summoning the strength to climb the stairs.

The morning was damp and chilly. At eight o'clock he'd hardly been able to glimpse the Elbe through its veils of fog. Mist snagged now in the unruly garden, muffling the sounds of kitchen clatter. The summerhouse was dank. Oskar wanted to go sit on the three-legged stool beside the kitchen stove, warming himself as he watched the girl roll dough across a flour-sown pastry board.

They had much to say to each other, Oskar and Reserl. But even their silences would be full of ease. Oskar imagined her performing her morning chores, her motions shaping themselves to his presence. A fiery tendril would evade her braid to sneak down the back of her impossibly white, smooth neck. Sometimes, so used to him beside her that she could forget he was there, she would start to hum, the sound of a breeze captive in her throat.

Mostly, though, he imagined the sound of their talk . . . Oskar and Reserl talking hours away in the warm kitchen. Oskar, lost to the murmuring, stood before the french doors of the summerhouse until his spine stiffened with cold. He could not make out a single word they might be saying.

It was close to noon by the time Oskar went to the house. He entered through a side door, avoiding the kitchen. The hallway smelled of soap and furniture wax. And perhaps ammonia? His eyes were stinging. Climbing the staircase to the General's room, he paused on the landing to listen. No sound suggested another presence in the house. Perhaps Reserl had gone . . . where on earth would the girl wander off to in the middle of the day? The very notion put Oskar out of sorts.

The door to the General's room stood open a few inches. The old man was likely asleep. Oskar peered through the gap. One lizardy eye, bright as a bead, stared at him from the bed. He's been waiting for me, Oskar thought. He opened the door wider.

"You did not discommode yourself by rushing, did you?"

Oskar started. "Did you need something?" He took a reluctant step inside. The room smelled of urine. "The girl seems to have gone out, but I—"

"Stay." The old man's hand fumbled under the blanket. "Don't move." He appeared to be seeking a weapon.

I have already been shot, Oskar imagined saying. *Don't trouble yourself.* He would describe to the old General how the bullet had entered his ear canal, sparing his life but stealing his balance. Now he inhabited a world perilously atilt. Its crazed angle could never be righted. For the first time Oskar felt a desire to explain to someone how he'd come to be so awry. He opened his mouth, but the old man's hard eyes kept the words backed up in his throat.

"Aslant, are you?" A smile cracked the lizard face into a million pieces. "They think I don't notice," the old man said. "Nothing escapes me."

Oskar nodded. "Lutsk."

He'd never before said it aloud, the name of the place where he'd been wounded. He wasn't sure why he'd feigned vagueness—with his family, with friends, even comrades—on details of the incident. But he knew. *Lutsk.* A bayonet thrust through his lung, and . . .

Somehow the old man knew all of it.

"Lutsk." The General nodded. "Who is your commanding officer, boy?"

"I haven't—"

"I'll not countenance evasion." Thunder boomed from the frail body on the bed.

"General von Bosch," Oskar whispered, "but I—"

"And you have learned nothing from such leadership?"

Oskar bowed his head. "Nothing."

"And so it goes." The General sounded delighted.

"I understand very little now."

"You supposed battle was staged for your education?" The old man chuckled. "Silly pup. The fact that war grinds you in its molars has nothing to do with you. Nothing whatsoever. Found that out, I gather? Don't say you've learned nothing."

"I barely remember," Oskar murmured.

"And never will." The old man smiled. "Not to say you'll forget."

Oskar raised his head. The General's dark eyes, lustrous and opaque, resembled Almi's black pearls. Oskar stopped breathing.

The old man's smile vanished. "But then you wouldn't care to." His voice became a young man's, uncertain and unguarded. "Forget. Surely you would not wish that?"

"No," Oskar said.

The cracked smile returned. "There is your education," the lizard said.

Downstairs a door opened. Footsteps skittered along the hall. Then, from the front parlor, the sound of shattering. *Minor damage.*

Oskar pictured the girl on her knees, bare hands scooping bright shards of glass from the tiled hearth. He imagined licking droplets of blood from the tucks between her small rough fingers. His tongue turned metallic and salty.

"She'll come up any minute." The old man was staring past Oskar at the open window. His eyes brimmed with yearning.

Oskar turned to look. The window framed the glare of an overcast noontime, calling undue attention to the Hofkirche's steeple, its usual grime. Nothing remarkable. His gaze returned to the bed.

"Why do you stare at me?"the old man said.

Oskar started. "I had understood you were no longer able to . . . converse."

The old General's lips were slightly agape. A trickle of saliva leaked from the corner of his mouth. "Very little remains to say."

After a moment Oskar nodded, then turned and slipped from the room.

Augustus Posse's eyes did not leave the smoke-colored sky.

The skin . . .

What stuff of this earth could replicate my beloved's incomparable skin?

We must do what we can, dear abettor, with such inferior materials as an imperfect world provides.

Commence, of course, with the most delicate of fabrics, yet with a texture . . . raw silk? Finespun linen? Possibly . . . but only should its substance prove buoyant and gossamer-frail.

I am, I confess, driven to despair's frontier by attempting to approach . . . so heavy and coarse, words, are they not?

I have consulted a chemist—did I tell you? He shall at my behest seek the proper adherent. Something to coax silk to cling to cotton underlining without betrayal of such fragile beauty as belongs to silk alone. What I seek is more likely to be produced by an alchemist, this man of science remarks, than by a practitioner of his own profane trade. Like any fool, our chemist is convinced of his own cleverness. His boisterous amusement further scants my scant hope, of course. Needless to say, our thick-headed accomplice labors in the dark, where the true nature of our project is concerned.

In any case, the approximation of complexion can best be attained, I believe, through the application of tiny swatches, meeting and overlapping and . . . imagine, if you will, the most intricate mosaic, made seamless. There can in our methods be no allowance for the broad or vulgar. (Do I blazon the flagrant once more?)

WEEKS SINCE HE LAST SAW HER, AND LITTLE TO SHOW FOR HIMSELF.

"Be sure to bring your portfolio," she'd written. "I must see your new work."

He carries instead a bedraggled wad of late lilies, picked to divert her attention. (Why, he wonders, should they remind him of toads?)

And why trouble himself over diverting Katja, who never has trouble diverting herself? In the past few weeks, while collaborating on a one-act play and extricating herself from a rather snarled *affaire de coeur,* she has attended a performance of *Carmen,* taken up cigarettes, and moved out of her father's house . . . all for the second time.

Her newly feathered nest consists of two cramped rooms tucked under the eaves of the same sprawling guest house Oskar once briefly occupied. Dr. Teuscher's sanatorium lay just across the Weisser Hirsch. He could probably glimpse it from Katja's windows. Not that he'd care to revisit the place. Treatment for combat's aftershocks . . . his memories of its particulars remain blessedly vague. If only his nightmares' horrid monotonies would desert him as well.

Near the end of 1916 Oskar had torn himself from Berlin to place himself in Dr. Teuscher's care. Not, certainly, the most opportune time in his career to remove himself from circulation. And Christmas was approaching. But Oskar was desperate by then.

Franz Teuscher, a hearty man with a strangely childish sense of humor, seemed an unlikely savior. The physician lacked sobriety. He laughed immoderately at his own jokes. He was, however, widely acknowledged as the foremost expert in the treatment of shell shock. His was a timely gift. The sanatorium's waiting list stretched across Europe and was said to be several years long.

Oskar had Fritz Neuberger to thank for his prompt acceptance as a patient. *He was not without friends . . .* These German doctors all kowtowed to one another, of course.

Not to say Dr. Teuscher wasn't dedicated. A wonder he hadn't collapsed by now, trying to reverse the Great War's devastation all by himself. His giddiness was likely a sign of exhaustion.

Teuscher's sanatorium first seemed an ideal haven. There, for the first time in nearly a year, Oskar was able to sleep. And eat. The food was bland and enticing, egg custards and creamed soups. In the afternoons he read, jotting promising thoughts in a little notebook with neat lined pages. He had, by the second week, begun to lose the cadaverous look that actually rather suited an artist, he thought. He scarcely noticed Christmas drifting past him, merely another restful day.

The lull in torment was short-lived, however. One otherwise uneventful night in January, the sanatorium, a wide-winged brick house with a stone foundation, started trembling beneath Oskar. All night the air whistled around his head. Morning, when it came, was no safer. Shrieks and detonations rode in on the light.

Confining Captain Kokoschka to his room proved unnecessary. By the time the order was issued, Oskar had already dragged the mattress from his bed and fashioned a bunker inside the wardrobe. No one could coax him out. Restraints and sedatives were applied. Nothing calmed him.

After a week it was recommended, not without regret, that Captain Kokoschka seek alternate lodging. His cries distressed the other patients, Dr. Teuscher said.

"They are easily alarmed, some of these boys." The physician offered a zany smile, and a handshake with a wintergreen lozenge tucked inside it.

Oskar continued for a few more weeks as a day patient. The Felsenberg Inn, hospitable and conveniently located, also proved economical, Dr. Neuberger being the most indulgent of landlords. Best of all, the foundations of the guest house rarely bucked beneath him.

The Felsenberg's other occupants, a rowdy band of young actors and musicians, took instantly to Oskar. The flat voice in which his war stories were recounted made them all the more hair-raising. He wore a fey mix of military and bohemian clothes. If his behavior was a little odd, all the more reason to embrace him.

Oskar remained desperate to believe in Dr. Teuscher's treatments, and Fritz Neuberger, alarmed by his friend's condition, encouraged him to continue. But faith best thrived, it seemed, in clinical isolation. Back in the world Oskar succumbed to skepticism. His new friends egged doubt on. A man whose livelihood and reputation rested on war was hardly, they said, to be trusted.

The parting of ways with Teuscher was not amicable . . . some dissent over fees? Oskar's memory is cloudy on this point. He must not have acquitted himself well, he gathers, for since leaving the sanatorium, he has twice encountered Dr. Teuscher in Dresden's streets. Both times the genial physician has stared right through him, as if he didn't exist.

Returning now to the Felsenberg invites a painful rush of feeling. Details and doubts best left in the dark. Had Oskar allowed himself to be unduly influenced? Behaved abominably? Defaulted on debts? A mercy, perhaps, how little he recalls . . .

There was a girl from Prague. A musician. Oskar remembers a halo of copper ringlets. Flora. Dr. Teuscher must be some sort of sadist, the girl claimed. Why dig up putrid things best kept buried? And those so-called sedatives, sleeping powders . . . one day he might wake from a peaceful doze to find his creativity gone.

"Not to mention your manhood." The boy, a French horn player from Magdeburg, claimed to be a pacifist. Oskar suspected he had a more than passing interest in Flora. Indeed, he could get rather bellicose about her. The sanatorium's capsules and tinctures had left some lads impotent, he claimed with a hopeful gleam in his eye.

The icy evening Oskar returned to the Felsenberg to announce severing his ties with Dr. Teuscher, the whole house (Dr. Neuberger was in Switzerland on business) celebrated with several bottles of Rheinpfalz and blithely went without supper.

It was after midnight when Flora led Oskar to her room. Her lovemaking proved less venturesome than her convictions. The sweet wine had left Oskar with a headache. Flora slept soundly, her body giving off a scorching heat. Her harp leaned, tipsy, in the corner of the cramped room. Its eerie gold shine ruined the dark.

"OSKAR?"

He spun around, turning his back on the windows, expecting to see Flora in her long faded-blue nightdress, her hair in raptures of abandon.

"Well?" Katja said.

Oskar folded his arms across his chest to muffle the thudding of his heart. "It's very nice," he said.

The small sitting room, scarcely more than the bedroom's threshold, was artfully littered with costumes and curios. Katja had, as usual, embraced her latest preoccupations with a vengeance. Spanish fans and Gypsy shawls abounded. A bust of Herr Richter looked down from a high shelf, mortified by a geisha wig and a false mustache. Everything wavered behind a scrim of yellowish smoke.

The room resembled a collage, Oskar thought, Katja's bare outline emerging, distorted yet recognizable, from the jumble. Nearly thirty and still auditioning new identities . . . not that he'd wish to rush the process. Should Katja ever settle on one version of herself, the drama of her life wouldn't likely offer him much of a role. He belonged to her wandering period.

" 'Very nice'? This is all the new voice of Dadaist theater can say?"

Oskar stared at her blankly.

"One expects an artist to be more observant." Katja waited a moment. When Oskar failed to respond, she pointed upward, as if reminding him Divinity hovered.

"Ah," Oskar said.

Bright billows of shiny fabric lowered the room's unusually high ceiling, filtered its available light. A tent. Of course. Oskar realized why, despite the obvious homage to Carmen, he'd had the sense of a Bedouin encampment. He smiled. Katja would ever be a nomad. There would always be a part for him.

"How on earth did you get up there?"

"I trust you are enchanted." She meant, he knew, to look mysterious. If only she were not so anxious for him to approve.

"Intrigued," Oskar allowed. "Is that a hot air balloon?"

"What remains of one. A gift to our abortive little theater company." The tender point of her chin rose in a sweet calculation of defiance. "Papa, sad to say, turned beastly. We'd hoped he could be counted on to donate a building. He has several."

Random bits of the saga began rising to the algaed surface of Oskar's memory—the industrialist's son grown tired within a fortnight of ballooning, the avant-garde theater company that never got off the ground, "Papa's" exhausted largesse. Oskar had heard the whole tale at some point. He hoped Katja wasn't about to provide a tedious recounting. He'd come for some cheering-up.

"Lovely how the color pools." Oskar's gaze roamed the room. "We are submerged." He smiled at her again.

Too late. Katja, set in her sulk, began beating the settee cushions into fluff.

"You've done wonders," Oskar said. "You've really a painter's eye, you know, when it comes to color."

Katja continued to slap at the cushions, but her expression softened. Gold hoops the size of napkin rings dithered from her earlobes. Her embroidered peasant blouse, deserting her shoulders, dared more bosom than was, even for Katja, customary. She turned and bent over a Chinese-red coffee table. Oskar spotted a fleeting pink shadow of aureole.

"So you are at least a little—"

"Enchanted," he murmured. "Helplessly."

Katja helped him off with his opera cloak, her birthday gift to him in March. Now, in late September, cold air had raced down out of the mountains, ushering in winter in a dreadful rush. Along the paths of the Weisser Hirsch, puddles were laced with ice. The ridiculous wrap could no longer be avoided. Leaving the Posse house, Oskar had car-

ried it rolled in a sack. The Direktor, observing him so negligently outfitted, had hinted more sensible dressing might lead to more robust
health.

Sensible? Would a sensible man sequester himself with the emanci-
pated Fräulein Richter in a cozy apartment on a cold afternoon? Would
a sensible man's fingers turn tremulous in their craving to reach a ring of
rosy skin peeking from a neckline's swoop?

"Whatever do you keep smiling about?" Katja's voice was sharp.

"Perhaps we should go out," Oskar said. "For coffee?"

"I have coffee. Some lovely Arabian."

His cloak, flung, fell upon the settee's flowery humped back. Costume absorbed into set. Dark wool turned back, exposing silk, a preen
of paisley. A prong of velvet collar pierced the lush crease of a peach
satin cushion.

Humiliating, how little it took to arouse him. Oskar forced his attention to a sketch above the hearth. It was ineptly framed and was not, as
a likeness, very good. Her nose had been prettified. The glitter of her
eyes looked brittle. Still, it was Katja.

"Wherever did you get that?"

"From your dustbin." The sound of her laugh, low and intimate, fon-
dled his groin. "The studio in Loschwitz. We'd met a week previous, I
think." Her eyes could indeed glitter like that. So hard. He'd forgotten.

Nails of light driven into the tenderness of . . . Almi, my beautiful eye.

"You'd made me look like a respectable milliner with a dirty mind,
you said."

"I said that?"

Her smile was insinuating. His arousal must be obvious. Oskar
turned back toward the window.

He'd been wrong about the sanatorium. It could not be seen from
here. But he knew it was there, just across the park, where someone was
always dying . . .

"I've missed you." Katja touched his arm.

He flinched.

"You wouldn't be keeping a lovely surprise from me?" she whispered. "From your chum?"

The warm press of her body to his back nearly unbalanced him. He
watched her small white hands begin to busy themselves with the front
of his trousers.

Fly buttons, underclothes . . . Katja's hands were swift and un-scrupulous. Hands that might have been his own, painting. Brush or palette knife dropping to the floor, as his soul gave itself up to the paint's seduction. Slippery, heady and warm as desire, the paint . . . thickening dark and deepening as with ecstatic fingers he stroked, caressing, and the canvas engorged with life . . .

No matter how he scrubbed afterward, his hands would not come clean. The paint's fleshy reek stayed on his fingers, dark rinds rimmed his nails. Days later, suddenly noticing the incriminating gore of color that spattered the floorboards around his easel, Oskar would feel shocked and shamed.

Women do not know such abasement, he thought. A woman's passions are not severed from will. *Phantom pain.* All over Europe now one saw it, stumps twitching with helpless desire.

He wanted her mouth on him. *Helpless.* He imagined his flesh cold and obstinate as marble against her tongue. He swallowed hard. His mouth was watering.

His arms, reaching backward, bent at impossible angles. *Not sensible.* The lenient shoulders of her blouse would sweetly yield, her nipples inflame at the chafe of his woolen lapels.

A sound like a hum trapped in Katja's throat. Behind him. His hands kept clutching at emptiness. Like Almi. Far back beyond his reach. He did not want to be here.

Oskar wrenched around. His teeth were clenched, his eyes closed. He heard the rip of cloth. The blouse fell to Katja's waist. The intake of her breath was short and sharp. He did not want to see or hear. He did not want her taste on his tongue, its desert heat bitter with to-bacco.

She was his one true friend. They were trapped in a tent of pitiless light, flailing through baffles of gaudy cloth and sexual puzzles.

"I do not want to lose you," Oskar whispered. He did not know whom he meant.

He knew he could not paint.

Must not touch the girl, nor wish to.

The sound of Almi's mocking laughter must be stilled, the Maestro's belittling breaths stifled. He would, failing this, go mad.

He did not want to hear the exploding air, the screams.

Nor to live on, alone, in a silent world.

Desire, like despair, was severed from will.

Oskar, helpless, tried to pull away. Katja would not let him go. He did not hear the cry wrung from him. But he felt the hot quick spill of himself, falling false and wasted into the deep scarlet folds of a Gypsy skirt, forever lost in ruined gaiety.

5

Astonishing, really, how seldom he recalled the lost child.

Lost? Not quite the word, perhaps. But what—abandoned? discarded?

I've done away with it was how she had put it.

Alma's face looked drawn when she returned. She seemed tired. He did not know where she had been. He recalled thinking her travels must have been more difficult than she'd cared to admit. A statement so simple and direct was unlike her. *I've done away with it.* His child. Theirs. And: *It was the best thing, of course.*

"The best thing?" said Oskar.

"The *only* thing," Alma told him.

The sound of his own weeping had alarmed him . . . something dire and inevitable heard at a vast remove.

His tears infuriated her. "You behave as if it is something that happened to *you,*" she said.

THEY HAD BEEN HAPPY, THEIR FIRST SUMMER TOGETHER, IN SWITZERLAND. Happy despite the constant intrusions of Alma's new friend. Lili was in love with her. Madly in love. She was very rich, Lili. Lesbians were curious, Almi said. So passionate. She found them amusing.

Alma never looked amused when Oskar entered a room to find her talking with Lili. Both women struck him as quite serious, in fact.

"Her devotion to me . . . surely you can see it is comical?" Alma's laugh weighted the air like expensive perfume. She shooed him from their bedroom. She needed to dress. Luncheon with Lili at the hotel. Oskar flustered her, she said. She would be late.

Day after day, his worn shoes trampled the lake's hem. The water was the dark blue of Almi's sapphire. Not long ago, in Vienna, she had forced the ring over the knuckle of Oskar's little finger. When it could not be removed, she had clapped in delight. "We are bound for eternity," she said.

A few weeks later, in a mood more pensive than petulant, Alma sent Oskar to the Molls' family jeweler. This jeweler was known for his discretion, as well as his artistry. The thin platinum band was easily cut and mended. The stone was an unusually fine one, the jeweler said. He hoped Frau Mahler, should she ever consider selling the piece, would offer him first opportunity to . . .

Sell it? Unthinkable! The sapphire was a gift from the Maestro.

Oskar's vagrant footsteps looped the deep blue lake. He suffered dizzy spells. The days Alma lunched at the hotel with Lili he found it difficult to remember to eat. Oskar wondered what women did together, how they arranged their bodies for pleasure. It embarrassed him that he did not know.

He'd known quite a few lesbians, actually. Particularly in Berlin. Else Lasker-Schüler, for one. He'd assumed so anyway, her marriage to Herwarth Walden notwithstanding. Else wore trousers and a turban and wrote poems combustible with odd, unruly passions. Her intimate friends called her "Prince Yussef." She insisted. Of course Else had a son. And was a genius. Which created some confusion. Still, genius or not, surely Else was a lesbian? Oskar wondered if Walden knew. Or minded. If that was the reason for their recent divorce.

Oskar had fallen a bit in love with Else himself, actually. How could he have helped it, hearing the gold bells jingle on her sandal straps as she traipsed between the Café des Westens's tipsy little tables?

By the time they met, he was already smitten with Lasker-Schüler's poems, their singular images, piercing and misshapen, that somehow seemed etched into the pages of *Die Fackel* and *Der Sturm*. That Else was old enough to be his mother merely made her checkered pantaloons, her morphine-glossed gaze more seductive. Before she came to his rescue, before she'd even spoken to him, Oskar's heart was enslaved. She called him, for some reason, *Vogelfänger.* Bird catcher? Else was not in the habit of explaining herself. The way she looked at him, the way her edgy voice softened when she spoke to him, made the epithet honorific. Yes, she'd seen the makeshift little portfolio of Oskar's portraits Loos had been showing around Berlin. Her hand, wizened and translucent as a sun-seared crab shell, seized Oskar's rough red fingers. Then, bowing like a footman, she kissed his right hand.

"You aren't left-handed, I trust?"

Oskar wordlessly shook his head. Then, unaccountably, he began to weep.

She seemed to read his tears, as if they were words written on his face. "Yes," she said after a moment. "Oh, *Liebchen,* I know."

Because he believed her, he told the poetess everything: How he had left Vienna with only a small satchel of shabby clothes and a loaf of his mother's *Schwarzbrot* in a paper sack and his father's insults— *Fehlschlag! Tölpel!*—echoing in his ears. And how—

"Fehlschlag?" Else Lasker-Schüler smiled. "An artist is *supposed* to be a disappointment to his bourgeois papa."

Ein Künstler . . . she'd called him an artist! For an instant Oskar imagined returning her bow, kissing the crablike hand.

"I know we've only just met." Reaching up with both arms, she blotted Oskar's eyes on her cuffs. Her purple sateen jacket was rather gladiatorial. "Still, I feel certain you are not a dolt."

Oskar told her the rest then: How, leaving the railway station, he'd found a barber to scrape the stubble from his skull; how the barber had preyed on his exhaustion and anxiety, convincing him of the need for tonics and pomades and elixirs (not to mention the sterling razor, the ivory-handled boar's bristle brush!) whose scents were (the barber hinted) the very essence of urbanity.

Else Lasker-Schüler did not laugh at him, even when Oskar confessed he'd noted neither the barber's name nor the address of his shop. Else simply ensconced the young painter between her long-legged self and her round-shouldered husband. Then, leaving the Café des Westens somewhat earlier than was their habit, Herr and Frau Walden took Oskar to their flat, fed him fried ham and boiled potatoes, and put him to bed on a rump-sprung brown sofa smelling of cats.

By the time Oskar awoke the next day, Else had already located the barber, returned the extravagant merchandise, and obtained a full refund—including the price of the shave.

Oh, yes, Oskar had a weakness for potent and passionate and peculiar women, lesbian or not. But Lili Leiser was not nearly so easy as Else to love. And no genius, except as a meddler perhaps. Lili was the sort of woman who made conversation by putting words in others' mouths. She thought nothing of hanging about for hours while Almi sat for him, freely partaking of their intimacy. Her eyes, blind to Oskar, sated themselves on Alma's flesh.

In Vienna, scant weeks before, painting Alma had nearly always led to lovemaking. Often rather quickly.

There must have been a dozen portraits—Almi on their hotel balcony, a snowy bust of mountains behind her. Lili appeared in none of them, but she was always there.

The lake licked the stony path. Oskar pictured Alma naked on her back on a striped mattress in a sterile room. Lili knelt between her knees, spreading her thighs, stroking them.

White as snow, Alma's thighs. Lili's head, dark and sleek and narrow as a seal's, lowered between them.

Oskar watched the mild amusement on Almi's face turn to pleasure. She moaned. Her hand, rising from the mattress, came to rest on Lili's dark glistening head.

Oskar would know, of course, the taste on Lili's tongue.

Alma and Lili frequently lunched together at the hotel. There was little else, really, to do . . . unless, of course, one should paint.

Reaching past Oskar to the breakfast tray, Alma dipped a finger into a cut-glass dish of currant jelly. It was all, wasn't it, just so peaceful? And yet invigorating, too . . .

She stared out the window for a moment, as she began to lick the bright red beads of jelly from her fingertip. The sapphire on her finger was the precise shade of a Swiss lake in late summer.

HE TIRED OF WALKING, TIRED UNTIL AT LAST THE LAKE'S COLOR WAS LOST on him.

Almi tired of Lili. She pressed her friend into accompanying Gucki back to Vienna.

"I'll join you there shortly," Alma said. "It would be such a help, dear."

Lili seemed never to tire of trying to please.

Gucki cried.

Lili was not good with children.

Alma needed, she said, to be alone for a while. Wasn't it all just terribly exhausting?

Lili herself had not found it so, but darling Almchen did look tired.

Where, Oskar asked, did she intend to go?

Perhaps Munich? Alma was not entirely certain. If I do not get some time for myself I shall go mad, she said.

Oskar spent another week in Mürren, alone. Switzerland, sadly, no longer seemed to inspire him. Its beauty lacks ambiguity, he thought.

He did not paint after Alma and Lili were gone. His meals remained irregular. He returned to Vienna a week earlier than planned.

Almi's return lagged several days behind his. She looked pale.

"I did away with it," she said, her tone matter-of-fact. Oskar's first thought, for some reason, was that she meant her sapphire ring.

The delusion survived but an instant, no more.

KATJA'S BEDROOM WAS, AS OSKAR HAD IMAGINED, A GOOD DEAL MORE spacious and functional than the sitting room. Its lack of frippery further enlarged it. The bed, a simple platform, was made of sturdy weathered planks. A stagehand Katja had befriended (and seduced, of course) had constructed it. The boy, a well-built lad from Thuringia, owed his wartime theatrical career to a suddenly fortuitous clubfoot.

He'd allowed his family the cherished illusion that he devoted his days to fashioning artificial limbs for those less blessed. His own favored fate the boy credited to Saint Boniface, after whom his devout Catholic parents had named him.

Arriving in Dresden with his improbable Thespian dreams, Boniface had allowed himself to be called Erich. A more *portable* name, a sympathetic producer had advised.

Aside from the foot, Erich's endowments were marvelous, Katja said. With one proviso, that is. One must remember not to use the boy's pseudonym. At the sound of "Erich," he sadly wilted.

This tale was widely known by now, in Dresden's cozy little bohemia. Oskar was being treated to his third account of *l'affaire Boniface* as Katja showed off her new bedroom. Her Gypsy costume had, piece by piece, been abandoned during their abridged liaison in the sitting room. Her nakedness now, Oskar assured himself, had no particular meaning. Seduction, effrontery, and primitive comfort could be all of a piece. Katja was by no means an uncomplicated creature.

Oskar, his scratchy trousers neatly rebuttoned, tried not to look ruffled as he eyed the legendary bed. "A testament to staying power, indeed," he said.

His praise for the bed's dimensions, its coarse grain and custom-made ticking, was unstinting. He tried not to imagine the Thuringian youth's endowments too clearly . . . aside from the fortunately flawed foot. But the inevitable images afflicted him. Oskar was, after all, something of a visionary.

The top of Katja's head barely topped his shoulder when they stood side by side. Once, caught in a downpour with her, Oskar had picked her up and carried her in his arms down the Alexanderplatz, merely for the sake of her ivory kid boots. In Berlin one could indulge such impulses. Before the war one could.

Now, at the foot of Käthe Richter's big solid bed, her rose-mottled body unwrapped beside him, Oskar felt small indeed.

Katja, as if sensing this, rose on tiptoe and kissed his cheek. "Don't, *Liebchen,*" she said.

"What?"

"Look sad." Her fingertip traced the flat line of his upper lip. "Don't *brood,*" she said.

The bed was so *brazen,* somehow. Flooded with unstinting daylight. Taking up most of the room.

Hushed and muffled, Alma's bed . . . bandaged in darkness.

She had, it turned out, little taste for afternoon lovemaking. Only by night's darkness, Alma said, could wantonness fully bloom.

There were, in any case, so many claims made upon Frau Mahler's afternoons.

Oskar was allowed, very occasionally, to sleep through an entire night beside her. He would wake in a panic, inexplicably certain morning had arrived, terrorized by the absence of confirming light.

Velvet drapes the color of ancient bloodstains concealed the four tall windows in Alma's room. Heavy silk cords dragged from the drapes. These cords were unused. The drapes were never pulled back.

Garlands and corsages, tribute from the bewitched and devoted, crowded Alma's dressing table. Bouquets cowered in corners in vases and baskets and bowls. She'd keep flowers long past freshness, rarely thinking to change their water. The room's overripe scent reminded Oskar of a swamp.

She found morning lovemaking distasteful. What use passion, she said, if all the senses were not fully awake? From time to time, she did submit, her thighs parting grudgingly to Oskar's odd craving.

Sometimes, bereft of morning's due light, he would start to weep at the moment of release. Alma beneath him, still and cool as stone. Tears streamed from his eyes. Sweat poured down his face. Oskar did not notice. He grieved for some part of himself lost deep inside her, left to bleed alone in the dark.

A swish of silk snatched Oskar from his trance. A glance at Katja told him his return was overdue.

Keeping her back to him, she stood before a pier glass. She had put on a black silk dress. Its high collar was locked tight with a staid cameo.

Eyes trained on her reflection, Katja began to pin up her hair.

Oskar stepped up behind her at an angle, keeping his reflection from joining hers in the oval of glass. "Forgive me," he said softly, "if I seem to be—"

"Unforgivable?" Her mouth was curt with hairpins.

"Perhaps I should leave," Oskar said.

Katja yanked a fistful of curls to the crown of her head and stabbed it with a beetle-black hairpin.

"You know I can't bear it when you're displeased with me." Oskar admitted a slight quiver to his voice.

In the mirror Katja raised her eyes and looked at him.

Oskar hung his head.

"I suppose we might," she said, "go out for coffee."

RESERL ROSE, ON MARKETING DAYS, WELL BEFORE DARK. THE MAKINGS OF a simple breakfast would be laid out on the dining table: bread and jam and cheese, a covered dish of simmered fruit. The silver urn would be filled with coffee. It was extremely strong, Reserl's coffee. By the time

Oskar and Hans Posse would come downstairs, it would have turned blacker, more bitter. But it would still be hot.

On Tuesdays and Fridays Oskar felt the stillness, the emptiness of Reserl's going, the moment he awoke. He'd loiter in his bed in the summerhouse, imagining her flight. She'd glance back before leaving the park. The house would, at a distance, look unfamiliar. Turning onto the broad avenue, she would begin to run.

She would reach the market stalls a step ahead of daylight, before the sun could wilt the vegetables, flies dance over the meat on their hairy legs.

Oskar never knew, of course, when Reserl left, nor when, exactly, she returned. He found this, for reasons obscure to him, unsettling. Oskar wished he could fasten a bell around Reserl's neck. Like a cat. A small silver bell on a blue satin ribbon, with a sound he alone could hear.

A disgraceful little fantasy, he knew it. The girl wasn't a pet, after all. He simply liked knowing she was in the house.

Mostly, though, he wished he could know when she was gone. Oskar imagined, on the mornings Reserl was out, slipping into her room. The door at the back of the pantry would stand ajar, as if he were expected. The tossed covers on the narrow cot would smell of her. Two of Reserl's three dresses would sag from nails on the wall, a third nail, unused and rusty, beside them. Seeing the two dresses, Oskar would be able to picture her precisely, a blue or green form on its rush toward the market. He would add to the picture a large empty basket, hooked over one arm. He would watch it catch on the snaggy cloth of her skirt, blue or green, as she ran.

Had Oskar only known when Reserl left, he might have gained an hour, at least, to study her few belongings. At his leisure he could have gazed into the sail-shaped shard of mirror, where her shadow might still flick like the wings of a fly snagged in a web . . .

He might have upended the thin mat on Reserl's cot, might even have rummaged at the bottom of the potato bin.

A thorough search might have brought to light a number of things. Such as:

Two tortoiseshell combs, relics of a mother whose long fall of dark auburn hair could, in time, have taught her child defiance . . .

Or a coppery likeness, perhaps, of a half-starved boy, his eyes downcast at a pair of tight hand-me-down boots, somewhere near the front . . .

Or an unexpectedly tender letter from a father who, had he, as a boy, been allowed to stay in school long enough to learn to write, might have grown into a man capable of forgetting his grievances, or coming to his senses, or entertaining second thoughts . . .

Imagine a book of recipes, filched from a neighboring farmhouse . . .

Picture a fetid green rag balled up among potatoes verdigris with mold or a blue-and-white prayer shawl with knotted fringes or a blessing for bread written in a foreign alphabet or a tangle of rusting hairpins or . . .

Who knows what Oskar might have turned up in the hour before Reserl returned?

She would, in due time, turn up, Reserl. Her basket would be filled: green flourishes of lettuce, a rainbow-scaled fish, a posy of scarlet radishes, their tendrils black with soil.

No line was drawn in Oskar between the imagined and the seen. He lay in his sweaty bed in the summerhouse and saw the girl with the sun in her eyes, saw her weave from stall to stall, foraging. A cluster of ink-dark grapes deep in her apron pocket for safekeeping. A pyramid of tiny apricots coddled in her palm.

But he did not know where she was, of course. Nor just when she might be back. Reserl could already be cutting across the Zwinger. She might or might not pause there, cooling herself in the palace's broad shadow. Perhaps, remembering her unmade bed, she'd start to run, tilted with the basket's weight.

Had she been given a pillow? Might its hollow still show where her head lay in sleep?

He sleeps little, battle's obvious residue. Oskar is always awake before dawn. How is it he never hears the girl leaving?

In her small room behind the pantry his dreams would not be able to find him. If only Oskar could be certain Reserl herself would not catch him there, resting for a moment, asleep on the cot whose patched linens still seem, impossibly, to hold the heat of her body, its mossy scent . . .

He sees her: She moves from stall to stall, taking her time now. The sun is up. She has what is needed. Why hurry back? Her absence will scarcely be noticed, so long as the coffee has not cooled.

A round pumpernickel loaf . . . carried like an infant in the crook of one arm, its still-warm weight against her ribs. Six brown eggs nested in a tea towel balance atop all else the basket can hold. She must not run. Reserl must be mindful not to run.

If only he could be certain she would not return and . . .

If only he could be certain she would return and . . .

She would find him there, succumbed to her scent's lullaby, his head fitted into the hollow her head has made and . . .

Dreams of the war would never find him there. Not in her small room.

Oskar never knows when Reserl leaves, not until after she is gone. There is no telling when she might return. He does not even know if she has a pillow.

THE KÜGELGEN HAUS HUNKERED AMONG THE DUSTY BOOKSHOPS ACROSS from the old market hall. Katja loved the Hauptstrasse. One day her statue, she said, would claim its own shady spot among the stone artists and goddesses that graced the street.

An inscription near the restaurant door distracted Oskar:

In Gottes Segen ist alles belegen . . . intriguing message to mark the spot where the painter von Kügelgen met his end. Shot more than a century ago by a soldier deserting a war far different. Still, an impersonal sort of madness Oskar felt he could comprehend. Wars laud acts of madness, so long as they aren't personal. *In God's sight are all things blessed.*

God will provide might, at the moment, bode better for him personally. There wasn't much money in his pocket. Katja was known for her expensive appetite.

As they stepped inside the restaurant, Oskar's dog-paddling spirit sank. Murals bloated with nostalgia for Old Dresden insinuated high prices and heavy cuisine.

An elderly gent, his face impassive and colorless as plaster of paris, relieved Oskar of his cloak. The flamboyant garment failed to impress him. They were led to a table at the back of the restaurant.

The hour was early. The place was uncrowded. Katja was visibly miffed. The kitchen door swung back and forth, each opening a rude announcement of clanging implements and hot air.

Before Oskar could object to the location, the old man had skittered away.

Katja settled herself in her huff. Oskar saw the hour he'd spent sketching her, burnt offering to her vanity, go up in smoke.

That the poor sketch of her must be replaced with a worthier portrait had been his opening gambit. But Katja's pouts were not easily checked. She stood beside the unrumpled bed, stiff in her ersatz widow's weeds. The usual enticements—teasing, flattery, apology—were not, Oskar guessed, likely to work.

Little wonder she found him unforgivable. A man with the least bit of chivalry would know better than to show a naked woman his back. Insult apparently accrued to injury when she'd observed him fussing with his cravat. He wanted to be Katja's *friend* . . . why couldn't she just *let him*? How had things got so balled up?

No choice, in the end, but to wheedle her out of the black silk dress. An operation not without risk. He'd first gently steered her back to the sitting room, away from the bed, making a game of it all. Punishment promised if she touched him, unspecified rewards if she did not. Katja adored games.

Oskar, his hands taking small mollifying liberties, arranged her on the garish settee. He'd turbaned her head in a silk scarf of gold and orchid stripes. The gold hoops she'd forgotten to remove in deference to the black dress turned perfect against her nakedness. Her eyelids reclaimed their sensual weight. Her full lips held to their pout, but loosely now.

What kind of a man would be able to resist her? So lost was Oskar in picturing her that he found no irony in the thought.

He stepped back to study her from the bedroom doorway.

He returned to the settee and ran his palms down her thighs. He might have been smoothing a cloth over a table.

Katja did not move, did not even breathe.

Oskar grasped her left leg, raising her knee, separating her legs slightly. Then, taking hold of her hips, he turned her lower torso just a fraction, bringing the dark plumage between her thighs to light.

For a moment his hand rested on the curve of her belly.

A flush rose on her chest.

"Ah," Oskar said.

This small benediction freed Katja's breath in a long, deep sigh.

Oskar straightened and backed away, studying the form on the settee. His eyes took full possession of her now. He watched the muscles in her fine-boned face grow lax and replete. He saw the tip of her tongue appear, a wet pink bud caught in her teeth.

He sensed, for a scant moment, the enormous effort in her stillness. Her body hovered, he knew, on the very cusp of release.

A woman would, without thought, yield to the rise and plunge. Her legs would open wide. Cries would abrade her throat. Hidden within her the tiny tongue . . .

A generous lover could have, *would* have, freed passion with a fingertip, the merest kiss.

The artist stared from the doorway of the bedroom, not yet quite satisfied.

His model held perfectly still.

Superb contrast, Oskar thought . . . purity itself, her skin, against the crass upholstery. And her delicacy of feature all the more emphatic for the turban's heft. Yet something . . .

Too conspicuous, somehow. Her nakedness. Too much too freely offered . . . there is no reward in it.

Suddenly Oskar was struggling out of his suit coat, tossing it to the floor. Then his fingers were tearing at the small satin-covered buttons of his waistcoat.

Katja watched, her eyes widening slightly. She did not otherwise move.

"Sit up." His voice was peremptory and flat. "Up. Come on."

Leaning over the settee, he pulled roughly on her arms, forcing them through stiff armholes.

"There," he said, pushing her back down among the cushions.

The vest was brocade, the color of bitter chocolate.

THE ODALISQUE WAS SKETCHED IN CHARCOAL ON COARSE BROWN PAPER. Amazing how deeply its crudeness pleased him. Its absent colors were indelible in his mind.

So much Oskar had come so close to forgetting . . . how the least act of creation could propel one beyond knowledge, intent, even identity. Art's imperious demands for *violation* in the smug face of decency, the forcible rediscovery of the soul's penchant for sacrilege.

Fräulein Moos grasped all this, of course. That companion knowledge in her was the seed that, conceived in Almi's likeness, would cure his sterility . . . *must* cure it. In time his Silent Woman would come. His potency would return. He would be released from this terrible shame that left him unfit for the least intercourse with . . .

He would not, for the foreseeable future, paint.

KATJA WAS AVID, OF COURSE, FOR A LOOK AT THE SKETCH.

"A mere study, *Liebchen.*" Oskar's thumb caressed her bare shoulder. "You must wait for the masterpiece."

Her expression hovered on the edge of petulance, then brightened. A central role in a masterpiece was worth some sacrifice.

He rather wished he could show her the sketch. Oskar imagined his smudged forefinger tracing the nuance of cleft at her breast, pointing out how the waistcoat's very reticence was what lent the wondrous debauchment to parted thighs, to pubic curl . . .

A phrase from one of his letters to Hermine Moos echoed at the back of his mind . . . *art drawn from our deepest wantonness* . . . was that what he had said?

Yes, the sketch's wantonness would delight and flatter Katja. And he might have educated her promising but undisciplined eye. But he mustn't risk it. She was no fool. She was bound to notice how her flesh had been softened, her frame amplified . . . Katja had spent enough time in his various nomad studios to recognize Oskar's one true model.

He had not, certainly, meant to allow it, Alma shoving Katja aside to usurp the sketch. He was simply unable to stop her.

"It's to be a surprise," Oskar said.

Katja, still naked on the settee, stretched deliciously. "I suppose I must wait, then." She raised one leg, arched her foot, flexed her long nimble toes.

LATER, AT THE UNDISTINGUISHED TABLE IN THE OVERPRICED RESTAURANT on the Hauptstrasse, Oskar watched with relief and gratitude as Katja dispatched a tureen of eel soup. Let food make his amends.

Katja's conversation grew more animated once their dinner plates arrived. She chattered vivaciously between mouthfuls, swiping bites from Oskar's neglected plate while emptying her own. How he coveted the resilience in her, the hunger! A remarkable creature, his Katja. A man with the least sense would not think twice about falling in love with her.

"Oskar, you've barely touched that *Bauernschmaus*." She'd ordered the dish—the Peasants' Feast—for him. It would cheer him up, she said.

"It's a bit heavy." He cosseted no nostalgia for Austrian cuisine.

"It is glorious." Katja speared a dumpling, relocating it on her own plate.

"I've not much appetite."

When Oskar looked up, the dumpling had vanished.

"When do you suppose you will finish?" Katja said.

"Finish?"

"My painting." Her teeth tore through a tender leaf of red cabbage to shred the beef inside. The savor of onion sharpened the air. Oskar turned his head slightly askance.

"You did say it would be a painting? I didn't misunderstand?"

"A painting," he said. "Of course. I can't say just when, but—"

"Soon?"

"I should imagine." Oskar pushed his plate away.

Katja reached over to it and pinched a bit of sauerkraut between her fingers. "Promise?"

So small, Katja's teeth, so white . . . "You have my word," he said.

"Ernst used to bring me here," she said. "Quite often, actually."

Oskar nodded absently.

"Now Ernst is off honeymooning with that flat-chested banker's daughter or whatever she is, while I—"

"You know perfectly well her father is a publisher. And given the political climate, the honeymoon is most unlikely. No one is traveling." Oskar smiled. "Nor, furthermore, were you ever the least bit in love with Ernst."

Katja gave up her pout with good grace. "I did *like* him, though. Do, I mean. Don't you think Ernst is too sweet to deserve a flat-chested wife?"

"But not sweet enough to deserve our Katja."

"Nor are you." Her eyes darkened. "Still I—"

The kitchen door swung open. A laden pastry cart swayed past on squeaky wheels. Katja's gaze followed it with conspicuous longing.

"Is a *Schillerlocke* called for?" Oskar said. "A consoling *Windbeutel*, perhaps?"

"They are very good here, the pastries." Katja sighed. "It's difficult to choose just one."

"You must have two, then," said Oskar, patting his flat pockets.

I GAVE AWAY EVERYTHING . . . YOUR BRACELETS AND BROOCHES, YOUR FILI-greed rings. With my teeth I unstrung your ropes of pearls. I scattered them like seed through battlefields fertilized with death.

I wrapped a beggar in your red coat. Its pockets filled with pus from his wounds.

The mouths of his bastard children I stuffed with sugared violets, garnishes pilfered from your cabinets while you slept.

I did not sleep.

Awaiting dawn, I staged our pain, choreographed our mutual torture. The audiences were rapt . . . particularly in Berlin.

I never slept.

In the end, I gave away everything. Even my memory.

Almi, my beautiful eye.

6

Hans Posse, spine erect inside his moleskin jacket's habitual slouch, buttered a crust of black bread, then set it back on his plate. When he noticed Oskar watching him, he picked the crust up again and moved it toward his mouth, then got no further. "I haven't much appetite this morning."

Oskar scooped a clot of jam onto the edge of his plate and studied it. Two pale gooseberries stared up at him like moist blind eyes. His gaze returned to Posse. "One needs to try." He smiled. "I believe it was you who told me that."

"You'll find my assertions tend to be most vigorous when undiluted by personal experience."

Posse laughed quietly. Oskar joined him for a moment. Then both men halfheartedly resumed the motions of breakfast.

There was nothing, really, one could say. Death was advancing on the floor above. The son could do little but stand watch. Oskar was monitoring the General's decline from downstairs. His host's face was a bulletin he scanned each morning. Casualties were clearly mounting.

"Do you know what he called me this morning?" Hans Posse said suddenly.

Oskar, imagining all manner of epithet, insult, and vitriol, went lightheaded. *Fehlschlag. Tölpel.* The old fool doesn't mean near half what he says, Romana had told her son. Dolt! Oskar blotted his brow with his napkin.

But Posse wasn't looking at him. "Birgitta," he said.

"*Wie bitte?*"

"My mother's name." This time the attempt to smile made Posse's face appear to writhe.

"He is . . . comfortable, I hope?"

"It is difficult to tell."

"Perhaps it comforts him to imagine his wife there, looking after him," Oskar said.

Posse shook his head slowly and looked away. "On the contrary, I'm afraid."

"I'm so sorry."

"Constant battles. Hostilities everywhere he turned."

He made it sound like a small joke. Oskar tried to smile.

"I wish I believed in the conventional pieties," Hans Posse said. "They should be a great help at the moment. Everlasting peace . . . that sort of thing."

Oskar waited.

"Have you an opinion at all?" Posse asked.

So little room for kindness, often, within the simple truth. Oskar closed his eyes. For a moment he wished he were the kind of man who found it simple, found it *possible,* to lie for kindness' sake. His throat constricted. "I wouldn't know," he whispered.

When he opened his eyes he found Hans Posse gazing at him with an almost tender expression.

"I wish I had assurances to offer," Oskar said.

"It helps to know someone else sits beside one," Posse said. "In the dark."

"If only I could provide a more *useful* sort of companionship, perhaps pull a candle from my sleeve, a match . . ."

Reserl materialized, an apparition framed by the kitchen doorway. Her face was the impossible pink of a Renoir infant's. Posse looked, beside her, like a ghost. She reached across the table, cupping the chased silver coffee urn between her palms, as if feeling for fever in a child's face.

"Thank you, Hulda."

Hulda. She and Oskar looked at each other with startled eyes.

"Bitte." She withdrew her hands from the silver pot and slipped from the room.

Oskar picked up the coffee urn, then nearly dropped it. It wobbled for a ticklish moment on its squat foppish legs. Dunking his scorched fingers into his water glass, he imagined a sizzle. He smiled.

The house was utterly silent. Hans Posse's eyes were on the ceiling, as if he could see through it. Oskar, too, looked upward. The gas chandelier's light trickled down like cloudy cider. A baldachin of spiderwebs stretched between two beams. He wondered if it had been spun overnight.

"He used to tell me sometimes, when he was still . . . cogent, that he was ready to die." Posse smiled. "I actually believed him," he said.

"But now—"

"It wasn't his intent to lie. He was simply mistaken." Posse picked up his cup and took a sip of coffee. "The idea of welcoming death is *hypothetical,* Oskar. I trust you understand this?"

Hans Posse had never before addressed him by name, not that Oskar could recall. He felt the consequence of it, a heaviness in the center of his chest. I am afraid, he thought. He did not know why.

"When do you intend to resume painting?" Posse asked quietly.

Oskar shook his head and looked away.

Upstairs the old man moaned.

Posse's gaze stayed on Oskar.

Footsteps, quick and light, ran up the back stairs. Oskar pictured strong scalded hands grasping the old man's shoulders, pummeling the knots from his flesh.

"I can't," Oskar said.

"Can't live without it," Posse said gently.

He would not, for the foreseeable future . . .

"You know that, of course," Posse said.

"I know nothing."

Posse smiled. "An ideal starting point for an artist, I should think."

Oskar, feeling mocked, turned away.

"What *did* you know . . . before?"

"Everything I knew before was false," Oskar said.

"Precisely."

Oskar looked at the older man again. His face, though gaunt and exhausted, looked oddly luminous for a moment. I would paint him as

Christ, Oskar thought. Once I'd have painted him as my sweet suffering Christ. Or someone's.

The sound of Posse's voice drew a veil over the portrait forming in Oskar's mind. "Can you rely, do you think, on your despair?"

"I don't understand you."

"What if despair, too, is only hypothetical? Are you willing to swear by it?"

"I haven't the words for this," Oskar said. "I am not a debater."

Posse stretched his hand across the table and touched Oskar's frayed cuff. "Isn't that what makes the painting so . . . vital?" he asked softly.

Oskar closed his eyes. He heard the clatter of his palette knife hitting the floor, felt the paint, fat and creamy on the tips of his fingers. Its scent was heady and rude. He imagined the colors thick on his tongue, as he licked his fingertips. He felt their flavors, countless and keen, flowing down his throat.

"Can you?" Posse whispered.

"Can I—"

"Live without it?"

Oskar stood up suddenly, his chair toppling backward as he pushed away from the table. The delicate spine of the spindle-backed chair cracked against the floor. Several pieces of rosewood inlay skittered under the table.

Oskar stumbled blindly from the dining room.

Hans Posse remained at the table, looking at the doorway through which Oskar had fled. He seemed, like Oskar, unaware of the damage whose sound died slowly from the air.

Upstairs, in the old man's airless room, Reserl began to sing softly. The song was a lullaby. She did not know the meaning of the words. She did not even know that she was singing. The sounds from below had not reached her. Reserl heard only the slowing rhythm of the old man's breaths, spiriting him toward the realms of sleep.

I put no sure credence in the existence of an omnipotent God. Nor, however, do I discount one. Indeed, as we struggle to emulate the myth of creation, more and more do I find myself inclined to belief . . . converted perchance by natural empathy for a Supreme Being who, until bringing beauty into being, could not rest . . .

If there is in truth a heaven, Fräulein, have we not cause to hope it must smile on an enterprise whose unabashed aim is perfection?

RESERL: EACH TIME HE CALLS HER BY THE NAME HE HAS GIVEN HER, HE claims a little more of the girl. They are both, Oskar and Reserl, shamed by this, by his claims, her yielding.

Why would you choose that name?

Why on earth? He has no idea. There is only his certainty that this is the name he must give her. The name she must accept. Reserl. No other name will do.

Why?

He would need time to think about that, Oskar has told her. This is a grave promise made to the girl, given in recompense for the old name he has taken from her. The more she yields to him, he knows, the more he is beholden. The debt is one he accepts.

Oskar tries to keep his promise. But no matter how long and deeply he considers the name he has given her, its reasons and origins continue to elude him.

Then, after more than twenty years, she visits him again: *Reserl.*

He was six, perhaps . . . seven? A skinny, quicksilver child who darted here and there, his mother said, like a minnow. Unmannerly and prone to mischief, yet rarely called to account, acquitted again and again by the misleading innocence of his true-blue eyes.

The Kokoschka home then lay on Vienna's western edge, so far from the city's heart that it felt like living in the country. The whole of the Galitzinberg Park had seemed to belong to him. Oskar was a proprietary sort of child.

It was the girl's red coat that had first captured his attention. The finest wool, not the squinting-bright red of Christmas ribbons and cinnamon candy, but a shade like the raspberry jam baked dark in a Linzer torte. The coat had a wide velvet collar and large black buttons that glistened. Its deep red folds flared out behind her when she ran. The girl looked, Oskar thought, as if she knew how to fly but did not wish to get caught showing off.

The little girl's mother was the most beautiful woman he had ever seen. Oskar knows that, still, though he no longer remembers whether the woman was dark or fair, slender or round, or what she looked like at all. Only that her beauty, at a distance, pierced his heart as nothing quite had before.

There were two daughters. The elder, called Lotte, had a suspicious and sullen air. Her coat, which she had outgrown, was the bitter color of brown mustard. Its hem skimmed a pair of fat, scabby knees. Lotte, who may have been ten, seemed huge to Oskar. Her sister, a year or two younger, appeared her opposite in every way: bright and lithe and inviting. She wore long white stockings and shiny black boots with pointed toes. Her name was Therese. Her mother called her Reserl.

The beautiful mother and her mismatched daughters appeared in the Galitzinberg Park each morning at half past ten. Each of them carried a book. They were accompanied by a stiff-legged Pomeranian on a very long leash. The leash, which was braided green leather, would have made, Oskar thought, a fine whip in his buccaneer games. Or a noose, perhaps. The Pomeranian's name was Leo. He seemed to belong to Reserl. She kept him on a short lead, the leash's excess wound around her right wrist like a pirate's shackle.

When the woman and the two girls reached the park, they went directly to a bench. The bench was low and stone and set inside a curve of thorny bushes. There were a number of benches in the park, but they never considered any of the others. The bench they occupied faced a small fountain, a little stone boy peeing into a pool. The pool was edged with tan stones that looked like loaves of bread stacked up around it.

The mother and Lotte walked in a measured pace and looked as if they were following two strict, straight parallel lines to their accustomed bench. Reserl and Leo ran and looped and jumped. That is how Oskar first learned the names of the little girl in the fetching red coat. "Reserl, do behave," the beautiful woman would say. And, when the girl and the dog kept running and looping and jumping: "Therese!" A peacock feather perched in the woman's blue felt hat. When she was displeased, she screeched like a bird.

Reserl, despite her long and looping route into the park, usually reached the bench ahead of her mother and her sister. She would drop her book on the end of it, sighing as if she had done her tiresome duty. Then she would unroll the green braided leash from her wrist. The leash was very long. Leo would sit and watch it unwind into a loose tangle on the ground. He would never run or even move until Reserl nodded at him. When Reserl nodded, the dog would prance and jump and bark and sniff the ground with great abandon. His little lion mane would flatten in the breeze when he ran. Reserl, her thin white legs pumping, would strain to keep up with him, never allowing the leash to grow taut. The dog seemed to forget he was tethered. Reserl's jam-red coat would flare out behind her limber white legs. If she'd cared to, Oskar felt certain, she could have flown.

By the time Reserl and Leo finished their first wide loop around the fountain, the mother and the sister would have arrived at the bench, brushed it off with their gloves. Smoothing their coats over their knees, they sat down, opened their books, and began to read. A stranger entering the park might not have thought the enchanting girl in the red coat and the little lion-ruffed dog had any connection to the two prim readers on the bench.

Oskar had learned to read before he went to school. When he was four his mother got him a little slate and taught him his letters, two each day. He loved the curves and spines and legs of the letters. He loved books. But whenever Oskar looked at the mother and daughter on the bench, their downcast eyes and stern stillness made him ashamed. He did not want to be like them. He wanted to be like Reserl and Leo.

Each day Oskar moved a little closer to the fountain. Reserl never seemed to see him there. Nor did Leo. Oskar wanted to go over and hunker down at Reserl's red hem and let Leo sniff his hand. But his mother, each morning as he left the house, made him promise that he would not talk to strangers in the park. This was a promise he supposed all mothers demanded of their children. If Reserl talked to him, he thought, her beautiful mother would surely look up from her book and start screeching like a bird.

After jumping and looping and keeping up with Leo for a quarter hour or so, Reserl would stand beside the fountain and would stare across the park's wide walking path at her mother and her sister. She would stare and stare at them without a word until one or the other looked up at her. If the beautiful mother looked up, Reserl would smile at her, then give Leo a nod and the two of them would again start to run.

If the sister looked up, however, Reserl would not smile. For a moment Reserl's eyes would plead with her sister in silence. Only after the older girl looked back down at her book would Reserl beg her with words. That is how Oskar knew the older sister's name. "Come play with us, Lotte," Reserl would say. "Please do."

Lotte, without looking up, would shake her head.

Reserl would stand still for another moment, her face a small pale precious thing Oskar imagined holding between his hands.

The mother never gave the least sign that she had heard or noticed the children's exchange. Beautiful women were untouched, Oskar saw, by heartache and lack. He would not have been able to put this in words then, but it was something he never forgot—that with great beauty came an immunity to others' suffering.

THAT AUTUMN THERE WAS NO SCHOOL. THE AGING SCHOOLMASTER, PUN-ishing his late-summer cold into pneumonia, had unleashed a wondrous permissiveness upon the district. Its children remained at liberty well into November, chastised only by a premature and exceptionally harsh chill.

Morning after morning, Oskar, bundled up beyond recognition by his thin-blooded mother, would lumber through the park's main gate at a quarter past ten. Then, making sure he was unobserved, he would duck into a heavily wooded spot behind the groundskeeper's shed. There he would divest his wiry frame of what weighed it down: the stiff boiled-wool jacket and quilted vest, a scratchy muffler, an absurdly tasseled stocking cap.

What Oskar hated most of all, though, were the thick brown mittens his mother had knitted for him. She might as well, for all his fingers could feel or do inside them, have cut off his hands.

His fingertips would be turning interesting shades of pink and blue and mauve by the time Oskar took up his position, each day somewhat nearer the peeing boy than the previous day's spot. While he awaited the arrival of the beautiful mother and her daughters and the little dog, he would be shivering. Oskar enjoyed shivering. It felt as if someone strange and exciting were dancing inside his skin.

Every morning was the same. They arrived at half past ten. The girl in the red coat never seemed to notice him. Her sister would never play with her.

After a week, lurking as near as he dared, Oskar devised a solution to the stalemate: If the girl called Reserl knew his name, she would be able to ask him to play with her. She would no longer need to subject herself to her sister's cold refusals. Her sad little face would no longer make Oskar's chapped hands long to hold it.

The next morning Oskar came earlier to Galitzinberg Park. He stashed his excess clothing in the shrubbery, as usual. He searched the wood's perimeter until he found a sturdy stick. The stick had a slender point on it.

A cinder path ringed the pool. It was edged, in spring and summer, with tight clusters of flowers. The earth now was frozen and dry. As a nearby church bell tolled ten, Oskar began to write his name in the cinders. He wrote it seven times across the path, spoking out from the fountain where, overnight, a pinch of ice had put a stop to the little stone boy's peeing. Oskar studied the stone boy's icy spout. It seemed terribly small. The ice made its size appear more normal. An excited stranger was dancing inside Oskar's skin.

When the spokes of his name were completed to his satisfaction, Oskar gathered up a fistful of pebbles from among the dry clots of dirt in the flower bed. Then, finding an almost flat stone at the top of the fountain's edge, he laid out his name there, too: O-S-K-A-R. She would know how to ask him, now, and her face would grow into its own brightness when he did not refuse her. Leo would race along between them and when they stopped to catch their breath, Oskar would hunker down and allow the small dog to sniff his hand, his muzzle warm and wet against Oskar's frozen fingers.

The next morning Oskar had to do it all over again, every bit of it. He didn't mind. He wrote his name larger this time, smoothing over the places where the prints of Reserl's boots and Leo's paws had scribbled through some of the letters of his name, leaving others there like a crazy code. This time his *O*'s were big around as skillets. He forked the tails of his *S*'s and thought, when he stood back from them, they looked like snakes. The pebble rendering of his name remained untouched on the fountain's rim. She never went close enough to notice it. After the second day, Oskar himself forgot it was there, an unclaimed message for the groundskeeper to discard in March, when the stone boy's pee would begin to spout again.

Nothing, in the end, worked out as he'd planned. Reserl didn't notice the spokes of his name on the second day, either. The third day, when she arrived at the park with her mother and sister, Leo was not with them and Reserl looked nearly as sullen as Lotte did. Oskar wanted to ask if the little dog was sick, or hurt, but he was afraid. Oskar was afraid Leo was dead. Afraid the mother would screech at him and flap her gloved hands to drive him into the trees. He was afraid his voice would come out so soft and uncertain that it would allow Reserl to act as if she did not hear him. Reserl was, for a young girl, extremely beautiful. So beautiful, in fact, that Oskar did not need to see scorn and callousness in her in order to fear them.

On the third day, when noon was approaching and it was nearly time for the beautiful mother to close her book and rise from the stone bench and lead her two daughters from the park, suddenly Reserl began to dance. Her pointed black boots leaped from spot to spot on the cinder path that ringed the fountain. Her red coat flared out behind her. Her face was cold and white and hard.

Three dozen meters distant, alert in a flimsy tent of tree shadow, Oskar felt Reserl's dervish dance beneath his skin, as her black boots scribbled over and stomped out the letters of his name.

He slinked out of his hiding place and began to run. The bundled clothes lay forgotten in the shrubbery behind the groundskeeper's shed. The park's wide-open gate suddenly seemed an obstacle, even a trap. From there he would have to double back to his house, an impossible distance, a terrible exposure on an avenue snarling with new electric trams and cranky old dray horses and neighbors ready to report to your mother whatever you were doing, even when you were hardly doing a thing but just running.

The wall around the park was not more than twice Oskar's height. If he got running very fast, he could vault over it on the palm of his hand. He'd seen Willi Huerter and his brother do it lots of times, and Willi was less than a year older than Oskar and hardly taller.

He heard footsteps running behind him. He glanced over his shoulder and saw a flash of red, a small white face. *"Halt mal, bitte!"* she cried. "Please stop!" He nearly did. He surely would have, if he'd heard the sound of his name.

"Reserl!" The screech of a great beautiful bird, every color in the world in its plumage.

Oskar ran faster.

Behind him the sound of footsteps stopped.

The wall seemed to be rushing at him, like a long white train.

Wait . . . please stop . . .

Oskar leaped in the air. His hand flattened hard against the pitted top of the wall. Something bit into the flesh of his palm. His fingers were numb. The wall was lukewarm with winter sun.

His feet arced up beside his head, then higher. He flew through the air. He danced, an exciting stranger. Oskar did not brace himself for the landing, not the least bit. He trusted the air to carry him.

There might, on the other side of the wall, have been stone or glass to crush or abrade him. His tender body might have been speared on a privet, steeled to winter. His mother could with ease have imagined endless specifics of countless disasters in the second it took Oskar to land outside the park that had been his first peek at paradise.

But not even Romana's strange Gypsy imagination could have predicted the softness and stink of his landing:

The decaying carcass of a sow had been left to rot on the grass . . . who knew for how long or why? Had there been no fringe of grass to screen it from view . . . had it not been the sort of thoroughfare where passersby moved so quickly, keeping their eyes straight ahead . . . had the city not yet outgrown itself, becoming a place where nobody was, it seemed, *responsible* for removing . . . for protecting . . . but who, really, could ever have imagined . . .

The dreadful collapse around him of the rotten flesh . . . the spurt of foul yellow liquid whose reek would remain somehow on him, *in him,* for all the eighty and more years of his life . . . and the way this prepared him for everything foul and humiliating and dreadful he would ever encounter . . . flies . . . disregard . . . putrefaction.

Someone carried him home. He never knew who. It would not, he knew, have been the beautiful mother and her two mismatched daughters. Even Oskar was not so fanciful as to imagine that.

He remained unconscious, or seemingly so, for three days. The doctor came and examined him. Nothing was found to be seriously amiss. The boy exhibited normal reflexes. His breathing was not impaired. There was no fever.

Oskar simply could not open his eyes. And, more disturbingly, he could not close his mouth.

He said nothing, of course, of the fly that occupied the root of his tongue, nor of its constant turning as it laid its grubs inside him. Nothing of the circles the girl ran around the fountain, obliterating the letters of him . . . nor the stone boy's spout sheathed in ice and the dog that was surely dead and the great screeching bird . . .

His lips dried and cracked and bled. His tongue was like sandpaper. His breaths made a rasping noise that made his mother weep. An odor emanated from his gaping mouth that made his mother, even his mother, turn her face away.

Oskar shivered. The maggots seethed in a larval dance beneath his skin. Their bore perforated his bones. His mouth opened wider. He made no sound.

A priest was called. He came and said prayers in Latin over Oskar's bed. After a while the boy began to breathe more easily. The priest slanted his face away and kept praying. His fervor drove Gustav Kokoschka from his son's bedside. Romana stayed, covetous of the priest's piety, furious at God's petty and inscrutable penalties.

Some of the rigidity at last left Oskar's face and body. The gap of his mouth narrowed slightly, perhaps. The priest departed at suppertime, possibly sensing the woman was too distraught to be thinking about meals.

The priest's fervor seemed to linger behind him, like something he'd wandered off without. Romana, whose religious devotions were casual at best, felt the priest's passion instill her prayers, a great blessing under the circumstances. For three nights she slept, if she slept at all, sitting upright on a stool beside her child's bed. Her husband and other children were left to fend for themselves.

On the fourth day Oskar nearly pressed his lips together, then slowly opened his eyes.

Afterward, when he was well again, he could not remember just what had happened. Or so he said. His mother thought it best not to ask too many questions. Except, eventually, as to the dire disappearance of his winter clothes.

Oskar did not know, he said.

Burdened with the unforeseen expenses of a new coat and a doctor's call, the Kokoschkas endured that year an especially severe winter. Occasionally, Romana Kokoschka remembered the religious ardor that, so briefly and brightly, had burned in her. She wished she could borrow it back again from the priest. But she did not see him for months at a time. Father Schimmel was not in the habit of aimless visiting, and Romana was not much drawn to church.

THE AGING SCHOOLMASTER, HERR RANKL, NEVER QUITE RECOVERED FROM his pneumonia. A new schoolmaster was found several weeks before

Christmas. His name was Lothar Schahlecker and he came from a village near Graz. Herr Schahlecker was a young man and not a good disciplinarian. The large dark birthmark that covered his right eye socket made him look like a terrier. The younger children loved him extravagantly. The older ones made fun of him. The parents agreed Herr Schahlecker wouldn't last, though they would never, of course, have said so in the children's hearing or to the teacher's marred face.

Oskar drew pictures of the new schoolmaster. He found this an endeavor far more absorbing than doing sums. He had already read the book his classmates were struggling through and found it altogether boring.

Herr Schahlecker knew what Oskar was up to. He didn't mind in the least. The boy had a gift, the young schoolmaster told his mother. Romana sniffed and tried to look neither flattered nor hopeful. Her husband was gifted, too, wasn't he? An out-of-work goldsmith so gifted that his hungry wife was forced to trade eggs to get a hand-me-down winter coat for their careless son.

One day in early spring Herr Schahlecker kept Oskar late. The boy, expecting to be punished, stayed at his desk as the other children filed from the classroom. He imagined them running outdoors, their coats flaring out behind them until they were lifted from the ground and found themselves flying through the blue-streaked air.

When all the other children were gone, the schoolmaster closed the door behind them. Then he went to his desk at the front of the room and took from a drawer a flat parcel wrapped in brown paper. "Come," he said.

Oskar approached the desk without dragging his feet. He *deserved* punishment, after all. He had been drawing unflattering portraits of the master for months. Toying with the canine resemblance. Disregarding lessons.

Oskar laid his fingers along the edge of the schoolmaster's desk and waited for the blow. The long flat parcel seemed odd. A ruler was customary. He wondered if this would hurt as much. It hardly mattered.

"This is for you," the schoolmaster said.

When the boy did not look up or move his hands from the desk, the man unwrapped the package himself. The paint box was black tin. Its lid had a silver fleur-de-lis border. A small peacock fanning out its tail formed a kind of cameo at the center.

Herr Schahlecker pushed the paint box toward Oskar. The boy's fingers pressed harder into the edge of the desk, whitening at the knuckle. The schoolmaster lifted the lid of the box. Three rows of coin-sized watercolors and six brushes were fitted neatly inside it. The box's interior was so white that it made Oskar squint and the round paints squeezed for a second into tight slashes of color that ran into one another and made him hold his breath.

"I will show you," Herr Schahlecker said. "May I?"

Oskar could not recall, later, a word being said after that. He remembered only the schoolmaster mixing the paints with water, dipping the little brush, its bristles fine as eyelashes, into a cloudy water glass.

Years afterward, Oskar hoped he said thank you, but he doubted he had. What came back to him most clearly was his shame, the clear red of it, and the sheer golden miracle of infinite color bringing things only he could see to light, to life, on the paper. Fixing them there.

Herr Schahlecker left at the end of that term, in June. Someone said, many years later, that the schoolmaster had been killed during the first year of the war. People in the small pockets outside the city were always saying such things, however, claiming truths no one could verify.

Oskar was forced to acknowledge that he had probably never said thank you to Herr Schahlecker, not properly. He had taken a sudden turn into shyness around that time, a turn that concerned her, his mother said . . . thank God he'd eventually grown out of it.

Before the schoolmaster with the kind, dappled face had left that summer, however, Oskar had wordlessly handed him a rolled piece of paper. On it he had painted a lively-looking girl in a long dark red coat that spread out behind her like wings. A dog that looked very much like a tiny lion flew along beside her, just under one red wing. The girl wore white stockings and pointed black boots that barely skimmed the ground. Her face was turned away, but something about the back of her head, its slight tilt perhaps, suggested impossible beauty.

The picture was extremely pretty, the schoolmaster said. He did not mention how mysterious it seemed to him that so bright a picture could carry such an air of heartache. An unusual boy, Oskar Kokoschka . . . one he was unlikely to forget.

Those few truly gifted pupils one was blessed to encounter now and then always seemed burdened by sadness. Lothar Schahlecker wondered why that was. He'd noticed that such children tended to bear

their sorrow with great care, as if sensing it, too, was a gift, as precious
as it was inconvenient.

*Let the fingers touch, Fräulein, what the inner eye must fail, in the end,
to imagine! Caress the tender stubble in the crease of a peach. Tickle the
raspberry's elfin bristles. When you deliver to me the bride I long for, you
will—you must—have a husband's knowledge of her.*

Will her mouth open?

*Might we devise the means, do you suppose, of steeping our darling in
the female odors? Not perfumes, I mean, but the musk, heady and distinct,
of a woman well loved?*

*I trust you are not offended that I raise such considerations? Indeed, it
is my fond hope that, given such sensuous puzzles, your erotic genius may
find itself aroused.*

THE SMALL STONE BATHHOUSE LAY JUST BEYOND THE GARDEN'S GREEN
pale. The bucket's weight was staggering. Six, she thought, six would
have to do. The Captain, for all his height, was a slight and bony man.

Evening sidled up to the trees. Blackbirds brazen with autumn appetite
perched in low branches. With sharp shameless eyes they watched her stumble
down the path. They are waiting, she thought, waiting for me to fall.

Reserl prepared his bath each evening at six o'clock. Oskar had never
requested that she do so. She had simply noticed his preference for
bathing late in the day. The habit seemed to restore him. She liked to see
him looking at her from the dinner table with calm clear eyes. The hot
water gave him better color. It may even have improved his appetite.

She shifted the pail from one hand to the other. Its heavy wire handle
had raised a welt in her right palm. The *Königinpastete* needed to
come out of the oven soon. The dumplings for the soup were not yet
started. The water had heated for a long time. Six bucketfuls, surely that
would be sufficient?

Reserl nudged the warped plank door with her shoulder. At the
door's unexpected give, water splashed over feet. Its scald cut through
the worn hide of her boots. She let out a half-stifled cry.

"Are you burned?"

She would not have dreamed of finding him there, let alone imagined
his nakedness, greenish-white in the mossy twilight.

Only once before had she seen a man naked. Memory had, instantly, dropped a veil over the sight.

Until now.

A huge wildness of animal fur and fat, her father's body. Only his clothes, a mercy, had spared her, until now, the sight. She remembered it all now, full and instant: the shame like dying in his howl, her flight. And her own name used for a curse and a lash, a sentence of banishment. *Hulda!*

He had stood on a riverbank at dusk, gleaming among dark trees on legs like marble pillars. His chest a tabernacle. *Hulda:* choking on her name, despising and disowning the blind girl child who . . . not quite blind, no, seeing all of him, but not understanding, scarcely believing, what was revealed to her.

He had only been bathing there, washing away the reek of his slaughterer's work. But the sight of his body, its brutish power . . . the forgetting of it had been a charity upon her frugal existence. She had a wordless knowledge of that now.

"Reserl."

The Captain made no attempt to cover himself. He appeared neither embarrassed nor surprised. Not angry, certainly. He stood on a scrap of ruined rag rug, thin arms flaccid at his sides. His gaze was both vague and intent, as if he could not recall a question asked of him, only its importance.

After a moment, he stepped over the edge of the round wooden tub and, folding his long thin body, sank down into the water.

She tried to look away.

"It's all right," he said.

She stared into the Captain's silvery long-lashed eyes. She felt the secrets of her childhood, the history of her wants, falling open . . . *It is I,* she thought, *who go naked. Now there is nothing . . . there will be nothing I can keep from him.*

Steam rose from the bucket. The flesh of her hand had split under the water's weight. She lacked the strength to raise the pail. The water in the tub was not enough. Its faintly murky surface revealed how little the murk could hide. Her arm trembled.

"It's all right," he said again.

"Sir, it's very hot."

He was waiting for her to empty the pail into the tub, but she could

not, could not raise the weight of it, and what if she should scald him?
"I cannot—"

He began, his hands gripping the tub's edge, to rise from the water.
Hulda shook her head.

The pale length of him, shining in a sheath of water like a fish, unfolded and rose.

"Perhaps you could just—"

She stood a few feet from the tub, paralyzed.

He smiled at her. "Never mind." He leaned out over the tub's edge,
reaching toward her with both hands.

She closed her eyes. She heard the caw and flap of the crows in the
trees. She heard rage, heard disinheritance in her father's voice, in her
name. *Hulda.*

"Give it to me," the Captain said. "Let me take it, Reserl."

Then the terrible weight was lifted from her hand and she had no
need to look to know the cleaving of her palm would at the end of her
life yet mark this moment.

She opened her eyes. A line of sparse dark hair ran from the center
of his chest to the joining of his thighs. His shoulders were narrow, his
belly flat. In his neck, beneath a faint rash of blood-shadows, tendon
strained. She saw the shape of a cry held fast in his throat.

He poured in the last of the hot water, wincing at its heat. The water
rose halfway, now, to his knees. Slowly, he refolded himself into it.
"Don't go," he whispered.

Like a child, she thought, he looks like an underfed child.

Reserl dropped to her knees beside the tub. Her hands slid into the
steaming water. When they returned to the surface, one held a sponge,
the other a square cake of soap. Both were the color of beeswax.

Slowly, she began to wash him. A scar gouged the left side of his
chest, a cruel blue gnarl defacing his fair skin. Something had pierced
him there, driven deep between his ribs with a ferocious will to breach.
He had been torn open. That much was clear. Reserl wondered if he
would ever tell her what had been done to him. She knew she would
never ask.

The sponge dropped into the tub, barely disturbing the water.

Gentle and insistent, Reserl's fingers probed the scar, sounding the
depth of the wound it concealed, gauging its scant remove from his kin-
dred foundling heart.

7

*You visited me in my private garden chamber after midnight,
Fräulein . . . quite wonderfully shocking behavior, may I say.*

*It was a dream, of course, that delivered you here . . . sleep's most mar-
velous illusion. Its benediction was to have us working together on our
beloved masterpiece, side by side and of a single mind. So attuned were
we, we did not need to speak. Indeed, our rare sounds were those of small
animals communicating each to the other approval, understanding . . . all
warm wordless murmurs and sighs.*

*But here is the truly extraordinary thing: We were, in this dream, both
blind. We could not see what we were doing, nor had we need. All was ac-
complished by* touch! *And I grasped, in a dream-being's infinite wisdom,
the absolute rightness (dare I say the* good fortune?) *of our shared im-
pediment. For the dream elucidated to me how we both—I as painter, you
as sculptor—have erred by our very reliance on our eyes.*

*I awoke, before dawn, in a pool of despair. Suddenly I understood how
genius itself, the genius of our vision, has been misleading us. Never,
Fräulein, shall our creation be granted the gift of life by virtue of the eye's
conviction. Who better versed than we, two artists of the visual, in sight's
mischievous proclivity to trick and take one in? It is not my eye that craves
its feast, dear colleague, but those parts and senses of a man harder to fool.*

Can art hoodwink tongue and fingertip, fill the emptiness of belly and
loins? Surely our task, resurrecting the heart and soul of this dead warrior,
is impossible. Yet the price of failure, Fräulein, is the eking out of my days
in a cramped and ignoble tomb.

   As we proceed, then, let us close our eyes. Common sight must be for-
sworn for the sake of that vital spark only flesh can verify. How my limbs
long for the unapproachable embrace!

Your ally in dream,

OK

HE AWOKE IN AN ASPIC OF DREAD. THE GIRL WAS GONE. HE KNEW IT BE-
fore he'd opened one eye.

A snarled bedsheet strangled his shoulders and neck. His armpits
reeked of his dreams. The girl, of course, had nothing to do with that.
What could connect Reserl to the spadefuls of Russian dirt weighting his
chest, his lungs' struggle for their fill of air? What severed his lips and
unhinged his jaw was no scream he'd ever for an instant imagine her
hearing. She was a schoolgirl then, Reserl, vacant-eyed daughter of some
listless village whose collective dreams could not have conceived a single moment of war, let alone whole battles . . .

The girl had nothing to do with any of this. It was just finding her
gone, how it wrenched open some door inside him, taunting the horror
he contained to escape . . .

He needed her.

Oskar twisted violently, tearing himself from the clammy bed linen.
Beneath him his right hand had gone to sleep. He flexed his fingers in
daylight's glare. Feeling began to return in pins and needles.

As the tingling subsided, Oskar began counting . . . Sunday, if his fingers were to be depended on. A second inventory brought the same con-
clusion: Sunday. She'd not have gone to the market.

Church? He supposed it was possible, though he couldn't quite picture Reserl in a church. The notion struck him, in fact, as an amusing
anachronism . . . as if her being predated Deity. Sacrilege! He waited for
the dance of a shiver and found himself laughing instead.

But the girl's absence this morning—his *abandonment*—was hardly a
laughing matter. The very suspicion made him ill. He did not need to see
her. He had no desire to talk to her. He simply required the certainty

that Reserl was there somewhere. Nearby. Within calling distance. He didn't understand it himself. She seemed to have grown, overnight, essential, vital to his well-being.

Oskar thought soberly for a moment of Dresden's various churches. He'd wandered through most of them, his first days here. He tried to envision Reserl kneeling before some half-recalled Baroque altar, imploring some blank-eyed gilt Virgin or saint. He glimpsed, for the fleetest instant, her upraised face, a dark speck against Chiaveri's fitful glitter. He felt her shudder before Augustus the Strong's pickled heart in its bronze egg cup . . .

Oskar's imagination swerved to the Alt Markt . . . Sunday, she cannot have gone to the market. He fancied the original Kreuzkirche, bombarded into oblivion a century and a half ago, restoring itself to receive her, heard the hosannas of a hundred boy sopranos entreating High Heaven in her name.

His name. The name he has imposed on her. *Reserl.*

Around him the bedclothes were fetid, chilly, damp. The summerhouse was silent and airless as a tomb. Oskar's body was clenched like a fist. The girl was not in any church. Absurd of him to think it.

His precipitous rise from the bed dizzied him. In an engulfing blackness he swayed on his feet. He would have to go find her. Vital. He would, if he must, grope through Dresden's tangled streets like some blind Homer investigating rumored approaches to eternity. The girl must be found. Must be made to understand. Ignorance of her whereabouts was simply intolerable. She could go where she pleased. When she pleased. Of course she could. He had no desire to impede or curtail her. His clear simple need was to know, always, where she was, only so he might imagine her there.

Oskar dressed in yesterday's stale clothes, not bothering to fasten the soiled cuffs of his shirt. His shirttail hung out in the back. His hair was starting to grow in. He raked it flat with his fingers.

In the unquelled rebellion of the garden, everything was wet. He'd barely slept a wink. How was it he'd never heard rain?

A small stone stoop squatted at the kitchen door, jutting out from the back of the house like a feisty chin. Reserl sat on the next-to-top step. The coarse blue hem of her least-worn dress (Sunday!) drooped between her knees like a hammock. Her head was lowered. Her lips moved silently, as if she were calculating difficult sums. Or praying.

A twig snapped under Oskar's scuffed boot. Her lips stopped moving. She looked up at him, then quickly down at her lap again. She mumbled something he took for *Guten Morgen*. He replied in kind and wondered if she heard his voice quake.

Of course she did, how could it escape her? She was looking up at him with startled eyes. Her face, offered up to the watery morning light, looked as if it had never met the sun.

Where have you been? Where in God's name did you run off to? Oskar closed his eyes and saw his ruddy overgrown hands grabbing the bodice of her blue Sunday dress, shaking her until her head wagged back and forth like a rag doll's. He took a blind step toward her and when his heel landed on another twig, he heard the bones snap in her neck.

When Oskar opened his eyes, Reserl was scrambling up from the step, her hands stretched out toward him. "You are ill," she said.

Oskar shook his head. A bolt of blinding pain shot through his left eye. His right eye saw her as thick swirls of blue and ocher paint sequestered in a dull gold square, a fresco of dark stones behind her. He smiled slightly.

She stood by the kitchen door now, one hand on its frame, skittish in her stillness.

"Where do you go," Oskar asked softly, "when you are not here?"

She looked at him without blinking, looked directly into his eyes in a way she almost never did. Her eyes were the color of port wine in an amber glass. "I am here," she said. "Always here."

The sound of Oskar's scratchy laugh pained them both.

"When you go to the market—"

"I meant—" A rose aquatint spread over her face.

"Of course," Oskar said. "But—"

Her body recoiled deeper into the kitchen doorway, but she did not turn her back on him.

"Will you go tomorrow?" Oskar said.

"If you wish," said Reserl.

"But I wasn't—"

"Do you need something?"

The sun was simmering the haze of moisture from the morning air. The glare sliced through Oskar's right eye. In the picture left behind she sprawled naked on a narrow bed, a damp twist of sheet teasing her thighs apart. A tussle of coarse blue wool was bunched under her head.

Her braids, thick ropes, bound her neck. There was no hair anywhere on her body.

"Sir?"

Oskar tried, for an instant, to look at her, to see her there in the weak sunlight on the porch, through his left eye, while his right eye kept hold of desire's willful picture of her. If he could see both falsities at once, he thought, some truth might come of the clash. But he had not yet mastered, it seemed, the duality of vision he longed for.

"Tell me," the girl murmured, "what it is you need."

Oskar shook his head as if trying to clear it. "I doubt there is anything . . ."

She turned away. The heavy oak door was swollen with dampness. She pushed against it with one thin shoulder. He heard bone grating on wood.

"If you would just let me know when you are going?"

"Yes, sir."

Reserl stepped into the kitchen, leaving the door slightly ajar behind her.

Oskar stood alone in the ruined garden. Steam was beginning to rise from the wet earth. He closed his eyes wearily. In the single picture of her that lingered, he watched the whole palette of bruising rise on one bare white shoulder: blue, red, and violet, yellow and green.

"HERR KOKOSCHKA?"

Oskar's gaze clung stubbornly to the young model. His homeliness was somehow endearing. As his students sketched desperately around him, Oskar studied the boy's legs, the unfortunate disproportion of bulbous thigh to stringy calf. Werner was a first-year student at the Academy. The modeling work reduced his fees. Oskar wondered if one got used to exposure.

Poised on one leg, frozen in flight . . . the pose captured a stoical grace that was almost heroic. The room was cold. The boy's sexual organs had all but disappeared. His feet were long and slender and perfectly shaped. The lad's entire little allotment of beauty resides in his feet, Oskar thought. How did it come to be November?

"Herr Kokoschka?"

The edge of panic in the voice cut through Oskar's absorption with the figure. He turned around quickly. His view of the speaker was blocked by an easel. For a moment he wondered if he would find any-one behind the huge sketch pad.

"I've done it again." A whisper now, but one he recognized. Oskar stepped around the easel and looked into the wide smoke-pale eyes of his youngest, perhaps brightest, and certainly most annoying student.

"What is the trouble, Hugo?"

The boy threw his hands up violently. Oskar pictured them flying away. Hugo's chin was quivering. He had been known to cry. But that, Oskar recalled, had been over a painting on which he'd worked for a week. This was only a sketch.

"It is always the same."

"How is that?" Oskar's voice was mild.

"The work comes to . . . finally I have done something right. I know it. The next moment I touch it and suddenly it is *ruined*. Utterly de-stroyed."

"Yes?" Oskar studied the boy's sketch for a long moment. "Yes, I see," he said.

The other students were beginning to slow or stop their work. Oskar glanced up, a severe smile on his thin face. His penetrating eyes fright-ened them. He knew and rather enjoyed this. "Your turn will come." Each thought he spoke only to him. Their attention quickly returned to their easels. Poor Hugo had broken into a profuse sweat.

Oskar laid a hand on the boy's bony shoulder. "It's all right," he said softly.

"Herr Kokoschka, you must help me!"

Hugo had stopped trying to keep his voice down. Ah, good, Oskar thought, he grows reckless.

He smiled. "Shall I erase what your hand has done, add a few strokes of what no eye but mine sees?" His voice was gentle but grave.

The boy's eyes filled with tears. He covered them with his hands.

"Don't tell me I cannot do this," Hugo said. "There is nothing else."

"Good." Oskar waited a moment, watching the boy struggle to col-lect himself. "Very good," Oskar said. "Shall we proceed from there?"

He dragged a stool in front of the easel. In spite of the scraping sound, none of the students looked up from their work. "Sit down," he said.

The boy thought it improper to take a seat while his teacher continued to stand. He gestured with one hand, offering the seat. Oskar shook his head. The boy's gifts would never amount to anything unless he learned to live with his discomforts. Forgot his damnable manners.

Hugo took the stool, nearly tipped it over in the process. Oskar resisted the impulse to reach over and steady him. He was pleased to see how quickly the boy, despite his embarrassment, was riveted to the easel.

Teacher and student studied the sketch for a moment. The model's disproportions had been belittled, making him almost attractive. Kindness or deceit? A little of both, Oskar suspected. Either would stunt and stymie the boy's ability.

"So it went awry." Oskar shrugged. "Show me where."

"You must show me," Hugo said.

Oskar stared, expressionless, into the boy's eyes. They were full of grief. "Show me," he repeated.

Hugo turned away. He stared long and hard at the drawing. The requisite patience and intensity are there, Oskar thought. He must learn to use them. To prize them.

Hugo appeared unaware of anything but the lines on the paper, unaware even of himself. He lifted one hand and moved it tentatively toward the easel. It hovered before the sketch pad for an instant. Then, very slowly, the boy's smudged fingertip began to trace the figure's spine, a muscular line feathered with shading.

"There?" Oskar said.

Hugo nodded. His gaze did not leave the drawing.

"What were you thinking then, Hugo? At the moment you drew that?" Oskar's voice was neutral, almost disinterested.

The boy closed his eyes for a moment. "I was thinking that a stronger line there would—"

"No." Oskar reached past him and ripped the sheet of paper from the easel.

"I meant that I—" The boy was stiff and white as a corpse.

Oskar crumpled the drawing, twisting it as if wringing the neck of something already half-dead. "You have no business *thinking*."

The paper dropped to the floor. Oskar grasped his student's right hand. He felt a tremor in the wrist. He watched the fingers quiver, then curl slightly inward, as if recoiling from danger. "What are you afraid of?" Oskar said.

Hugo, staring down at his own hand, seemed to stop breathing.

"Look here." Oskar uncurled the stiff fingers, wrenching the boy's hand open. The creases in the palm and the whorls in the fingertips were sooty. The nails were bitten to the quick. "What is it thinking?" Oskar asked.

"What? I—"

"Your hand," Oskar said. "What is it thinking?"

The boy seemed near collapse. Oskar waited. The only sound in the room was the whisper of charcoal and soft lead stroking textured paper. But the other students did not exist. The teacher and his student inhabited a privacy inviolable and absolute.

Oskar loosened his grip on the boy's hand but did not release it. Slowly the bony smudged hand was guided toward the blank page on the easel. Something in the boy let go. Oskar felt it.

Then Hugo's hand took the lead, guided them both over the contours of the figure that, unseen and palpable, filled the empty white space.

Oskar Kokoschka watched closely as his student forgot him. The boy's face turned stricken and lost and ecstatic, as his hand, on its own now, moved across the paper, conforming to the texture and shape of what he alone could see.

Oskar stepped back.

Hugo, groping for a stub of charcoal, did not notice his teacher leaving.

HE'D TAUGHT BEFORE, OF COURSE, FIRST AT SCHWARZWALDE, LATER AT the Kunstgewerbeschule, the School of Applied Arts, where he'd been a student himself. But that was different. That was Vienna. That was only drawing. That was before the war.

Waiting for his duties at the Dresden art academy to begin, Oskar had been unable to imagine himself teaching there: painting, and not an acolyte this time, but a high priest: *ein Meister,* Professor Kokoschka, who (presumably) painted.

Classes at the Academy would resume in the second week of October. As Oskar waited, each day of his existence had felt like the epilogue to a nightmare. He could neither recall nor rid himself of his dreams. Nothing made sense. Everything terrified him. His attempts at conversation were vague, futile, inarticulate.

The only forum in which he had seemed at all capable of explaining himself was his correspondence with Hermine Moos. His letters, longer and longer, sped with greater and greater frequency to Stuttgart.

The dollmaker's occasional replies were terse and so dispassionate that Oskar began to wonder whether he was making his wishes—indeed, making anything at all—clear to her.

The fetish was coming along nicely, Fräulein Moos assured him. But "fetish" was his term, of course. "Our endeavor," she wrote, "ought to be completed in . . ." What, another month perhaps? She gingerly inquired as to what arrangements might be made for "shipment of the work."

Shipment . . . as if his beloved were freight! The very word, rendered in the dollmaker's spinsterish hand, sickened Oskar. How little she understood him, after all. The "dear abettor" to whom he'd been disclosing his soul was as much a fantasy as the idol he'd commissioned her to create. The landscape of his life was populated with bloodless companions on whom his every passion was lost. He was not unaware of that. But *shipment?*

That he would travel to Stuttgart to call for her had always been his assumption. A private coach on the express train, no matter the cost . . . his bride must be escorted properly to her new home. Fringed silk would cover the seat on which she'd recline; he'd found a Chinese piano shawl among the props at the Academy that would do beautifully. Pillows of velvet and tapestry would lushly brace her. A basket of cherries and clementines imported from the Crimea, a tin of the Viennese cookies she loved, sprays of autumn flowers to freshen the air . . .

He'd see to all that, of course. Oskar pictured her face slanted toward the train window, saw Fräulein Moos's dainty lace-edged handkerchief waving a discreet farewell.

If only the dollmaker had bestirred herself to finish "our endeavor" before the Academy's term began, in full compliance with his dreams. Now he was no longer free to travel, however pressing the reasons. He was saddled with obligations. Oskar was a teacher.

He had angled shamelessly for the faculty appointment. He had even prayed for it. So much had seemed possible then, when everything was theoretical. Even an attentive God had, now and then, fallen within the realms of imagined possibility.

But Oskar could not quite see himself as a teacher, no. He envisioned instead a studio overcrowded with talented youngsters avid for his attention. Public successes in Berlin had left him giddy. Not to mention the rapt and rowdy audience at the Vienna lecture . . . surely students would flock to, would *adore,* him. He worried only for his privacy. A band of zealous disciples could be a serious distraction. Adulation could so easily divert one from art's true work. Look what Klimt had become in his last years, posing in his embroidered vestments—high priest indeed! Posturing and lofty pronouncements didn't hide what his work was coming down to. An artist whose bold vision had—it had to be said—returned to art its rightful erotic soul, and in so doing had redefined painting for a new generation!

Though it would not do to say so just now, particularly of one who had been so generous a mentor, the real tragedy of Klimt was not his death at fifty-five. It was the sad unspoken truth that had the master lived much longer, he'd have been remembered merely as an expensive decorator. Klimt was a teacher, all right. His very life was a lesson in what became of an artist who let himself be persuaded by the flattery of disciples.

As it turned out, however, humility was low on the list of Oskar's needs in the autumn of 1918. By the time he was due to report to the Academy, he doubted he could teach anyone anything, let alone mesmerize, seduce. He couldn't even persuade the girl to cut back on the starch in his shirts. His neck was raw. He had not painted in months. Why in the world should serious art students respect him?

So Oskar's shriven spirit approached Dresden's altar of art and learning in sackcloth and ashes. All he had to offer his students was his humble attention. In possession of no answers, he shared his questions with them. Naturally, they adored him from the start.

Not that his students amounted to a throng. There were less than a dozen in his first group. The Academy, insofar as was possible, permitted the students to select the teachers with whom they wished to study. The preferences of those longest enrolled were given priority. Nine of the ten in Oskar's charge were beginning their first term. He was no one's first choice.

Just as well, however, if his following was neither large nor vigorous. Studio space was also determined by seniority. Oskar had been assigned a cramped room with a stingy ration of northerly light.

Still, the students' faces seemed to illuminate the regrettable space. Oskar taught for two and a half hours each morning, beginning at half past nine. No matter how early he managed to arrive, the students would already be there. Awaited, he had merely to step through the doorway, it seemed, to be found riveting.

Each morning ten young faces upturned, opening to him like flowers to the sun. Their eagerness to sanctify his most dubious utterance more appalled than flattered him. Could he actually have fretted over how to gain their respect? The difficult part of teaching, Oskar soon saw, would be inducing his students to abandon respect. *Art abhors reverence,* he wanted to tell them. *Would* tell them, eventually. When they were ready. When *he* was ready. When he could be sure their blindness could no longer break his heart.

For the dreadful lesson Oskar had learned, his very first week at the Academy, was how utterly he'd mistaken the nature of his task. He was not needed here to teach the students how to draw or to paint. Most of them worked quite adeptly with charcoal and ink and pastels. Some already showed mastery in oils and tempera. A couple were finer watercolorists than he himself would ever be. These hatchling artists had worked hard. Their gifts had been incubated like baby chicks, cosseted and dropper-fed and prized. When it came to matters of technique and theory, some of these youngsters likely knew more than he did. Several may even have been gifted—a matter of speculation that meant, in his opinion, little. For the dreadful truth was, not one of his pupils *knew how to see.* I have my work as a teacher cut out for me, Oskar thought.

The second great shock came blessedly close on the heels of the first, however: Oskar soon realized he loved this work. He even, with a sweetly distant distraction, loved his students. Their optimism and energy amused him, even as he envied them. They jousted and jockeyed for his attention. Oskar was both gratified and irked. But he cherished their passion, their innocence. And in their bouts of despair his soul found a kind of companionship he'd encountered only once before: the first weeks at the sanatorium, when the cries of others' seizures and nightmares had been his greatest comfort. The incomparable solace of quarantine among those identically afflicted.

"YOU ARE MAKING QUITE A NAME FOR YOURSELF," HANS POSSE SAID.

Oskar's smile was bemused.

"At the Academy. The estimable Professor Heiner dropped by the museum. He tells me the students are already forming lines for your studio next term."

Oskar shook his head and glanced away. The Direktor was distressed to see a flush rise in his guest's hollow cheek. He had meant to encourage, not embarrass, him.

"You are rumored to be some kind of *Zauberer,* do you know that? Heiner's jealousy was quite obvious." Hans Posse chuckled. "Subtlety, of course, is not his strong suit. As you've likely observed."

Josef Heiner, the Academy's senior professor, was a pompous and small-minded character. His reputation for flattering portraiture of minor nobility was vastly overshadowed by the blatancy of his social ambitions.

Zauberer . . . wizard. The man was a fool.

"Not a favorite of mine, Heiner," Posse said. "Though one can't but pity him, now that there's no court to toady to. Perhaps he can paint the new industrialists . . . make them look like royalty. That should be lucrative."

Oskar rubbed his brow as if he had a headache. "I haven't actually met the man."

"Well, he's quite aware of you, my friend. He was trying to wheedle something, God knows what, out of me. Some secret he thinks you possess."

Oskar's ice-blue eyes were startled.

"Do you?" the Direktor asked lightly.

"Whatever could he—"

"Did you know I taught for several years myself? Astonishing, how ill-suited I was for the work. My tutelage was nearly as inept as my painting! You may not persuade me as to magic, but if there is a secret, I wish you would confide it to me."

Oskar looked cornered and trapped.

"Listen here—" Posse faltered, at a loss to make clear the harmless teasing he intended.

"I make them cry." Oskar shut his eyes. "Not that I mean to. It just seems to happen."

The older man had no idea now what to do or say.

"After that," Oskar said softly, "they look at me differently. As if they belong to me." His face was still and pale. "I don't know how to make them stop," he said.

"My dear boy—"

Sorcerer to fools . . . Oskar opened his eyes. "I am becoming a charlatan, I'm afraid," he said.

Posse looked stricken.

"They worship a false idol, these novices."

"I expect you might not feel so," the Direktor said gently, "if you were painting."

Oskar winced.

"It is difficult to speak of it," Posse said. "I know this. And I've hardly the right . . . I wish I knew a way to help you, that's all."

Oskar shook his head. "There is no help for it," he said.

He was lying. The help required to return him to himself was forthcoming. From Stuttgart. *Shipped*—dreadful word—in a coffin-sized packing crate, laid out in straw bedding perfumed with the costly French scent he had already provided.

He had advanced a portion of the trousseau, as well. By now Fräulein Moos would likely have received it: the cashmere traveling suit the color of Bordeaux claret. Within the dark frame of its astrakhan collar the face luminous as a star. The skirt was stringently—fashionably—hobbled. What need for his love to walk? He would take her everywhere. He would carry her in his arms. Soon she would arrive. She would never leave him.

And soon Oskar would be painting again, his every deficiency and doubt addressed, his terror sent packing . . . she would recline at her ease on the divan in the corner of his room, his muse, overseeing his every stroke with loving eyes. Sight would return. Then his gifts, set free, would soar.

Everything had been seen to now, nearly everything . . . he had only to figure out how to prepare Hans Posse for her arrival. To wrench out of circumstance some means either of concealing or explaining her . . .

How the impossibility of either would have delighted his Almi! But the respectably bourgeois Frau Mahler-Gropius, keeping house now in Vienna, would play no part in these desperate shenanigans.

Katja would adore the intrigue, perhaps . . . yes, wouldn't his darling Katja throw herself and her considerable talents headlong at deception's disposal? But jealousy might make a traitor of her. No, Oskar could not afford to enlist Katja as ally . . . not yet.

And a man as respectable and preoccupied with responsibility as

Hans Posse should never be burdened with so volatile a secret as the *Schweigsame Frau's* clandestine arrival in staid Dresden. Oskar simply could not imagine how to tell his host that his shabby summerhouse was about to become a honeymoon cottage, nor . . . well, it simply would not do. Never. He was tolerant, perhaps to a fault, the Direktor, but he lacked whimsy.

Oskar was going to have to use every bit of his devious ingenuity to guard his beloved's privacy here. His itchy secrets would have to be kept.

And if Fräulein Moos's niggardly dispatches were to be credited, little time remained for plotting . . . *the shipment* could arrive in another week or two.

Hans Posse was gazing at Oskar with a worried expression.

Oskar could, for the moment, only apply himself to the task of summoning up a lighthearted smile. For Posse's sake. What with the lizard slowly expiring upstairs, the poor man had quite enough on his mind.

"I expect it's this headache I woke with," Oskar said. "My outlook today must seem a bit bleak."

"Let me get you something." Posse started to rise from his chair. "Dr. Neuberger has given me a powder that—"

"Don't trouble yourself. It's nearly gone." Oskar's disingenuous smile shimmered. "All in all, I am a good deal improved since the teaching began, wouldn't you say?"

Posse's weary eyes brightened. "You do appear stronger," he said.

His host's eagerness to join in the duplicity was touching. I might even spend an hour daubing some paint on one of those canvases he so pointedly left stacked in my cupboard, Oskar thought. Just to ease his mind . . . tomorrow afternoon, perhaps.

He hadn't the slightest notion of a picture in mind. Still, it might be a diverting exercise, trying to duplicate the color and texture of the cashmere suit, the hue deepening within the exquisite fabric's folds . . .

The Direktor leaned into the fan-shaped back of his parlor chair and opened his newspaper with a sigh of relief. "I'm pleased, in any case, that the teaching goes well."

"And I am pleased if it seems so," Oskar murmured.

How would he ever leave his bed, once she lay in it beside him? He hoped love would not make a truant of him. Had he remembered to counsel Fräulein Moos she mustn't be frugal with the perfume? Surely his love's scent, rising from the packing crate, would bring her to life before he laid eyes on her . . .

The faint rose-gold of her skin, the merest hint of down inviting his fingers . . . gold dust diluted in apricot nectar . . . a rush of vin rosé in the cheek, Manzanilla pooling in the hidden tucks and creases . . .

"Yes, indeed," Oskar said, "I believe I am much improved." *Der Zauberer.*

. . . Do not distress yourself, should our goddess display a disinclination to stand. What need? My duty and incomparable honor shall be to serve as her conveyance, sole and constant . . . let her be a creature with a singular gift for reclining.

Pliancy of limb, then, must supersede backbone's rigor. Such suppleness as allows her arrangement in comfort . . . for her comfort is, of all requirements, first and most implacable.

What need, dear Fräulein, for a goddess of love to stand?

When shall all I desire recline in the desperate hollow of my embrace? Do not dally, I beg you! I know only too well, as an artist, both the vileness and the inefficacy of nagging the deviser. But so long has my heart lain fallow I fear only wasteland, soon and permanently, may occupy the vast spaces within, where wild desire once spawned monstrous beauties . . .

Thus do soul and voice, once at art's disposal, trespass upon all that is yours, crying, Hurry, Fräulein. Please hurry!

Your desperate OK

HE STOOD FACING THE STREAKED WINDOWS, HIS BACK TO HER.

The canvas before him was almost exactly the size of the window in her little room, half a meter long perhaps, and a bit less wide. He was dragging haphazard streaks and smears of paint over it. An ugly shade of paint, faded purplish red. Like a stain that would never come out, she thought.

The coarse bristles of his thumb-sized brush slapdashed the paint across the textured emptiness of the canvas. But the Captain appeared languorous, almost dreamy, as if unaware what his hand and the brush were doing. Now and then Reserl stole glances at the easel, watching for some shape to emerge from the spreading stain. But nothing seemed to come of it, nothing at all. He did not notice her watching. It pleased her when he seemed to forget she was there. *Herr Opfer.* Mr. Casualty.

Rain had fallen all morning. Now, in midafternoon, a weakening autumn sun preened listlessly, mirrored in the garden's puddles. Washed in milky sunlight, everything inside the summerhouse appeared more soiled and worn.

Dusting, Reserl dawdled, lavishing care on the Captain's shabby things. It was not that they were sacred to her. Really not. He simply had so little and could not, she felt, endure more loss. She was thankful for the way her usual clumsiness seemed to desert her at his threshold.

She held a feather duster in one hand. The gritty rag in the other was drenched with lemon oil. Feathers danced over the bed's satinwood headboard. Reserl's dark eyes widened. Forest creatures—fairies and elves, toadstools and small furry animals—hid in the wood's mazy veneer. She wondered if the burled eyes bothered his nights, fussed his sleep. Even the toadstools had eyes. She rubbed her dustcloth hard across the wood, but its oil just brightened the eyes, making their gaze more piercing.

She backed away from the bed. No wonder the poor Captain always looked exhausted. Who could sleep with such hubbub around his head?

"I don't suppose you've ever seen it." His voice, oddly, did not startle her. She was merely disappointed. He had not forgotten she was there after all.

Slowly Reserl turned around.

"Painting," he said. "Have you ever seen it done?"

"I have been in one, sir." She blushed. *Unnütz.* Vain.

"Indeed?" He sounded amused.

Reserl stood a little straighter. "I have," she corrected herself, "been in *two*. Two ladies near my village . . ."

The surprise of it came back to her, stumbling upon them in a clearing in the wood: their thin white dresses, the wide straw hats trailing ribbons over their shoulders.

Hulda had been out gathering wild mushrooms for her father's new wife. How strange she found the little upended white tables on flimsy wooden legs . . . sticks sprouting coarse hair at one end like homely expired flowers in the ladies' dainty hands.

She scarcely remembered the ladies themselves, only that when a breeze tipped their hat brims back, letting the sunlight fall on their faces, both were younger than she'd have guessed. They were guests of the manor house beside the lake, they said, friends of the doctor's daughter. Their brittle smiles told her they meant to take something from her.

"Two ladies painted you." It ached inside her, the disbelief in his voice.

"I must pretend I am a statue." Reserl said. "They tell me this and for so long I do not move that when they say to go, my feet forget how to walk."

Oskar laughed. He was starting, she saw, to believe her.

"They give money to me, a strange kind of coin. I cannot show it." She lowered her eyes. "I must give it to my father's wife," she said.

Oskar shook his head. "That hardly seems fair."

Reserl smiled at him.

"But perhaps you are in a museum."

She looked startled. "I am here, sir."

He laughed again, kindly. "You have never been in a museum?"

"No, sir."

"But you know what it is?"

"Where Dr. Posse goes each day. He is the Direktor."

Oskar nodded. "You must go with him one day. Or I'll take you, to see. Perhaps you'll find yourself there."

The ache returned inside her. "You think I am foolish," she said.

"No," he said. "No, Reserl."

She slanted her face away. Her eyes teared.

"Beautiful things are put in museums so that people may look at them," he said.

She said nothing.

"You are beautiful," he said.

"You must not say this."

"Why ever not?"

She shook her head.

Oskar set his brush on the easel's ledge and moved toward her, holding out both hands.

"No." She took a step back.

"You are," he said. "Beautiful. It is the truth."

She was still shaking her head, more agitated. Tears spilled from the corners of her eyes.

"You must not think I do not know what I am," she said.

"You know what you are inside, yes." Oskar's hands dropped to his sides. "But I must tell you what you are in my eyes."

"I am afraid," she whispered.

His face went wan with sorrow. "We are both afraid," he said. "It's the blood we share."

The truth of it stole her breath.

"Isn't it so, Reserl?"

After a moment, she nodded.

"Come." He held out his hand.

She pretended she was a statue.

"You must see the painting," he said.

She took a step toward him. She felt his large hand close around hers. Her fingers were cold. His were colder. He led her around the easel. They stood side by side before the painting. He did not let go of her hand.

Reserl looked at the painting in silence for what seemed a very long time. Streaks of the ugly reddish paint dashed and scattered in every direction. In some places the paint was so thin the canvas's pale texture showed through. In other spots the paint had clotted. She did not know what she was supposed to see in it. What she felt from it terrified her.

The Captain was waiting. If she spoke he would see how stupid she was. An oaf. Like Hulda. But she was Reserl now, his Reserl, who must not lie to him.

She drew in her breath. Humiliation weighed down her head. "What is it?"

Oskar smiled sadly. *Das Blutbad,* he said.

Carnage.

She did not know the word as such, but its parts were simple enough. Their meaning seemed clear:

Bathed in blood. Reserl pictured the quick, clean slice of her father's slaughtering knife severing the throats of kids and lambs.

But it wasn't so, was it? What sense in killing small animals, so little to feed on? Her father was a close-fisted man. He'd not have done such a wasteful thing. Sometimes she remembers things, Reserl, that did not happen. Sometimes Hulda lied, *die Stiefmutter* said.

She studied the paint a while longer. Its color seemed all wrong. When the knife made its swift impeccable cut into the throat, what followed was a bright uncomplicated flow. Its red was pure, *das Blut.* Nothing like this raw, wayward shade.

Yet it reminded her, this painting, its color, of something . . .

She waited, her gaze steadying on a spot near the middle of the canvas. The paint, mucus-thick, was already coagulating there. Ropy strands of it trailed down to the bottom of the splattered canvas, dripping off its edge.

Reserl began to feel light-headed. When her eyes closed, they remembered.

"Die Eingeweide?" she said.

Entrails.

She opened her eyes and looked at Oskar.

He nodded.

He'd got the color right, then.

8

He had, after a long stalemate, struck a bargain with insomnia. A compromise.

Now, after months of sleepless nights and tortured dreams, Oskar slept, every third night, profoundly. Every third morning, for an hour or two, Oskar was allowed to remember how it felt to be fully alive. The way he would wake, those mornings, kept him from total despair.

General Augustus Posse died, at last, on one of those precious nights when sleep was granted, a dispensation. Oskar tried not to resent the old man for its disruption, but found this difficult. *Die Eidechse* had known so much about him. Surely he had known this, too: that by robbing Oskar of these rare hours of rest, he left his hold on life even more tenuous.

When the old man died, Oskar, the most cloddish of dancers, was waltzing.

All of Vienna looked on, suddenly, uncharacteristically free with its adulation. Oskar, Alma amply contained in his arms, whirled in widening circles around the center of a huge ballroom. Its floor, made of glass, was very slick. So swift and sure were Oskar's large feet, however, that there was no danger. He could not slip. I must have very good shoes, he thought. He wished he could recall how he had acquired them, for he would have liked to put by an extra pair.

The rapping of Hans Posse's knuckles on the summerhouse's warped door was not able to intrude upon the dream.

Alma's silver satin gown mirrored each prism of the huge chandelier overhead. The air around them shrieked with light. There was no music, only the sound of breathing. Spinning Alma across the glass, Oskar felt his arms begin to grow heavy. The Maestro had arrived. Oskar sensed his overbearing presence somewhere in the room.

Oskar awoke in a pant, sitting bolt upright. Icy fingers dug into his shoulders . . . death's grip. For a moment there was no fear, only a resigned sort of sorrow: He was going to have to slay the Maestro now. Whole symphonies, blameless, would die with him. The blood of unborn beauty would forever stain Oskar's hands.

"Oskar?"

He was reaching for Hans Posse's throat when the gentle voice extricated and absolved him. The dream's glittering shards shattered and flew.

"I need you, my friend."

Oskar's hands, retreating, clutched at the bedclothes. He was suddenly mindful of his nakedness. Hans Posse was lighting the oil lamp beside the bed. It glowed too brightly at first, smoking one side of the glass chimney. Posse lowered the wick. Oskar saw by its steadied light that his friend had been weeping.

"My father . . . it is finished."

How curious, Oskar thought, that so sensible a man could not bring himself to say *dead*. But we are none of us, are we, sensible through and through? He wondered if, in these first moments of loss, Posse felt like a child again. He looked, by the lamp's murky light, suddenly aged, as if the departing father had bequeathed a portion of hoarded years to his son.

"I am sorry." Oskar's voice, hoarse with sleep, sounded as if he too might have been weeping.

"You offered to make a drawing . . . it should have been done then. Now—" Posse, his voice breaking, moved away from the bed, tucking into shadow.

Oskar remembered the Maestro's death mask. Cast in bronze, of course. Alma had displayed it on a marble pedestal in the foyer of the house on the Elisabethenstrasse . . . Gustav Mahler's closed eyes, his grim mouth and lowered brows . . . all the strict straight lines in parallels too perfect and complete for anything but death.

No matter how gay the occasion, Alma's guests passed through her door attired in mourners' faces and manners. Oskar had once summoned the temerity to suggest the display was morbid, that the death mask might better belong in a more private region of the house.

"The bedroom, perhaps?" Alma's wicked smile sobered. "The respect is due him," she said. And: "Gucki must not be allowed to forget her father."

Had she never noticed, Oskar wondered, how the child averted her eyes passing through the wide hall? It was not her father's blind gaze Gucki was avoiding. It was death's.

The observation might have shored up his argument. But there was no arguing with Almi, of course. Oskar knew better than to revive the subject. He had always wanted to know, however, who had done the original mask. Had an illustrious artist been called to the house the moment the Maestro gave up the ghost? Had Alma been making plans in advance for posterity? He supposed she had.

And perhaps she was, in her unreasonable and haughty way, correct: Immortality was Mahler's mere due. The Second Symphony alone would have earned it for him . . . *Resurrection.* Had there never been a Third, a Ninth . . .

Not to mention the *Kindertotenlieder.* Their beauty so glorious (one critic's conceit) that the seraphim by this one exception had admitted to the celestial repertoire lamentations unto eternity.

Yes, Gustav Mahler was surely among those worthy of *Totenmasken* . . . and perhaps General Augustus Posse was, too. But even if not, Oskar thought, the least office that might ease his gentle son's bereavement must be taken up with gratitude.

The prospect of entering the stuffy little death chamber, however, of placing his fingers on flesh already engaged in the process of decay . . .

Oskar shuddered and pulled the bedsheet tighter around his bare shoulders.

"I don't suppose you have plaster of paris?" he said. "If there is a quantity of paraffin in the pantry, that should do. Or—"

Once, as a student in Vienna, he had been required to practice the technique. The master of the anatomy class was a grim, unimaginative man. The cadaver, that of a nameless pauper, had possessed a nose of astonishing proportion. The whole enterprise had been regarded by the students as something of a lark. Oskar wished now that the specifics of the casting process would come back to him as clearly as the jokes at the corpse's expense.

"I believe I'll need cheesecloth," he said. "Or gauze. Something on that order. And—"

Hans Posse had turned around and was staring at him. His expression was horrified. He was evidently speechless.

"What is it?" Oskar, for some reason, imagined he was bleeding somewhere. He opened his hands and looked down at his unmarked palms. He remembered the self-portrait that had brewed such tempests in the teapots of Vienna and Berlin: the thorny crown, his pierced side. Something salty dripped from his forehead into his eye.

He blinked. When he opened his eyes he saw comprehension on Posse's worn face. "It's good of you, my friend, but I wouldn't ask it." He tried to smile. "I only thought if you could manage a sketch or two, before—"

"Drawings," Oskar said. He would not have to touch him. "Of course."

Posse left him to dress. Oskar wondered where he would go. It was just after two o'clock in the morning, four hours and more until sunrise. He hoped the Direktor would return to bed, but he doubted it. Perhaps he meant to observe the tradition of sitting up all night with the deceased. Oskar wondered if he'd be able to draw death's likeness, should all that living grief be keeping watch beside the bed.

He left the oil lamp burning on the bedside stand as he went out, a light to welcome him when he returned. The chill night, close on the heels of an unusually warm late-autumn day, had sent fog creeping through the stalks and stems of the neglected garden. The moon, swathed in clouds, left a purple bruise on the sky. No light shone from the little rectangular window that marked off Reserl's room. Oskar imagined her awake, listening to the uncommon activity moving through the house. What might she make of it? Would she fear thieves, vandals, or murderers? No, he thought. Reserl would need no announcement of death's arrival in the house.

One arm encumbered with hastily gathered drawing materials, Oskar groped his single-handed way through the kitchen's blackness. The room proved more familiar than he'd have guessed. He steered surely between table and stove, chair and chopping block. Then, only slightly misjudging his own footsteps' angle, he shouldered, hard, into the frame of the hallway's narrow door.

The crack of meagerly padded bone against wood sounded like a book ungently returned to its shelf. A bolt of pain shot down his arm. The darkness was powdered for a moment with stars. Oskar imagined Reserl cowering on her cot behind the pantry. "It's all right," he whispered. "It is nothing."

The house's back stairway tapered and kinked, its treads smoothed perilous by a century of servants' feet. In foreign territory now, Oskar climbed as a small child would, taking each step with his right foot. It was a measure of Hans Posse's distress that he'd neglected to light the way. *Then again, I might have had the foresight to carry my own lamp, mightn't I?* The thought made Oskar smile at the dark.

From the stairway's final turn a spill of secondhand light laid a path to the old man's room. Oskar moved faster down the corridor, trying to discern Hans Posse's hovering shadow. But when he reached the doorway he found a room occupied only by what General Augustus Posse had abandoned to stale bedding: his husk.

Die Eidechse: That which, half an hour before, still breathed, now looked dried out, petrified and nearly transparent. *Nothing to him,* Oskar thought. But that was untrue, of course. It was simply that what there had been to him was gone now . . . and only deference to what had vanished demanded heed or homage to that which remained.

Oskar's mind could not seem to embrace the dead man at all. He found himself wishing only that he'd better tried to understand the bereaved son. For the nature of Hans Posse's desire for a last likeness of his father was unclear: Did he want the old man fixed in his final moments of life? Or captured as he appeared in death? These are two different men, Oskar thought, and I cannot take it upon myself to choose between them.

He stood just inside the doorway, at a distance from the bed, for several moments. He recalled his first sight of *Die Eidechse:* a skull in a nest of pillows. He was, in truth, little more than that now. But the sound of the old man's voice remained in the room. The General was, even now, not one to be easily dismissed.

Over and over again Oskar apprehended his own skittish gaze, trying to make a getaway. He tethered it tight to the old man's face. My eyes must be made to *listen,* he thought.

Surely you would not wish to forget?

After what seemed like a very long time, Oskar crossed the room, drew back the drapes, and opened the room's one window. Up here, high above the deserted street, the night air was clear. A swatch of cloud slipped past, baring the moon. Its light drifted down like a slow flurry of snow, dusting the Hofkirche's steeple. Oskar wondered if Augustus Posse had ever noticed what his small window had been offering up to him. If he'd been informed of the Armistice to which an exhausted *Vaterland* had acquiesced days earlier, and if its sad terms had figured in the old soldier's slipped hold on life. But perhaps it was just peace he was waiting for, Oskar thought. Peace of any stripe.

He turned and studied the old man again. His face looked quite different from this new vantage point. He appeared, in fact, less dead. For a moment Oskar saw the lizard's bright beady eyes peering keenly at him. *I'll not countenance evasion.*

Oskar, one arm still encumbered with his sketching materials, pulled a straight-backed chair close to the bedside and sat down. The room's meager light, provided by two oil lamps, was poor for sketching. Yet the idea of bringing new light into a room so recently visited by death seemed an outrage. Oskar contented himself with moving the oil lamp on the bedside table a finger's length closer to the old man's face.

He set a cigar box on the edge of the mattress, at the General's elbow. The box held a motley hoard of chalks and pastels, stubs of pencils, rusted nibs. Oskar did not open it. He found a well-worn piece of charcoal in his trouser pocket. Charcoal, more pliant and forgiving than lead, seemed the proper initiation for so sober and tentative an undertaking.

Oskar opened the sketch pad, leafing quickly through its used pages. The blur of his eyes' past dalliances—naked bodies and bowls of ripe fruit, serried market stalls and histrionic self-portraits—embarrassed him. Their ruddy infatuation with life seemed uncouth.

Three quarters of the pad had been squandered on the impossibly common. The artist who had frittered away these sheets was a youngster, entranced with surfaces, parading as passion what was mere energy. So it was not simply a matter of seeing, was it? *I must listen with my eyes,* Oskar thought again.

At last he found a blank page. He folded back the cover, smothering the unseemly exuberance of all those wasted sheets. He shifted closer to the bed. He bridged the last bit of distance with the sketchbook, its bottom propped by his knees, its top by the edge of the mattress.

Slowly, his eyes began to make peace with their lot: the room's dearth of light, a life's sad leavings.

Somewhere unseen, a shape was starting to form. It was unlike a portrait. Closer, Oskar thought, to a still life. Then he willed himself to stop thinking altogether.

Little by little, the life of Augustus Posse was moving toward him, all of a piece, in a single sure line. Then the line, in a silent collision, ran up against all Oskar had seen, heretofore, of death.

Oskar Kokoschka had, for a young man, seen a great deal of death. But war's cacophony had first muffled death's sound. And later, in cowardice, he had covered his ears. Now, keeping company with the old General's remains, Oskar saw the truth of his own petty wounds and losses, the frantic sham of his need to hum and wail and drum death away. That the solace of such noise was no longer allowed him was something he neither knew nor thought, but simply felt now in the artless core of his soul.

Oskar sat for a very long time—perfectly still, listening—before the first soft dark true line made itself fully known to him. Then he began to draw it.

THE NEXT THING OSKAR KNEW, THE SMALL ROOM WAS CROWDED WITH dawn's shadows and Hans Posse stood beside him, weeping.

Oskar opened his mouth to speak and no sound came out. His tongue was gritty. He felt the skin at one corner of his mouth crack and begin to bleed.

Balls of paper, loosely crushed, lay about the bed, a mass beheading of white peonies strewn over the dark carpet. Dozens of crumpled sketches littered the blanket covering the General's bony legs. But Oskar and Hans Posse were not looking at the dead man on the bed. Both men saw nothing but the drawing that occupied the last sheet of paper in the sketch pad, its slant still secured between the deathbed and the artist's knees.

The figure in the drawing was not a corpse. Nor was its face that of a stern old man full of secrets taking his sweet time dying. Oskar had not, in the end, been forced to choose. Indeed, there had been no choice in any of this. Oskar felt as if he had been, at best, a lowly apprentice, holding steady the plane on which a master, ancient and unknown, had drawn.

Hans Posse studied his father's final face, his own face bathed in tears. There was something almost rapturous about his weeping. He was, like Oskar, unable to speak.

Finally, dizzied by the room's stuffiness, Oskar stood. His stiff limbs straightened reluctantly, as if against excruciating pain. He handed the sketch pad to Posse, who with both hands clasped it to his chest. His mouth shaped the simplest word for gratitude. The rapture of tears persisted on his face. His deep gaze acknowledged the valor of Oskar's journey.

Death's borders had been penetrated. Posse knew this. He recognized the hostage Oskar had rescued from oblivion not as the man who had lived, nor the father who had died, but a third man, eternity's being.

Oskar circled to the far side of the bed.

Posse bent down and touched the hem of the bedsheet that lay across his father's chest.

Oskar picked up the other side of the sheet.

Together they covered the castaway face.

The hallway outside the old man's room was stippled with early-morning light. Medallions of gold sunlight and green shadow littered the steep back stairs. Oskar's hands brushed the wall, steadying his descent. The charcoaled pads of his fingers left dark moth shadows among the wallpaper's sallow petals.

He knew she would be there, just as she was: Reserl, attentive to grief, waiting at the foot of the stairs. The folds of her dress were the blackish-green of the moss inside a well. An outlandish rag of the same shade covered her hair. The perfect appropriateness of her covered head shocked him.

Her arms rose, as if ready to catch him. He took the last two steps with an invalid's stiff exactitude. Her arms dropped to her sides. Her small rough hands vanished inside the frayed sleeves of her dress.

"It is nothing." It was her face, buttermilk pale, that extracted the foolish words from him. Her small sad smile understood this and he swallowed a silent recanting.

"You must eat," she said.

He shook his head and stood a little straighter.

"Something. You ought to."

His relief was nearly like joy. No need, with her, for either display or disguise. His weakness was simply a part of him, unremarkable as his voice's pitch, his body's heft.

"Come."

He followed her into the kitchen, where a single place had been set at a small marble-topped table beside a window.

They were hers, this table and the corner it straddled. Here she rolled out pastry, set bread dough to rise. Pies and coffee cakes were left to cool on the veined slab of marble, meats to steep in spiced concoctions of blood and wine. Once, entering the kitchen in flight from a restless dawn, Oskar had found her, wobbling on a fickle stool as she ate oatmeal from a dented tin measuring cup. So he had known Reserl took her solitary meals at the same table where she worked. But he'd never again caught her in the act of eating.

The table's chipped marble top was spread with a blue linen tea towel, upon it a cracked plate and a frazzled napkin. The ungainly spoon, tarnished and bent, and the flushed clay bowl were never meant for tableware. They, too, would be hers, Oskar knew. Yet he somehow understood the place was meant this morning for him.

Reserl reached behind the pantry door and dragged out the same perilous stool he'd seen her occupy. Before Oskar could move to take it from her, the stool had bumped over the brick floor and come to a tipsy stop beside the table. Reserl pointed to it. The round seat favored a giddy tilt. By the time Oskar had himself safely balanced, she stood at the stove, her back to him, inciting the flame under a scorched cast-iron skillet.

The same covered pot sat in its usual spot on the cold back burner. Sometimes, passing through the empty kitchen, Oskar would lift its lid and look inside. He always found the same thing. The prunes were simmered to softness. Curls of lemon peel floating in otter-brown water. The liquid smelled like sweet wine.

Even when he'd touched nothing else on the heavy trays the girl wrestled up the stairs, the old man had nearly always eaten the prunes. Now Oskar stared into the clay bowl in front of him, picturing the dark fruit floating there. He would refuse it. He would not taste the dead man's leavings.

Oskar closed his eyes and sat perfectly still, hands keeping his balance on the table's edge. A soft fabric of sound wound around him: birdsong, heavy footsteps overhead, a lid's clang closing over a pot. A street away, wooden wagon wheels gritted over cobblestone. Liquid poured from one receptacle into another. I must bathe, Oskar thought.

The mossy scent of her, close by, yanked him from the verge of a doze. Oskar opened his eyes. In the rosy clay bowl raspberries floated in heavy cream. It was nearly winter. Where in the world would she find raspberries? The cream was tinted pink with their juice. I am in a dream, Oskar thought. Then he heard a sputter behind him. The air turned salty with ham.

Then Reserl, her eyes intent on him, was touching his sleeve.

Oskar felt his throat close. "I can't." He turned away, his raised hands a charade of helplessness. The stool seesawed, pitching him toward her. Reserl caught him under the arms. For a moment, his weight seemed more than she could bear and she nearly toppled back into the window. Oskar pictured her small form flying out into the morning light on wings of shattered glass.

Then Reserl regained her balance.

Oskar recovered his more slowly. "I can't," he repeated.

Her gaze, for the merest instant, dropped to the bowl of raspberries and cream. Her lips lapsed into the shape of sorrow, a sorrow Oskar recognized but failed to understand. It seemed to him he ought to say he was sorry.

But before he could speak, Reserl took the words for her own. "I'm sorry."

Oskar bowed his head. He felt her hands letting him go. Warmth lagged in the bones of his rib cage, just under his arms, where she had held him.

Then she was leading him by the hand, blind, out the kitchen's back door and through the back reaches of the garden, where the bathhouse would be cold and damp and still, where his scalded eyes might be entrusted to the mercies of only so dim a light.

EVENING HOVERED WHEN OSKAR AWOKE. FROM HIS BED IN THE SUMMER-house neither sky nor river lay in sight. The nameless hue of the scant light slanting through the shutter slats announced the day's passing. Soon an inflamed sun would lower itself into the Elbe, blistering the river's surface as it sank from view.

Scraps of dreams littered the foreground of his mind. I have been ill,

Oskar thought, have forfeited a day to delirium . . . any number of days. Fretting, he touched his forehead. His brow was cool.

This must be an ordinary evening, then. The old General might already be cursing his supper tray under the eaves. Soon Hans Posse, charming patronage over aperitifs in some café or drawing room, would glance at his gold pocket watch and lament the late hour.

Oskar felt as if he had not eaten in days. He pictured Reserl's upper lip dewy with kitchen heat as she grated onions and potatoes, whisked flour into spitting fat.

Reserl did not, in Oskar's picture of her, wear anything on her head. Why smother the sparks in her hair? Woeful enough, their stern plaited confinement . . .

For a moment the mystery of it diverted him from his sense of lost time. Why on earth should he be thinking of a dirty scarf covering her hair?

He tried to dismiss her, send her away, but the girl, her head covered, kept picking at loose threads on the ragged edge of consciousness:

Chill silky hands like fish in the warm water, pale shadows flickering in the greenish dusk . . . in the morning, when Oskar never bathed . . . not his habit . . . and death a reek no water could dilute . . .

Would Reserl have touched him? Not there, not in that way. Nor held him. No more than he himself, in her presence, would have wept: sounds ripped from the cold cavity that houses his heart.

How silly, all of it, simply the stuff of dreams:

Stemless peonies, linen-white, strewn upon a mound of venerable bones.

A bowl of garnet berries adrift in clotting pink cream.

Hans Posse's face a cracked glaze of tears.

Steeped in death's stench, Oskar sees himself in a tub, wreathed in steam. He is shivering. A palsy so violent might crack and splinter bone.

The girl's dress, dark and eerie as a thundercloud, rises over her head. Her naked body floats above him, then lowers.

How should such a delicate web of limbs manage to enclose him? Only in the calculus of dreams . . .

So white, Reserl's body, in the patinous light, an overlay of verdigris on copper nipples, and on her body no hair, no hair anywhere.

A caught breath of lavender, the water.

Her head wrapped in cloth so rancid that, awake, she'd not allow it to wipe ash from a grate. Proof enough, that filthy bandanna: what he remembers could only occur in dreams . . .

Oskar: tearing the sordid cover from Reserl's head, filling his mouth with her hair. And Reserl: taking death on her tongue, swallowing it.

Somewhere, someone has died.

9

He will never love me.

She knew this as, for the first time, she lay beneath him.

What she recalls of that moment, however, holds no thought, only a voice. Days later, she hears it still: a voice so clear, so certain and wise, it could not be her own. It wakens her, the voice. It warns her. He will never love you. It blames her, in advance, for everything she will suffer, for all she will, of necessity, go without.

HIS SKIN, IN THE BATH, HAD BEEN KEEN WITH GOOSEFLESH. HER SMALL rough hands sleeked his shoulders, his back. He was bristled and bony. Hungry and cold. An orphan boy had, all along, huddled inside his respectable clothes, a child she had somehow always known. She opened her arms to him without a thought.

The warm water, the morning sun, had not touched his chill. Cold had sunk deep roots in him, binding his vital organs. The quilt she'd warmed beside the stove while heating the bathwater scorched her fingers as she laid it over his bed. Its heat would not penetrate him.

He would, without touch, soon freeze. Succumb to the cold he carried within. Reserl saw his long sad face encased in ice, his eyes frostbound, inclement.

Her hands, slowly lowering, squandered their warmth on his belly, his hips, his thighs . . . *he will never love me . . . you . . . never.* The chill of his flesh crept into her fingers.

Eyes peered out at her from the polished headboard of the bed. Mouths hooked with mockery in the gnarls of veneer. Reserl turned her back on the bed and began to remove her clothes.

Sauces never tasted blemished her apron. The crudely mended holes in her stockings climbed her legs like centipedes. Bared, her legs bloomed with bruises the colors of Alpine flowers.

No man had ever looked upon her nakedness. Reserl had never looked fully upon it herself. Behind her, on the bed, Oskar kept his eyes tightly closed, his head wrenched toward the shuttered windows.

She imagined another woman in the room, taking inventory of her deficits with placid molasses eyes. The woman, watching Reserl remove her clothing, laughed without making a sound. But the rippling silk of her flesh seemed to sing with amusement. Reserl, wrapping her thin arms around herself, covered her breasts.

Reserl and Oskar were alone, naked, in the summerhouse.

There was a woman in the room, watching Reserl emerge from her sour and shabby clothes.

Two truths bound to kill each other . . . Reserl did not ask herself how it was that both could survive.

The Captain trembled with cold. At her back the bed's tricky headboard rattled.

Shivering, Reserl climbed onto the bed and laid her newfound body over his. His eyes stayed closed. She wondered if he had stolen a glance while her back was turned, already seen her nakedness. Would he pity her? Perhaps he had looked into the molasses eyes, laughing soundlessly with the silent woman.

His shivering began to slake. In time he lay nearly still. He might, but for the occasional shudder, have lain dead beneath her.

Reserl lifted one hand from his shoulder and laid it along the side of his face. Her chapped fingers smelled of onion and garlic. She wondered if the scent repulsed him, if he noticed the roughness in her touch. His lips were slightly parted. She covered his mouth with her own and breathed into him.

His eyes remained closed.

She might have been a blanket.

Reserl twined her arms and legs about his body, lifted her mouth from his. His breath grieved like a high and distant wind.

He will never love you.

An ache spread out from her center, until the whole of her being was overtaken. Reserl recognized the cramp. Nights long ago, as a child, she had groaned and writhed with it. *Growing pains,* her mother had said.

I must grow larger, Reserl thought. If I am to hold him.

She must not think.

He will never love you.

Her body slipped from his. She lay beside him for a moment, on her back. Her eyes filled with water. Her heart was slamming into her ribs like a fist. She saw slight white shoots of bone inside her chest, trampled and torn. Water was pooling in her eye sockets. Reserl lay very still to keep it from spilling.

His weight came as a shock. He was such a slight and bony man. Her heartbeat had only begun to slow and even. As he rolled on top of her, his eyes did not open. His hands did not touch her. The weight of him slammed down on her, as if he were hurled from high above. His weight pushed the breath from her, in a sound like a small hopeless sigh.

He would never love her.

SHE HAD GATHERED A STORE OF NOTIONS ABOUT IT, WHAT ONE DAY SOME man would inevitably inflict upon her body, claiming it.

Reserl had seen when she was young, as farm children cannot help but see, the violent and exciting ways of animals in the mud of spring. She had heard the cries like death and been astonished when, dirtied and torn, females of various species staggered up from the earth, a kind of ruined fury about them. It had hardly surprised her, at nine or ten, when the village boys began whispering of such spectacles as they fled the schoolhouse, their laughter muffling but not drowning out the loud truth of their boasts and threats.

Someday you will belong to someone, her mother had once told her.

I am already yours, said Emil. Be mine.

You will be ruined, *die Stiefmutter* said.

It would be beautiful, swore Frieda, the friend who made mistakes but never told lies.

A father would never, of course, have discussed such things. Nor would a daughter have asked it of him. But Hulda had seen the stallion's parts loose between his haunches. She did not need her father to explain what bred in the nest of coarse hair, the dark flesh's purpose.

The pain of it, though, nobody had shown or told Hulda of that. The pain was Reserl's own notion.

Oskar lay beneath her, a marble altar, cold and unmoving.

She had somehow assumed there would be heat.

The heat, when she offered herself, was entirely her own.

Then the weight of him fell upon her, stealing her air and stifling her heart.

After a time, Reserl, with great caution, began to move. Bone grating against bone made her believe a spark would soon be struck between them. She wondered if she should be afraid.

That a fire sufficient to warm him might reduce her to cinders was not unthinkable. She probably should be afraid. Skin heretofore untouched must be easily rent. Had she only thought of it.

She must not think.

Hulda would have been afraid.

Reserl moved bravely, her hide a sacrifice laid on the icy altar of his bones.

He did not touch her.

And the pain of that, of giving herself to a man who either could not or would not touch her, was one for which nothing, not even her own notions, could have prepared her.

THE DIREKTOR'S FINE FACE WAS MANGLED WITH GRIEF. HIS CUSTOMARY reading chair, a haymow of worn brown horsehair, sat uncustomarily close to the hearth. Its displacement seemed to set the whole parlor at odds with itself.

Reserl, peering in from the doorway, for a moment imagined looters stealing through a window, breaching a household engrossed in mourning. But the mantel's scrolled ends were still weighted with silver candlesticks, the escritoire's shelves still hectic with figurines. The figurines needed dusting. Nothing really amiss, apart from the Direktor's pallor, the occasional spark menacing his heavy chair.

The day lay dim and disordered in Reserl's memory. Closing the summerhouse door behind her in midmorning, she had run off confusion and shame with worries over lunch. Sherried consommé and poached fish, currant buns . . . perhaps coddled eggs? Light, nourishing food to lure the Direktor back toward daylight, to sustain him through the chores of arranged mourning . . .

It was nearly noon when the men in dark clothes came to bump the General down the stairs. He was removed from the house in a lidded rattan basket shaped like a rowboat. The men moved slowly down the straight front stairway. The long basket left scrapes on the wallpaper. It would never have made the tight turns on the back stairs.

There were three men. Two struggled with the basket, their knees buckling. The third, who wore a dusty black suit and black bowler, held their dark cloth caps. Twice Reserl heard him say, in a voice like a growl, *Beeilen Sie sich,* Hurry up! He also whispered the word *Vorsichtig* repeatedly, as the huge basket jolted down the steps. *Careful,* the way he said it, sounded like a prayer.

When the men with the casket reached the foyer, the man who held their caps told them to stop. The two workmen were sweating. The third man removed his bowler, held all three hats over his heart, and bowed his head. Reserl was surprised to see thick wavy red hair covering his scalp. In the hat he had looked like a man whose head would be naked, pink and shiny.

After a moment the man raised his face, returned the bowler to his head, and growled at the other two men, telling them they must go out the back door. He nipped at their heels all the way through the kitchen. At the back door, he turned before going out. He bowed to Reserl, without looking at her.

THE DIREKTOR DID NOT APPEAR.

An hour after the men had taken the General away through the back door, the brass bell at the front door sounded. Reserl, dreamy over her simmering stockpot, jumped. When she answered the door she was trembling.

The Direktor's friend Herr Hoffenmeyer had come to offer condolences, he said. He did not say how he had learned of the General's death. His nankeen coat was rumpled. His deep red cravat, fine spatters of black paint on it, suggested pickled beets.

Although Reserl did not know just where the Direktor was or what he was doing, she said he was resting. "Do not disturb him," Herr Hoffenmeyer said.

Hoffenmeyer was a soft-spoken man with rounded shoulders and sad eyes. His long sharp nose looked like something he had borrowed, under duress, from a more severe man. Reserl wondered whether she should call the Direktor, at least tell him his friend had come. Herr Hoffenmeyer seemed like a man who would be good at giving comfort.

But Reserl did not know how to take back her lie. The Direktor was resting. Well, perhaps it was not a lie. She looked down in confusion. A gardenia plant in a blue-glazed pot sat beside Herr Hoffenmeyer's scuffed black boots. The pot and plant were quite large. Reserl wondered if Herr Hoffenmeyer could have carried the plant all the way from his home, for she had heard the Direktor remark that his friend lived on the other side of the Loschwitz Bridge.

"You have brought this?" she asked softly.

Herr Hoffenmeyer looked puzzled. Then he looked down and saw the plant. He shook his head sadly. "I should have brought something," he said.

After he left, Reserl picked up the gardenia plant and carried it inside, placing it on a small table in the parlor. How odd that no card or note accompanied the plant. The Direktor would want to know who sent it. She felt ashamed that she would not be able to tell him. She hoped the plant's weight was not too great for the little table. She imagined its spindle legs trembling.

WHEN, BY HALF PAST ONE, HANS POSSE HAD FAILED TO COME DOWNSTAIRS and Oskar had not appeared in the house, Reserl emptied the urn-shaped soup tureen. The dining room table was relieved of its small cut-glass bowls of relishes and condiments. She hoped both men were sleeping. They must be very tired.

At three o'clock Reserl ducked into her little room behind the pantry and lay down herself. She did not sleep, however. She simply tried to empty her mind. Reserl lay on her narrow cot and pictured herself lagging along the dusty twist of road into her village. She wondered if her father still lived there with his new wife, if they would know her, should she appear at their door.

Lying stiffly on top of her rough blanket, still wearing her boots,

Reserl reached into her apron pocket. She had replaited and pinned up her hair before leaving the summerhouse. The kerchief must still be out there, fallen under the bed or ensnared in the linen. Reserl, her hand tucked inside her empty pocket, tried to imagine the green wool balled up in the Captain's long, slender fingers as he slept.

She closed her eyes. Against the webbed red backdrop of her eyelids Emil's face appeared. How young he was. So young. Emil's face glowed like a moonstone. His eyes overflowed with belief. *We shall marry in spring . . . roast lamb and dancing beneath a huppah of blossoms . . .*

He would not know me now, Reserl thought.

THE DIREKTOR, STARTING AT THE SOUND OF HER SIGH, GLANCED TO THE doorway. His slight nod, his murmured *Guten Abend,* were the reflexes of inborn courtesy. In his eyes Reserl saw that she might have been a stranger.

She bowed her head. "You will have dinner, mein Herr?" Her whisper floated, then settled in the room like more dust.

"Wie bitte?" Hans Posse was staring into the fire.

"Möchten Sie etwas essen?" she asked, her voice a little stronger: Wouldn't you like to eat something?

The Direktor smiled vaguely at the hearth.

"Let me just fix a little something," she said.

Reserl hovered in the doorway for another moment, in case the Direktor might reply. The gold mantel clock ticked strictly under its cloudy glass dome.

"What has become of him?"

Reserl flinched and backed away from the parlor's brassy light.

"Oskar," Hans Posse said. "Herr Kokoschka."

The fire seemed to reach across the room, touching her face with heat. "Shall I call him for you, sir?"

"Please. Don't disturb him."

The Direktor's face looked like wax. Reserl imagined it melting. "I'll just call him," she said, backing farther into the foyer.

I'll just knock on his door, just once . . . if there are no lights I'll knock loudly . . . I will not knock unless . . .

I'll call out to him . . . I will not call him Captain . . . I will not have him laughing at me, will not allow . . .

I will call him by his proper name . . . will call him like a proper servant . . .

I will knock but I will not call him . . . will not call out.

The day was drained of light, all but one gold thread to the west, stitching the river's shining far edge to the purple sky. But for the reflected glow of the parlor windows, she would not have seen him.

Oskar lay under a barren tree that rested one thorny elbowed branch on the kitchen's low roof. A stained blanket was spread beneath him, useless against the damp ground. His eyes were closed.

For a moment Reserl stood paralyzed, her stare begging his neck for a pulse, his chest for breath's rise and fall. His body seemed to move not at all. She dropped to her knees on the edge of the blanket and took his face in her hands. Master.

Oskar smiled dreamily and murmured something. *Almosen . . .* alms? Was that what he'd said?

Then he opened his eyes. Reserl saw in Oskar's eyes that she was not what he expected, not what he desired.

"Come to the house," she said. "You must come in."

He nodded.

"Dinner will soon be ready, and you—"

Struggling to her feet, she stepped on the hem of her dress. She grasped at the tree for balance. The end of a branch snapped off in her hand.

Reserl, despising her own clumsiness, caught her balance. He was watching. She let the branch fall to the ground.

"You are awake now?" she asked softly.

Oskar nodded. His eyes were looking past her, as if what he needed lay behind her, in the dark.

Reserl turned back toward the kitchen, leaving him there. Leaving his dreams to beg alms from the dark. Would he fall back to sleep? If he did, she wondered, should she try again to wake him?

His simplest needs twisted and tangled inside her, making impossible knots. I should fear him, Reserl thought. I need to be afraid.

She ducked through the back door. The kitchen was a cave of warm light. *Noodles in sour cream, a dust of nutmeg, a strewing of parsley . . .*

Spätzle would have been perfect. For a moment her fingers, sticky with a paste of flour and egg, ached with need. Powder-white hands, grace knuckling through the soft dough . . .

But there was not time for that now, of course. No time.

In the overheated parlor the Direktor coddled new shoots of grief, while in the gone-to-seed garden the Captain dreamed of charity . . . and she, Hulda . . . while she . . .

Reserl struck a wooden match and touched it to the stove. A flame huffed under the copper stockpot. Everyone was hungry. They would begin with the consommé. *Nahrhaft.* Nourishing.

THE NEXT MORNING, THE DIREKTOR LEFT FOR THE MUSEUM AT THE USUAL hour, Oskar for the Academy, as if nothing had happened. From what Reserl had been able to hear from the kitchen, the two men had talked very little over breakfast. But that, too, was as usual.

Without the General to look after, Reserl had time on her hands. Still, she rushed through the customary morning chores. A great many visitors were bound to enter the house over the next few days. She gave the parlor an especially vigorous dusting. She overturned nothing. Nothing broke.

On Thursdays both the Direktor and the Captain were expected home for lunch. Reserl quickly assembled the ingredients for salad and an omelet. Then, with an hour left to the morning, she meticulously sponged and pressed each man's best black suit.

Both her mother and her grandmother had been hurried into the earth before the setting of the sun. No one had ever explained this urgency to the child. Other village families took their time with death. Sometimes, if the weather was not warm, three whole days might pass before the living would let go of the dead.

Now, in the city, it occurred to Reserl that the interlude between death and burial might measure the dead person's importance. The General had been a very important man, of course. The Direktor also was. The weather was cold. A funeral might not take place until . . . perhaps Monday?

Still, Reserl must be prepared. The Direktor and the Captain must be ready. It would shame her if either should appear disheveled or worn. Reserl hung the suits, one fine, the other a bit shabby, back in their wardrobes and checked on the condition of the best collars and shirts. This afternoon she would begin the baking.

Would she, as a member of the household, be expected to attend the funeral? Reserl rather hoped not. Though there were bound, in the case of so important a personage, to be speeches. And a great many flowers. It could be a pleasure to hear learned men explaining the General's greatness while breathing in the perfume of flowers, she supposed.

Neither speeches nor flowers had attended the deaths of her mother and grandmother. The two women were buried side by side in a small walled-in square of earth that lay, almost hidden, outside the village. Speeches would have seemed silly, Reserl thought, out in the woods. And who in the village would have known how to make one? Hulda loved flowers. Their beauty might have consoled her. But tearing flowers from the dirt only to return them there . . . where was the sense in that?

But perhaps there had been flowers. Perhaps her father had wept for his wife. She recalled so little of all this, Reserl . . . not even whether Hulda had cried . . .

Only the ground behind the wall in the woods, how pure black and wet . . . she remembers how small the plain pine box being lowered into the mud, her mother inside it. All of it so fast and the box so small . . . Hulda did not quite believe, as the box sank and vanished, that it could hold inside it all there was of her mother.

When, similarly and soon thereafter, her grandmother was also disposed of, Hulda was less shocked. Death's indelicacies had grown familiar. Her disbelief, however, was even stronger. The wide-hipped woman who was her mother's mother would never have fit in the box.

Yis'ga'dal v'yis'kadash . . . below monstrous shadows men's voices low and rough as rocks. Death had its own language, then.

Hulda heard but did not understand it. Hulda was only a child.

Reserl barely remembers it. Yet she hears it now, for a moment, again.

Will there be chanting? When will the old General be tucked into the ground? She wishes the Direktor would tell her. Perhaps he has forgotten. Surely he would wish her to know.

Small things tend, in death's presence, to be overlooked.

AFTER A WEEK, WHEN ALL THE SCHEDULES AND ROUTINES OF THE HOUSE-hold stubbornly persist, it becomes clear to Reserl that a funeral is not to be. A few visitors come around in the evenings to sit with the Direktor. She serves them the *Bienenstich* and ginger biscuits, the *Hefekranz* and poppy-seed cake she has baked. The visitors sit in the well-dusted parlor and eat her cakes and pastries and drink Turkish coffee from the

tiny gold-rimmed cups whose fragility makes Reserl pray as she washes
them. When she carries the cups back out to the kitchen, two at a time,
one in each hand, dark grounds fine as pollen swirl inside them.

In her village a very old and ugly woman named Helike used to claim
that for a coin or two she could read messages in coffee grounds. Helike,
the village children knew, was a witch. The men laughed at her great sag-
ging breasts, at the burl of a mole sprouting hair on her chin. The village
women gave Helike their coins. After Helike delivered her messages,
wives sometimes forbade their husbands to leave the house after dark.
Sometimes a mother might begin mourning for a perfectly healthy child.

Sometimes terrible things happened. Sometimes the messages were
true.

Once, when Hulda was small, she was carried in her mother's arms
through the kinked doorway of the old woman's cottage. Helike had
stared at her with piercing eyes and made her cry. Later, when Hulda
was growing up and her mother was dead, the old woman always looked
away and pretended she did not see her.

Reserl wondered if the memory of old Helike was what stole her
hands' steadiness as they washed the small cups.

But it might have been the cups' way, when she held them up, of
turning transparent against the light, like the skin of newborn babies.

New mothers must be frightened all the time, Reserl thought. How
easily babies could be broken or crushed. She herself would have no babies. She knew this, though she did not know how she knew. She knew
it more surely than if Helike had read the indelible message in the
grounds in Hulda's cup.

Reserl did not drink coffee. Coffee tasted bitter. The Direktor's visitors said the coffee Reserl made was very fine. Rich and mellow. No bitterness, they said. The important thing, Reserl knew, was to let the coffee
neither boil nor cool. A delicate business. Like a baby. She wondered if
it might be a blessing, knowing no babies would come to her. If her fears
grew too many, she would no longer be able to count them. Which
would be a terrible danger to her.

THERE WAS TO BE NO FUNERAL. RESERL, AFTER A NEARLY USUAL WEEK,
knew this.

She was afraid the Direktor would waste away if he did not begin eating.

She was afraid the Captain would never again look into her eyes, would pretend he did not see her.

She was afraid more flowers might mysteriously arrive. What if cold night air should freeze the petals, blacken the leaves, before she found them?

Each afternoon the week of the General's death Reserl opened the front door many times. She would glance out at the iron steps and, finding them empty, would close and lock the door again.

She did not go to the summerhouse. Each afternoon at five o'clock she would carry heavy buckets filled with steaming water to the bathhouse. Six buckets in all. When she poured the last one into the tub, the Captain would not be there.

Each morning, while Oskar and the Direktor were taking breakfast, Reserl would return to the bathhouse. As the two men drank her fine hot black coffee in the dining room, Reserl would empty the cold gray water, bucket by bucket, into the tangled shrubs at the back of the garden. Wraiths of vapor would dance over the frost-glazed ground.

Reserl was afraid the old General's spirit, discomfited at not having been laid properly to rest, might afflict the house. She dreaded all that a spiteful spirit might cause her to do: pour salt into the sugar bowl, crush the eggshell cups in her bungling hands, fall off chairs and speak out of turn and . . .

Such mishaps, countless and terrible, often befell those to whom old Helike had delivered messages.

Reserl was waiting for a message. From the General.

Or the Direktor, perhaps. These days Hans Posse barely spoke, apart from perfunctory courtesies. Sometimes Reserl feared there *had* been a funeral, that the Direktor had simply forgotten to inform her of it. Now he might be put out with her for failing to attend. Her employer was, as ever, kind. But he never seemed to look at her. She rarely broke anything anymore. She wondered if he noticed.

No more flowers or plants, once she went on the lookout for them, arrived at the house.

Returning from an anxious foray to the front steps one day, Reserl found her green kerchief in the kitchen. Folded into a lumpish triangle, it lay on the chipped marble tabletop in the corner.

She stared at the rag. Tree-shadow fell through the window and appeared to stain the dark wool.

Reserl grabbed the scarf and ducked into the pantry, where she shoved it into the back of the potato bin.

Why hadn't she simply left it there? She could not remember. Something about death.

Reserl was afraid.

The most terrible thing would be if the Captain's silver eyes should never look into hers again. Could the old General's spirit cause such a thing?

Reserl was always afraid.

WHICH MADE IT RATHER ODD THAT, RETURNING TO HER LITTLE ROOM ONE night and hearing her name, a hiss in the dark, Reserl felt no fear.

It was nearly midnight. An unusual number of visitors, six, had stayed unusually late. Two of the visitors were ladies who seemed to be friends of the Captain as well as the Direktor. One had a clutch of speckled feathers pinned in her rambunctious golden hair. The other, who was very thin, wore what must have been boy's breeches. The young lady in the yellow breeches was surprisingly quiet. The other one chattered a good deal and shook her hair and made everyone, even the Direktor, laugh.

Both ladies had left pretty pink kisses of lip rouge on the rims of their coffee cups. One of the men smoked a pipe that veiled the mirrors in strange fruity smoke. Reserl let the parlor air out while she tidied up after the visitors. It was late, but she did not mind. The lady with feathers in her hair had called Reserl's poppy-seed cake *himmlisch*—heavenly! And how lovely hearing the Direktor's long-lost laugh rumble out of the parlor and down the hall.

When the house was set to rights, Reserl closed the windows and doused the lamps. Then she made her bedtime visit to the privy behind the house. No light shone from the summerhouse as she crossed the yard. The Captain had drunk more brandy than coffee. He must have tumbled easily into sleep.

The night was moonless. The garden was unusually dark. Reserl was thankful she'd troubled to carry a lantern. Rats sometimes chewed their way into the privy and waited there to surprise her.

The house had, of course, a proper commode, one water rushed into when a chain was pulled. But *das Klosett*, as the Direktor called it, was on the second floor. A similar toilet had been installed in the summer-house, once Oskar chose to stay there. The Direktor, who was extremely considerate, said Reserl must feel free to use the upstairs water closet. Not being accustomed to modern conveniences, however, she was content with the garden privy. If only the rats did not want to share it with her.

But the outhouse was, on this late night, her own . . . its stench hers, too, she supposed. Who else ever used it? Returning to the house, Reserl stopped to splash water on her face under the pump at the kitchen sink. The water was freezing. Drying her face on her apron, she slipped into her room.

"Reserl."

She had left the extinguished lantern in the kitchen. What need for light in so small a room, its contents so few and familiar?

The room was far blacker than the night outside. She did not need to see, of course, to know Oskar's whisper, to hear that it came from her cot. She had never imagined him there. Still, she had somehow known to expect him. She was not afraid.

Reserl felt her way through the blackness. His hand groped for hers and guided her to sit beside him on the edge of the cot. Saying nothing, she waited.

Again he whispered it, the name he insisted on: *Reserl.* Then: *I need you.*

"Reserl, I need you," the Captain said.

She nodded. Then, realizing he could not see her, Reserl whispered, "Yes?"

"Someone must help me," he said. "I am sorry, there is only you."

She caught her breath for a moment.

"All right," she said.

If only he was not sorry.

THE NEXT DAY'S BLAZING LIGHT SHARPENED THE EDGES ON EVERYTHING. The sun bullied her, trying over and over again to persuade her that nothing she recalled from the dark could be true:

A woman was coming to live with him, the Captain said. They loved each other desperately, could not live apart, yet their union must be hidden, could not be blessed . . .

"She is married to another man," he whispered. "But she is my bride . . . only mine."

He sounded as if he were choking. Reserl reached through the dark and stroked his throat. He leaned close, his strangled breaths hot and damp on her face. Her hands moved up and covered his cheeks. His face was wet with tears.

"I need you," he whispered again. "Help me. Please."

Reserl went very still inside. She knew how to give fear and sorrow the slip. There was no breath in her stillness, no language or thought. In a cultivated lull she mimicked death.

When the stillness inside her felt trustworthy, Reserl ventured a small breath. "How?" she asked. "How am I to help? You must tell me."

Oskar shuddered, his relief so profound it shook the cot. Its flimsy frame bucked and bumped the wall. "No one must see her," he said. "Only myself. And you."

Reserl waited.

"She is a goddess," he whispered. "You understand this?"

He seemed oblivious of her failure to reply.

"We shall serve her, you and I. Shall worship her, Reserl. Our adoration shall restore her to life!"

She was dead, then, his goddess?

Reserl gathered herself inside her stillness.

He needed her. How? Why? In time he would show her . . .

There was no reason for fear.

"She arrives next week," Oskar whispered. "On Tuesday. In a packing crate."

The stillness shattered. "I don't understand," Reserl said.

"The Stuttgart train will bring her." As if this explained something. "The train arrives in early afternoon. The Direktor will be at the museum. A wagon has been hired. They must come up the alley, I've told them, and—"

She could make no sense of it. Strong drink, Reserl knew, might rob a man of sense. In the first weeks after her mother died, her father had often come home weeping, mumbling words without edges or shape, before falling soon and mercifully, suddenly and deeply asleep.

But the Captain's words were different. They raged through the dark like a fire. Reserl's stillness exploded. Its slivers left her bleeding, alone and afraid.

He needed her.

Reserl.

There was no one else.

"You must tell no one," he said.

LIKE SOMETHING SHE MIGHT HAVE DREAMED, YES. BUT SHE HADN'T. HE had been there, the Captain, in her room. Proof in the scent of his hair tonic still drowsing on her pillow at dawn. And in his smile this morning, for the first time in weeks looking into her eyes when he thanked her for his breakfast plate.

One could see he had not slept. Her own face felt as if it must have the same drawn and shadowed look.

You must help me . . . must . . . no one else, I'm sorry.

Asleep on her feet before a choir of white shirts singing on the garden clothesline, Reserl stares into the sun. She faces daylight and swears allegiance to all that transpired in the dark.

"SILK." HE WHISPERS, TONGUE LOITERING, MAKING A SOUND LIKE A SNAKE. Then he dispatches the word more forcefully. "Silk—you do not, I suppose, know it?" He looks discouraged.

Reserl straightens her shoulders. *Seide,* she knows it. Her father's wife brought with her one dress of such fine cloth. The dress she would have worn to marry, Reserl supposes. Hulda did not witness the marriage but often imagined it: the magistrate's overheated parlor in another village, *die Stiefmutter*'s black eyes cold and satisfied as the vows were sealed. The dress was a muddy rose, the color of tainted pork. A yellowed lace collar rimmed it like a rind of fat.

When the couple returned, newly wed and full of surprises, Hulda's father slaughtered a hog to make a celebration for the whole village. The rose dress posed stiffly below a trellis and a lukewarm smile.

All pork was tainted, Hulda's grandmother claimed. *Treyf,* she said. Something like that.

Treyf? *Was bedeutet dieses Wort?* Hulda, still something of a child, was fond of strange words and kept a place for them in her mind.

Her grandmother closed the subject with a sniff. *Verboten,* she said. The old woman and her granddaughter attended the nuptial celebration but did not partake of the meat. They were not, they said, terribly hungry.

Reserl glances now at the Captain's discouraged face, then looks down modestly. "I know *Seide,*" she says. "It is most delicate, yes?"

The Captain is surprised and pleased. They both smile.

Draped on the divan, a tea gown preens. Its silk does a brazen dance between green and blue. Like the eyes in the feathers of the peacocks that patrol the Zwinger Palace. The birds behead whole regiments of summer flowers. They scream and show Reserl their fancy backs.

The iridescent silk winks at the lamplight.

The bed's headboard is rueful with dust.

The room is full of eyes.

"Yes, extremely delicate," the Captain says.

HE HAD STOLEN INTO THE KITCHEN AS SHE WASHED THE LUNCHEON dishes. The Direktor had perhaps retired to his study, she could not be sure.

The Captain kept his voice low but did not whisper. "You must come to me," he told her. "This evening."

Reserl, unsure of the Direktor's whereabouts, wished the Captain would whisper.

Her wary look amused him. "It is time we begin." Oskar was smiling like a bridegroom. He held a letter in one hand.

"Begin?" Reserl barely breathed the word. Had his beloved arrived unnoticed and unattended, left to freeze like a gardenia plant outside the door?

"To prepare for her." Oskar's expression grew stern. "You must be taught a number of things. So little time." His fingers crimped the letter. "You will come?"

"To your rooms?" Reserl thought of the eyes in the headboard. She was afraid, yes, and ashamed of her fear. He needed her. "When?" she asked.

"After dinner." Oskar slanted his head toward the dining room door. "Once you are certain the house is . . . quiet."

"It may be very late then."

He smiled.

She wondered if he would touch her, might need her laid over him again like a blanket.

She hoped, if she did so, he would not punish her afterward by refusing to look at her.

I will rub the juice of a lemon on them, she thought. My hands must not smell of onion.

"I will come," she said softly. "When the house is sleeping."

His silver eyes, two tiny shining mirrors, reflected his smile. Standing closer, Reserl thought, might she see herself there? For a moment she imagined Hulda in one mirror, Reserl in the other.

But in his eyes she would be Reserl, of course. Only Reserl.

"YOU REALIZE THE SILK MUST NOT BE WASHED?"

Reserl nodded. She knew this, yes.

"Nor the wool." A storm-cloud-gray cloak with velvet-covered buttons hung from the open wardrobe door.

"Ich verstehe." I understand.

"Ordinarily, one might hang things out to air. But as no one must see . . ." He shrugged. "Perhaps before an open window now and then, when we can be certain the Direktor is away from the house, but—"

His fretting distressed her. "I shall take every care," she said. *She no longer broke things.*

"It's just with the dampness . . . things grow musty. And the moths, the mites!" He looked, for an instant, like the hero of a tragedy, crestfallen but resolute. "No sunlight must touch them," he said. "I live in terror of fading. Once color is gone, one cannot . . ."

Emboldened by his helplessness, Reserl touched his arm. "I will see to it."

"I know." Suddenly something, a glimpse of his own foolishness perhaps, made Oskar smile. "You'll find her extremely demanding." His laugh was high and giddy.

Might he be ill? His eyes did look feverish. Reserl covered her mouth with a lemon-scented hand and coughed softly behind it.

"Gesundheit," the Captain said, still laughing.

HER LACK OF SUBTLETY, OF GUILE, CONCERNED HIM, OF COURSE. THE GIRL was simple. Yet her simplicity was what she had to commend her in the end, an existence dedicated solely to doing as she was told.

That there was no one else to whom he could turn, this was also in her favor, obviously.

Oskar tried to think of Reserl as a new canvas, its value utterly depending on the vision, *his* vision, imposed upon her. The metaphor tripped and tumbled, however, over the notion of color. The girl had none. Earthy and pliant, she was more like clay awaiting his hand to give her shape.

Surely anyone could learn to lie? To conceal and, at least mutely, mislead?

Alma, of course, would have been the ideal tutor. Such a glorious liar, his Almi . . . worthy of sainthood, were duplicity a gift from God. Alma's extravagant lies had often seemed without purpose, tossed off for sheer pleasure. Her Italian gardener had six bambini? She gave him eight. Whole fanciful wings were added to houses she'd occupied, centimeters subtracted from her small waist to swell her ample bosom.

Once, in the reckless phase of early widowhood, Alma had appended a pair of symphonies to the Maestro's opus. Naturally, a great tizzy ensued in the musical world. Lost scores? We've yet to hear the last of Mahler? Alma's mysterious smile fanned the flames of rumor until, grown bored, she denied ever having made any such outlandish suggestion. An elderly critic's faulty ear trumpet was conveniently blamed. Ridicule hastened the poor man into provincial retirement.

Oskar had served as audience to many such dramas: little loaves and fishes of truth . . . Almi seizing and serving them up in feasts of deception so sumptuous as to seem miracles. Her lack of scruple more awed than appalled him.

Pointless, in any case, to dwell now on such things . . . Alma would have had no patience for so dull a pupil, Reserl no need for such elaborate skills.

The girl was not without talent, however. Her talent was devotion.

She simply needs direction, Oskar thought. She is already mine.

10

Katja's chartreuse eyes shimmered. Suspicion animated her face. "You are up to something, *Liebchen,*" she said.

"I am simply trying to understand your art," Oskar insisted. "The process of it, if you will."

Katja rose to her toes and whispered into his ear.

The term he heard belonged more to a barnyard than an art gallery. Oskar, laughing, glanced around uneasily. Those in his view seemed utterly absorbed in the borrowed Dutch drawings . . . or at least in the challenge of appearing to be so absorbed.

"There's a level beyond which mastery trespasses upon dullness," Oskar murmured. "Excruciating dullness."

Katja laughed boisterously. "This theory is your own?"

"I cannot imagine anyone else would care to claim it." He squeezed her plump bare arm. "I have missed you, my gypsy girl."

Katja snorted. A man in a black suit and a silver brocade waistcoat frowned in her general direction, then looked away. Katja and Oskar smiled at each other.

"I have," he insisted. "You are just what I've needed. I should have known."

Tactless remark, he realized as soon as he'd made it. Being overlooked was a form of torture to her. Katja's mind, fortunately, remained engaged with an earlier point in their conversation.

"I am to tell you exactly how a lady's maid behaves. And you do not intend to tell me why you need such information?"

"'Need'?" Oskar said. "I don't remember implying that I *needed* anything."

"Well, let's not go off onto that field of inquiry. What you may *need*, my muddled darling, could keep us here bickering for several years!"

Oskar, studying a small drawing of a naked male torso, frowned. Such meticulous beauty . . . why should it fall flat?

"What?" Katja picked at his sleeve.

"It may be that perfection is intrinsically vapid. Do you suppose?"

"What I suppose," Katja said, "is that you are ruthless and will stoop to anything to drive me back to your chosen topic. Even the mores of the lady's maid are, I'll grant you, fascinating compared to these quackish theories of art you pretend to espouse."

Oskar studied his friend for a moment. "Where is your devotion, my angel, my muse? Couldn't you just humor me?"

His smile ventured nowhere near his eyes.

SHE DID, IN THE END, HUMOR HIM, OR TRY TO. BUT KATJA TURNED OUT TO know less than either of them might have expected, when it came to the practical ways of personal servants. Fräulein Richter had been born to a bohemian ménage, albeit a rich one . . . not lacking in domestic staff, certainly, but with less than proper regard for formalities, perhaps.

"This upstairs maid," Oskar said, "how does she address your mother? Simply as Frau Richter, or—"

"As *du*, mostly." Katja's smirk was calculated to annoy him. "Or Rozsi. Hilma's been in charge of Mama since the nursery, still thinks of her as a spoiled child. Which is just what she is, of course."

Oskar sighed vigorously, attempting to stem another tedious examination of Katja's poor mother, an ineffectual and largely inoffensive woman. Katja lacked empathy, that was the heart of the problem. If she could not sense the gravity of *his* needs, she could hardly be expected to notice those who existed merely to serve her. Spoiled child, indeed. An *actress* was meant to discern the feelings, the concerns and motivations, of others, was she not?

"Oskar, don't be cross with me." She lisped like a little girl and leaned into his side. "Am I to be blamed for an unconventional upbringing? I didn't choose it, you know."

Oskar looked down into her face. Her eyes looked gold, like a cat's, under the gallery's amber chandeliers. She swayed slightly, her soft bosom bobbing against his breastbone. He saw her lips part, felt her breath quicken.

"A black dress," she whispered. "Very severe, I should think. With wisps of white lawn for an apron and cap. Shiny black buttons, a hundred of them, small as currants, to undo the front of the dress. And miles of petticoats under my skirts."

The least shift in his footing touched his groin to her hip.

Katja smiled.

Around them, Dresden's pompous little art world kept redesigning itself in new patterns, a kaleidoscope. A toy.

Reclining on the velvet divan, waiting each night for him there, his odalisque . . . a window of firelight the stove . . . a raspberry's elfin bristles and the tender stubble in the crease of a peach . . . no need for our goddess to stand . . .

Oskar's eyes were closed.

"Is there something I may have the honor of providing for you, mein Herr?" Katja's whisper borrowed the rough edge of a rustic Saxon accent, promised prodigal pity.

She was, empathy or not, a rather extraordinary actress.

HE EXPLAINED NOTHING. HE SIMPLY USHERED THE GIRL INTO THE SUMmerhouse, shut the door behind her, and pulled from his trouser pocket a measuring tape.

His hands were efficient and impersonal upon her. He became thorough and judicious, pausing to jot each dimension in a small notebook. Its speckled pasteboard cover reminded her of an egg she'd found in the woods as a child. The egg came from a stork, Frieda's mother had said.

Reserl, wearing just her coarse chemise, which she only now remembered had a smear of menstrual blood at the back, was shivering. After a while the Captain perhaps noticed her chill, for he turned and opened the stove's small door, allowing more heat into the damp room. Then, turning her by the shoulders, he faced her away from him. Reserl tried not to think of the stain. She felt his index finger pressing one end of the tape measure to the knob of bone where nape ended and back began.

Die Wirbelsäule . . . yes, the spine. Hers was always torturing her, Hulda's grandmother used to say. "As your own will one day," she promised. *Die Folter.* "Torture. You'll see." The old woman always laughed, though, as if she found pleasure in her own groaning. *Die Folter,* the child inferred, was nothing to be afraid of.

The Captain's hands settled for a moment on her shoulders, then gently turned her to face him again. "What are you thinking, Reserl?" There was a vague tenderness in his smile. He was looking into her eyes.

"I am thinking of Bubbe Etta," she said.

He raised his eyebrows.

"My grandmother."

He nodded, then picked up the dark heap of green that was her dress and handed it to her. "Get dressed," he said absently. "What is her name?"

His mind was awry. How could she have failed to see that before? "Etta," she said. "Her name was Etta."

"Was. So she is dead?"

"*Ja.*"

She stood very still, waiting. He would say he was sorry. Sorry her grandmother, Etta, was dead. It seemed to Reserl that, without realizing it, she had been waiting for this moment for years, waiting hopeless and unsettled as she waited now for the old General's funeral rites that would never occur.

"Put on your boots," the Captain said. "We are finished for now."

THE NEXT DAY HE RETURNED FROM THE ACADEMY SEVERAL HOURS EARLIER than was usual for a Friday.

There was to be a reception at the museum that evening; the Direktor would not be home until late.

All day she had been fretting over what to prepare for the Captain's solitary dinner. Reserl had an uncanny instinct for the Direktor's tastes— "You know what I want before I do," he told her sometimes. Reserl, unless otherwise directed, relied on this alleged instinct to plan the day's menus. The Captain's tastes, however, remained a mystery to her.

Oskar's appetite had slowly improved in the months since he had joined *der Haushalt.* He looked less spectral, certainly. But he scarcely noticed what he ate. Should she serve him no dinner at all this evening, Reserl doubted he would mention it.

So her surprise at finding the Captain in the kitchen doorway at half past two on a Friday afternoon breezed away in a huff of relief. He must be here to clarify his desires: a fat *Zungenwurst,* perhaps, pale chips of tongue glistening in the dark blood pudding, and the skillet of hot fat singing. Served in a nest of *Geröstete,* the shreds of potato crisp and brown as leather bootlaces. Red cabbage . . . a bowl of *Blaukraut* cheered a table more than roses, the Direktor said. She'd chosen some lovely late *Mirabellen* at the market yesterday. The meal would be filling. The little yellow plums would be a lovely dessert.

"You are smiling, Reserl."

She flinched, as if caught at something shameful.

Oskar chuckled. "I suppose you have guessed, then," he said.

"Sir?"

"That I have brought you a gift." *Ein Geschenk.* He was leaning against the doorframe, the sun behind him, like the dark silhouette of a dandy in a haberdasher's handbill. He straightened suddenly and stepped aside, revealing the brown paper parcel he'd been holding behind him by its loops of twine.

The sight of the package unaccountably frightened her. "What is it?"

Oskar's arm swept forward, dangling the parcel in front of her. "A surprise, my girl. A surprise."

He wished her to reach for it. She could not.

"Go on," he said, smiling.

She drew back slightly. The stove's heat rose around her. She had been about to bake the bread. Reserl imagined scrabbling inside the oven, seeking sanctuary in the fire.

Oskar reached around her and closed the oven door. "You must be careful," he said.

Reserl lowered her eyes. "I don't know what you wish for dinner." His boots were run-down at the heels and in sad need of polishing.

"Reserl?" he said softly. "What is it?"

"A surprise." Her look accused him. "I don't know what it is," she said.

"Oh," he said. "I see."

He saw, he *understood,* nothing.

Reserl lifted her chin, held her spine very straight. She gazed past him. The afternoon sun was making a spectacle of itself beyond the kitchen door.

"You don't care for surprises," he said gently. "Is that it?"

That he understood even that much amazed and moved her. Still, she would not look at him. He will ask me why, she thought.

"Now that I think about it," he said, "I don't much care for them myself."

Reserl turned slowly, opened the oven door, and placed two round dark loaves inside. Then she shut the oven door. She kept her back to him.

"Sardines," Oskar said. "With onions in vinegar and a boiled egg. I'd prefer to take dinner in my room. Will that be all right?"

"At what time, sir?" Reserl asked without turning.

"Would six o'clock be too early?"

"I shall bring a tray at six. Will there be anything else?"

Sunlight poured into the kitchen, spilling over her back. Its warmth seemed to soak through the coarse fabric of her dress and soften her spine. When he touched her back, a patch of coolness stayed there, like a shadow.

"I would like you to eat with me."

She did not turn. She did not answer him.

He did not, in any case, wait for a reply.

Behind her she heard the small scrape of the door, closing.

The parcel was, for the moment, gone. Reserl did not ask herself what might have been inside it, or whether his request might be a joke, nor if she should comply with it.

She went into the dim pantry. She found two small jars of sardines on the lowest shelf. They shimmered yellow with oil when she carried them out into the sunlit kitchen.

She wondered if he mightn't be pleased to find the plums on the tray, although he had not requested them.

THE FIT OF THE DRESS WAS PERFECTION. ITS BODICE TAPERED, JUST SO, TO the delicate dimensions of her upper torso, the skirt flared over her hips.

Her hips were a bit wider than he'd have guessed, her legs more sturdy. Her proportions were full of exquisite little surprises. Had circumstances been otherwise, he'd have pined to paint her, have clamored and hankered and pestered and raved. But of course he must not . . . must not even think of it.

So much depended, now, on the girl's innocence.

He had already, of course, lain naked with her. Oskar knew, if barely remembered, this. The incident seemed long ago. A forgivable infraction, he told himself. An understandable lapse of shock and grief. But he hadn't actually penetrated her. Had he? He was thankful recollection was dim. The more detail recalled, the harder forgiving oneself. One could not go back and erase what was done.

Now, studying the girl before him, Oskar might have been seeing her body for the first time. There was an almost heartbreaking purity about her form. Her posture was docile. Yet the black dress gave her . . . what was the word Katja had used? *Severe,* wasn't that it? Yes, Reserl in the black dress looked almost severe . . .

Like the pilgrim nuns. He and Alma had nearly stumbled upon them one afternoon in Venice. Twin shapes, long and dark and flat against the rose-veined marble floor. They were prostrating themselves before the Virgin at a side altar in San Marco. Bizarre custom. Oskar remembered their bare upturned soles, pitted and filthy. And Alma's delight at the arcane spectacle the two women made. Peals of laughter, contained barely long enough to flee the church . . . they'd sent the pigeons into a panic . . . a low gray sky filled with dingy wings and Almi laughing.

The tap of raindrops on the roof returned him to the summerhouse, to Reserl, to the row of tedious little buttons whose undoing he would have to watch her fumble . . . unbearable prospect, when time was so short. But she'd need to learn, and the dress could not be soiled or mussed, not now. The laden tray sat there, heavy as obligation. They would have to eat, he supposed he owed her that . . . she must not be allowed to eat in the dress.

"Wait," he said.

The girl looked up in alarm. As if she'd go anywhere . . . as if bid to stop breathing.

"What?" she said. "What is wrong?"

"I forgot." Oskar rifled through the swaths of brown paper on the bed. Then, something white and insubstantial in his hands, he circled around behind her.

The apron was organdy. Stiffer than lawn, more diaphanous. A conceit of ruffles. Merely decorative, of course. Oskar tied the sash tight. His bow was flamboyant. "A work of art," he said. "But—"

For a moment he studied her. "Your hair will not *do,* my lamb." *Mein Lamm.*

Her shoulders, just beginning to relax, stiffened again.

"You don't care for my endearments?" He remained behind her. She could hear his smile, the strain in it.

"Shall I cover it?" she asked.

Why on earth should she sound so anguished? "It's just a little wisp of a thing, Reserl. A *filament.*" He strained the word through what was left of his smile. "You won't even know it is there."

Then, hairpins occupying his teeth, Oskar stopped talking.

The braid's weight, when he lifted it from her back, amazed him. For a moment he shifted it from one hand to the other, admiring its heft. But it would not do for what he now had in mind. A less pastoral look.

His fingers took exceptional care, removing the greasy snip of rawhide from the braid's end. Thick and soft and straight, the tip of her braid was like a superb paintbrush, better than anything he could afford.

"I'm not hurting you?" he mumbled through the hairpins.

Reserl shook her head. He enclosed it between his hands, gently stilling it.

Oskar ran a finger through the center of the plait, unraveling a few inches at a time. He had positioned the girl between two wall sconces. Their buttery light toyed with the colors in her hair as it was released. Reaching the braid's thick topmost part, he used both hands, all his fingers. The strands, parting, flowed over his wrists and arms before tumbling down the straight and narrow of the girl's back.

Hairpins slipped from between his lips and scattered on the floor. Oskar barely noticed. He stood behind Reserl, watching colors run and hide through her rippling hair. Its darkness sparked with incendiary shades—reds and oranges, yellows and golds. But he caught flashes of blue there, too, nuances of violet, undertones of green. Imagine capturing it in paint, such a rebellion of color! The least attempt would court despair. Oskar was thankful this task, sacred and hopeless, need not befall him.

He did not know how long, lost in her hair, he'd forgotten her.

"You have a remarkable aptitude for stillness," he said.

Her reply, a slight lift of shoulder he took for a shrug, set her hair rippling again. Oskar, forcing his eyes from the sight, bent and picked up the hairpins from the floor, clamped them between his teeth.

He first attempted the loose pouf and lax chignon Alma so favored . . . the style, he amended, that so flattered *her.*

Oskar smiled. This little fit of cool objectivity pleased and surprised him. Frau Gropius was no longer a girl, was she? Her lips, when last he saw them, were starting to thin. Her nose looked almost . . . *blunt.*

The girl's hair, at any rate, hardly lent itself to Alma's style. Reserl's hair was too heavy, too dense. Her solemn little face got easily lost. Like Gucki's. She might have been wearing one of those absurd fur helmets Cossacks sported. When Oskar tried to anchor the little lace cape on top of it all, the poor child turned into a squat table with a doily on it.

He was forced, in the end, to acquiesce to simplicity. Two plaits, lighter and more pliant than the one, inclined naturally to her head. The lace cap rested easily within this wreath. A faint blue tracing of vein pulsed at her nape. The back of her neck a milk-white stem . . . its tender beauty struck him like a blow.

Oskar lifted an escaped tendril of hair there. He had used up all the hairpins. He wheedled the strand of hair with his finger, coaxing it under the braid.

Then his fingertip encountered something on her scalp, a bump, a scaly patch . . . yes, a scab.

"You've a little wound here," he said. His finger traced it, probing gently. "Have you hit your head?"

"It is nothing." Her voice sounded cold.

Oskar withdrew his hand and took a step back. He looked down and found blood on his finger, already drying. He put his fingertip into his mouth and sucked away the stain.

"We will eat," he said. "I haven't forgotten."

She said nothing.

"Turn around, Reserl," he said. "You'll hardly know yourself."

She seemed to shudder as she turned to face him.

"Over here." He guided her toward the mirror.

He'd resurrected the old pier glass from the one room in the summerhouse still reserved for storage. Its oval mahogany frame was an abomination of cherubs, garlands of unlikely blooms. Swatches of silvering had flaked from the back of the glass, leaving the mirror's images full of holes.

Oskar adored the mirror, had grown possessive of it overnight. He wondered if Hans Posse might be induced to sell it to him, when it came time to leave. The Direktor, generous soul with little regard for furnishings, would likely insist he accept the piece as a gift.

Leave? Darkness fell upon the little scene playing out in Oskar's mind. *I shall never leave here,* he thought.

Never.

His hands, holding Reserl's shoulders, persuaded her toward the mirror.

"Look at you," Oskar said. "Oh, Reserl, just look at you!"

Her face, in the pitted mirror, was small and white and lacy.

He'd been quite right, of course. She hardly knew herself.

THE SILVER EYES WATCHED WITHOUT MERCY, WATCHED AS IF THEY WERE searching for . . .

Reserl pinched a bit of black bread from a round loaf and pushed it into her mouth. What could he be looking for? The longer she chewed the morsel of dough, the less likely it seemed to fit down her throat.

She took a desperate sip of water. The lump of bread lodged halfway down, around the spot where, in the Captain's skinny neck, an Adam's apple bulged. She imagined she must look as if she'd swallowed a frog.

Oskar picked up a green goblet and sipped his wine. His head tipped back to swallow, he kept his gaze on her face.

The bread saddened her. It had gone cold while he fussed with her hair. Bread tasted so much better when it was hot.

He was smiling at her.

She took another sip of water.

"You haven't much appetite, Reserl?"

"I am thirsty," she said.

He nodded.

She looked away.

A pair of shabby brown carpet slippers poked out from under the bed. They looked a good prospect for the dustbin. Reserl hoped she'd find them when the Captain decided to discard them. She would keep the slippers in the potato bin, wrapped in her head scarf. Now and then, on very cold nights, she might set the slippers where her feet, leaving the bed, could find their way into them. She would not have to lace her feet into her boots first thing in the morning, still cramped and blue with night's cold.

She wondered if Emil had slept with his boots on, and if The Front was in a cold land. Very likely so. It was somewhere to the north. She could not be sure of the season when Emil had died. News was slow to reach her village.

What had she done with all the hours in all the days when Emil was already dead and she did not know it? This was one of a number of things Reserl wished she knew.

For a moment she imagined not their wedding, but their life . . . Emil as a husband, herself a wife. The bread would come hot to the table, always hot. He would have carpet slippers. She would tease him about them. "You are a dandy," Reserl would tell Emil, her husband. She would keep his slippers in good repair, embroidering fanciful designs over holes and thin spots. And after she died—she must die first—her Emil would have the slippers to warm an old man's bony feet.

"What is it?" Oskar said.

Reserl blinked. *"Wie bitte?"*

"You are smiling," he said. "You were."

She shook her head.

"I have confided in you my greatest secret, Reserl. You should trust me, too."

He meant to sound playful, she knew, but his words hummed with urgency. They both heard it. *What was it he expected of her?*

"Never mind." He'd noticed her skittishness, her confusion. "I do not wish to take anything from you, Reserl." He purposely chose the strongest of terms, *ergreifen* . . .

I do not wish to seize *from you anything.*

She sighed softly.

She must be tired, he thought.

"I know," she said.

"Come," he said. "Have one of these lovely plums. I'll make us some tea. Do you drink tea, Reserl?"

Too many things at once, and none of it what truly preoccupied him . . .

"I have a little pan here. It boils water quite fast. I just set it here on top of the stove . . . you see? Perhaps I should open a tea garden."

"I want nothing." Her voice was hardly more than a whisper.

She was tired . . . but of course she was, exhausted and aching. Prolonged stillness took more of a toll on the body than exertion, as any life-drawing model would attest. And here Reserl, this inexperienced girl, had held still longer than any professional model would have stood for. Not to mention the day's labors, laundry and baking and . . .

"Poor lamb." Oskar pulled out his pocket watch. Hans Posse would be out for another hour at least. "If you don't wish to eat any more, then . . ." He stood up and brisked his hands against each other.

Reserl watched a little flurry of bread crumbs sift down onto the carpet.

"We'll just go over the rest of the wardrobe," Oskar said. "It isn't extensive, but the requirements for proper care . . ." He pulled a flowered hatbox from the top of the wardrobe, a pair of ivory kid boots from a drawer, a striped carton from under the bed.

He looked feverish again. He was not, could not be, entirely well.

"Perhaps, to begin, lingerie." His long reddish fingers caressed the striped box. "Made in France, by hand," he murmured. "All of it. In Paris. But the lace was imported from Alsace . . . no mean feat, given the sorry state of trade since the war."

The war would never end.

Oskar removed the box's lid and tossed it aside. Several sheets of tissue wafted to the foot of the bed.

"The French make the most acceptable maids, too, she used to say. Not that she actually finds anyone, in the end, acceptable. I wonder who she has doing her bidding now? Besides her new husband, of course."

His animation flagged for a moment. He sat down carefully on the edge of the bed. *Not entirely well . . . no.*

"I do know a bit of French." His face brightened. "Rudimentary, of course. Still, I might teach you a phrase or two, if . . ."

His hands delved inside the box. He closed his eyes. A tremor moved up his arms. *"Oui, madame,"* he said. *"Merci, madame. Je regrette, madame."*

His features twisted, imposing on him an old man's suffering face. *"Je t'en prie, chère madame,"* he whispered.

His eyes opened slowly. He took something from the box and got to his feet again.

The silk camisole was the color of a modest blush. No shade so extreme as embarrassment's, but . . . yes, the silk seemed to glow with shy pleasure.

Oskar held the garment by its flimsy straps.

A pale rose was appliquéd on the breast.

He let go of one strap. His hand, making a soft fist, filled one side of the camisole's emptiness.

"Cold water." His face was bone white. "The soap you use must be extremely mild."

"All will be as you wish, sir."

The silk seemed to breathe in Oskar's trembling hands.

"Je t'en prie," he whispered.

A delay, you say, dear Fräulein. A delay? As if this were a business transaction, simple and routine? Am I to accept this without question? Can you expect such equanimity of a soul in torment? Had you supposed my heart could bear the blow when the appointed day arrived and my goddess did not?

Surely it must have occurred to you that I . . .

I confess, Fräulein Moos, that the confidence you have encouraged me to place in you now lies inside me crippled and bleeding. A casualty of dashed hope. How, then, are we to recuperate, you and I and our once-vital collaboration?

"She is not all she should be," you say. No, let me correct myself, for I wish in quoting you to be scrupulous. "It is not all it should be," you claim. As if what my heart hinges on is receipt of some object.

Of course you know better, Fräulein. Your syntax makes light of me.

Please reply without delay to this letter. Address forthrightly—do not spare a sensibility already mutilated—my most urgent concerns:

First, what has gone wrong? Have you somehow ruined the work of these many months? Have you given up? Has courage deserted you? Have thirty pieces of silver induced you to turn your back on me? But who—

Forgive me, dear friend . . . before the ink I use to write these words has dried on the page, I see how they impugn and betray you. Make allowances, I beg, for a mind ruptured by the strain of . . .

Disappointment. Extremes of disappointment, just now, I admit. But that does not justify scattershot blame, I know this. May I apologize? I acknowledge your integrity. Just tell me, please, what has gone wrong. Hope, Goethe claims, is "the second soul of the unhappy." Only knowledge, knowing even the worst, can resurrect this second soul in me. Whatever the setback or damage, surely we can devise its remedy. Have we not already, together, surmounted impossible obstacles?

Then, having clarified the nature of the trouble, would you be so good as to estimate when I may hope to receive her? Even if you must guess . . . even if the delay is bound to be lengthy . . .

Quantify my hope, Fräulein, with a number I may circle on a calendar to hang above my bed, whence it might choreograph my dreams and set some lyric to my days. Just give me some estimate of when I might behold . . . when I might hold her . . .

Je vous en prie!

OK

11

Christmas came, to scant notice, and passed by. The Direktor, so recently bereaved, had no heart for a season of celebrating.

It was not in Hans Posse's nature, however, to forget the matter of gifts for his little household. On Christmas Eve, after a simple luncheon of cheeses, herring with apples and onions, and a nice bottle of Moselle, he presented Oskar with a small painting by Anton Maulbertsch, an artist they both admired. The piece, though fine, lacked sufficient distinction to earn a place in the Museum (an assessment shared by both men, but mentioned by neither). The Gemäldegalerie's early-eighteenth-century collection, largely acquired by Posse's easily cowed predecessor, was capricious and already cramped.

The Direktor's gift touched and mortified Oskar. He'd overlooked the season entirely.

His protests and apologies were murmured away. A token remembrance, Posse said, hardly more.

I'll make him a gift of one of my pictures, Oskar thought, when I am able to paint again. Of course the death-drawing of the old man, already given . . .

Oskar jumped as Reserl, clearing the luncheon plates, brushed his shoulder with her sleeve.

"Entschuldigung." She whispered the apology.

"*Gern geschehen.*" Don't mention it. Oskar suddenly felt an almost excruciating desire to laugh. He hadn't the slightest idea why. He pressed his lips together. His eyes teared. Perhaps it was the need to weep . . . *I am hysterical,* he thought. For a moment he was frightened. A mossy scent, not unpleasant, wafted past his face. He stared down at the table. A blue dish of little white star-shaped cookies appeared before him.

"*Zimtsterne.*" Cinnamon stars. The Direktor had a weakness for cookies. His sigh was almost blissful. One recovers, Oskar thought. Eventually one can recover from anything.

Behind him the kitchen door stuttered softly to a close.

"Our Hulda," Posse said. "How should we ever get along without her?"

THE DIREKTOR GAVE HULDA A SOFT RED LEATHER COIN PURSE THAT FAS-tened with a pearl button. A generous bonus, in bills, was crisply folded inside. Posse mistrusted the new currency. The paper had a temporary feel to it. Still, the old currency of the Empire would do the child little good. He hoped she would spend the gift quickly, before the paper money, too, turned worthless. He wondered what Hulda might want. From what one could see, she needed everything.

Late in the day on Christmas Eve, Oskar rushed from one flower stall to another. An old woman with very few teeth surrendered to him the last red roses to be found in Dresden. She let them go for half price; both she and Oskar could see the petals were half frozen. The old woman cackled joylessly, admitting the damage. A blast of cheap brandy fumes nearly sent Oskar reeling backward into a fruit cart.

The flower vendor wrapped the bouquet in a cone of damp paper tied at the bottom with some wrinkled green ribbon. "No extra charge," she said, thrusting his pitiful purchase at him and laughing again.

Oskar naturally intended to present the flowers in person. He hadn't seen Katja in . . . could it be nearly two weeks? She must be dreadfully put out with him. Nearing her father's house, where she would be in-stalled for the holiday, Oskar decided to drop his inexcusable gift on the doorstep and flee. With the right combination of luck, nerve, and stealth, he might get away without being observed.

Katja would recognize the poor gift as Oskar's. But if he did not appear, she could delight in tormenting her parents and the inevitable suitor or two with larcenous hints of anonymous admirers . . .

At least that way I'll have given her something, Oskar thought.

THE YEAR CHANGED WITHOUT FANFARE IN THE POSSE HOUSE.

Oskar had not seen Katja for nearly a month.

Occasionally, glancing up from his work, a monograph on C. D. Friedrich, the Direktor would be surprised by a small square of deeper blue on the faded blue wall beside his desk. For a moment or two he would be unable to recall what used to hang there.

He hoped Oskar would not be forced to sell the Maulbertsch. The market was not advantageous just now. The Direktor could hardly help but notice the frequency with which certain bills kept arriving for his young guest, whose debt for room and board also had fallen into arrears. Not that Hans Posse would dream of mentioning it. Indeed, he wished he might find some tactful way of suspending the obligation altogether. The money, negligible, was a nuisance. He wondered if Oskar was painting . . .

The Direktor's concerns were not fiscal in nature. It simply worried him that the boy seemed, still, after so much time, so lost.

Oskar was scarcely a boy, of course. Hans Posse wondered why he kept thinking of him as one. Perhaps because he himself was starting to feel so old. Well, the world these days was full of worries . . . the childlike painter with his oddness and wounds just happened to be one of those parceled out to him. It was good having someone to look after, now that his father was gone. His boarder's presence provided not only company, but a kind of security against the breakdown of orderly habit. Left to his own devices, to the mercy of his worries, Hans Posse hated to think what might become of him. The whole of Europe was falling into chaos. No need for his little *Haushalt* to abet the general upheaval.

In Dresden, one felt the disintegration of the known in mostly small ways, *vielen Dank*. The letters the holiday season customarily brought seemed reduced this year, and slow to arrive. More than one friend's Christmas note had delivered unhappy news. Financial reverses spread. The same Spanish influenza that had abbreviated Gustav Klimt's illustrious oeuvre had, it was becoming clear, traipsed through much of the continent . . .

On the feast of the Epiphany Hans Posse realized with some consternation that he had received no holiday greetings from his sister-in-law. Nor had he thought to write to her of the General's death. Trudl's attentions to the old man had been more dutiful than fond. Still, she should have been informed. Might even Pirna's bracing rustic air have been hospitable to the epidemic? Posse worried. Surely Trudl would have left instructions that he be notified if . . . her sister's widower, strictly speaking not kin, was the only family relation Trudl could claim.

A high wind blew down on Dresden from the mountains that night, bringing not snow but ice. All night, as needles of ice tried to pierce the drafty old house, Hans Posse lay awake, thinking of his late wife's sister. For the first time her poverty of charm saddened him. He saw his annoyance with her as petty. For a few cold hours the impossibility of loving her seemed an authentic tragedy, not only for Trudl, left to face death alone, but for himself.

Several days later, the customary letter and parcel arrived from Pirna, the customary fruitcake wound in its brandy-stained cheesecloth shroud. Trudl was well, she said, aside from the indescribable pains of lumbago, nobly borne.

Posse did not care a bit for fruitcake, even exceptionally good fruitcake, which Trudl's was not.

He left the cake in the kitchen, hoping Hulda would know what to do with it.

The fruitcake was never seen again, nor mentioned. Except in the Direktor's customary letter of thanks, of course.

> *I surrender, mein Fräulein. No more might I hope to subjugate your will to mine than might any poor mortal expect to escape an omnipotent Deity's reach. I am skittish with total dependence—upon your volition, your power, your mercy. (You will, I pray, show mercy!)*
>
> *My gracious thanks for your most temperate reply to a letter whose slights and excesses I soon, if too late, regretted. Little wonder the delay of your reply. Fancy too easily imagines my disruption of your peace. Did my envelope wail with anguish before your first cut to open it? A man so ill in spirit as I, Fräulein, cannot cage his symptoms, and so must go about begging forgiveness for their frenzied intrusions in others' lives. The pardon I sense between your few supple lines has administered sedative to a heart in desperate turmoil.*

*And I must, of course, bow to your superior discretion in the matter of
what my heart so immediately and heedlessly craves.* Our Schweigsame
Frau *is not yet ready for her journey to me, you say. Would I wish to receive her in a less than perfect state? Of course not! When at last in perfection she joins me here, I shall sing hosannas of thanks and praise to the
one whose provident insistence spared these adoring eyes any glimpse of
nascent flaw.*

THERE WAS A SMALL RENT IN THE LUMPY MAT ON HER COT. THE RED
leather coin purse just fit inside it. The money's principal value resided
in Reserl's delight at knowing it was there, beneath her when she slept.
And in her wonder, which was exorbitant.

Reserl loved thinking about the money. She did not, however, know
how to think about spending it. She had three dresses, two blankets,
whatever she cared to eat, even chocolate. Sometimes at night, as she was
falling asleep, Reserl told herself tales about what she might buy with the
money on which she rested. Things that might comfort and amaze the
Captain: a pair of excellent boots, a vest woven from the soft hair of
goats, a watch fob spied in a jeweler's window—a gold-dipped tooth!

Each tale had the same beginning: A warm afternoon when the Captain walked with her in the garden and told her he loved her. This love,
having just dawned on him, had left him pale with surprise. Money
would be good to buy things for someone who loved you, Reserl
thought. Yes, having money for that would be lovely.

OSKAR HAD PURCHASED BLACK SILK STOCKINGS AND THIN BLACK BOOTS
with pointed toes and narrow laces. He gave the boots to Reserl the day
after Christmas. The Direktor was visiting a friend near Schloss Pillnitz.
The stockings, in tissue, lay inside the boot box, which was wrapped in
silver paper.

When the Captain handed the parcel to her, he said, "Happy Christmas, Reserl," and apologized for the lateness of the gift.

Reserl looked out the window of the summerhouse. The garden had
vanished in a sudden snow squall. Christmas, she knew, had slipped the
Captain's mind.

Whatever the box held had been purchased some time ago. The

wrapping was an afterthought. Reserl wondered who had done it. She doubted a man could have made such a handsome job of it.

She thanked Oskar politely before opening the box.

When Reserl saw the boots and stockings, she had no need to try them. They would, she knew, fit perfectly. She also knew they had been purchased not for her own needs and desires, but for the Captain's.

He did not love her and never would, except in stories. She knew this, too, of course.

"Don't you like them, Reserl?" the Captain asked.

She had taken great care, opening the package, not to tear the paper. Her hands smoothed it now, flattening the creases. She nodded to his question.

She is still shy with me, Oskar thought. How shy she is.

Her eyes cast down, she asked him something. She rarely spoke up. He was seldom quite sure he'd heard her.

"I beg your pardon?" He must be courteous with her, always. How was the girl to grasp the conventions of politeness, if not from him?

Her chin lifted slightly. She repeated the question.

"For you to keep?" Oskar smiled. "Of course."

It was not until a moment after he replied that he realized the nature of her true desire—that its object was the silver paper.

ONE MORNING RESERL, COMING IN TO TIDY THE SUMMERHOUSE, FOUND A large calendar hanging on the wall beside Oskar's bed. She took great care, removing it from a nail in the wall and leafing through it. Its dark thick-lined drawings showed muscular peasants engaging with unlikely joy in varied seasonal labors. The drawings seemed a poor advertisement for the fine inks and writing instruments Beucher & Sons claimed to purvey. The calendar's pages were laced together at the top with hairy-looking brown twine. Each month consumed a full page.

It was February when the calendar appeared in the Captain's room. Reserl might hardly have noticed it, had the displayed page not so insistently proclaimed April. The peasants were plowing an endless rutted field. Below them, in the fourth square on the second row, the number 15 had been heavily circled. The circle, which was purple, appeared more likely to have been made with paint than Beucher's fine ink.

That evening, for the first time in several weeks, the Captain asked

Reserl to visit the summerhouse. After dinner the Direktor begged
Oskar please to excuse him, and if Hulda would not mind bringing coffee up to his study . . . The Friedrich monograph was coming along
nicely, might soon be finished if only . . .

"Felicitations!" said Oskar.

Posse blushed. "Most kind, but I fear premature." He paused for a
moment at the foot of the stairway. Then, sighing, he reached for the
banister and began his climb. Oskar wondered how old the Direktor
was. It was not a question that had ever occurred to him to ask.

The night was unusually chilly. Upstairs Reserl stoked the study fire
for staying power as the two men finished their exchange of pleasantries
in the hall below. She must hurry, she chided herself. The Captain
needed her. She mustn't keep him waiting, dawdling over the dishes,
further chapping and reddening her hands. Still, it was bound to be difficult, leaving the warm soapy water, to face a bitter wind bent on ran-
sacking the night.

SHE SAW HIM IN THE WINDOW, WATCHING FOR HER, HIS FACE A PALE SPI-
der in a web of white lace and frost. Before she reached the door he'd
flung it open, reaching out into the dark to grasp her hands, pull her inside.

He fastened the latch on the door.

Reserl tucked her raw hands under her apron.

"So much to do!" He clapped his hands together. His eyes were too
bright. His voice was brittle.

On the other side of the window something creaked, then shattered.
Reserl and Oskar both started and froze.

"An icicle," he said after a moment. "Jumping from the roof." His
laugh, high and giddy, made her cringe.

One winter night when Hulda was a child, a man in her village
passed out in the snow in front of the tavern. An icicle long and heavy
and sharp as a sword had dropped from the roof, piercing the man's left
eye and entering his brain. He was not found until morning, a veil of
pink ice over his face. Herr Gernreich had an uncommon love for plum
brandy. Drink was bound to be the death of him, Hulda's grandmother
said.

"You are grave this evening." The Captain's face, slanted toward the stove, looked sharp and thin. Firelight gleamed in his eyes. "I've been overzealous perhaps . . . is it too warm? Shall my poor lamb roast in here?"

He liked to tease. Reserl recalled the young lady with feathers in her hair, her laugh, each time the Captain spoke to her, like singing, and how quickly and lightly she returned words to him. How wonderful, Reserl thought, being able to think and speak and laugh all at once. A man would be bound to love a woman with beautiful hair who could manage so much as that.

"You will teach me teasing?" she asked.

"What?" Even he seemed slightly taken aback by his bellowed laugh.

"Teasing," she repeated.

"Teasing would not suit you, Reserl." He spoke quietly, as if atoning for his noise. "Come." He pulled one hand out from under her apron and led her toward his writing table, where an ink-black wig slouched comically on what resembled a huge wooden egg.

Reserl looked at his face, hoping it would tell her . . . if this was more teasing, she ought to smile.

"A few simple lessons in fixing a lady's hair," he said. "Coiffure is the elegant term for it."

He suggested she repeat the strange word after him, several times: *coiffure.*

Her first few attempts did not please him.

"You must hold the tail of the word in the back of your throat. Like this." He said it again.

She tried.

"*Mein Gott,* Reserl, you sound like you are being strangled!" He was not teasing.

She covered her mouth and coughed.

"Once again, please?"

Before she could open her mouth, he pressed his fingertips to the soft hollow in her throat. "The end of the word ought to purr," he said. "Right here. Like a cat with a secret. Now."

"Coiffure," Reserl said.

His fingertips, leaving her throat, swept tenderly along her jaw to her cheek.

"There, my lamb," he said. "Your first French lesson. Now for the crimping." He smiled.

Reserl had never before seen such a thing. A curling iron appeared a cruel and dangerous device. The Captain, too, betrayed some leeriness in handling it. By the end of the evening the large egg had its featureless face turned to the wall in shame. Its corona of ringlets, unevenly sprung, gave off a scorched smell.

The Captain, however, had grown downright larky in the face of mishap.

"We need practice," he told her. "That's all. There is plenty of time."

His nonchalance did seem . . . a bit high-strung. Still, it was good to see him laughing. He'd been withdrawn and sad since before Christmas.

Reserl was thankful to the wig.

What men will try to take from you . . . what men are always after . . . you will be spoiled then and no one will . . .

Die Stiefmutter's dire predictions always had somehow to do with Hulda's hair, her shameful, beautiful, dangerous hair . . .

Reserl, leaving Oskar's room at midnight, glanced back at the curling iron. Escaping into the frozen garden, she cast over her shoulder a wordless blessing upon the vicious instrument, now harmless, cooling on the stove tiles . . . and the wig, butchered and burned, scapegoat for her own unholy hair.

The steps to the kitchen were slick with ice. The cold of the brass doorknob felt like burning against her hand.

His voice collared her, sending needles of ice down her back. "Good night, Reserl." He sounded pleased and harmless . . . as if he meant her no harm at all.

"OUR MODEL, LADIES AND GENTLEMEN." ALL SKIN AND BONES, ALL SHINE and shadow, all appetite and sneer.

The room simmered down, apart from the radiator's hiss. The students sidled toward their easels.

"Ulrike," he said. They must know, from the start, that the body of which they were about to make use, in lead or charcoal, pastel or paint, did not lack for a name. He must, as their teacher, make this clear to them. "Ulrike," he said. "Ulrike . . . *Luft,* was it?"

Her startled look was a giveaway. She'd offered no surname, nor been asked. Just "Ulrike." Not that he particularly believed that, either.

Oskar smiled at her. Eighteen, she said. Fourteen at the most. She looked twelve.

Ulrike looked him over with impassive violet eyes, then smiled back. He was up to something. She'd probably never run into a man who wasn't. She nodded.

The students, of course, took in this silent exchange with prickling attention. The least promising of them made Oskar the key figure in the tableau. A couple, those with some measure of talent, acknowledged the girl.

Only Hugo Birnbaum—rehabilitated crybaby, artist in chrysalis, Kokoschka disciple for life—showed no interest in his teacher's introductory rites. Hugo was already engaged with the girl's skeleton, splaying her pathetic little bones across his blank sheet to posture and dance as they might, there below him, while his gaze stayed with the real thing.

Her lack of grace was riveting, her lack of self-consciousness more so. She slipped off her robe without being invited. She threw herself into a glorious adolescent slump. It gave her belly, thin as she was, roundness. It humped her back and spread her thighs and made her small breasts nearly disappear.

She was, she claimed, an experienced model. Well, she *would* say so, of course. That and the requisite age, eighteen . . . or the Academy would not have hired her.

The students, all but Hugo, froze like statues while the little model turned and moved and shifted and swung . . . every sort of movement except *natural*. Oskar's long face struggled mightily to maintain a neutral expression against her contortions and his students' embarrassment.

"Just a moment," he said at last, gently. He could bear no more. "Please."

The students cast their glances down or away.

Only the girl's face aimed at him now, small and barbed and dangerous. "Keep moving . . . wasn't that what you said?"

"Yes, of course."

"I do as I'm told." She bared her teeth in a mean little smile. Her teeth were sharp and yellow and crowded together in front.

Her kimono, cheap imitation red silk, lay in a heap on the platform beside the girl's dirty bare feet. An embroidered dragon breathed fire across its back. Oskar leaned down and retrieved the robe. "It is cold." He laid it, dragon up, in her hands.

"I get paid whether you use me or not." The chit was spoiling for a fight. "I've got a signed paper, mein Herr." Her sneer was irresistible.

She'd insisted she was French—ridiculous. To forestall any checking of references, he supposed. As if models were expected to tote pedigrees in their satchels. She was a Bremerhaven wharf rat, of course. He could hear it every time she opened her mouth.

"There is no dispute. We are honored to have your services, mademoiselle." Oskar made, without sarcasm, the slightest bow.

The child's eyes may have softened a bit.

"But my students . . ." Oskar shrugged. "We are not yet so greatly experienced, some of us. We must prepare ourselves." He said this in a low confiding voice, though any student who cared to hear the exchange surely could. "And the class, as you know, lasts two full hours. Each day through the week. You must not so soon exhaust yourself."

He pulled a rickety chair with a flaking gilt back from the perimeter of the room. He set it beside her and motioned for her to take a seat. The students cut their eyes at him, at her, but no one stared openly.

"*Merci beaucoup, mademoiselle,* for your patience."

For the first time her face admitted uncertainty. She suspected his courtesy of ridicule, and yet . . .

"May I ask you something?" He spoke as if they were alone in the room.

She shrugged, her nonchalance stiff, unconvincing.

"Would you mind telling us what you are paid?"

"For this? Here?"

"Modeling for us here, yes."

The girl narrowed her eyes. "You ought to know."

Oskar hunkered down beside her. "Yes," he said softly. "I really ought to."

She shrugged again. He could not hear her mumbled reply.

"I'm sorry?"

She glanced past him, indifferent. "One mark fifty." She lifted her chin. "Each hour," she said.

Oskar nodded slowly. "And so, for this morning, three marks?"

"You cannot change the agreement."

Would to God he could.

"I would not dream of it, mademoiselle."

He could say nothing else, not with the child sitting here before them. But these students of his, hardly more than children themselves, did they begin to grasp the disgrace? Three marks . . . not the price of a first course in a modest restaurant. To exploit, to humiliate, to turn a living soul into an object of convenience . . . did they recognize the scandal of it? Did they understand it was only the practiced and selfless devotions of true art, art's obliteration of ego, of self, that might in any way redeem this sin of which only the child was innocent, in which all of the rest of them, and he most of all, were complicit? Did they *see*?

Oskar, as he rose and turned to face his students, seemed to undergo a metamorphosis. His body grew larger, harder, more sharply made. The face that an instant ago, level with the girl's, had been all calm and chivalry, was now edgy, almost belligerent.

"You think you know already what you are going to do, most of you." His voice was barely louder than the one he'd used with the model, yet taunt was plain in it now, and urgent.

He had captured their attention. Some of them were afraid, their eyes skirting his . . . the worst offenders, he thought. The hopeless cases. He could have assembled a list without looking.

Oskar stepped off the platform, into their midst. The quiet was suffocating. He waited until each of the students, whether in fear or respect or courage or simple curiosity, had found within themselves the means to look into his eyes. He stared back at them.

His clap was a whip crack.

Several students visibly recoiled.

"You know nothing," he said. "Can you try, please, to understand this?"

Oskar waited, watching his students' faces.

Kristofel, his small gifts crippled by an exorbitant eagerness to please, looked lost—excellent.

Hugo had the good grace to look abashed . . . relying on his intellect again, he knew better. Thinking was a kind of cowardice . . . a safe harbor from the terrors of all one can't possibly know.

Rosalie, one of the youngest, currently squandering her talents on a flirtation with the Fauves, wore a dreamy look. Her ripe lower lip drooped with sensuality. Then she noticed Oskar staring at her. A deep flush flooded her heart-shaped face. You'd think he'd caught her masturbating. Oskar fought a smile. He knew what the child was up to . . . turning poor Ulrike into some sort of fanciful animal, no doubt. Primary colors and unnatural vegetation. Playing with her.

"This is the truth to which you must surrender: that you know, in advance, nothing. This is clear?"

Kristofel nodded first, Rosalie last. Hugo ripped a sheet from his sketchbook and let it slide to the floor.

"Good." Oskar allocated the moment a modest smile. "Now perhaps we can begin."

Behind him the chair creaked. The girl was growing restless. Oskar turned to her. "Mademoiselle Ulrike?" He made a courtly gesture, not directing, but inviting her to rise.

The girl stood up abruptly and began to unfasten the sash of her robe.

"Please." Oskar raised his hand. "Not just yet."

She narrowed her eyes, but acquiesced.

"Merci." Oskar turned to his students. "What now?" he said. "Would someone tell me, please, what must be done first?"

Rosalie opened her mouth, anxious to redeem herself, but could not quite face the risk of a wrong answer. Oskar smiled at her. "You do not know, Fräulein? Splendid!"

Several of the students laughed.

Someone spoke from behind an easel in the back. "First we must see."

Matthäus. The boy studied so hard, could parrot Oskar's every word. He was a draftsman, at best, no painter. He will wind up a critic, Oskar thought.

"So easy as that?" he asked. "Now we have only to *see*?"

Matthäus looked as if he'd been betrayed. Nearly all of them did, even Hugo. *Seeing is everything* . . . by now he'd taught them that, if nothing else.

"Of course seeing, yes. But that can take a very long time," Oskar said. "To see is to reach a destination, is it not so?"

They wait like baby birds, he thought, hungry and helpless and blind. They wait for me to drop into their little beaks some tidbit they think they can survive on. Oskar wanted suddenly, desperately, to leave the room, to abandon them, keeping what little was left of his ruined and exhausted spirit for himself. No wonder he could not paint . . .

"Sehen." The voice behind him, low and rough, was out of patience. Oskar turned around slowly.

"You are not going to see, are you, unless you *look,*" Ulrike said.

"Say again, please?"

"Sehen." She spit the word at him, at all of them. To look. To perceive. To behold.

"Ganz richtig!" Oskar said. Exactly. He did not look at the students. He had no need to witness their humiliation. "We thank you, Fräulein. If you would be so good as to disrobe now, I believe we can begin."

The girl seemed, in the interlude, to have inhabited a different body, the one she was born with and was growing into and would carry with her to her death. Her movements now, her smallest gestures, were fluid and natural. Incorporating the sum of her experience, they attained a perfect equipoise of suffering and joy.

After the first few minutes there was no further need to ask her to change position. Ulrike gave herself to motion, her measured movements in such accord with his own aims and instincts that Oskar felt as if they were dancing together, had been doing so for years.

Leaving the platform to her, he roamed through the studio, scanning his students' work. He did not comment on what he saw. He reminded them only to keep moving, just as Ulrike was, not to linger too long in any one place, not to belabor, *not*—please, God—to analyze or criticize or think.

Some struggled longer and harder than others, but eventually each managed the essential feat: his students forgot him. Their eyes did not stray from the platform now. Their eyes belonged to the girl. But Oskar did not need to look into the fledgling artists' eyes to know they were seeing. The work on their easels made that plain.

Beyond the studio's grimy windows, the morning had begun to clear. Forgotten by his students, Oskar warmed himself in a patch of sunshine as he watched frayed clouds being whisked away by diligent breezes. The studio was drafty. His shoulders ached. But the room, as the sun rose higher in the winter sky, was warming. He wondered if the girl was cold. She must be. But then she would be used to it.

Oskar pulled out his watch, a shoddy steel-cased thing befitting the lowliest clerk. The plain stocky numbers on its flat face announced it was nearly eleven. There should have been a break by now, if only for the model's sake.

He glanced around the studio. The intensity of the young artists' concentration for a moment seemed to him a beautiful object, faultlessly shaped, its facets polished to a hard bright shine. Something he had created. How could he bring himself to tamper with, to *risk* its perfection, born of the passionate conjoining of will and pure desire?

He turned to the back of the room. He returned his watch to his pocket. He did not look at Ulrike. The girl was not reticent. Surely if she needed a break she would demand one. Oskar closed his eyes, relishing the sun's rising heat. Soon it would be midday. He heard, behind him, the sweet friction of charcoal and lead and brush against paper's grain. He imagined he heard the quickening breath of one student, then another . . . the flap of a flipped sheet . . . a sigh . . .

Rosalie's plump lower lip would soften and dip . . . a tiny crystal of saliva glistening, unnoticed and unprized, at the corner of her mouth.

While at the next easel the skinny, silent lad from Crimmitschau would feel a tightening in his groin . . . for once ignore it, possessed by another lust, lost to the dusky clefts and curves of his own hand's making . . .

How it felt . . . he remembered it, yes. Oskar, his eyes still closed, tilted his face up into the light. Dark lines and shapes, endlessly moving, coalesced and scattered on a crimson scrim. There could be no release . . . better if the passion were gone, he thought.

He heard, though he knew he made no sound, a deep groan inside himself. A pitiless sound.

He slipped his hand into the deep pocket of his trousers, just to feel for a moment the heat and hardness . . . to believe again, if for the merest instant, that whatever accounted for human passion could still somehow, after everything, return to him . . .

What his fingers enclosed was round and flat, heavy and cold.

One day I will find another gold watch in my pocket, Oskar thought. This one will be my own. It will be thin as one of Reserl's vanilla wafers, and have graceful Roman numerals that I, lost to painting, will forget to consult for days on end.

"It is noon." The rasp of the girl's voice more annoyed than startled him. He had not forgotten her, not entirely.

He turned neutral eyes on her. Her skin had a bluish cast. Had her face, a couple of hours ago, been so thin, so pale?

"I am free to go at noon, they said."

How could he, at the start, have failed to notice the bruise at the left side of her rib cage? It was big around as a soup cup and rife with unsavory colors, the muddy greens and brownish yellows of homely condiments. He wondered if someone was mistreating her.

"You are, yes. Free." He nodded, his gaze still hovering around the girl's ribs. "We are all free."

His hand emerged from his pocket and waved vaguely, as he wandered, first and alone, out of the studio.

The disposition of lower limbs continues to trouble you? Refer again, please, Fräulein, to my earliest sketches. These were rendered in hope's insolence, I know, undaunted by practicality. Still, these first sketches remain, to my mind, the most accurate and inspired rendering of her legs' flawless lines: the fragility of ankle, the flirting ovule of knee, round thigh's receptive flesh . . .

The quest for words to approach such an ideal of form . . . need I report to you, my collaborationist, how soon and hopelessly I am lost in the brambles of exquisite arousal? Release me, I pray, from the tedious obligations of language. Look to the drawings. Dwell there. Only then, freed of words' failings, might you find approximation of such impossible beauty.

But have I remembered to tell you—forgive me if I repeat myself—how essential to my satisfaction is the complete and flawless articulation of the toes? My darling's fair feet are, even in winter (perhaps I have confided this?), fond of truancy. To chase her, barefoot, through these rooms! The middle of April, you say? No later?

The motion of each toe, anyway, please remember, must be entirely independent of any other. And the curl and peak of the littlest toe ought properly to resemble a rose in its first hours of budding . . .

You must, of course, rely on your powers of recollection here. It would be unspeakable cruelty to delay, for such lessons as summer's roses might teach, what you have sworn to send in sweet advance of spring's first blooms.

You will honor your word in this, I know!

Your faithful OK

"A BRIEF WORD WITH YOU, PROFESSOR KOKOSCHKA, IF I MIGHT?"

Oskar, caught in a daze before a grimy window, laughed. He did not mean to. Particularly not before seeing who might observe him from his studio doorway.

He put on a sober expression, suitable for making amends. He turned around. "Ah, Karl." He bowed and started laughing again. "Professor Löwenblatt."

Karl Löwenblatt, the only one of his colleagues as lowly in age and experience as Oskar, looked bewildered.

" 'Professor,' " Oskar tried to explain. "I don't expect I'll ever grow used to the title."

The other man sighed. "Nor I."

Behind his slumped back, the students called him *Blätterteig,* Puff Pastry. Oskar hoped that, if aware of the nickname, Karl also knew it was not given without sympathy, affection, even respect. Löwenblatt, too, had tasted the mustard gas, had seen the carnage. His timid and conventional appearance disguised an artist of singular and truly horrific vision. He served art loyally, bravely, and without the least hope of being understood. He simply had not developed the means of concealing the fragility of his self-confidence.

"Am I disturbing you?"

"Hardly." Oskar thrust out his hands, then let them drop to his sides. "Idleness . . . the very devil, just as Papa predicted."

"You work very hard," Karl said kindly.

"Teaching? I do not call this work."

"Nor I." Löwenblatt smiled. "I expect we will, given another year or two."

"If they keep us that long."

Oskar watched with a stab of remorse as his colleague seemed to shrink before him. "I meant myself, dear man," he said. "Not you."

"Still, it's altogether obvious how little I belong here."

"That is nonsense," Oskar said.

Karl Löwenblatt wandered to a spot near the window. Where my easel should be standing, Oskar thought. It had been a dismal winter day. Now late-afternoon light seemed to tarnish his colleague's wan face.

"Hearing your laugh just now, when I called you 'Professor'? I envy you. Hearing myself so addressed makes me weep." Karl stared out the window, squinting as a sudden shaft of sun pricked through a purple cloud. "I've instructed them to call me Karl. Not appropriate, of course, but an outburst of sobbing would be less so, don't you think?"

His cunning smile caught Oskar by surprise. He hadn't suspected Karl Löwenblatt of concealing the weapon of irony. *He'll be all right,* he thought.

And: *Perhaps we could be friends.*

"I'd thoroughly enjoy their deference, of course," Karl said, "were it even slightly merited."

Oskar nodded, his face pained. Regard should have been invigorating, after so long being found, in Alma's eyes, perpetually wanting, falling short of every mark. But unwarranted deference was oddly enervating. Between Hans Posse's civility and the students' veneration, Katja's endless seductions and Reserl's dumb homage, Oskar felt like a flower pressed in a romantic's diary, suffocated and reduced.

"I don't paint any longer," he said suddenly. "I suppose that's been bandied about?"

Karl Löwenblatt, staring at Oskar with wide shocked eyes, shook his head.

"You must be truthful." Oskar smiled. "Otherwise . . ."

"I rarely lie," the other man said. "I am very poor at it."

"Dodging lies and hitting upon truth are not the same thing, of course."

Löwenblatt nodded and licked his lips.

"'Puff Pastry.' You know, I suppose, that's what they call you?"

Löwenblatt flushed. "I know, yes."

"There it is, truth bald as an egg. Now it is your turn."

Karl Löwenblatt seemed to stop breathing. His slight body, without moving, betrayed both the desire to flee and an unassailable will to stand its ground. To possess in oneself such courage . . . Oskar's covetousness was, for an instant, sickening.

"Truth?" Löwenblatt's voice quaked slightly. "You are slightly deranged," he said.

"Ah!" Oskar beamed.

"I hadn't finished," Karl Löwenblatt said.

"Excuse me," Oskar said.

"The war may, to some extent, be blamed for your condition of mind."

Oskar nodded. "That is one nice thing about war," he said. "It conveniently excuses a number of . . . irregularities."

Löwenblatt had a surprisingly charming laugh. "Your second feat of truth!" he said.

"But I interrupted yours."

"Yes, before resolution fails . . ." Karl Löwenblatt took a deep breath and straightened his shoulders.

"In fact, it is love that's deranged you," he said. "Or so word has it in the basement, among vapors of tobacco and tea."

Oskar, his face impassive, turned and stared out the window at the encroaching dark.

"And what do you think?" he asked finally.

"My personal opinion?"

"Yes."

Karl Löwenblatt waited until Oskar looked into his eyes. "Allowing love to derange us . . . well, it's a kind of holiness, isn't it? What else, in the end, does a saint amount to?"

Oskar's silver eyes glowed. "I'm not the only one here who's deranged, then."

"Of course not." Löwenblatt swatted the obvious away with one hand. "The fact is, people are always oversimplifying holiness, confusing it with *goodness*."

"Well, obviously it—"

"When in fact they are opposites."

Oskar, a dizzying lightness in his head, waited for the other man to go on.

"Pure and restful and healing and—" Löwenblatt made a spitting sound. "Ordinary as water, goodness."

He took a step toward Oskar, then another. His breath, scented with cinnamon, was oddly pleasant.

"I recognized you immediately," Karl Löwenblatt said. "Before we met. Years ago. Your work in the Hagenbund . . . can you imagine what a relief it was?"

"I'm sorry," Oskar said, "I don't—"

"I saw there was someone else in the world who knew what I did," Karl Löwenblatt said. "That holiness is fire."

THEY WOULD, BOTH OF THEM, LATER MAKE LIGHT OF IT, HOW KARL HAD wandered into Oskar's studio believing him gone for the day, hoping to filch a rag and some turpentine . . . and how that absurdly inauspicious errand had led to a lifelong friendship based upon the conviction, in each, that the other was thoroughly, reassuringly, marvelously deranged. It was a discovery both men promptly accorded the status of assumption, thereafter taken for granted and seldom requiring discussion.

Oskar found, in Karl Löwenblatt, a soul whose dimensions could accommodate his own limitless passion . . . if not quite understanding it, accepting it nonetheless.

And in Oskar Kokoschka, Karl Löwenblatt recognized a similarly commodious receptacle into which, now and then, a measure of his own unearthly passion might be poured.

Both men lived to be very old, attaining the age from which the absurdity of one's youth acquires a patina of bravado and charm.

12

He would, if only she were beautiful, love her.

Sometimes the voice told her lies.

The wedge of spotted glass on the wall of her room returned Reserl to herself in small pieces. These, too, might be less than truthful. Hulda? The girl was forever gone.

The Captain was sick with love. For love of a beautiful woman he had given himself to madness.

He looked at Reserl. Sometimes he almost studied her. But he did not seem to see her.

She did not want him to.

She was not beautiful.

He would never love her.

THE LADY WITH THE RAMBUNCTIOUS GOLD HAIR CAME BACK, NOW AND then, to visit. About every other week, Reserl thought, though she could not be certain. Had Reserl dared mark the Captain's calendar, small dark dots like moles might have recorded these visits. Reserl's body was sprinkled with moles. Her arms and chest and shoulders looked as if they were starting to spoil.

The lady wore no more feathers in her shining hair. The skin on her chest and throat gleamed like pearls. She'd stay for several hours, sitting with the Captain in the parlor where they would drink Turkish coffee with the Direktor and make him laugh.

Sometimes, however, the lady came in the afternoon, before the Direktor was home. The Captain, smiling, would rush to the front of the house to receive her. Then he would lead her by the hand to the summerhouse, where he would heat water in the little pan on top of his stove to make tea.

Once the Captain asked Reserl to bring bread and butter and jam. When she stood at the door of the summerhouse, waiting for it to open to her elbow's inconvenient knock, she heard the Captain and his visitor laughing inside. Their laughter, Reserl knew, had nothing to do with her. Still, the sound of it, as she waited to be let in, left her feeling sad and small.

The lady with the golden hair caused Reserl a certain puzzlement. For she was very beautiful, with her sparkling eyes and pearly skin, her vivid heart-shaped face and small high bosom. The Captain smiled often when she was near him, especially when her hands touched him, which, even Reserl could see, they often did.

The lady visitor spun a web of desire over the Captain. Reserl saw how desire thickened the air around him whenever she was near.

It was rude, of course, to stare. Reserl carefully slanted her glances when the visitor was there. Reserl spied on beauty and desire from the corners of her eyes.

It pained and puzzled Reserl, the lady's golden beauty, because the Captain clearly saw it, of course, and desired it, yet he did not love the young woman with the golden hair. Despite her beauty. Despite desire. Reserl knew but did not understand this.

Reserl wondered if the lady knew about the Captain's goddess. Perhaps it had all been explained to her, how his love belonged elsewhere, it could not be helped.

Reserl wondered if the beautiful visitor understood this better than she herself did and whether, in spite of it all, she wished, as Reserl did, that a little of the Captain's love might be left over from the goddess so that he could, at least a little, love her, too.

Still, he had said, had he not, that only she, only Reserl, could help him? *I need someone . . . there is only you, I am sorry.* She knew what he had said. His words were still there in her room, in the dark. *Only you.* If only he was not sorry.

He called the lovely woman who visited *Liebshen*. The Direktor called her Fräulein Richter and greeted her by kissing her hand. She came to call four times, four little dark moles invisibly spoiling the Captain's calendar, before Reserl learned her name:

Katja. Finally Reserl heard the Captain murmur it. His visitor had just arrived. *A delightful surprise*, the Captain said.

It was late afternoon. The Direktor would return soon from the Museum. They stayed in the parlor. The lady sat close to the Captain on the settee, speaking in a low warm voice. She laid her hand on his chest. Her pale fingers crept between the mother-of-pearl buttons of his shirt. The Captain gently lifted the hand and, even more gently, set it back in her lap.

"Katja," he murmured.

Then he noticed that Reserl had come into the room. She offered the guest a Meissen plate strewn with forget-me-knots and butter cookies. The Captain's smile, drifting between the two women's faces, looked like something broken and ineptly mended.

The lady, Katja, refused the cookies with a toss of her head that made her golden curls shiver in the dim silver light. The parlor was webbed with desire, a desire chilly as frost.

"Shall I light the fire?"

Neither the Captain nor his visitor seemed to hear Reserl, nor to notice when, leaving the plate on a rosewood table, she lit a lamp and left the room.

THAT THE CAPTAIN COULD DESIRE THE BEAUTIFUL WOMAN NAMED KATJA without loving . . . how by the light of such beauty to make sense of that? Might love and desire be entirely separate things? Perhaps so. Reserl began to revise the stories she told herself. In the new stories, the Captain loved her without desire. He touched her body only to shelter it, without thought of possession, kissed her with lips whose light touch was dry and cool against her brow.

These new stories did not unsettle and keep her awake the way her first stories of the Captain's love had. Lacking experience in comfort and passion, Reserl found them difficult to imagine. Comfort, she supposed, would be the sweeter and less demanding of the two, less stern in its demand for beauty.

Reserl was hardly to blame if, in the stories devised for her comfort, she remained, still and always, beautiful. Reserl was hardly more than a child.

THE UNFAMILIAR WEIGHT WAS A PLEASURE DEEP IN HER APRON POCKET. Reserl quickened her step through the market, nearly running from stall to stall. The faster she moved, the harder the soft red leather purse's thump against her thigh. She imagined the bills inside rubbing together, whispering.

It was well known that the widow from Pillnitz, Frau Gruen, had the best veal and pork. This week, however, her meats looked poorly, juiceless and limp, rather like the old woman herself.

Reserl ducked into the shade of a fruit cart's makeshift canopy, hoping the old woman hadn't noticed her. She wouldn't want to hurt her feelings. But nothing Frau Gruen had to offer this morning was worthy of the Direktor's table. Too bad. The schnitzel he loved would have to wait until next week. For now, perhaps some fish . . .

Reserl began to search for the fishmonger's wagon. The skinny, sunburned, moody man's wares never sat twice in the same spot. The place where she last recalled seeing him was occupied by a pair of brownskinned children in gaudy rags.

The children were hanging ribbons and laces and trinkets from the lower branches of a skimpish tree. Reserl's run slowed to a walk, her walk to a loiter. The red purse slipped into the corner of her pocket.

It was a clear brisk day in early March. A breeze was trying mightily to make off with the children's wares. A dozen ribbons fussed among the dry twigs, tangling with lockets and watch fobs, fichus and bootlaces.

The clash and blend of the ribbons' many colors cast a spell on her eyes. Reserl forgot where she'd been going, what she'd meant to find. One ribbon, in particular, seemed to pull her toward it. As she stared at it, the others seemed to vanish. The ribbon was velvet of the same candid blue as the early-spring sky. It glittered in the sunlight. Stepping closer, Reserl discovered the blue ribbon, unlike any of the others, was shot through with silver thread.

She touched the ribbon and felt a kind of dizziness. She shut her eyes for a moment against the morning light, the ribbon's silver-blue beckoning. When she opened her eyes, she turned away from the tree and stepped quickly into the stream of market traffic.

Fish, she thought. *Makrele or Zander . . .* perhaps trout. The Direktor had a fondness for eel, but the very idea of touching it . . .

"Wait, Fräulein!"

She began to run. She did not know why. With each step the red leather purse bumped her thigh. Why had she brought it? The Direktor provided the marketing money. He always gave her more than enough.

"Please, Fräulein . . . wait."

A hand grasped her wrist, a small brown hand with filthy nails.

The child wore ragged tan breeches and a voluminous shirt, once white, a man's shirt hacked off to accommodate a small boy's height and motion. Yet Reserl somehow knew—before she felt the softness of the child's hand clasping hers, before she saw the gold loops threaded through the small ruddy earlobes—that the child was a girl.

"Our prices are fair." She sounded huffy, as if in the midst of a quarrel. She might have been eight, perhaps ten. She was very small. But the face was not a child's, Reserl thought.

"We keep the best things in a box." The grip of the girl's hand was fierce.

Reserl bent her head slightly to hear.

"People steal here, Fräulein."

Reserl felt accused. She shook her head and tried to withdraw her hand, but the girl would not let it go. She looked up and smiled. Her eyes, black and shiny as olives, reminded Reserl of old Helike, of secrets that could not be kept from her eyes. The child was a Gypsy, of course.

"Come. You will see everything," she said.

Reserl allowed herself to be pulled toward the bent and stingy tree. A boy a year or two older than the girl crouched on a horse blanket in its spotty shade, sorting out an unruly display of trifles and oddments.

"My brother." The girl made plain this was a regrettable fact that could not be helped. "Enrique," she said.

The boy, looking up, seemed ready to accuse her of something.

"Sehr erfreut." Mere politeness. Reserl was not at all happy to meet him.

The boy's attention returned to his work, aligning tortoiseshell combs in pairs along the blanket's edge.

With a soft click of her tongue the girl consigned the whole of the male species to derision. *"Die Schachtel,"* she said.

Her brother looked at Reserl. When she met his stare, he jumped up and darted into the crowd. In less than a minute he was back, a patched black pasteboard box tightly gripped in his grubby hands.

"Gib es mir," his sister said, stretching out her hands.

He handed over the box, then stood with his shoulder nearly touching the girl's, his arms folded over his skinny chest, vigilant chaperon to his sister's risky ventures.

Reserl smiled. "What is your name?" she asked the girl.

"What is *yours?*" the boy growled.

His sister bumped him with her shoulder and he lost his footing.

"Stelle." The child's dark eyes, glittering, narrowed against the sun. "I am named for the stars," she said.

Reserl nodded solemnly.

The boy made a disgusted sound and returned to displaying his merchandise.

"What are you named for?" Stelle asked.

"I don't know," Reserl said.

The girl's face went still and sober. After a moment, setting the box in the dust between their feet, she hunkered down and began to unfasten its worn leather strapping. "I will show you," she said.

Reserl squatted beside her. "I don't need anything," she said.

The child glanced in her brother's direction. The boy's back was turned, conspicuously ignoring them.

The girl smiled and raised the lid of the box.

The tangle of jewelry and trinkets and trimmings caught the sky's blinding glare and threw it back up into Reserl's face. She squinted. The day seemed to dim.

The girl's face was a dark shadow above her, the sun blazing behind it.

"I can't see," Reserl said.

"Ja."

Laughing softly, the girl tipped the box. Strings of glass beads and tarnished earbobs, buttons and brooches and corset laces, tokens and amulets and whalebone stays, clattered into the flighty hammock of Reserl's apron.

A few feet away, the ribbons blew a breezy music. Reserl's eyes, yearning toward them, could no longer find the blue one. The colors had all run together, like an ignorant bride's ruined laundry.

"I don't need anything," she whispered.

SHE ACCEPTED, IN THE END, WHAT THE CHILD CHOSE FOR HER: A HALF dozen wooden buttons carved in the shapes of flowers, a pair of silver earrings, a string of yellow glass beads. The earrings were hoops the same size as Stelle's gold ones, but these fastened with tiny screws in the back. The girl seemed to pity Reserl, as if her unpierced earlobes were an embarrassing disfigurement. There was no pity in the child's hands, however, when she fastened the silver rings to Reserl's ears.

"Too tight."

"It hurts?"

Reserl, wincing, nodded.

"If they do not hurt, you will lose them," Stelle said.

When Reserl tried to remove the earrings, she succeeded only in further tightening the small screws. Perhaps she would get holes in her ears after all. She cast a longing glance over her shoulder at the ribbons.

"I'll give you a gift." The little girl began scooping handfuls of merchandise from Reserl's apron, tossing the trinkets carelessly back into the box. "Whichever you choose," she said. "For nothing."

Even with her lap emptied, Reserl found she could not stand.

After several strenuous attempts to pull her up, Stelle called her brother. The boy, his face surly, came over and yanked Reserl to her feet.

"*Danke.*" She wiped her hands on her apron before taking the red leather purse from its pocket.

Stelle stared at the bill she was offered, her face shocked. She ran over for a whispered consultation with Enrique. They appeared to argue, but Reserl could not understand their words.

Was it possible that the bill, a significant portion of the Direktor's gift, was less than they wanted for their trinkets? So I'll give more, Reserl thought. What matter? There was nothing she could buy for the Captain, nothing she needed herself . . . buttons and beads and earbobs. *Vergeblich.* Useless. All she wanted was to leave.

Hot whispers hissed under the tree. Then Stelle returned with a fist-sized drawstring bag of coarse gray cloth. She loosened its puckered mouth and emptied a stream of coins into Reserl's apron pocket.

"*Zuviel,*" Reserl said. Too much.

The child shook her head. "Not enough." Her eyes skirted Reserl's.

"It is fine." Reserl turned to go.

"A ribbon." Stelle's voice was gruff like her brother's. "You must choose."

Reserl slowly turned around. The wind had died down. The ribbons hung limp from the branches, as if the tree were dying of thirst.

Reserl shook her head. "I don't need anything."

The little girl in boy's breeches looked up, squinting, her eyes chips of jet. Old Helike, Reserl thought.

Muttering under her breath, Stelle moved back to where her brother was building a pyramid of embossed tin matchboxes in a pool of sunlight.

You need to know your name.

Could the child have said such a thing?

Suddenly Reserl was running. Forgetting the temperamental fishmonger and the year's first radishes and a nearly empty potato bin, she took the shortest route out of the market. She felt, with each step, the drag of her apron's weight, heard the coins clanking like chains.

THE SIGHT OF THE DIREKTOR IN THE KITCHEN HORRIFIED HER. THE DIrektor rarely entered the kitchen.

"Oh, there you are, Hulda! You are just getting back?"

What time must it be? Her string bag dangled from her hand, nearly empty. She opened her mouth as if doing so might lure a useful word to her tongue.

But Hans Posse was smiling. "Professor Kokoschka has left us."

The string bag slipped from her hand and hit the brick floor. Reserl heard an egg break. She did not look down.

"He is gone?" Why on earth would the Direktor be smiling?

"For the weekend," Hans Posse said. "To the country."

"Alone?"

"With a companion, I believe." The Direktor smiled.

Reserl blushed.

"You mustn't worry so about him, Hulda."

"Yes, sir," she said.

"He's a good deal heartier than he was when he came to us. It is all to the credit of your care, I'm sure."

Reserl looked down. A clot of egg white was pooling beside her bag, as if some lout had spit on her immaculate kitchen floor.

"Hulda?"

She started at the tentative touch to her shoulder.

"If anyone here looks frail these days, it is you," the Direktor said.

Coiffure . . . ensemble . . . toilette. Merci, madame . . . Merci beaucoup, madame . . . Je vous en prie, madame . . . We shall learn more français at the weekend, Reserl. Madame vastly prefers it. There is so much more I must teach you, the Captain had said.

"I am well, sir."

The Direktor's hand withdrew discreetly. "But you look very tired," he said. Then he patted his stomach in a comical manner. "So it is a good thing I'll be dining alone for a few days. Soup and a bit of bread will do nicely." His waist was barely wider than her own. "While our guest is away, I shall get fit and you shall get rested."

She opened her mouth to protest.

He laid an ink-stained finger over his lips.

The summerhouse could have a good airing. The weather now was cool and dry. The wardrobe doors left open might freshen up Madame's things, too. The bed's headboard could be waxed and polished, the linens soaked overnight . . . some lemon in the water for freshness. Had the Captain worn his best boots? Surely he would for a journey. She would polish the poor ones he wore to the Academy, would somehow remove the spattered paint, would give them new laces. He would tease her: *Some fancy gentleman has left his boots in my cupboard, Reserl!*

The Direktor was looking at her with concern.

He would return on Sunday. Reserl would be wearing her blue dress. The silver rings would dance in her ears, the glass beads shine at her throat. And the buttons like flowers might . . .

On Sunday he would come home.

"Are you listening?" the Direktor asked gently.

He will never love you.

"Yes, sir. I am," she said. Her eyes were mournful. She'd forgotten the fish.

KATJA'S SULK, IN THE TRAIN'S CLOSE QUARTERS, WAS UNRELENTING. "AND not even a wedding invitation," she said.

Oskar was by now well acquainted with the ostensible cause of her pique. She'd discussed little else the last two times he'd seen her, barely diverted even by the extravagant napoleons he'd carried to her in the Café Parisien's beribboned pink box. Katja's sulks were more than he could afford. He should have known this by now. What made him think a few days in Thale might purchase her good humor?

She pouted her way west-northwest from Dresden, past Leipzig, and into the Harz Mountains. At the sight of quaint hamlets and glistening rivers she turned up her nose. The train compartment was overheated, she said. And furthermore, Ernst did not *love* this homely heiress, he never would; couldn't Oskar see she was heartbroken?

It took Katja a mere instant to deem Thale, as a resort, overrated. Bourgeois, she said, and prissy. The locked door between their adjoining rooms in the guest house was a personal insult. Not to mention a major inconvenience. The bathwater was tepid and the food inedible and the sight of the mountains unsettling.

Oskar's mouth was very nearly watering . . . at last to see with his own eyes the Hexentanzplatz he'd dreamed about since first reading, as a youth, Goethe's *Faust.* Katja's refusal to consider the excursion came as a shock. The short hike would be invigorating.

It would be the ruin of her dainty footwear, Katja said.

"'The Place Where the Witches Dance,'" Oskar wheedled. "*Liebchen,* where is your sense of adventure?"

Katja sniffed and stared out the window of the guest house dining room. "Run along," she said. "Don't let me detain you. I'll just sit here and . . . read a book or something."

This Oskar knew he could not afford.

"Let me buy you new boots," he said. "Something stout and comfortable."

"Clodhoppers," Katja hissed.

"Will you have more coffee?" The proprietress maintained a wary arm's length from Katja's side of the table, having already received a tongue-lashing on the subject of the bath's inadequacies.

Katja, ignoring her, stared belligerently out the window, as if to intimidate the cliffs towering over the Bode Valley.

"Thank you," Oskar said. "I think not."

The start of their first day in the idyllic spot and he was more than a little out of sorts himself, having been awakened by Katja's knock at two o'clock in the morning. He had jumped from his bed. An inferno . . . an intruder . . . The guest house was a fanciful tinderbox that resembled a cuckoo clock. The guests were provided no keys. "Crime is unknown here," the motherly Frau Schinkel had said.

"Oskar!" Katja had sounded desperate.

"What?" His own voice frightened him in the dark. "In God's name, what—"

She could not sleep. The unfamiliar surroundings unnerved her. The room was cold. Was he sure the door could not be unlocked on *his* side?

"Go back to bed." Oskar tried to make himself heard through the door without raising his voice. "Please, *Liebchen.*" Everyone in the guest house must be awake by now, a rapt supine audience to Katja's little drama.

"I want to sleep with you!"

Oskar cringed. Years on the stage made projecting her voice second nature, he supposed. In the morning, eating breakfast, he would be surrounded by strangers who—

"Oskar?" Yes, the way her whisper could carry to a theater's back row was a marvel. Everyone said so. "Are you there?"

And Katja's beauty, glimpsed by morning light, would only make him look worse. What sort of man would refuse her invitation?

"I'm here." His misery, at least, was audible.

As was, in the silence, her fury.

She needed reassurance. This Oskar understood. If only she did not imagine the slight of a former lover's fortunate marriage could be redressed by a night in Oskar's bed. A mere two hours past midnight and the day had already exhausted him.

And what was he to say to her, with the very darkness listening? He couldn't think . . .

"Good night," Katja said.

The door between them was not, in fact, locked. Oskar had investigated it upon taking occupancy of the room. He'd been both amused and relieved to discover the door, which was rather flimsy, had been not locked but nailed shut. He saw no need to point out this distinction to Katja.

"Good night," she repeated. A well-practiced pathos lodged between them, smoldering like a cinder behind panels of parched walnut.

Oskar's murmured benediction upon his friend's dreams was not, that he could hear, returned.

RESERL FOUND HIM IN THE KITCHEN ON SATURDAY EVENING.

The few supper dishes had been washed and returned to their shelf. On the back of the stove, dough for the Sunday-morning rolls was rising in a cracked yellow earthenware bowl.

The Direktor's cherished cup of warm honeyed milk had just been delivered to him before the waning fire in his study upstairs. His courteous *Danke* and *Gut' Nacht* had been reassuringly absentminded. His attentive concern for Reserl had been lulled by two days of rote exchange and calm routine. Reserl had even forced herself, overruling pride, to serve the simple meals the Direktor had requested. But what about Sunday dinner? Would the Captain be there or not?

There he was on Saturday night, on her stool in the corner, when she returned to the kitchen. His face looked gray and drawn, his eyes feverish. A balding carpetbag the color of lichen lay on the floor at his feet.

A roasted capon, Reserl thought. The rosemary had, with ease, survived a mild winter. Now, with the promise of spring, the thyme was perking up.

I shall rise early. I shall make no sound. By the time they come for breakfast, the capon shall be clean and white, its filled belly stitched closed with basting thread, and the kitchen shall smell like a garden.

Oskar slid from the stool. He swayed for a moment, as if the rosy bricks under his feet were fitful. Then, looking at her, he steadied himself.

Reserl thought of the silver earrings and yellow beads tucked into the rent in her mattress inside the red leather purse . . . her blue dress, freshly laundered and hung all afternoon to dry in the March sun. If only he . . .

"It is only Saturday," she said.

Oskar nodded.

"Have you eaten?"

His eyes alone, their stillness, dismissed the question.

She did not know how to talk to him, she never had. Reserl lowered her chin. The odors of sweat and yeast and cooking fat rose from her clothes. Had he returned an hour later, she would at least have been freshly bathed. She would never know how to talk to him.

"Reserl."

She looked up.

He held out his arms, the palms of his large chapped hands laid open. She thought of the figure of a starved man she had, despite her grandmother's warnings of the evil eye, once sneaked inside the little Catholic church in her village to see. Reserl did not remember the man's face. She recalled only the thinness of his limbs and chest, stretched taut across two rough planks, each rib distinct and visible from the back of the dim church, dark spikes piercing the palms of his womanly long-fingered hands.

Hulda had wanted to venture closer. His head drooped. His face was in shadow. Were his eyes open? Crouched behind the last high-backed wooden bench, she couldn't tell. But what would that have told her anyway? Death did not close the eyes. The living had to do that. Hulda's grandmother had closed her mother's eyes, had weighted them with coins. Had anyone closed her grandmother's eyes? From the back of the little church Hulda had stared at the man splayed on the crossed planks, stared at the spikes driven through his oddly dainty hands and feet, and hoped that he was dead.

"Reserl."

What was she named for? She wanted to ask him.

Hulda had longed to walk to the front of the church but feared the evil eye would follow her. The church was *verboten,* Grandmother had said.

The Captain's silver eyes drew her forward. Reserl surrendered to them. *He will never love you.*

"I cannot go away from here," he whispered. "I should not have tried."

Reserl thought of all he might have meant. Perhaps, in time, she would make stories of them, the many things he might have meant but did not.

She stepped into his arms in the corner of the kitchen, held by him, holding him up. He was shivering. She felt how, sinking into her, he grew heavier. She regretted her smell and rejoiced in her steadiness and thanked her legs for their strength.

13

Katja's farewell had been a masterpiece. Her unexpected self-restraint forced a hush upon the guest house. Its floorboards stopped creaking. In the dining room the clink of china and the clatter of silver ceased. The stifling upper hall was perfumed with her bitterness.

The mountain air might do her good after all, she'd decided. Oskar's sudden and urgent need to return to Dresden showed disregard for her health . . . rather typical, sad to say.

She did, he thought, look pale. The curtain at a nearby window cast an ornate lace of shadows over her face.

She had money . . . enough, certainly, for stout boots. What matter if they were unflattering? She would scale the Rosstreppe cliffs without him.

"Please try to forgive me," Oskar begged. "I cannot stay. Something is wrong with me."

Katja nodded. "You are not a man," she told him calmly, "but a boy."

Her face, translucent and white as the frozen pond beyond the window, suggested dark depths.

HE ALLOWED HER WORDS, ALL THE WAY BACK TO DRESDEN, TO TOY WITH him. They left him, to be honest, more intrigued than shamed. Not a man . . . Alma, of course, had made the same charge. But that was long ago, before the war, before . . .

Not a man? Perhaps. Katja had a facility for backing into truth, particularly where Oskar was concerned.

What use, in any case, being a man in such times? Vienna, Berlin . . . the fortresses of European culture had become rowdy playgrounds. Petty anarchies were a matter of empty boast, parading as conviction, as honor. Men misbehaving like boys . . . how was one to tell the revolutionary from the militarist?

Kraus, peering down the steep slope from his vast intelligence, was very likely right. The sole surviving relics of Habsburg glory would come down to spas and operetta, self-indulgence and treacle. *Die letzten Tage der Menschheit . . . The Last Days of Mankind,* indeed.

To be an artist in such a sorry, ruined age . . . what he'd hoped to be a life's vocation, was it more than a child's pastime now? The boundless humanity of a Rembrandt, the moral lucidity of a Brueghel, appeared obscene by the light of what passed these days for European civilization. The Renaissance might have been some lunatic's wine-soaked dream. How to explain to his students, to anyone, a world without the least coherence or reverence . . . let alone convince so bankrupt a world of its need for art?

A teacher, bereft of conviction, was no better than an impostor. I shall teach you *to see,* he'd said. And so had he begun to . . . Watching as his students' eyes opened, he'd lulled himself to a degree of satisfaction. Sometimes he might even, for a moment, rejoice. But then would come bouts of excruciating clarity: Make them see? He'd better equip them for the world they were bound to inherit by teaching his students to close their eyes, to bury their heads in the sand.

None of which had a thing to do, really, with Katja and her flimsy boots and the Hexentanzplatz . . . nor in any way explained what had put Oskar in flight back to Dresden. Why had one wakeful night in a stuffy guest house dismantled him? He was well used to Katja's histrionics. There had been a time when he quite enjoyed them.

The error had been leaving Dresden, Oskar thought. Stepping outside the web of fantasy he'd spun around himself there. Lying wide-eyed in a cramped, unfamiliar room, he had caught an unfortunate glimpse of himself in the dark. Seen what was becoming of him. Oskar supposed he should be grateful he had at least enough good sense left to be afraid.

Pathetic enough, his past and present—doomed love for a cold and selfish woman and his frantic efforts, now, to perpetuate that fruitless passion. The real horror, however, was the blank space Oskar envisioned as his future. All well and good to realize he was devoting himself to fantasy and falsehood. But what, without them, could he hope to amount to? How to keep himself alive?

He had known, as a boy, the sort of man he meant to become. And yes, he had idly entertained a boy's dreams of a world that would heap on him riches and rewards. But Oskar had, even as a youngster, known the difference between dreams and devotion. All he had truly asked of life, in humility and good faith, was that he be allowed to serve beauty, and to love in purity and truth.

Fighting a lost war, sharing close quarters with death, had changed him, of course. Oskar sometimes thought he'd become an old man overnight . . . was that the kinship *die Eidechse* had spotted in him, the bone-weary soul's dim beam from within a young man's gaze?

I shall never be the same, Oskar thought. He could accept that. Whatever the war had done to him, it had not altered the nature of his devotion . . .

It was the world that had changed. Dismembered by war, disfigured by greed . . . nothing was familiar, not even one's homeland. *Especially* one's homeland.

Now, as a painter, one could only choose between false reverence for what no longer reflected the world accurately . . . or a ruthless will to destroy, hurling fragments of a smashed culture and claiming art in the arc of one's aim.

But more ignoble still, his choices as a lover—submitting either to Katja's fickle impulses or to an inert embrace of horsehair and feathers and wax. Were I able to pray, Oskar thought, I should bless heaven for my lethargy. What, otherwise, to hinder suicide?

What was to become of him? Barely past thirty and his heart as crippled and cold as a codger's. The doctors were only too eager to make his excuses—Baranyi and Teuscher and Neuberger behind him like a Greek chorus divested of moral perspicacity, chanting of war and shell shock, grenades and gases, assuring him forgiveness of anything.

A blanket of forgiveness, the war, his wounds . . . a boy's dream, a man's downfall. His melancholy, his indolence, his lack of manners and the goddamn perpetual ache in his head . . . it was all the war, wasn't it?

Only the war? How could he refuse to huddle under the thick blanket of their mulish *understanding*?

It isn't the war, Oskar thought, as the train noisily bundled what was left of him back to Dresden. Not the war, but the wanting. The months of waiting, at the mercy of his merciless longing, for her. The laughable futile belief that any day she would return to her senses and come back to him. And lending insidious substance to that hopeless hope, his fanciful scheme to *create,* out of scrap and delusion, the love he required.

Die Schweigsame Frau . . . his compliant Silent Woman: The excitement of creating her, if only in his mind, had made him buoyant for a time. But now she was beyond his reach, clutched in the hands of a Stuttgart spinster who, a certain skill notwithstanding, knew little of eroticism, less of true passion. Oskar had, for too long, tried to cajole himself out of seeing all Hermine Moos lacked. Her letters, stiff and stingy, were uninspired. She was forthcoming with neither the details of her progress nor the causes of its lack. She offered nothing to nourish confidence or hydrate hope. His spirit had been forced all these months to feed off itself. Little wonder that spirit had gone starved and gaunt.

And to whom might he have turned in despair, if not to his most intimate friend? Like a drowning man he'd reached a frantic hand toward Katja, who—

Staring out the window as the train hurtled past Halle's industrious outreaches, Oskar collided suddenly with an unwelcome memory . . . *a drowning man.*

Could nearly a year have passed now without thought of it? He'd never, except in the war, witnessed something so horrific. Even at the Russian front . . . one *expected* brutality in combat.

One did not expect it in Dresden.

Dresden, his sanctuary . . . Oskar, waiting for his teaching appointment to commence, had daily paced the staid city he was not sure he cared for but seemed, by default, to have adopted.

The last hours of those negligent and restless days were given to the river. One evening, heading back toward the Zwinger through filaments of dwindling light, Oskar started across the Augustus Bridge. Of what had he been thinking? Trying various names on the Elbe's ambiguous tint at that moment, perhaps. He was, in any case, preoccupied.

Oskar was well onto the bridge before he noticed the crowd lining the river's banks below. The shouting had sounded mischievous to him, lighthearted . . . some obscure local holiday or festival? The thought made him feel more than ever like a stranger.

He stopped and leaned on the bridge railing to watch. He felt the flicker of a smile on his face . . . the smile of one waiting for the meaning of a joke to dawn, aware that he might be its dupe.

Then shots rang out, a sharp report that finally clarified what his eyes were seeing.

A round-faced man was flailing in the middle of the river. His gold-rimmed spectacles flashed queerly in the dusk. The man appeared unable to swim. Several times the pale circle of his face disappeared under the water's surface, then popped up again, the water shattering around him like an ill-omened mirror. Oskar, seeing the man cough and sputter, imagined, through the yells and taunts of the mob on the shore, the sound of choking.

With a frantic effort that somehow looked hopeless, the man neared the western shore. Touching a shallow spot, he lurched upward for a moment against a welt of inflamed sky, escaping the water just enough to make evident how stout he was, how thoroughly weighed down by his dark and sodden clothes. Then he sank again, his face barely afloat on water gone ashen.

Finally, just as his feet seemed to gain lasting purchase on the river's muddy bottom, more shots rang out. The unfortunate man plunged back into the depths that, after a few more minutes of struggle that seemed endless, swallowed all of him.

Oskar stood paralyzed, his grip fast on the railing. The massive bridge seemed to hang above the river by a thread. Only doubt, in the end, set him moving. He told himself he'd imagined what he had seen. There was no longer any crowd. What had appeared an ordinary sampling of Dresden's populace intent upon drowning a man? Not only failing to rescue him, but preventing his least chance of saving himself?

Fanciful and morbid, Oskar chided himself. Fanciful in the extreme. The sloping banks of the Elbe were, on both sides, deserted.

He wished he could say he'd been dreaming. Misinterpreting what he had observed, perhaps? Oskar rushed across the palace grounds and into the house to give the Direktor a breathless account of what had occurred. What *may* have occurred . . .

Hans Posse listened, his face keeping its composure as it lost its color. In the silence that followed, Oskar entertained inane hopes. The

Direktor, a sensible man, native to Dresden, would produce a reasonable explanation—an outdoor morality play, a Saxon rite of spring.

This Posse could not, of course, do. He offered the next best thing. Though the indulgence was customarily postprandial, he pressed a brandy on Oskar. He'd join him, in fact.

Posse waited until their glasses were empty. Then, in the most tactful of terms, he expressed his concern not for the drowned man (that is, the man who may have drowned) but for Oskar.

Delusions were not uncommon, certainly, as battle's nagging aftereffect. And in a man who'd also suffered a head wound, well . . .

Clearly, Oskar was not yet recovered. Not fully. Still, the Direktor could not help hoping this disturbing episode might be attributed to something less alarming than hallucination . . . the surfeit of imagination, for instance, not untypical in artists . . . or (he did not actually voice this possibility) the storyteller's inability to resist embellishment, perhaps?

IT WAS NOTHING OF THE SORT, OF COURSE. WHAT OSKAR HAD REPORTED was, as the Direktor had most feared and somehow known, the truth.

All Dresden was, by the following morning, aware of the lamentable facts. Some middling official or other (Oskar was never entirely clear on details the Direktor was entirely too distressed to discuss) had been pressed into service as scapegoat to the popular mood, which was decidedly unpleasant. All over Europe, the war's epilogue was the breakdown of order, of civility. The currency of reasonable explanations devalued further each day.

Oskar had seen, precisely, what he had seen.

And he kept seeing it. For days afterward all he had to do was close his eyes or, distracted, stare off into space, and the hapless bureaucrat would sink once more below the water. While he himself hung, mute and impotent, above him.

The next afternoon, Oskar's solitary stroll led him to the Grosse Meissner Strasse, where freshly printed public notices fluttered from its numerous pillars and posts: authorities seeking witnesses who could furnish reliable accounts . . .

Sickened now by the sight of the river that in recent weeks had been his one consolation, Oskar ducked inside the Jägerhof. Dresden's folk art seemed, overnight, to have lost its charm. Indeed, something disturbingly devious appeared to infect the entire collection. Malevolence tinged the faces of peasants. Violence animated their labors and even their dances. Their children had the stares of idiots, their villages the tidiness of tyranny. Oskar left in a quarter hour, ashamed that such art could ever have diverted him.

"I suppose I should make a report," he mused over dinner that evening.

Hans Posse looked up from his noodle soup with a blank expression.

"Yesterday's incident."

"You suppose you possess useful information?" The Direktor's flat blue gaze reminded Oskar of the Jägerhof's portrait gallery. "Could you actually identify any of the—"

"I saw a man drown," Oskar said.

"I believe they are aware of that much." Oskar had not before heard sarcasm in the Direktor's voice.

Posse must have noticed it himself. "Forgive me," he murmured. "I simply don't wish to see you involve yourself . . ." For a moment he looked away. "There are certain elements, matters of a local nature, I fear you may not grasp."

"Elements that make murder an acceptable form of expression?"

The Direktor looked stricken. Now it was Oskar's turn to apologize.

"I am not a political animal," he said. "If that was your meaning, you are entirely correct. But mob violence—"

"Don't think I condone it." Posse winced. "I could not bear to have you think that of me."

Oskar, speechless, shook his head. One hand, of its own accord, reached ineffectually across the table as if to calm and comfort the older man.

"You have not been here long," Posse said. "You have been distracted. As a witness to the unfortunate events, you could do no more than confirm what is already known. A man was drowned as others, at the very least, stood by."

"And the shots," Oskar said.

Posse nodded sadly. "You have some idea where they came from? Could indicate a direction or identify the nature of the weapon, perhaps?"

Oskar shook his head.

Posse nodded again. His gaze was steady, yet there was something skittish behind it. *Devious,* Oskar thought, then felt ashamed.

"I merely suggest that by putting yourself forward, you might find you occupy an untenable position. What would be cowardice, if you actually possessed useful information . . ." The Direktor shrugged. "I should call it merely good sense to stay out of an imbroglio such as this when to enter it would, in the end, benefit no one."

"No doubt you are right."

How to argue? Oskar himself was hardly eager to become involved, to dwell on events he'd prefer to forget. Still, Posse's vehemence troubled him, for Oskar sensed in the Direktor a lack of forthrightness he'd not have guessed at, a suggestion of self-interest in his eagerness to keep Oskar from the fray. Perhaps he feared the Museum's fortunes might suffer for political taint, no matter how far removed.

Hans Posse was, in any case, correct: such information as Oskar could offer would hardly have been useful. Nor, given his current instability, was he in any position to assume the least role in any controversy. The death throes of the Empire and the birth pangs of the Republic were turning all of Europe into an arena of upheaval and suffering. Naive to presume Dresden exempt from what, by all accounts, was making Berlin a bloody battleground.

Oskar, of course, had quite had his fill of battlegrounds.

And had, as it turned out, an unforeseen aptitude for forgetting.

In a coach car returning him to the Elbe nearly a year after he'd watched a human life vanish under its treacherously calm surface, Oskar examined that aptitude. Was forgetfulness a character flaw or a saving grace?

That would depend, he supposed, on the nature of what was forgotten.

VERLORENE EIER . . . EGGS GENTLY COAXED INTO THE BOILING BATH, SOON to be rescued, soon, the moment they are white. White and fluffy, rumpled and soft, like tiny bath towels, the Sunday eggs. And again the tender coaxing: slipped from the cradle of a wooden spoon into spinach nests tucked under snowy blankets of cream sauce. A breath of nutmeg, the merest sigh, then the heat of plates warmed in the oven that will sear her fingertips, will leave shiny red patches if . . .

She must move swiftly, swiftly and smoothly to—

Reserl's arms spread over the table like wings. Plates are set before both men at the same moment, a synchronicity so perfect that two dishes touch the linen with a single sound. Her fingertips are scalded, Reserl knows without looking. Their sting and stiffening please her. She would be ashamed if, allowing the burn to rush her, the plates had settled with a thump or clack.

Breakfast late on Sundays, dinner early. This was the way of *der Haushalt,* not that the Direktor had thought to say why. No one went to church. In her village many people went to church. Reserl liked Sundays without quite understanding them.

Larger, more elaborate Sunday meals put her skills as a cook to better use. (Should there be a failure, of course, two meals meant one less chance to redeem herself. But rarely, in the kitchen, need Reserl seek redemption.) Sundays encouraged rich desserts, welcomed florid vegetables unknown in her village. The vendors at the market, old country women mostly, and great talkers, were only too happy to teach Reserl the names of foreign vegetables and how best to prepare them.

Sundays also justified the best cuts of meat, the costliest fish, and most succulent game birds. One could, on the Sabbath, serve delicacies without appearing spendthrift . . . could take the blue dress, saved through the week, down from its nail . . .

Yes, almost like holidays, Sundays in the Direktor's house. Had the Captain stayed away in the mountains, what would have become of this Sunday?

The two men, absorbed in conversation, did not look up when the hot plates came to rest before them. Nor did Reserl look at them. It was improper for a servant to gaze directly at those she served. Except, of course, when being addressed . . . in which case, of course, it was rude *not* to look.

Tutoring her in the ways of a lady's maid, the Captain had unwittingly crushed her.

"You must never speak, unless she speaks first to you . . . but you know this, of course," he said.

Reserl, at pains to conceal her shock, keeps her eyes downcast, her face expressionless.

Unfortunate, then, the Captain's suggestion of "practice," a bit of playacting . . . harmless:

Reserl is directed to smooth the counterpane (it is not rumpled) on the bed, to wipe from the dresser nonexistent dust with an invisible feather duster.

She busies herself with it, he laughs at it: nothing. He bursts into song, claps a hat on his head before reading a newspaper, a clown. Reserl must not look at him . . . must not notice his hat is on backward, his newspaper upside down.

The moment he addresses her, however, Reserl must suspend what she is doing, turn in his direction. Very well. "But look into my eyes, right into them, here." Smiling madly, he points at his eyes, silver darts.

To look, of course, is her undoing. Her eyes swim with tears. His face shimmers. He is testing her. She must not look away.

"Reserl, are you crying?"

"It is nothing, sir." Surely this is the proper response?

He steps closer. Too close. She cannot see his eyes.

He touches her arm.

She looks down. How strange his hand looks on the ragged green sleeve of her dress.

"This is not a game now," he says gently. "All right? You must tell me what is troubling you."

"Would it be all right if I do not look at you?" Reserl whispers.

"That doesn't matter. Not now." Warm fingers bracelet her wrist. "Only tell me what has upset you, Reserl."

She bows her head, spilling the tears from her eyes.

"I have looked at you as I wished . . . I did not know I did wrong."

"No, Reserl," he says. "Not wrong."

She lifts her face and braves his eyes. "I am ignorant."

"I didn't mean—"

"I shame the Direktor." She sounds heartbroken.

"No." His grip tightens on her wrist. "Reserl, listen to me. I was only talking about . . ."

Oskar glances at the divan in the corner, as if someone were there. A sealskin cape, newly arrived from Paris, glistens in the lamplight. He closes his eyes. "We must not forget this is a game," he says.

She does not answer.

"It is only a game, Reserl. Isn't it?" In the dim lamplight his silver eyes look tarnished.

"I do not believe so," she says.

A sudden gust of wind rattles the flimsy windows of the summer-house. Oskar, shivering, lets go of Reserl's arm and steps closer to the stove. He stands there for a moment, keeping his back to her. "You understand," he says, "far more than I've a right to expect."

What could he have meant?

Turning, he reached for her hand. He raised her hand to his mouth. He kissed the inside of her wrist.

Later, Reserl remembers this, telling it to herself over and over, until it seems more like a story than something that could possibly have happened.

The sad tenderness of his lips on her wrist was very much like something Reserl might have imagined.

His lips were cool and dry.

Her wrist, branded by her clumsiness, was ugly and raw.

This much she remembers.

As long as he was not addressing her, she was not, if she understood, obliged to look into his eyes.

Reserl seems to recall staring into the fire, awaiting further instruction.

Weeks later, she is waiting still.

A SECOND BATCH OF HOT ROLLS HAD JUST FLOATED ON A CLOUD OF STEAM and fragrance to the table, when Reserl, refilling the coffee cups, remembered the letter.

It had arrived just after he left. It should, when he returned, have awaited him on his desk, not been left to languish on the silver letter tray in the front hall. She knew how he yearned for each day's post. What had she been thinking? The Captain almost never used the front door.

Should she mention the letter now, Reserl wondered, or wait until he finished his meal? Her hand shook. Hot coffee splashed into the Meissen saucer under his cup.

The Captain seemed not to notice. Reserl dabbed at the spill with the corner of her apron, the white linen apron saved only for Sundays, when . . .

Holding the apron's stained corner away from the skirt of her blue dress, she backed into the hallway. Had he smiled at her as the door swung closed? Her face was on fire.

Reserl soon returned, apronless, to the dining room carrying a small envelope. The paper was thin and the color of buttermilk.

She held it out to him. *"Verzeihung,"* she whispered. Forgive me. She did not look at him. She tried to imagine him smiling at her.

"A fine meal, Hulda," the Direktor said.

The Captain's hand, snatching the envelope, trembled.

"It is nothing," Reserl murmured.

"It is splendid," the Direktor said.

In the refuge of the kitchen, Reserl's hands moved without thought. She heated the water for washing the dishes, put the remaining eggs and butter and cream in the cold pantry. He must be so angry with her. He . . .

By the time she thought of her white apron, tossed to a chair, the coffee had begun to dry. Reserl listened for sounds from the dining room. The two men seemed to be finishing their meal in silence. Once a stain set, you could never get it out.

Perplexed and unsettled by the silence, she waited a long time before returning to the dining room.

The Captain had eaten little. He had not even finished his coffee. The Direktor, on the other hand, appeared to have swiped his plate clean with the last of a roll. The porcelain's cobalt scallops and swirls glistened under a veneer of butter.

Both men had folded their napkins. Like children in a fairy tale, they'd left a litter of bread crumbs behind.

Many Sundays, if the weather was not unpleasant, the Direktor and the Captain would stroll the Zwinger grounds together after their late breakfast.

The March morning was reasonably mild, but the wind was rollicking and rude. She stood at the dining room window, watching rough-and-tumble clouds bump heads as they bullied their way west. The sun looked sallow and out of sorts.

Stillness sat heavily upon the house, stealing its breath.

Reserl imagined the two men in the Grosser Garten, the Direktor pleasantly conversing, while the Captain tried to follow, to grasp . . . while in his pocket the letter, still sealed, smoldered.

Behind him, in cages, captive animals pacing, pacing . . . he did not like to see animals behind bars, the Captain once told her, yet again and again he found himself drawn back to the cages. "When I look into their eyes I feel what they feel," he said. "There are screams in the sounds they make. No one else hears them. All around me children are laughing, while I am—"

Wahnsinnig, Reserl thought. Frantic.

While I am frantic.

HE SNEAKED UP BEHIND HER. HIS RIGHT HAND WAS A BLINDFOLD, HIS LEFT a muzzle. His arms bound her shoulders and waist. He waylaid her like a mischievous boy.

Reserl did not struggle. He had startled her, yes, but she was not afraid. She knew, by now, his scent . . . knew, too, that he must not be angry, for anger would have kept him far away. He was close. He was wrapped around her. The air she breathed was balmy with coffee, with anise candies, with the witch hazel from the green bottle beside his shaving brush.

Chilly fingers slipped from her face, an arm from her shoulders. Still held by the waist, Reserl let herself be twirled from the stove, spun past the pastry table and nearly into the pantry.

The oven door yawned, squandering heat on the kitchen. The prongs of a meat fork were stuck deep in the meat. Rivulets of blood ran into the roasting pan, hissing.

"Freitag, Freitag!" Hot breath sang against her ear. "On Friday she comes, Reserl!"

Upstairs one boot thumped to the floor, then another. The Direktor would be retrieving his carpet slippers from the hearth. He would, in moments, fall asleep in his chair, a book on his lap.

"Hush," Reserl said softly.

"I got him thinking." Oskar laughed. "He hears nothing when he is thinking. You know he doesn't."

He choreographed another giddy whirl, returning her to the stove's hot clutches. Releasing her, he banged the oven door shut. "You must be more careful, my girl." His severe look collapsed in laughter.

"Friday?" Reserl felt dizzy.

"We are not ready, of course, but—" His eyes were glittering. He was flushed. "And bless our dear Direktor, who shall by Friday be safe within Leipzig's walls, haggling over some manuscript . . . or is it a score? Convenient, his business there, whatever it may be." He laughed again.

What on earth was he talking about? Reserl, keeping her eye on him, opened the oven, reached through the heat and wrestled the fork from the roast. She set it carefully on top of the stove. Then, without flinching, she plunged her scorched fingers into the basin of cold water where her apron was soaking. Her gasp made a sizzling sound.

Oskar, naturally, noticed none of this. "On Friday she will be here," he said. "*Mein Gott,* Reserl, we have everything yet to do. Everything!"

He began to pace. *Frantic.* As if the kitchen were a cage.

"I shall have to purchase new bed linens, I think, don't you? And a nightdress, at least one nightdress . . . those I ordered from Battenberg have yet to come. The post is so fickle . . . God knows the local merchandise is far from distinguished . . . I shall have to ask Katja where, I suppose, though how I can broach the subject of nightdresses and pillow slips without arousing her suspicion . . . supposing Katja is still speaking to me, which I suspect she is not."

He was addressing her, yes . . . but really, *was* he? Reserl's gaze, set adrift, wafted to the window. He wasn't looking at her anyway. A slight drizzle was falling in the garden. She'd hoped her apron might dry outdoors. Now it must hang from a hook in her dim, damp room . . . would never smell as clean and who knew when it might be dry? A brown shadow shaped oddly like a large nose on its lower right corner . . . no longer fit, no matter how faint the stain, for Sundays.

Nightdresses from Battenberg . . . soft and white as flour, and fluted at wrist and neck and hem with lace. Battenberg lace, unlike any other . . . incomparably beautiful for its simplicity, the Captain said.

He kept talking.

Reserl turned away.

Reaching into the cold water with both hands, she chafed a block of coarse yellow soap against the stain on her apron. Maybe later, soaked in bleach, not too long, not too much, just . . .

Or salt.

Or the juice of a lemon, perhaps, the light of the sun.

Behind her he whispered and paced.

Wahnsinnig. Frantic.

As if she were not there.

14

Each day, all day, she waited. Some word from him, some sign that would tell her that he wanted her, in the evening, to come to him.

None was given. Not a word, not a sign.

Reserl scarcely saw him, in fact, except at the table. The Captain ate little, ate quickly, returned as soon as possible to his rooms. His windows long past midnight blazed with light.

So much for her still to learn . . . had he forgotten? *Someone must help me . . . there is only you.* Perhaps he had changed his mind. Perhaps he was angry with her after all.

He left in a rush each morning, a film of distraction over his eyes. Each evening he returned later and later until, but for spring's stretching light, he would have come home in darkness.

He arrived, as it was, in twilight. He stepped inside quietly, his arms loaded with parcels.

"Ah, there you are!" The Direktor, idling over some journal while awaiting the call to dinner, looked relieved. His *Guten Abend* was pleasant. Had the Captain enjoyed the day? Feeling well? he hoped.

Oh, yes. Quite well. Quite well indeed. Oskar seemed vaguely startled, as if Posse did not belong there, in his own parlor.

Neither man made reference to Oskar's encumbered arms. The packages caused less curiosity than fret. The Direktor could not help worrying over his guest's financial straits. It was not a subject he'd dream of alluding to, of course.

IT WAS WEDNESDAY EVENING. HANS POSSE WOULD LEAVE IN THE MORNING.

Leipzig's lure was, in fact, a manuscript, a Schiller fair copy whose provenance was in some doubt. The Gemäldegalerie could hardly afford it in any case. Still, it would be a treat, the Direktor thought, to examine it, to rub elbows over it with colleagues he hadn't seen in too long. The trip would freshen his mind.

Reserl, whisking clean shirts to his room, found the Direktor packing. The sleeves of the shirts, stiff with starch, flailed from their hangers as she hung them in the wardrobe.

The Direktor, stuffing rumpled pajamas into his bag, thanked her absently. The scuff and slouch of his leather valise reminded her of an old saddle.

"Let me do that for you," she said.

Hans Posse looked startled. "There's no need," he said kindly.

The Captain had, several weeks ago, shown her the niceties of preparing for travel—tissue-wrapped garments rolled rather than folded, to prevent wrinkling, soft flannel bags to keep shoes from soiling the clothes . . .

"I know how to do it properly."

Her quiet certainty surprised him. "I'm sure you do." Hans Posse smiled and took a shirt from a hanger. "I am nearly finished, in any case," he said.

"Shall I turn down your bed?"

"That won't be—"

He saw her need to do something for him. "Yes, Hulda. Thank you," he said.

A solid four-poster of pecan wood dominated the room. The bed had come, with his wife, from Pirna. He watched as the girl pulled back a brown worsted bedcover. He remembered how different the room had looked when his wife shared it: a pale flowered quilt, rosy silk lampshades. It had not been Hans Posse's intention to change things, yet it seemed he had. The room, become his own, had turned spartan and subdued. For years an embroidered cloth had draped the nightstand, its scalloped hem dragging on the floor. What in the world had become of it? How many other reminders of my Marthe, he wondered, have I care-lessly ruined or discarded or mislaid?

Hulda, turning back a triangle of gray woolen blanket, exposed fresh linens the color of cream, pillowcases worn soft, sheets often darned.

"You take such good care of me," he murmured. "Of us."

Her reply was low. His hearing was starting to fail, he thought. He watched how the girl's mouth shaped thanks, *Danke . . .* carefully. Does everything, our Hulda, with such care.

"What a wonderful wife you will be." A natural thought, a sincere sentiment . . . but he hadn't meant to say it aloud. Now the girl was blushing. An apology would merely prolong her embarrassment.

"You'll find money with the matches in the tin on the parlor mantel," he said. "For anything that's needed while I am gone. I'll be back Satur-day . . . I can't say just when, but surely before dinner."

"Yes, sir." Reserl smoothed the pillows, straightened the hem of the top sheet.

"Hulda?"

She had crossed the room to close the heavy drapes. Her fingers seemed reluctant, letting go of the cord. She turned around slowly. She is starting to feel at home here, the Direktor thought. She must be. Her gazes lately, when he spoke to her, were less bashful, steadier and more direct.

"May I take you into my confidence?" he said.

She waited with the attentiveness of a wild creature hearing a footfall in a forest.

"I am concerned about Professor Kokoschka," Hans Posse said. "The past week or so, he seems . . ."

Something like fear perturbed her gaze.

"I don't mean to suggest—" He cleared his throat. "Does he seem to you more . . . perhaps I imagine it, but . . . less sturdy, somehow? More as he was when he first came to us? He worries me."

The girl did not move. Her stillness was effortful, will pitted against the desire to flee. Surely she didn't think he was blaming *her?*

"You do all you can, Hulda. I know that. I only wondered if you . . ."

Her hands were clasped in front of her. Her knuckles whitened.

Suddenly the Direktor found himself missing his wife, longing for her in a way he had not in years. A difficult woman, Marthe, but intelli-gent, insightful. Someone with whom a man could *discuss* things. He sighed.

"I fear the Professor is still more . . . fragile, I suppose, than I cared to realize. Likely time will do more for him than you or I can. But if you observe anything . . ." Hans Posse shrugged with resignation. "It would not be improper for you to report to me, should there be cause for concern, Hulda. You understand?"

She nodded. Nodded perhaps too quickly to assure the Direktor he'd made himself clear.

"Well." His sigh excused her. He returned to his packing with a kindly and hopeless smile.

Reserl went to the window and finished closing the drapes.

"Is there anything you need, sir?"

"Everything is fine," Hans Posse said.

She was looking into his eyes again, but now seemed unaware she was doing so.

The Direktor looked down into his bag, trying to recall . . . had he included socks? "Good night, Hulda."

He felt her pass behind him. He did not hear her reply. But that is my fault, Hans Posse thought, not the girl's. He hoped he was not on his way to becoming one of those cranky old men waving an ear trumpet about like a weapon . . . they never seemed to hear anything anyway, poor souls, and spent their last years terrorizing everybody with their frustration.

The Direktor dropped a pair of boots into his valise. He did not notice the gray imprints their heels left on the front of an Egyptian cotton shirt, generously starched, impeccably pressed.

ZERBRECHLICH, THE DIREKTOR HAD SAID. FRAGILE.

Brittle. Something too easily broken. Like the tiny gold-rimmed coffee cups she fears might shatter in her hands. *Does he seem to you . . . less sturdy somehow?*

And he saw, the Direktor, who thinks she is still Hulda . . . he saw that she shares his fear. Reserl, too, is—yes, afraid.

She tries to imagine . . . how did he put it? *Reporting to him,* yes? The Direktor said, *It would not be improper . . .*

Reserl tries to think of words that might fashion a credible account of all she knows but does not understand of the Captain: *goddess* and *love* and *serve* and *heart* and *help me* and *no one else* and *sorry.* The

Direktor is a learned man, a man of much experience and understanding. Still, Reserl cannot imagine what he would make of the story she might fashion of such words, the more true the less believable and . . . he could, in the end, only send them away if he knew, banish both of them—Reserl and the Captain . . . and what of the goddess in her packing crate?

Friday. The Direktor would send them, all three, away, if he knew.

THE SUN IS SINKING. THE CAPTAIN HAS RETURNED, WEIGHED DOWN WITH more parcels. A spray of spring flowers in a cone of violet paper has disappeared into the summerhouse with him, one pure white petal dropped at the threshold like a clue.

Fog paces through a garden heedless of flowers. Its beds are promiscuous but barren. Reserl, snatching the Direktor's blue-striped pajamas from the clothesline one step ahead of evening's dampness, keeps glancing at the petal on the mossy stone step. She wants to claim it, rescue it from the crush of his heel. But what if he should open the door and find her there?

She returns, dejected, to the kitchen, where she stirs the veal stew he is sure to rebuff. He eats nothing. Next to nothing. She covers his neglected plates, saves the food as if he might ask for it later, as if she might eat it herself. She waits until the food spoils. Then she adds it to the compost heap at the garden's back corner.

The Direktor is gone. Tomorrow is Friday. This evening the Captain will surely call for her . . . any moment now he could come looking for her.

Then it is dark. The summerhouse windows glow, a mute cry of light. The Captain does not come to the house for dinner. Should she call him? He has always, despite a fickle appetite, come in of his own accord. Each evening between half past six and seven he appears.

Reserl goes to the parlor and looks at the ormolu clock above the fireplace. It is after seven o'clock. She returns to the kitchen. There is numbness in her fingertips. Her hands are not accustomed to idleness. She touches her earlobes often, and her collarbone, surprised each time by the earrings and the beads. She has until now worn the ornaments only in her room, where the skin of her ears and neck appear white as potatoes in the sail-shaped mirror.

I must eat, she thinks. But she is not hungry. And what if the Captain should rush in to find shreds of meat in her teeth, grease on her lips? Why does he not come? Reserl is certain that putting food in her mouth will cause the door to open, letting dampness creep in from the garden . . . letting him catch her . . .

She opens the back door just wide enough to look through the crack with one eye. The dim light seems to flutter, as if inside the summerhouse a single flame is fanned by a frenzy of wings. Reserl closes the door and, for a moment, leans against it.

WHEN NOTHING IS LEFT TO SHINE, WHEN THE SILVER AND MARBLE AND brass gleam throughout the house and all the polishing cloths are black with tarnish and grit, when the parlor clock announces midnight, Reserl goes at last to bed.

She will not sleep. Reserl knows this as, still dressed, she lies on her cot and covers herself with the blanket. She will not sleep. She does not care to. She simply does not know what else to do, so she lies down.

One . . . two . . . three . . . a chime, sweet and distant, keeps strict account of the hours. She observes each by rising, going to the window. Two parallel swatches of frail light waver over the garden. She tries to imagine the Captain inside, doing . . .

Reserl cannot imagine what he might be doing.

She repeats her ritual observance when the clock chimes four. This time, however, when she leaves the window, Reserl does not return to her cot. Grappling with the dark, she finds her boots, slides her bare bone-cold feet into them. She leaves her room, crosses the kitchen, and goes out the back door. Her untied laces drag behind her.

In a patch of dirt, bereft and weedy, she crouches below the window. The blunt toes of her boots sink into the damp earth. She steadies herself by holding on to the sill. Her hands will be filthy. Her heels do not touch the ground.

Reserl, peering in, thinks, *I am seeing a dream.*

Candles flicker everywhere, burning low with the waning night. Every flat surface the room has to offer is engraved with ornate drips of melted wax. It is as if the world's last light has come to this room to die.

This room . . . *his* room . . . the Captain's room in the summerhouse. Reserl knows where she is, but nothing is as she knows it. This must be a dream. Surely she is dreaming?

The bed, from the arched top of its high headboard to its scrolled foot, is draped. A gush of cloth the color of currant jelly overflows the mattress, swirls in eddies on the floor . . . bolts and bolts of glistening cloth, the bed a waterfall, shining red.

And gold: lace and satin and ribbons and fringes of it. Gold pillows in a mound at the head of the bed. On the divan, more gold: pillows heaped at each end. And above, on the wall, imprisoned in golden fili-gree, a painting.

Though half its length and breadth, the painting seems to dwarf the bed. The moment she sees it, the rest of the room fades. Naked, the man and the woman embrace, a dance of melding flesh, entwining limb. But they are not dancing, no, their feet are rooted. Their legs rise out of the ground, solid and defiant as ancient trees. The air around them blooms, fertile and turbulent. Bold slashes of color hint at the taste of fruits, the fragrance of flowers.

The woman's face, cold and white and beautiful, is the face of, yes, a goddess. The man's face, hollow and haunted, could be no one else's.

Reserl is overcome suddenly with horror and shame, as if by giving herself to the painting, she has intruded upon their coupling. Closing her eyes, wrenching her attention away, she turns her back on the painting.

Through a scrim of yellow candlelight, she sees that the writing table has stepped out from the wall to claim the room's center. How does she even recognize it, his homely desk, in its disguise of parchment-colored lace? Its squat and sturdy shape, perhaps? The cloth is embellished with gold thread. Its edge, a golden blade, slices into the blood-red carpet.

A crystal decanter, two glasses like long-stemmed crystal flowers, iced cakes on a cut-glass plate, fluted silver bowls of candies and nuts, dried figs . . . the table's glare and plenty make her wince and she wants, for a moment, to close her eyes once more. Surely she is dreaming . . .

Except in a dream he would not be . . . would not have . . . would not look so . . .

She rises from the flower bed. The hem of her skirt is wet against her calves. She enters the room without making a sound.

He stands beside the stove, dim in its shadow. His trousers, loose at the waist, hang low on his hips, black suspenders dragging from them. He wears no shirt. His feet are bare. Heating something in the small nicked pan, he spreads his large red hands over the heat. His head hangs as if under the weight of a dreadful accusation he cannot deny.

Reserl would never dream him this way . . . her Captain.

Has he no awareness of her, behind him? She wants to touch the back of his neck. *Zerbrechlich,* she thinks. Brittle. She looks down at her hands. She imagines his spine snapping like the stem of a feather at her merest touch.

"When will you sleep?" she whispers.

He does not start or turn around. "There is no time." As if she has been there all along.

"What more can be done?" Her voice remains hushed, as if somewhere in the room someone is sleeping.

He turns to smile at her. "You don't see?"

"It is beautiful."

He shakes his head sadly. "I have burned up all the candles."

"There is money," Reserl says after a moment. "I will go when the shops open. You must sleep."

His laughter is not cruel, but like something he wishes to share with her. He looks steadily into her eyes. Like music, his laugh. Relieved of words, Reserl smiles at him.

He glances around the transformed room, shaking his head as if trying to clear it. He does not look at her again. Reserl bends down and pulls off her boots. The carpeted floor warms her feet as she walks through the room, blowing out the candles.

A fat pillar of beeswax in a pewter holder with a handle shaped like an ear burns beside the bed. Reserl leaves this one candle burning. Its flame is bright and constant.

She turns back the brocade spread and folds it neatly at the foot of the bed. She removes all but two of the pillows and folds back the sheet.

"You must sleep now," she says.

In a pirouette of smoke he turns to her. "That is impossible," he says.

The thick, soft carpet seems to give off its own heat. Her cold toes burrow into its nap as she crosses the room.

There is no use to argue. No place in this for words at all. Her feet, her hands, her whole body oddly supple and sure now, she is relieved of the need for words. She imagines ancient roots under her legs. He does not resist her when, grasping his shoulders, she steers him toward the bed.

She feels the force of the painting above the bed, trying to pull her into it. She imagines her face concealed by a mask of ice. Unfastening his trousers, she pulls them down, taking his drawers with them. When she touches his ankle, he steps meekly from the pile of cloth.

She gestures with one hand toward the bed. He sits on its edge, sighing deeply. His legs, all bone and skin, put up no fight when she lifts, then lowers and covers them.

"The linens," he whispers.

She can see they are new, of course, and costly. A border of embroidered plumes, fine silvery stitches, for a moment steal her gaze from his face. Pale-gray thread . . . silk, she thinks. Feathery shadows scattered over linen so white . . . *it will never be so white again, the linen, and*—

"Reserl?"

"Close your eyes," she says.

"There will be creases."

"I will take care of it."

"Everything must be perfect."

She nods.

She understands.

Slowly his eyes begin to close.

"Sometime after two o'clock," he murmurs. "No later, surely, than three."

She leans down. Her lips are close to his ear. The scent of gardenias drifts up from the pillow. "It will be perfect."

All she means to promise him does not fit into the words she whispers.

He seems not to notice. Or perhaps, trusting her, he simply does not mind that the words fall short.

The flame burns low and steadfast above the solitary candle. Light pools on the bed. Reserl, barefoot, hovers at its edge, looking down. His face is yellowish against the pillow slip. There are sooty smudges around his eyes. Just as in the painting. She does not look up. She sees nothing but his face.

She waits for a long time. When his lids seem to float upon his eyes and his lips softly separate to ease the passage of his breath, Reserl blows out the last candle.

SHE STANDS OUTSIDE IN THE COLD DRIZZLE OF MORNING. WATER TICKS from the roof of the summerhouse. It is nearly half past eight. If she does not wake him now, this moment, he will not arrive at the Academy in time to meet his class. Each morning he leaves, without fail, before nine. Even if she wakes him quickly, there will be no time now for breakfast.

Reserl presses her ear to the door. Perhaps he is dressing. She imagines him shaving in haste, starting at the sound of her entrance. She pictures the razor slicing into his cheek, drops of blood springing up along the gash, glistening red as pomegranate seeds. She shivers.

There is no sound. Only the *tick-tick-tick* of the water hitting the stone step, flicking the glossy new leaves of the bushes that wreath the summerhouse. She looks down. The white petal is gone.

The door groans open. She winces. The mound on the bed does not move. Reserl crosses the room on silent feet and stands beside the bed. Only when she stops breathing can she hear the soft ebb and flow of his breath. Then she is able to breathe again.

The room's light is like pewter, burnished and gray. The air smells smoky. Still, there is a clarity to the room that betrays the night's secrets, the candlelight's disguises. The red drapery, the gold pillows and tassels are raveling and dull, the carpet in spots stained and threadbare. Lumps and drips of melted wax deface the tabletops.

He lies on his back, one bent arm thrown over his face as if to ward off a blow, a blinding flash. His mouth, slightly open, is twisted in something resembling horror. Reserl tries to imagine what he might see in dreams. She wonders if, awake, he tells himself stories, gentle tales to drive off all that assaults him in sleep.

She looks at his face and thinks, I must wake him. Right now. She imagines pulling his hand from his eyes, welcoming him in a soft voice back to a washed and wakened world. *Friday,* she would whisper. She is coming. *Today.* But her hand will not move, her voice cannot be found.

She will not, cannot, wake him.

THE RAIN, AS SHE STEPPED OUTSIDE, QUICKENED. BUT SHE DID NOT TURN back for an umbrella, for an oilskin to huddle under. No time. Cold rain streaked her face, invaded her clothes. Icy fingers of water crept down her belly and her spine.

The grand, widely spaced houses of the Zwinger looked incidental against the great green sweep of the gardens. The palace was a distant-looming shadow. Abandoned. The rain made everything look deserted.

By the time Reserl reached the home of the Direktor's nearest neighbor, Dr. Hagedorn, her hair was streaming, her clothing drenched.

"Hulda! *Mein Gott,* what has happened?" The alarm on Valda's chubby face did not quite conceal a certain hopefulness. The doctor's young housemaid was ravenous for gossip. Catching a whiff of the least drama or disgrace, her nostrils would flare, making her look like a horse.

She cannot help herself, Reserl thought. She touched the girl's hand to reassure her. Valda flinched and let out a shriek.

"It's all right," Reserl said.

"A hand like a corpse is all right? Blue lips, too, I suppose are fine?"

Reserl's smile felt stiff. "Herr Doktor Hagedorn, he is in?"

"Someone is ill . . . Herr Posse?"

Reserl began to shake her head, then reconsidered. "The Captain," she said.

Valda gave her a blank look.

"Our guest."

"The young man with the odd silver eyes?"

"The Professor," Reserl said.

"He looks awfully shabby, doesn't he, for a professor." Her disappointment at provoking no reaction was obvious. "He is very ill, then?"

"Only a little, but to teach today? Not in such weather."

Valda looked amused. "You have become a mother? *Alles Gute!*"

"He is feverish." Heat bloomed in Reserl's face.

"You might have drowned."

"The Direktor has gone to Leipzig."

"What is in Leipzig?"

Time was flying past. Reserl could almost see it, as if from a speeding coach. The kitchen was warm. She was sweating. "I must send word—"

"To Leipzig?" Valda looked scornful.

"To the Academy," Reserl said. "The Professor cannot—"

"Ach, you wish to borrow *Die Heuschrecke!*"

Jakob, the doctor's yard and stable and errand boy, was an orphan from Valda's home village. She called him "the grasshopper" for his nervous habit of standing on one foot and rubbing his legs together.

"I am sorry to ask this," Reserl said.

"Perhaps a walk in the rain will wake him up." Valda laughed.

The boy, too, seemed delighted by the prospect of an errand. He did not mind a little rain, he said. Reserl followed him outside, ducking under a waterfall from the house's high eaves. Valda was watching from the kitchen window. Reserl waited until she and the boy were out of sight before reaching into her apron pocket for the red coin purse.

Jakob looked at the note she handed him as if he had never before held so much money in his hand. And perhaps he had not, Reserl thought.

"You will hurry?"

His quick nod might have been a tic.

"You remember what to say?"

"Professor Kokoschka is ill. He apologizes to his students."

Then the boy seemed to wait for something more. Not more money, surely? "Yes?" Reserl said.

"Who do I tell this to?"

"Oh," she said.

The boy shifted to one leg and stared at her, as the heel of his boot scraped up and down his shin. His wiry, fox-red hair had gone flat and dark in the rain. His bones showed through his soaked shirt. He could not be more than twelve, Reserl thought.

"I'm afraid I don't know," she said.

He stood on two feet again. "I'll tell someone," he said.

Beneath a ragged parasol of dripping linden branches, Reserl watched Jakob bound toward the avenue. He leaped like a stag over puddles that looked, through the rain, like mirrors. How wonderful, she thought, to run so lightly, not slowed in the least by uncertainty.

The resemblance dawned on her just as the boy was on the verge of disappearing—the flame in his thick hair, the sharpness of his bones. She might have been his sister. But Reserl, even as a child, had lacked Jakob's nonchalance. She walked slowly through the downpour, in each step the weight of all she could not know.

OSKAR AWOKE TO WINDOWS STREAKED WITH RAIN. BEHIND THEM THE SKY was so dim he took it for dawn. I've barely slept, he thought. I have not slept at all. He groped on the bedstand for his pocket watch. Its face sent him into a panic. Nearly noon . . . half the day gone, so much yet to do, and his class . . .

No, no, his class was seen to, of course. He'd told his students he'd not be able to meet them today, that Professor Löwenblatt, whose own class met in the afternoon, would stand in for him.

Der Blätterteig had naturally been curious, but too courteous to inquire. Oskar was glad he'd not had to tell his friend the shoddy story he'd concocted, an imaginary funeral . . . such fabrications, his mother warned, teased fate. Many a fib turned into prophecy. Utter nonsense, of course. Oskar did not believe in curses. Still, there was just enough of Romana's Gypsy blood in his veins to make him shudder. Today, of all days, to flirt with a hex . . .

As he leaped from the bed, pain shot through his head. Had he drunk a whole bottle of wine last night? He looked at the lace-covered table. The glasses were clean and empty. A fresh bottle, its cork intact, stood between them. Slowly Oskar's eyes surveyed the room. The writhing veins, the puddles and stubs of melted wax were gone. Dozens of white candles stood around the room, their curling virginal wicks like haloes.

Reserl, he thought. She could shock him, now and then, with the depths of her understanding, her resourcefulness. But—

Oskar frowned. She should have wakened me hours ago, he thought. So much yet to be done and she will arrive in three hours, could be here in two. There were not enough flowers. The linens could not be laundered, too late for that now, even without the rain. He'd never imagined rain, had always been certain she would appear on a spring afternoon spendthrift with sunshine and birdsong and bloom, while now—

A low rumble of thunder drew his eyes to the window. A frazzled wire of lightning twitched through the sky and left him close to weeping. Oskar, lowering his head to his chest, became aware of his body, its nakedness, its bitter and brackish odor. I must bathe, he thought. The rest—

He was no longer able to remember the many other pressing things for which he'd reserved the morning that, now, was lost.

Reserl, her hands occupied with a small silver tray, entered without knocking. The tray, highly polished, pierced the dim room with a glare.

"My head," Oskar said.

"You must eat something," Reserl said.

Neither seemed aware of his nakedness.

She set the tray at the foot of the bed.

"For God's sake, be careful," he said.

Smiling, she lifted the crowned lid of a small silver pot. The brisk savor of coffee enlivened the air.

"I must have a bath, Reserl."

She nodded. "The water is heating," she said.

He stood at the foot of the bed and tried to think what he was supposed to be doing. "I am so tired," he said. He was shivering.

"Here." She handed him a silk dressing gown, a paisley of brown and gold and blue.

"Where did this come from?"

"The Direktor keeps it for guests." *Für die Gäste.*

"I am *ein Pensionär,*" Oskar said. A paying guest, though God knew how long it had been since . . . he studied the embroidered hem of a sheet.

"Put it on," Reserl said. "You are chilled."

He did as he was told.

She would prepare the bath while he ate, she said. Oskar smiled. *I will move the water* were the words she used. He watched her wipe a speck of dust from the headboard. He saw nothing but devotion on her face. She probably is, in an odd way, beautiful, he thought. If he painted her, her beauty would become apparent to him. He had sworn, had he not, that he would not paint her. But why? He could not recall his reasons, only his vow.

"I will see to the bath now," she said.

She would move the water.

She would, Oskar thought, move heaven and earth if he required it.

The door closed behind her.

A breath of rain had entered the room.

Oskar tightened the sash of the dressing gown. He warmed his hands on the coffee pot's silver belly and wondered if he shouldn't, after all, try to eat just a little something.

A WONDER THE WAIT, HE WOULD LATER THINK, DID NOT DRIVE HIM MAD. By the time she arrived, it was nearly five o'clock. The train had been delayed for several hours outside Crimmitschau, where the track had been occupied and mistreated by a herd of petulant cattle. Charolais, to be specific. But Oskar could not, at the time, have known such details.

Not to say possible explanations did not occur to him:

Fräulein Moos, a shameless schemer, had betrayed him—why?

His Almi, so easily seduced, had been spirited from the train by a dashing young cavalry officer with a scar on his cheek. The scar was surprisingly attractive.

Customs agents, suspecting contraband, had seized the crate.

Unless, of course, it had fallen off the freight car.

Hermine Moos? No dollmaker by that name was known in Stuttgart.

Stuttgart? Herr Richter recalled providing no address. Why, Oskar's very description of the exhibit (dolls? in a prestigious gallery of the avant-garde?) suggested, did it not, the fanciful spasms of an overheated imagination?

All too easily could Oskar's imagination conceive of ruin, many and various its forms. A train impeded in the middle of nowhere by cheeky French cows, however, was not among them.

The packing crate, when at last he spotted two young louts in tight breeches and insolent caps jarring it down the alleyway, nearly made him cry out. It was half the length it should have been to contain her comfortably. Picturing his beloved doubled up inside this cramped receptacle, Oskar nearly vomited.

The delay, however, brought one benefit: The rain had been wrung out of the clouds. The afternoon had given way to warm sun and a glossy blue sky. Persian, Prussian, cerulean . . . *bleu lumière,* Oskar thought, as he ran through dizzy circles of gold and azure light to unlatch the gate.

"Herr Kokosnuß?" one of the youths inquired.

His cohort guffawed. "Mister Coconut!"

The color of the sky was piercing as a whistle. Oskar closed his eyes for a moment. "Right here," he said.

"You don't want us to bring it inside?"

The sun was burning a hole in the crown of his head. *A corona of flame bursting from his brain like . . .* "I am going to faint," he whispered.

Then he felt her firm grip on his arm, heard her voice, soft and certain and sane. "Yes, inside the small house, just here," she said.

"Our pleasure, Fräulein," said the taller youth, the one who had been laughing.

By the time the spell of dizziness passed, the crate had been bumped through the door and Reserl was still holding his arm.

"I am all right," Oskar said.

She nodded and let go of his arm. Then she reached into her apron and fished out the scuffed red leather pouch. The pouch rustled and clanked with currency.

"They have been paid," Oskar said. "In advance."

Neither Reserl nor the youths seemed to hear him. She sorted through the purse and produced two bills, handing one to each boy. *"Danke,"* she said. *"Vielen Dank."*

The tall one pulled some sort of small crowbar from the waistband of his breeches. "We shall open it for you?" He was looking at Reserl with an odd intensity. Lovestruck, Oskar thought. How peculiar to see anyone, even so raw a lad, look this way at his Reserl.

"No," Oskar said.

"You are very kind," said Reserl. "But it isn't necessary." Her smile turned the boy's sallow face gaudy.

Then they were, all three of them, gone, evaporating like gnomes in a fairy tale, and Oskar was inside the door throwing himself on the crate, clawing at its slats, tearing his nails, driving splinters into his fingers.

The wood, frail as it appeared, defied him.

"Wait."

He looked down. Blood dripped from his fingers, dropping onto the crate. He was sobbing.

"Let me help you." Her right hand clutched one of his old palette knives. Yes, his. But where had she got it? How? Its handle was spattered with an ancient gore of paint.

The nails, parting from the wood, groaned. One by one the slats clattered to the floor. He would not have guessed so slight a body could contain such force. "Thank you."

She stepped back then, allowing him to lift away the top she had freed.

Oskar, leaning forward, placed his hands on it. Reserl was looking at him, her face small and pale and oddly blank. Then everything turned black and tiny pins were pricking him from his scalp to the soles of his feet.

"No," he said. "It can't—"

She grasped him, with both arms, from behind. Holding him in a grip that made his ribs ache, she kept him, just barely, from sinking to the floor.

Then, somehow, he was in a chair, his head between his knees. Waves of nausea and faintness broke just above him. Fingers dug into the tendons at the top of his shoulders, the base of his neck. She was hurting him. The pain was his thready tie to consciousness.

"All right now?" she asked after a while.

"Better, yes." He began to lift his head, then quickly dropped it again. "You mustn't let me go," he said. "Not yet."

Keeping her hold on him, she edged around to the front of his chair. "You need water."

"No," he said. "Wait."

He concentrated on breathing, small scuds of urgent air drawn through his nose. He kept his lips pressed tightly together, as if the smallest chink between them would be a surrender to sickness.

He did not notice when she let him go, nor wonder, when at last his eyes opened, how she had come to be crouched in front of him. She held a glass of water to his lips. She did not release the glass when his hands reached for it. Her fingers, beneath his, were warm and dry.

Oskar sipped slowly. The dimming and sparking in the air around him stopped. The crate was somewhere behind her. Her face loomed before him, blocking his view. Her mouth was pilfering his air. Her breath was stale, her flesh musty. He imagined, for an instant, shoving her backward. He saw her sprawled, small and still, among the splintered slats on the floor.

"I am fine," he said.

She sighed softly. As if making restitution for breaths she'd robbed him of.

"It's all right, Reserl."

When she did not move or release him, his gaze shifted reluctantly, resentfully, to her face. She was too close for clarity. Could he have imagined her beautiful? Such docility in a woman's eyes was cloying, such softness in a mouth humdrum.

"Let me up." He jumped to his feet as if she were not there. Had she not so swiftly removed herself, he might have toppled her.

He returned to the crate. Her assumption of a place beside him there enraged him. Unreasonably, he knew. Fury flexed in his chest like a muscle.

"Reserl," he said, "look at the way you are dressed."

She looked down in confusion. The skirt of her blue dress was pressed. Her apron was spotless.

"When Madame first lays eyes on you, surely you wouldn't wish to be seen without your proper—?"

Her fingers fidgeted at her earlobes, her throat. Her face hid nothing—distress and humiliation at being deemed unsatisfactory, of course. But also betrayal: Why had she not been told before now?

"Shall I wear the uniform, then?" she asked softly.

"And the hair." He stared. "Something must be done about the hair."

She nodded, her eyes lowered, and began to turn away.

"Wait."

So cool and quiet a voice . . . it seemed to startle both of them. She froze beside the door. He lunged toward her, as if she were about to flee. His hand reached for her throat. "This will not do." His fingers closed around the cheap glass beads.

How readily the string broke.

Bright bits of yellow scattered around them like seed. The beads, so tawdry against her scrawny white neck, on the carpet fell into a kind of beauty.

Oskar's gaze returned grudgingly to her plain face. "Earrings?" he said. "A proper maid does not wear jewelry. What were you thinking, Reserl?"

He was being cruel. He knew it. But kinder, he thought, than Almi would be. She would need a tougher hide, Reserl. He had her best interests at heart.

She mumbled something—some little apology, no doubt. Her eyes were quick and bright with tears.

"No harm done," Oskar said. "I'll take care of things here." He smiled at the packing crate. "Go make yourself presentable. When we need something, we'll let you know."

He supposed she left quickly. She left without making a sound.

He was, understandably, distracted. And still recovering, of course.

Had his darling, Oskar wondered, observed his little bout of faintness? I mustn't be embarrassed, he thought. His dizziness was not so much a sign of weakness as a gauge of passion . . . she fainted herself, Almi, with some regularity. As befit a creature of such titanic passions. Delicious to recall . . . to *anticipate,* he corrected himself.

Oskar clung to the crate's edge and, doubling over, rested his damp brow on the hard ridge of his knuckles. He wanted to remember everything, for only the senses' recall could substantiate yearning . . . without the lips' memory, the eyes', the tongue's, what was to set apart expectancy from mere fantasy? What was to authenticate *hope?*

His mouth filled with her taste. His lungs hoarded the scent of her.

Oskar lifted his head and straightened his back. The crate, stunted and crude, was like a pauper child's coffin . . .

The child would be nearly six now.

What was he thinking? The child never came to mind. The child had never existed.

Late daylight slanted in through the summerhouse windows. The sunset must look like a blood orange, Oskar thought. Its light, already crimson, poured over the carpet, hunting down each escaped bead, tinting the saffron glass to tangerine and marigold, Tangier and Spanish ocher.

Almi, my beautiful eye.

15

The sunset was, in the end, disappointing, a faint blush on a twilight placid and wan. Reserl, awkward in the unfamiliar black dress and thin stockings and delicate boots, vacillated in the dining room window, watching the western sky. She thought of the old General, how in his last weeks there was each morning less and less color in his face. When he had at last died, his white cheeks had the same grayish cast as unbaked piecrust.

I shall bake a pie. Tomorrow the Direktor will return. Tomorrow before the light leaves the sky. An apricot pie and the whole house will smell, as he comes through the door, of butter and sugar and fruit and spice. All is well, she will tell him, and he will say, How glad I am to be home, Hulda, and sitting across from the Captain at the polished mahogany table he will, the Direktor, taste the pie and look up and see her and smile.

A sound in the garden banished the smile. Reserl, her whole being given to listening, stopped breathing.

Nothing.

Why had she been thinking about tomorrow? Because I am waiting, Reserl thought. I do not know what I am waiting for and so I don't know how to think about this day, its next moment. *It is all I know how to think of . . . tomorrow.*

Again a sound in the garden, louder this time, no blaming imagination. Sharp and wild, the sound, like the bawling of the wolves that roamed the wood outside the village, and even her father some nights, hearing the cries, was afraid.

There were, Reserl knew, no wolves in Dresden. Only the one in his cage in the Grosser Garten and he was bound to die soon, the Captain said, unless the zookeeper found him a wife. *Without a mate he will pine away,* said the Captain, making the Direktor laugh and making Reserl sad and worried. "Such a romantic you are, Oskar," Hans Posse said.

A romantic meant something like a hero, Reserl thought. The Captain was a hero, yes. The Captain had been a hero in the war.

The dining room windows were draped in heavy velvet. The velvet was the color of moss. The fringed gold cords tying back the drapes were nearly as big around as Reserl's wrists. Folds deep enough, she thought, to hide in.

Again the sound. Reserl reached, without meaning to, for the sash of a drape, then found she could not let go. She must look . . . she must go see what was making the sound of wolves in the garden.

Are you laughing, Fräulein? Is this a joke?
Please tell me this monstrosity is not the final outcome
of your labors and my dreams.

Yours in despair,
OK

HE WAS NOT IN THE GARDEN. THE SUMMERHOUSE DOOR REMAINED CLOSED. The shutters blocked the windows. He would call for her, he said. He had told her to wait. The sound like a wolf could have been laughter.

But it was the Captain. And she knew the sound. Reserl knew the sound of grief.

Only not just that, no. Something weightier, more cruel and more final, than grief. *Die Verzweiflung,* she thought.

Despair. It was not a word of much use, apart from stories. She wondered how she happened to know it at all.

He lay on his back on the scarlet-and-gold bed. As if a giant had flung him there from a great height. He looked broken. His eyes, closed, were streaming. His face, swollen and mottled, barely looked like his own. His mouth, though silent, seemed warped to the shape of the cries that had brought her.

Yes, *die Verzweiflung,* Reserl thought. She had not mistaken the word.

Still, none of this frightened her. It was not until he opened his eyes that Reserl was truly afraid.

His eyes were drained of all light. He is dying, she thought.

"What?" she whispered.

He could not speak. She knew that. She doubted he saw or heard her, so that when he pointed, back behind her, she forgot her fear and was for a moment amazed.

She turned slowly and saw it on the divan. Something monstrous, inhuman. I am right, she thought, to be afraid.

"What is it?" The words escaped with her breath. The question was unintended.

"My love."

Then, again, the sound. Reserl pictured the wolf in the jaws of a trap, blood and entrails splattered on the ground around it, life pouring out too quickly and amply for the earth to absorb . . .

But it was only an instant's release, the wildness of his grief, the repletion of his loss. He wept then the tears of an ordinary man. And the narrowness of his chest, the flatness of his belly, seemed to drive despair deeper inside his body, where its measure could only be guessed at, not taken.

Reserl's hand yearned toward his face but did not touch him. His face looked as if a finger's weight could shatter it. He closed his eyes again, as if shutting out the sight of her could send her away.

His dismissal curiously relieved her. She did not wish to touch despair with her own hands. Reserl turned from the bed. Slowly, steadily, she approached the divan where his goddess waited to—what, receive her? Repudiate her? Devour her? *I am right to be afraid.*

Only the gravity of despair, behind her, kept her from laughing. More animal, surely, than woman, his goddess, and yet . . . even the dumbest animal possessed some warmth, some grace, some promise in its presence of comfort . . .

What sat stiffly upon the bottle-green divan, propped by a golden range of pillows, was no being at all, but simply an object. A horrifying object, Reserl thought, though one that might, to another's gaze, in another room, appear comical.

Fear deserted her. She took a step closer. Something small and hard, like a pebble, dug into the supple sole of her boot. Reserl picked up her foot. The forgotten beads, scattered around her feet, glistened. The candles, she realized, had not been lit. The room blazed with the lamplight of an ordinary evening.

By the light of six dozen pure white tapers, might the monstrosity on the divan more easily have passed for a bride? Reserl was grateful for the lamps' common and unsparing light. She moved still closer to the divan and looked down. It seemed many years ago she had lain in this room, lain under his weight, imagining the eyes of a beautiful woman mocking her from this corner.

Dark and beady, the eyes that stared back at hers were no more capable of ridicule or meanness than of tenderness. The face, stiff with paint, suggested no thought or feeling. The limbs refuted the very idea of motion. Still, she might have been beautiful, his goddess, in the cold and imposing manner a statue could be beautiful, had she been fashioned of marble or metal or wood.

Reserl glanced over her shoulder at the bed. He had not moved. His eyes were closed.

Reaching down, Reserl touched the creature's breast. Its stuffing, dense and lumpish, was mounded under a coarse nap of . . . what her skin might be made of Reserl could not guess. Her flat palm followed the steep downward curve from breast to boneless rib cage to bumptious curve of hip.

Nudged by her hand, the goddess's arm sprang off the edge of the divan to wag impishly in the air, before reaching its limp equilibrium just above the floor.

When Reserl lifted the arm and tried to return it to the divan cushion alongside the body, it swung out stiffly again, as if it meant to hit her.

Its weight amazed her. A living arm its size might, she thought, have weighed half as much. The whole of the creature . . . how in the world had the Captain managed to lift her, lift *it,* from the crate? Could he have carried . . . he must have dragged his goddess to the divan, Reserl thought.

She turned and again, surreptitiously, surveyed the room. The crate had indeed been dragged, she saw. Bits of excelsior laid a trail across the carpet. At one end of the divan a vase of flowers had tipped. The tiles around the stove glittered with shards and fine splinters of glass. The wineglasses were gone from the table. Reserl wondered what had become of the bottle.

At the window she shifted one shutter. Night had fully fallen, a night that, from what she could see, promised no moon or stars.

The Direktor would be home again before another sundown . . . tomorrow. A blessing his absence . . . had he not gone to Leipzig . . .

It would not be improper for you to report to me, Hulda, should . . .

Reserl looked across the room at the body strewn across the bed.

It would not be improper . . .

I should, she thought. He could be dying. I would call the Direktor to come now, if only he were here, would ask him what to do, for how can I . . .

But she knew, Reserl, that she would not . . . despair was the Captain's secret. He had entrusted it to her. Only to her. She must keep it, must not disclose it. Not even if he were dying.

She had promised him.

The Direktor . . . that was different, not a promise. She would tell Dr. Posse nothing. What could he do anyway? Despair could not be helped, could it? The idea that the Captain's despair could be helped was just a story, something she told to calm herself, as she tried to imagine what she could . . .

How was she to keep him from dying?

"WHERE ARE YOU, *LIEBCHEN?*"

Reserl was on her hands and knees, wedged between the divan and the carved edge of the low coffee table.

Her hand trembled as she dropped the last of the scattered beads into her apron pocket. She stood up slowly, not wishing to startle him. She knew she must say something. It was hard to think what, without knowing . . .

"Were you calling Madame?" she asked softly. *She* liked that, he'd said. *Madame.* Such a civilized language, French, and by far the most felicitous choice for dealing with servants, should one be so fortunate as to find a servant with the intelligence to—

His laughter terrified her. "You, Reserl. I wanted *you.*"

"I am here," she whispered.

"Come over here where I can see you." No longer laughing, no, yet sounding still amused. "I won't bite you," he said.

The bed seemed a raft afloat on a pond of light. Reserl waded into the light warily. "I am here," she repeated.

He lay on his back, smiling up at her. "You always are," he said, "aren't you?"

Yes, always. She remembered the missing bottle of wine and wondered if he could be drunk.

He laughed again, as if reading her mind.

Reserl's face felt hot.

"What did I expect?" Still softly laughing, he pushed himself up to a sitting position. "So you and Madame have met?" His eyes did not venture near the divan. "Rather beastly, isn't she?" His face was taut. Its white planes looked polished. Suddenly, though he continued to smile, tears began to slip down his face.

"Have you nothing to say of her, Reserl?" He seemed unaware of his weeping. "Don't tell me she has already mistreated you?"

Reserl shook her head mutely, but he was not looking at her. His tears, in the lamplight, had the hard shine of cut glass. She saw the tight smooth skin of his cheeks slashed, trickling blood. She imagined his soul rising, preparing to leave the room.

She must say something. Something to hold him here.

"I have helped her to dress for dinner."

Though she spoke softly, he flinched as if she had shouted.

"Don't," he said.

"I suggested the dressing gown, since the journey has tired her. But her first night here . . . the black silk. She insisted."

"Stop it, Reserl." His voice was choked. His stunned gaze was drawn to the divan. "You dressed her."

"She wished it," Reserl said.

After a moment, he nodded.

She went to his bureau, opened its top drawer, and found a handkerchief. She wondered if he had noticed the blue initials she had embroidered on one corner. She had copied them from a painting the Direktor had shown her before the Captain had come. The painting was odd and dark. But the letters were made in the simple, slightly crooked way of a child. "Our guest is a very important artist," the Direktor had said. Reserl had thought then he must be an old man.

She unfolded the handkerchief and handed it to him.

He blotted his face.

"What time would you like to dine, sir?"

He looked blank for a moment, then slanted his head toward the divan and chuckled. "What does *she* say?"

"She says . . . whatever is your pleasure."

His smile was zany, off kilter. "You have prepared something?"

"A pheasant," she said. "Lovely. Quite plump."

It was only a capon, in fact, but who would taste it to know the difference? *I am learning to be a fine liar . . .*

For a moment Reserl felt as if she might weep.

But the Captain appeared delighted with her. "She is partial to pheasant, Madame. It is stuffed with wild rice?"

Reserl nodded. "And morels."

"And what of dessert? She has, you know, a sweet tooth."

She had not thought of dessert. Only the Direktor was fond of sweets. She smiled. "A little surprise," she said.

He jumped from the bed. His face, vivid and animated, hardly seemed to belong to the man so recently splayed on the mattress. "I can see that you have things in hand," he said.

"It shouldn't be long. Shall I bring a tray at—"

"By no means!"

"Sir?"

His eyes were red, but his grin was prankish. "Madame and I shall, of course, dine in the dining room."

"Of course," Reserl said.

"It is already late," Oskar said gaily. "Shall we say nine o'clock?"

The question, somewhat rhetorical, was addressed to the vicinity of the divan.

Reserl paused for a moment before leaving, listening for some sound of quibble or dissent.

"Of course, my darling."

The Captain kept nodding, rapidly and repeatedly consenting to things Reserl could not hear.

SOMETIMES HIS GRIEF WOULD CRY OUT, ROUSING AND DRAWING HER IN THE middle of the night.

He kept his despair caged. Despair paced in a cage somewhere deep within him. It did not again, after the day the beast-goddess arrived in Dresden, see the light.

He mourned like an animal, alone in the wilderness, in the dark. Reserl, asleep on her feet at the window, would flee her small room, finding her way to the summerhouse, where she would snatch him from nightmare.

His arms, seeking comfort, rifled the dark. Finding Reserl would quiet him. Sometimes, once sure he was awake and aware, she would allow him to remove her clothes and pull her into the bed.

Barely awake, flat on her back, she would assume his weight. Her legs would disjoin to the thrust of his flesh. She gave herself to him simply and without a sound. But only after he was awake, grief recaptured and locked again in its cage. Grief, isolated, might dwindle and die. She did not know how to keep him from dying. But she understood despair must not be given a mate.

WITH THE SILENT WOMAN IN DRESDEN, OSKAR KOKOSCHKA SEEMED, BY the light of day, transformed. The melancholy and uncertain young man who had left for the Academy each morning in dishevelment and diffidence now bounded from the dining room to the door, sometimes still carrying on a conversation as he reached the street. At the table Reserl would find the Direktor laughing, the Captain's breakfast plate polished clean with a crust of bread.

His spirits, when he returned in the evening, seemed even higher. He came home giddy with gossip, jokes, and politics. He could eat a horse, he often said. Causing Reserl, before the Direktor gently enlightened her, to serve a stew of the strong-tasting meat whose aroma turned the entire household queasy. Her embarrassment at the misunderstanding was vastly outweighed by relief. Eating horse meat was, in her village, considered savage and unclean.

"Our guest certainly seems to be thriving." Hans Posse was only too eager to credit another miracle to her cooking. "Hulda, you have worked wonders," he said.

The undeserved praise made Reserl miserable, of course. How could the Direktor fail to see that the Captain's high spirits were an affliction? The higher they soared, the more she feared for him. It relieved her that, at least in his sleep, he cried like a man whose heart had been broken.

"The war is finally beginning to fade," Hans Posse said.

Reserl, clearing the Saturday luncheon plates, pretended not to hear.

Oskar's gaze was attentive and polite. What on earth was his host talking about?

"The experiences of battle cannot be erased, Oskar. I am, believe me, aware of that. But as they fall farther behind you, their edges, I hope, are less sharp?"

Oskar smiled vaguely.

"And such marvelous turns your life has begun to take! I can't tell you how it pleases me that your genius is starting to be recognized."

"Oh, it isn't—" Oskar's cheeks were pink, his eyes flighty.

"Oh, but it *is*." Posse chuckled. "Young though you are, it is overdue, my friend. Schmidt acknowledged your brilliance at the Sonderbund . . . how many years ago?"

Oskar shrugged.

"Now Westheim and Tietze, two critics of the highest discernment, both devoting major attention to your work in a single season and—"

"Good fortune has the dangerous habit of . . . bunching up," Oskar said. "I should be in a sorry state if I started thinking this means very much."

"Two of your plays in production in Berlin," the Direktor said. "Mere accident?"

"A fluke. The Kammerspieltheater audience is negligible."

"A minority perhaps, but one that constitutes the heart of Berlin's intelligentsia!"

"I am a *painter*," Oskar protested. "No playwright."

"Indeed!" Posse looked delighted. "So shall we discuss Gurlitt's publication of your Bach portfolio . . . or perhaps the Franzen commission?"

"A miracle if I paint a picture Herr Franzen fails to despise . . . particularly should I also unwittingly avoid clashing with the fashionable Frau Franzen's new love seat."

"Such disdain for the golden goose!" Hans Posse smiled and shook his head. "I admire the way you take all this in stride. No doubt it's for the best. Success is as fickle a mistress as—"

The Direktor, beginning to perspire, fell silent.

Reserl, busy at the sideboard with the coffee service, kept her back to the table. She knew the unvoiced name. The dining room seemed, for a moment, to echo with it.

Alma.

At Oskar's burst of laughter the sugar tongs slipped from her hands. "I'm sorry," she whispered.

"I likely could help, if you lack a name to complete your analogy." She imagined the Captain smiling behind her.

"Forgive me, my friend," Hans Posse said. "How tactless you must find me."

"Tact is the thing you least lack, sir."

The Direktor sighed.

Reserl picked up the pot and poured coffee into a gold-lined porcelain cup.

"Nothing in the past matters so much, finally."

His voice was high and thin and false, like a hidden puppeteer's. Reserl imagined children laughing.

"Matters far less, in any case, than your return to painting," the Direktor said. "You know, I hope, that I rejoice for that?"

"I've come back from the dead."

Reserl wished she could have seen his face. He did not sound, she thought, like a man harboring a ruined heart.

But then he was not, by daylight, the man who cried out in the dark.

IT DAWNED ON RESERL, ONE DAY IN MAY, THAT NOT ONLY THE CAPTAIN had changed. The whole world around her was altered. How could she have failed to measure . . . to mark the moment?

At first it had seemed spring's side effect, the trail of visitors creeping like ivy up the steps, through the door, along the hall and into the parlor. Sunny afternoons and mild nights, budding trees and intoxicated birds lured all manner of life from winter's burrows. Even in her small village, spring had been so.

And the Posse house, lolling on the Zwinger's idle emerald lawn, must seem more welcoming now, Reserl thought; no old soul muttering upstairs, quibbling with the Angel of Death. Sometimes she missed the General, though she could not have said why.

The house was still far from done with mourning. The Direktor's grief might have no end. Nor, surely, the Captain's. Still, springtime seemed to usher in fresh air, reminding the house of its original design for cordiality.

Guests made more work for her. Reserl did not mind. When the Direktor said he might give a dinner party, she forgot her bashfulness and clapped in delight.

She would cook for a week. Freed from the constraints of a small household and modest appetites, her hands would take butter and spice on a spree. The Direktor would be proud, the Captain—

"A roasted lamb, I should think," the Direktor mused. Asparagus, perhaps? New potatoes? The details he would leave to her. "Your instinct for a menu is unerring, Hulda," he said.

Baby peas, she thought, so sweet when they are small . . . a salad bright with new radishes, spring onions . . .

"Except . . ." the Direktor said.

She was lost in clouds of steam and popping fat. In the soup perhaps . . . would he object? She saw slivers of asparagus, tiny green boats adrift on a sea of cream . . . lily pads of melted butter . . .

"One thing I should have mentioned, Hulda."

She startled. "Yes, sir?"

"I hardly expect you to do all of this yourself," he said. "You mustn't worry."

But he'd just said . . . was he asking her to leave?

The blow's landing, swift and without warning, left no time to prepare her face.

"Hulda, what is it?"

She looked down. The floor needed scouring. No wonder he thought her incapable.

"My dear, you won't be worked ragged. I mean to hire extra help. Two, do you think? One to assist with the cooking and one to serve?"

A dark blemish, spilled coffee or gravy, on the brick. She hid it with the scuffed toe of her boot. She should, for a party, wear the dainty boots the Captain had given her, the proper black dress with little buttons, the ruffled apron and cap. But she could not, of course. The Direktor would demand to know where . . .

Yet his friends must be served by someone properly dressed. Naturally. *Bonjour, madame . . . Merci, madame . . . Très belle . . . Très bien . . . Je vous en prie, madame.* If the Direktor knew how many French words she could say, he would see there was no need . . .

"Hulda?"

She ground the toe of her boot into the stain and lifted her head.

"There seems," he said gently, "to be some misunderstanding."

"Please."

No wonder, misunderstanding, when that was all she could say. Reserl begged the Direktor with helpless eyes.

"I do not want to distress you. I would sooner forget the party than—"

"Please," she said again. "Just allow me to—"

"You want to do everything?" He looked alarmed. "Yourself. Is that it?"

"Yes, please," she said.

He studied her for another moment. "Such a large undertaking . . . you are certain you do not want . . ."

She smiled. "I am certain."

The fat on the lamb roasted crisp, black with pepper . . . a sigh of sherry in the soup. Surely by then strawberries at the market, the small wild berries whose flavor shocks the tongue. Topfenstrudel, *the Direktor's favorite sweet, each fat white slice jeweled with a perfect berry . . . dimpled macaroons dripping bittersweet chocolate . . . almonds bronzed in burnt sugar . . .*

She saw the Direktor in his stiff white shirtfront and black cravat. At the head of the table, of course. He could, from there, see every guest. He bestowed equal measures of charming attention on each.

And at the table's foot the Captain, smiling over a cut-glass bowl of perfect spring flowers. Smiling at Reserl with warm, astonished eyes . . .

Astonished and, yes, a little ashamed.

How for a moment could he have found her . . . wanting?

THE PARTY HAPPENED MUCH AS SHE IMAGINED IT. BUT EVEN LARGER. Lovelier.

She had never seen the mahogany table stretched to its full length. How could Reserl have imagined eight chairs fitting perfectly along each side? A mint-green tablecloth and eighteen napkins with scalloped edges . . . that such fine linens could lie so many years forgotten in an attic trunk and come to light without mildew or must? She would never have dreamed it.

Nor, even in a story, would Reserl have seen herself in one of Frau Posse's dresses.

The dress, though black, was otherwise quite unlike a maid's uniform. Its round crocheted collar was nearly as wide as a washbasin. A broad grosgrain ribbon banded the waist.

The morning of the party the Direktor had come downstairs carrying a small bundle loosely rolled in yellowing tissue. Reserl was polishing silver. "I thought perhaps you might like this. For the party." He held the parcel out to her.

Something for the table, Reserl thought. She quickly rinsed and dried her hands.

The table was, except for the dessertspoons she was just seeing to, already set. Whatever was in the bundle, she hoped it would not mean changing everything.

As she pulled back the wrapping, the black dress seemed to unroll of its own accord. The deep, flat folds of its skirt reminded her of the dining room drapes.

The Direktor looked hopeful and a bit embarrassed. He looked, Reserl thought, like a boy.

"Frau Posse was not quite so small as you," he said. "But nearly."

"Your wife's dress?"

"I thought you might like to wear something . . . different," he said. "For the party."

He did not wish to be humiliated before his friends by the way she . . .

"*Danke,*" she said somewhat stiffly.

"Had I only thought earlier," he said. "In time to get something new."

Reserl saw in the Direktor's eyes the gift's simple and singular purpose: to please her.

"It is very beautiful," she said.

A half hour before the guests arrived, she caught sight of herself in one of the parlor's long, spotless windows. The figure she saw there was graceful, slender, and almost tall. The collar was a carved ivory frame around her face. Frau Posse's dress made her nearly beautiful. For a moment Reserl wished that, this one night, she might have worn the bright glass beads.

The Direktor came down in his best dark suit. He had even thought to clean his spectacles. Behind their polished lenses, sorrow dimmed his eyes at the sight of her in his dead wife's dress.

Then he smiled. "All is ready in the kitchen?"

"Everything," she said.

"Good," the Direktor said. Then he asked Reserl if she would please stand beside him in the front hall to greet his guests.

The evening was cool and damp. As each guest came in, Reserl took the wraps. "This is Hulda," the Direktor would say, "our housekeeper."

Not *das Stubenmädchen,* maid, but *die Haushälterin.* Reserl hoped the Captain, serving drinks in the parlor, heard what the Direktor called her.

AND HOPED, LATER, THAT HE HAD NOT. RESERL HOPED (MIGHT HAVE prayed, had prayer been her habit) that the Captain had not heard, that he was not thinking of her as Hulda, *die Haushälterin,* when, between dinner and dessert, he appeared in the kitchen.

Not *appeared,* no. She did not see him. She was entranced by the pastry tray, the lovely task of its last embellishments. Maraschino cherries and candied chestnuts lightly scattered among the cookies and cakes.

The warmth of his whisper flowered at her ear. "How lovely you are, my Reserl."

A cherry slipped from her grasp, leaving a bright wound in the soft white flesh of a cream cake.

By the time she turned around, he was gone.

It was not a story. He had been there. He had been beside her in the kitchen. He had found her, for an instant, lovely.

By the light of that moment, all else Reserl recalled of the Direktor's party turned shadowy and dim.

He had seen her.

He would paint her.

"A marvelous evening! Everything was perfect, Hulda," the Direktor said.

"AH, THERE YOU ARE," HE SAID. "AT LAST." HIS EYES AND HIS VOICE, BOTH cool, rebuked her. He had, since his goddess's arrival, grown prickly and finical. His tongue was barbed. He could be impossible to please. Not like himself at all. More like *her.* While at other times he—

It was as if there were two of him now, two very different men.

There was the Captain, a quick and rather noisy fellow whose conversation made the Direktor laugh and argue and throw up his hands and clean his plate, who charmed a snaking vine of visitors into the house to keep the parlor lamps burning past midnight. He was, this man, a bit of a dandy. He had suddenly begun minding his trousers' crease, his shirts' well-being. A spot on a lapel could put him out of sorts.

This man, recently arrived, was a professor at the Academy. He was, moreover, a painter of growing renown, Herr Posse liked to say. As such, the Captain was called upon, with increasing frequency, to travel. He acquired a new portmanteau of pocked ostrich hide, the gift of an unspecified friend he seemed to regard with fondness. The scuffs of each journey must be rubbed out with saddle soap and neat's-foot oil. Good luggage was, he remarked, the sign of a gentleman.

The gentleman who now breakfasted with the Direktor before venturing forth into busy days differed markedly from the man who, arriving rather earlier, had installed himself in the summerhouse. The man of the summerhouse was no man of the world. Indeed, he seemed scarcely a man. He was more a boy—frail and uncertain, lovesick and dreamy.

The boy in the summerhouse looked peevish this balmy evening. His silver eyes were dim and dark-edged, as if the man's late gadabout nights were depleting him. And love, of course . . . he would by now be worn out with love. Between midnight and dawn, the boy howled back at the storms of love that battered him. Reserl often heard him.

He was thinner than ever. The fringed sash of the hand-me-down dressing gown, wrapped twice around him, still draggled to his knees. The paisley silk gapped on a chest that was bony and white. The food the man took in with apparent relish seemed to make no difference. Somehow the boy's body defied nourishment.

"So at last you come." His stare narrowed. "But too late, I'm afraid. Madame has retired."

It was often like this. When he shouldered the burdens of another's displeasure, Reserl had learned to be cautious.

"Madame wanted me?" Her eyes were downcast. "She is not unwell, I hope?"

"Not unwell, no." How chilly he sounded. "But gravely unhappy, Reserl."

Madame's displeasure: he staggered under its weight. Now Reserl must shoulder it, so that he might sleep.

"I am sorry," she said softly, "to make Madame unhappy with me."

"Unhappy, I'm afraid, with all of us."

"The Direktor needed . . ." Her hands knotted under her apron. "Perhaps tomorrow I can explain—"

"Explain?" He smiled bitterly. "Madame has no stomach for explanation."

Reserl bowed her head. "I am sorry."

His gaze skittered to the divan, to the mound under a rose satin comforter. "We are, all of us, endlessly sorry," he murmured. One corner of his mouth quivered.

"Perhaps if we put her properly to bed, Madame will feel better in the morning," she said.

His eyes narrowed now on Reserl. "If we wake her, she will kill us."

"We shall not wake her." Reserl's breath waited for his nod.

At the divan he seemed to ease back the comforter a centimeter at a time. There was a slight tremor in his hands.

Reserl was surprised to find his goddess fully and elaborately dressed. There were by now a number of beautiful white nightdresses. Even after those he'd ordered arrived from Battenberg he kept buying new ones. He changed her clothing several times each day. Madame found her wardrobe, he reported, still far from adequate.

Angled over the divan, he gazed down upon the grotesque face, its mouth and cheeks eerily bright, metallic lids mercifully closed over keen glass eyeballs. How, Reserl wondered, could he bear it, looking, always looking, at that terrible face? But his eyes saw something else, of course.

He dreams, she thought. Asleep he howls, awake he dreams . . . how to keep him here, keep him from dying?

"Perhaps we should slip Madame into a nightdress?"

He blinked himself back from wherever he'd gone. He shook his head sternly. *If we wake her, she will kill us . . .*

His lips were slightly parted, the muscles in his cheeks slack. The face's spare flesh seemed to collapse downward, as he leaned lower. Gingerly grasping the unyielding shoulders, he began to lift the monstrous woman from the divan.

At his nod, Reserl grasped the ankles. Her fingers recoiled slightly from the bristling, the poor stand-in for skin, the absence of bone. *She could not wake . . . could not be killed, nor even hurt.* Legs like logs bound together by a hobbled skirt, fine linen the shade of a wren in winter. Impossible to keep linen from wrinkling. Madame was rumpled. Reserl was strangely pleased.

Her grip on the misshapen ankles less than gentle, Reserl hefted the mannequin's lower extremities. Carrying her slowly and soundlessly, they crossed the room, then lowered the deadweight to the bed.

He had turned back the covers on the side where he did not sleep. His tender fuss arranging the pillows under the lifeless head made Reserl turn away.

"What are you doing?" His tone was exacting.

"Did you not wish me to go?" she said.

"And leave her like this?" His narrow lips, pressed into a tight line, paled. "You must help me undress her," he said.

She had done so before, of course. But then there had been a light-heartedness, a shared sense of absurdity. Assuming Madame's voice, he would make outrageous demands, criticizing the clumsiness of Reserl's every gesture. Before, it had been a game.

This moment seemed terribly different. He looked ill. She felt close to weeping.

"Die Stiefel," he hissed, thrusting his chin toward the figure's impossibly dainty feet.

The boots. They were new. Reserl had not seen them before, nor in fact seen anything like them, ever. Oxblood kid softer than the finest glove. Narrow velvet ribbons for laces. Amber beading on the toes.

The knots were stubborn, the ribbon frangible. Reserl's hands removed the boots with impeccable tact. Then she waited to be told what more he required of her.

But she had been forgotten.

The tiny pearl buttons did not impede him. The linen shirtwaist conspired with his practiced hands. The tight cuffs opened easily. Pushing up the sleeves, he caressed the pale furred arms. The collar came loose at a touch. Pearls slipped, one by one, from the loops that had held them.

Beneath the prim linen, silk's laxness and flush . . . she had seen it months before, had almost forgotten it: the camisole, the knuckled proxy of his hand filling the rose-appliquéd cup.

As in the familiar dream where all one dreads bears down, Reserl found herself unable to move. She wanted to turn away. She could not even lower her eyes.

The slender straps slipped from the sloping shoulders. Then he paused, gazing down with vague and dreamy eyes. His mouth was soft. His lips looked swollen. He might have been a boy.

"Isn't she beautiful?" he whispered.

His eyes worshiped for another moment. Then his fingers, with great delicacy, invaded the camisole's lace-crimped top edge. Slowly the silk eased down. The breasts were two frozen mountains fleecy with snow.

He bent low over the bed, an acolyte at an altar. His eyes were closed. One hand dipped and disappeared between the woolly white thighs.

His mouth wrenched in a mute cry. His head fell upon one breast. Spit glazed his lips. His teeth, yellowed by lamplight, looked small and sharp. The nipple his mouth devoured looked like a store-bought confection, pallid chocolate and dyed marzipan.

I lie down, I confess, with what you have sent me. Long before daylight I rise, wakened by my own screams. I draw the drapes while dark reigns, for I cannot risk dawn's first ray . . . cannot now bear for the sun's least light to touch the sullied pelt that covers a blasphemous heart.

No doubt you consider me mad, Fräulein, have always thought so. And you are perhaps not wrong. For what was it if not madness, entrusting you with my soul, investing my last hope in your crass and cynical hands?

Yes, I must be mad. But not so lacking in sanity that I fail to recognize unnatural acts. I know the name of my sin, Fräulein. It is bestiality. And it is you who have damned me to its helpless practice. Yours is the name my cracked lips shall call out from that cage assigned me for all eternity.

How, I wonder, shall that hell prove different, except in duration, from the one I now inhabit?

Shall I find you, my once collaborator, beside me in its fires?

16

The Direktor would, as was his habit, escape to the mountains for a month in late July.

"Come along," he had urged Oskar. "As my guest, of course." The view from Rathen . . . the Bastei would inspire him. Spa waters, mountain air, the occasional bracing hike—nothing too strenuous, of course—would restore him. They would hire a rowboat to paddle over the Amselsee. They would make an outing to the Königstein. (Oskar had not seen the fortress? But he must!) The local wines, likely overrated, would test their palates' discernment.

"A most generous offer," Oskar said. "It is too much."

"I would be glad of company," the Direktor confessed. "I have not much enjoyed my holiday since . . . without my wife," he said.

Oskar might, had he believed this, have felt guilty. But the Direktor was simply too kind. And he himself had commitments. He had, above all, to work.

"It goes well, then, the painting?"

"Never as well," Oskar said, "as one hopes."

The Direktor smiled. "Of course."

"I really must start to . . . *apply* myself," said Oskar. "I must bear down and not squander these weeks I am free."

"The teaching begins to grow burdensome?"

Oskar laughed boisterously. "I adore it," he said. "Which is precisely my difficulty."

How could the Direktor, in the end, fail to understand, to agree? Delightful and salutary as the mountains might be, what Oskar most needed at the moment were solitude, routine, concentration. He needed, as he put it, to remember how to be a painter again.

So Professor Kokoschka would remain in residence in Dresden. Perhaps fortunate, then, that Hulda had declined the Direktor's offer to send her home to her village for a month. For which time she would, of course, be paid.

"No, thank you, sir," she had said, rather quickly, when the proposal was made.

Hans Posse was taken aback. "You have been here more than a year," he said. "Surely your people must miss you."

"I don't believe so," she said.

"Your father—" He tried to catch her eye.

Shaking her head with unusual vigor, the girl stared at the floor.

"Hulda, I can hardly leave you here alone for a month."

She looked at him then. She looked frightened.

"All right," the Direktor said. It was only the start of June. Surely something could be arranged. "If you are certain you don't care to go home."

"I am certain, sir," she said.

So the girl would not, as it turned out, be left entirely alone. And his guest would have someone to see to his laundry and meals. Not an ideal arrangement, certainly, but it would have to do. He ought to feel relieved and grateful, the Direktor supposed. He hadn't the slightest idea what might have been done with Hulda had Oskar agreed to accompany him—ask neighbors to keep her? She could hardly have been dragged along. A lovely young girl traveling unchaperoned with two men? Even in bohemian circles . . . No, things had worked out for the best, really, under the circumstances.

And it was not as if Oskar and the girl would actually be sleeping under the same roof, was it? Hans Posse wished he could dispel his uneasiness about the arrangement, could rid himself of the suspicion that something untoward . . .

No, that was putting it too strongly. Hulda was a good girl, Oskar a decent fellow, a reputable artist, not the sort to take advantage of innocence. But every now and then Hans Posse thought he saw a look pass between the two . . . not lascivious, no. Not even flirtatious. But a meeting of eyes that hinted at familiarity, collusion . . .

Collusion? *Gott in Himmel,* that sounded as if they were *spies!* Yet some suggestion of . . .

Doubtless nothing.

How I agitate myself over needless things . . .

The Direktor smiled. It had been too long, several years, since he'd last found himself absurd. It was actually rather pleasant. Perhaps I am not yet so old, he thought.

HE SMILED, HIS GAUNT CHEEKS POUCHED WITH STURDY RYE CRUST, POORLY chewed.

Her face pinched with attention, she poured the coffee.

Their eyes conspired down the polished length of the dining room table.

The Direktor, fortunately, was distracted. The hired car would arrive any moment. His bulging bags, three of them, sat by the door. Their aged leather (how strangely insistent Hulda had been about oiling them) gleamed in a patch of morning sun.

"I hope this will be a true retreat," Oskar said. "I did not like to say so, but you have been looking tired."

The Direktor smiled. He might have asked if his guest had looked in a mirror recently himself. But teasing with too much truth, his mother used to say, was like sauerkraut with too much vinegar. "I intend to devote myself passionately to idleness," he said.

Oskar's smile was abstracted.

Hulda had noticed that the Direktor was scarcely eating. The prospect of an absence from home always made him a bit squeamish. But the girl looked distressed. Posse picked up his butter knife as if he intended to do something with it.

"Now you have several envelopes I've addressed to myself at the resort," he said to the girl. "You must not hesitate to . . . send me a message if . . ."

She was nodding. *Ja, ja,* they'd been over it several times. Thank heaven he hadn't slipped and said she must *write* to him. He wasn't sure she could.

"I'll send more money if it's needed."

She smiled as if he'd made a joke. Which in a way he supposed he had. Between her thrift and his worry, an unspent fortune must be stashed about the house in various jars and tins.

"All will be well here," Hulda said.

She seemed almost happy that he was leaving. Proud, perhaps, being entrusted with a sizable house. The girl did seem, the Direktor thought, to be gaining a degree of confidence.

A BLESSING, RESERL THOUGHT, THAT SHE NEED NOT GO. SHE COULD NOT imagine riding in a motorcar. Spying out the parlor window, she watched it pull away, a huge shiny black insect making dreadful noises. She pictured it skittering up the side of a mountain, tipping, sliding down on its back.

The Captain, alone on the cobbled street, looked forlorn. The car, the Direktor, had vanished. Reserl hurried back to the kitchen on wobbly legs. The Captain must not come in to find her daydreaming at the window. The kitchen was where she belonged. She wondered what he would like for dinner.

There were veal chops, two of them, pale and solid. The egg noodles she had rolled and cut yesterday were drying on racks in the pantry . . .

What if he stopped eating altogether, now that the Direktor was gone?

She heard the thump of the front door closing, the clank of the turning lock.

"Where art thou, *mein Lamm*?" He sounded playful, carefree. His lamb. He sounded like a boy.

She saw the gleaming bright motorcar bouncing over the rocky cliffs. The hair prickled on the back of her neck.

"I am here," she said, as he bounded into the kitchen.

"Ah, yes." He laughed. "Where else?"

"You will have lunch?" she said.

"But I have just had breakfast!" He laughed some more. "Never mind about food, Reserl. We have so much to do."

She waited.

"To begin, the dining room must be rearranged," he said. "Entirely."

"The dining room?"

"Of course! Come, let me show you."

He took her hand and tucked it into the crook of his elbow. He escorted her from the kitchen on his arm as if she should have expected as much.

"In here I think we can achieve something more . . . intimate, don't you?" Her hand was still captive in the tuck of his arm. "Less staid and formal a setting?"

Removing the candelabra from the table . . . was that what he meant? Hardly! Could there be too many candles?

"The furniture must be moved," he said. "I wish some of it could be thrown out."

Her shocked expression greatly amused him.

"Let me show you, *Liebchen*. Here."

Within half an hour, both were sweaty and disheveled. The leaves had been taken from the mahogany table, leaving a modest oval. The extra chairs were stowed in the Direktor's study, a room for which they'd have no use, the Captain said. The table fit neatly into the windowed alcove, taking the place of the marquetry sideboard that, at some peril to its fragile contents, had been wrestled to a side wall. To Reserl's vast relief the breakfront was permitted to remain where it stood. She shuddered to imagine the Meissen's decimation.

The Captain appeared delighted with the effects of their exertions. Reserl thought the room looked sad. The crystal chandelier now swooped down over nothing. The table legs had left hoofprint-shaped dents in the carpet's Oriental maze.

"There must be flowers, of course. Banks of them. I'll bring in the candles . . ." He lowered his voice. "While Madame is sleeping. And some of that gold cloth, I should think, for the table."

Reserl nodded uncertainly.

"So subdued, *mein Lamm.* Don't tell me my plans have already tired you?"

The Meissen, complete service for twenty-four, crashed down a rocky slope. A sharp deluge of French crystal, bright needles of rain, pelted the summer-green valley.

"I am not tired."

A blessing, she thought, his failure to insist on moving the breakfront.

"You are not used to freedom." He sounded as if he pitied her.

The Direktor would return in a month. The twenty-ninth of August, he said. It would be nearly autumn then. The market stalls would fill with apples, scarlet and golden and green. She would make for the Direktor's Willkommen sheets of strudel, strudel fat with raisins and the white flesh of early apples. The pastry like ancient parchment, yellow with butter and flaking away as . . .

"I will teach you to love freedom, Reserl," the Captain whispered.

Her captured hand was folded into his arm.

The black car lay, flat and crumpled, at the foot of a steep jagged slope.

MADAME WOULD, OF COURSE, EAT NONE OF THE DISHES SHE ORDERED prepared. Sitting stiffly at the small, opulent table, Madame seemed to look down her nose at her plate.

Madame's nose was quite beautiful, meticulously molded under a powdering of something that shimmered like gold dust. The Captain confessed he found Madame's nose captivating. Madame's nose was, he told Reserl, famous throughout Europe's capitals (what was left of them).

"Not petite," he said. "But perfect, no?"

"Yes, sir," Reserl said. "A lovely nose." It was. Although it did not look, in harsh light, quite *like* a nose. Not exactly. Perhaps it was the haughty angle of its display. Madame wore her nose like a costly piece of jewelry.

Reserl, of course, would not have entertained this thought. She did not know *what* to think where Madame was concerned.

It was the Captain, actually, who observed that Madame's nose flaunted itself on her face like a diamond brooch on a large bosom. It seemed he could not help himself. Now and then, late at night in the summerhouse, the Captain made jokes at Madame's expense while Madame was asleep. Mockery right under her nose. Teasing.

No jokes were made in the dining room, but sometimes while she stood at the sideboard outwaiting Madame's displeasure, Reserl would remember something the Captain had said in the summerhouse. She'd have to take pains with her own face then. An unseemly smile in Madame's presence could be perilous.

"The beets are quite nice, Madame says. You mustn't mind her not eating them. They clash with her lip rouge."

Sometimes in the dining room the Captain's comments were as funny as jokes.

They were not, however, meant as jokes. To smile would be unseemly.

"Madame requests a moratorium on spinach." He could, as her spokesman, be quite severe. "Her teeth are turning green. Reserl, that will not *do.*"

"Forgive me." The apology was addressed to Madame, whose dainty teeth were unnaturally pointed and white. "Entirely my fault," Reserl said.

Accustomed by now to the rearranged dining room's empty look, Reserl did not mind her lowly part in the charades there. Nor did she mind in the least the odd and troublesome meals the Captain requested in Madame's behalf. With both the Direktor and the Academy on holiday, the Captain now scarcely went out. He'd canceled a planned lecture in Berlin, as well as a family visit to Vienna.

Much of each day he painted. When the weather was fine, he set up his easel in some sunlit spot on the Zwinger grounds, never far from the house. When the heat of the sun drove him inside, his easel stood in the summerhouse window. Over and over and over again he painted the ruined garden.

Reserl never disturbed the Captain when he was painting. Yet she found comfort in knowing where he was, what he was doing, and that he was near enough for her to hear if he called for her.

Sometimes on days when rain kept him indoors, he'd come to the kitchen and forage, helping himself to what he needed or desired. Odd and homely objects seemed to make sudden claims on him. He'd stare at them the way he sometimes stared at Reserl's hands, turning them over, examining their every surface and flaw as if his fate were encoded there. After choosing and studying these things—a brown-spotted lemon, a chipped butter crock—he would arrange them on a little table in his room. He once carried off a beheaded chicken she'd just started to pluck. Reserl had to find something else to serve for dinner. The chicken, kept in his room for several hours, quickly began to spoil from the heat. It left a wing-shaped bloodstain on his desk.

The Captain's paintings of plain and unremarkable things fascinated Reserl. Ugly objects turned strangely beautiful. Yet his touch left beauty tainted. What he painted could nearly always be recognized for what it was. A bruised pear was still bruised, still a pear. Yet he seemed to draw out of each thing he studied an immediate and startling resemblance to some other object, something quite unlike it. The commonplace lost its ordinariness. Everything he painted somehow became something else.

One day he would paint her. One day Reserl would sit on the grass, keeping her back straight, not dropping her head like an oaf. She would watch him for hours with steady eyes and he would not mind and time would evaporate like cologne in a flask with a loose-fitting stopper.

Each morning from the kitchen window Reserl would inspect the sunrise. If the sky looked sheer, the light transparent, she would think, Perhaps today . . . he will ask today if he might paint me.

She imagined his gaze shy, his words clumsy, and her own perfect stillness as his silver eyes burned into her like mirrors igniting sunlight.

She wondered what she might come, in his painting, to resemble.

She hoped he would let her wear Frau Posse's dress.

MADAME SEEMED TO NEED A GOOD DEAL OF SLEEP, WHICH WAS CONVENient. She never appeared for breakfast or lunch. Of course, the Captain often did not, either. His attendance at lunch was especially fitful. Reserl could, most days, fuss over dinner all day. The evening meal was worth every effort and care, for when he dined with Madame, the Captain had a voracious appetite.

Sometimes, having finished the food on his own plate, he would reach with a lover's nonchalance across the table to pluck succulent bits from Madame's. These thieved morsels and shreds he consumed with particular zest, licking his fingers and smacking his lips.

It was rude, Reserl knew, to stare, especially while someone was eating. Sometimes she could not look away. Not that he seemed to mind. If the Captain noticed Reserl watching him eat, he'd smile and lick his lips. He smiled as if sharing a secret with her. His tongue, lapping his lips, was slow and wet and agile.

She recalled one winter morning when he'd come into the kitchen and stood watching her spread buttercream between the layers of a torte. The kitchen windows were webbed with frost. She was shivering, Reserl remembered, when he plucked her hand from the bowl. The knife slipped through her fingers, flinging thick white spatters across the rosy brick floor. Sometimes, watching him eat, she could still feel his tongue sliding in and out between her fingers, grainy with sugar, sleek with cream.

WHEN RESERL CARRIED THE DINNER PLATES FROM THE DINING ROOM, ONE was often empty, the other almost full.

Many such evenings, after carting a sleepy and sulking Madame to the summerhouse, the Captain would return to the kitchen. Reserl might be washing silverware, scrubbing a pot. Finding the plate of food on the small corner table, he would smile.

Sometimes he would even joke.

"Madame sends her compliments," he might say.

Or: "We shall have to loosen Madame's stays. She has gorged herself again."

Then the Captain would fish Reserl's hands from the scalding water and, claiming them as if they were his own, he would pat them dry with a tea towel.

When her hands were dry, he would study them, turning them this way and that. Reserl wished her hands were soft and white, wished so hard that the wish could close her eyes.

When Reserl opened her eyes again, he would still be studying her palms. The Captain inspected her palms like a gypsy in pursuit of a vagrant curse.

Keeping hold of her hands, he would coax her into the corner. There, taking hold of her waist, he would hoist her onto the wobbly stool.

"You are hungry, my Reserl."

She would shake her head and press her lips together. She was not hungry.

"No?" He would filch from the plate a particularly juicy morsel, a gravy-soaked bite of meat, a soft little dumpling, a dripping mushroom. Pinching the bit into a mouthful with the tips of his fingers, he would slip it onto his tongue. His smile would look a little wicked, a buttery gloss on his lips and teeth.

"You must be." Still chewing as he spoke. The tip of his tongue sliding over his lips. "I know you are hungry, my dove."

His fingers would pluck another nosegay of food from the plate. Grasping her chin, he would tease her mouth open.

It was unmannerly, speaking with food in one's mouth.

With bite after bite of Madame's food, Reserl was silenced, until nothing was left.

RESERL AND HULDA . . .

The man and the boy . . .

Not to mention Madame and her imperious entourage of moods.

Occasionally Reserl heard the old General, pacing in the rooms above. Still waiting for his funeral, she thought.

The house at times seemed crowded.

The Direktor, most days, was scarcely missed.

There was, in each day, so little time, despite summer's protracted light. Such a poverty of hours when the Captain's guest . . .

Was Madame a guest? A guest could be counted on, in time, to leave. Reserl devoutly hoped that Madame was a guest.

She was, the Captain's guest, so demanding.

And everything took longer, somehow, in a deficit of certainties.

From the moment she rose each morning, Reserl felt doubts drag at her heels. Things that should have been clear and simple were opaque with confusion, delayed by fret. Even the commonplace of dressing for the day was a forest beset with traps.

Madame preferred Reserl's blue dress for morning, regardless of the day of the week.

Serving dinner, of course, called for the proper uniform. Several delicate sauces had scorched of an evening, while Reserl grappled with a rank of exacting black buttons. The apron needed, almost daily, to be washed and starched and ironed.

Oskar was ambushed by a wistful longing for the green dresses, their mossy color and scent. How their cloth seemed further to fade in sunlight, as if not to rival her hair's bright fire. Hadn't she, in a green dress, darker eyes? Both calm and alert then, his Reserl's eyes, their watchfulness for his every desire and need, his alone. These days she looked skittish, distracted.

As well she might.

The man, each evening before dinner was served, inspected her. Every crease and nuance of her uniform, the smoothness of her stockings and hair, nothing escaped him.

The boy, blind, stripped away her clothing and hurled it into the dark. He scoured her face with the grit of his beard. He pulled out her braids and made a commotion of her hair.

Hulda had come to Dresden with three dresses, two green, one blue. The blue was, of the three, the least disreputable, Madame said.

Reserl kept her maid's uniform in pristine condition. She wore it each evening serving dinner. Its sleeves were long and snug. Its buttons were irksome. August was unusually hot in Dresden that year.

The Direktor would return on the verge of autumn. Cooling nights and apples in the market and a strudel for *Willkommen*. The Direktor had given his late wife's dress to . . .

Hulda, *meine Haushälterin,* was a marvel in the kitchen. *What a wonderful wife you will be.*

The dress of the Direktor's late wife had a collar like a carved ivory frame.

How lovely you are, my Reserl.

Someone—the man? the boy?—once said so.

Was she meant, Reserl wondered, to keep the dress? Perhaps the Direktor had simply forgotten to ask for its return.

She wondered if she would ever wear the dress again.

The Direktor was scarcely missed.

The General paced.

Madame did not touch her food.

The Captain searched Reserl's palms, conviction of doom in his eyes.

She dressed more slowly each morning.

The boy cried out in the night.

Only Madame slept well. Madame was always sleeping.

Not a sauceboat or a butter plate had been broken.

It was a particularly hot August.

The house was always crowded.

Did it please you, as you fashioned this abomination I am now obliged to love, to imagine my suffering in this or any world? Have you found in ridicule, Fräulein, a worthy consort?

At last your art reveals to me, reveals in relief so sharp as to incise my very soul, the poverty of your spirit . . . a spirit so dwarfed and crippled it can have known nothing bearing the least resemblance to love.

Only a woman deprived of all passion could find passion laughable. Amuse yourself as you will, as you have. But may you know, Fräulein, that

even as you have destroyed this heart, its capacity for feeling remains suf-
ficient to pity you pity's lack.

I may seek my poor solace in the arms of the graceless thing your scorn
has made, my need an indelible stain upon her furred thigh. Do I thus
mock desire? Profane love?

It may be so.

Yet any just God must judge you, Fräulein, the true abomination. You
and your pitiless stone heart.

Mine, on the other hand, even in madness and depravity, remains

Ever faithful,
OK

RAPIDS OF WATER RUSHED FROM THE EAVES, SPLASHING DOWN ON BEREFT
flower beds, leaving craters in the dry, neglected earth. The path from
the kitchen steps to the summerhouse was a muddy stream. I have
waited too long, Oskar thought.

Each morning for more than a week, he'd promised himself he would
do it that day, would paint the palace rose garden. Its extraordinary pro-
fusion and palette, the pinks and scarlets and corals and golds, the flowers like faces, petals like scallops of skin . . . each morning pictures
bloomed in his mind, one upon another, appearing so fast they blurred.

But the blur, regrettably, brought on a headache . . . the heat, the insect buzz . . . really, wouldn't the peak of flowering be *tomorrow*?

Now downpour was stripping the flowers, trampling petals in the
mud, and what might be left tomorrow would be . . .

Interesting?

Possibly.

Oskar saw it in his mind: a chiaroscuro of sharp thorns and twisted
stems, petals crushed and bruised. Like a derelict grave, he thought, and
felt for a moment happier.

Such rain could not last long. He would paint the rose garden tomorrow. A much more *original* approach, really, examining ruin. Only what
was left of the roses could truthfully immortalize them. Any fool could
ape perfection. Flawless beauty was insipid. Not to mention unconvincing. Tomorrow he would not wait for the sun to put its false gloss on
everything. He would present himself in the gardens, barefoot, at dawn.

The wet morning eagerly conspired with the heat that, after a month, seemed imperishable and hopeless. Mildew flourished in every crease and corner. The summerhouse windows, shut upon the slanting rain, were filmed with steam.

Oskar unbuttoned his shirt. Looking down, he saw rills of sweat straying down his pale chest. He tore off the shirt and used it to blot his face and neck, the wet hollows around his navel and under his throat and arms.

Almi avoided the tropics, despised deserts. The Mediterranean was habitable only in late autumn, she said. She would gladly die without seeing Tangier. Her appetite for travel was finical, craving only art and music and mountain air . . .

Honeymooning with the Maestro, she had glittered, a jewel in the ornate setting of Saint Petersburg. She recalled each detail—the steps of the Hermitage glazed with ice, the sly clasp on a Fabergé egg. A certain member of the Imperial family had been quite taken with her.

The liveliness of cities incited her own natural animation, filled her with a gaiety that men, in particular, found irresistible. Vienna, of course, had always thrown itself at her feet. Alma, in a cultured city, burned like a torch among tapers.

But summers in Maiernigg . . . all dullness and humidity . . . in the Maestro's summer retreats Almi had made her acquaintance with despair. She'd recounted with a kind of horror the flat blue line of the Wörthersee, herself staring out at it from the veranda of that philistine pile of stone and wood he called a villa. Almi, ignored for days (and nights!) on end as, locked away in his beloved little *Häuschen* on the lake's edge, the Maestro sweated and thrashed and moaned over his precious Fifth Symphony's gestation. As if *his* were the belly stretched and swollen and hot, his the agonizing labor that . . .

She had, throughout those summers, slept alone, Alma told Oskar. Her room was not even on the same floor as her husband's. No comfort at hand when, jolted awake before dawn, she would heave and gag and . . .

But that was Maria, of course. Their precious Putzi. Could her mother regret a moment's suffering, even if that first summer might have killed her?

And it had, Maiernigg, nearly been the death of her . . . summer after summer the white hot sun on the level blue lake, nothing around her but tangled woods and the welter of ugly furniture his tasteless, tyrannical sister had chosen. But for heaven's grace, Almi said, I might have gone hopelessly mad.

In time there were the children, of course, sweet little girls both, and company of a kind. But babies were exhausting—one without his own could hardly be expected to understand. The pains she'd taken, from dawn to dark, to keep their least sound from the refined ears of their father, her husband wrestling with the Angel of Genius in his homely little lakeside hut (where she, his *bride,* had been given to know she was not, without express invitation, welcome). The Maestro—well, she had worshiped him. As everyone well knew. But Gustav was, to say the least, *difficult* . . . a difficult and self-centered genius with the great good fortune to have found a wife whose first talent was for devotion. (Not to say there weren't others . . . young Alma Schindler's startling promise as a composer, perhaps a poet. She'd even shown—not to boast—some aptitude for art, if . . .)

If only she'd been able to breathe, to stretch . . .

If only she'd had a proper summer home, a place to restore herself . . .

If only she'd had a refuge in the mountains!

Mornings in Mürren reaching for Oskar as she woke, devouring him with a hungry mouth . . . then her rush to the balcony, naked under her dressing gown, leaning over the railing, her bare feet planted wide, and the touch of cold dry air everywhere upon her. The rich breakfasts she consumed those mornings she would, in Vienna, have reviled.

Yes, Oskar had seen his Almi's exquisite arousal at higher altitudes. He pictured the flare of her, ripe and rosy and plump against the mattress ticking, saw Lili's head, narrow and smooth as a seal's, delving between pale floes of thigh . . .

If he had not ceaselessly pestered her with his tedious jealousies . . .

If they'd been able to escape Vienna's summer heat . . .

Had the war not made travel to civilized cities so difficult and had Gucki not come down with a small fever and had Oskar not insisted on painting the most grotesque aspect of all he saw and had he not been too distracted by that fool Kammerer to notice Gropius waiting in the wings of her attention, waiting all along to insert himself between them when the slightest gap . . . had Almi's talents included the least aptitude for *faithfulness* . . .

Oskar glanced at the divan in the corner. She was not there. For a moment his heart stopped beating. She was always leaving him . . . would never stop leaving him.

Ah, but Madame was only asleep! Of course. It was barely nine o'-clock. She rarely stirred before noon. In this heat his Almi would have no interest in breakfast.

Oskar went to the bed. A bank of soft white bedding left visible only the crown of her head, its tangled topknot in the loose grip of a pair of silver filigree combs. Had her hair always been so coarse, so dull? His hand hovered near, but did not touch, her head.

On the coldest nights she would luxuriate in linen's fine friction against her keen and tetchy hide. Sometimes the pure pleasure of shivering nakedness made her writhe against the mattress, a snake trying to shed its skin, her abandoned nightgowns ruffled ghosts cast to the cold floor around the bed. Alma was a creature that thrived in chill.

But the heat made her . . . difficult, his darling. It was the curse of a sensitive nature, she'd often said so, feeling things so much more intensely than others did. It left you at the mercy of . . . *everything,* really. It made life trying. Especially when it was hot.

So hot. Such a ripe odor to the air, as if the room were sweating. Rotting. Rain poured from the roof, scattershot the windows. Oskar closed his eyes, imagined the moistness between her breasts, her thighs. The taste of salt was on his tongue.

She sighed, his Almi, in her sleep. She murmured something. His name?

Oskar opened his eyes. How she hated the heat. He lifted the blanket, peeled back the sheet. He folded the bedding at the foot of the bed.

She lay on her side, one stiff arm thrust out in front of her. Her eyes, thank God, were closed. Expensive mechanical eyes that did not always work properly. Sometimes she kept staring at him when she must have been asleep, he knew she must. Almi, my beautiful eye . . .

Oskar's eye, for one swift and terrible moment, lost its gift for transformation. He saw that the thing on the bed was absurd. He felt ill.

It is only the heat, he thought. He quickly circled the bed. When the face was no longer in view, he touched her. He ran one hand along a broad white curve of haunch. If his touch moved with the grain, her flank felt silken, smooth. Almost like . . .

Minden Lo . . . *Liebchen.*

He remembered the sorrel mare that had escorted him to battle. A stallion would have been preferable, of course. Still, beggars couldn't be . . . He'd gone into debt for the sweet, unlucky beast, cadging an embarrassing loan from his friend von Ficker to buy her . . . then forced to beg another handout from Loos, and another, just to keep her in oats.

Within days, the creature's lovely sepia hide was torn and festering from the wooden saddle's rub . . . he'd seen signs of lameness even before leaving the cavalry school at Wiener Neustadt. A bad bargain all the way around, that horse. But without a decent mount, there would have been no place for him in the Imperial Cavalry, no officer's sky-colored tunic.

Oskar had never bothered to learn the name his mount had arrived with. He thought he might call her Minden Lo. But the first time he did so, aloud, he knew he had made a dreadful mistake. To display his least affinity for the beast, in even so slight a way, was foolhardy and dangerous. To love something, he'd learned, was to number its days. He vowed to regard the animal with pure indifference. It was the only protection he could offer her.

In the end, however, without meaning to, he had sometimes called her *Liebchen,* despite his best intention to call her nothing at all.

She was not really a beautiful horse, his *Liebchen,* apart from the gleam of intelligence in her eyes. Because she was somewhat stocky, she appeared far sturdier than she'd prove in the end. They'd endured months of indignity and deprivation together, Oskar and his horse. Both were jumpy and worn down by the rigors of training long before arriving at the front.

When the horse was shot out from under him at Lutsk, Oskar was almost relieved, for by that time her lameness was a clear liability. When struck, she screamed. Her anguish had an eerily human sound. Oskar went down with her in silence, as if the horse's scream sufficed for both of them.

Both casualties of a single instant, Oskar and his expensive, perishable mount. That he'd been the one to recover and survive had seemed, at the time, a fortunate accident. Incredibly fortunate. Later, lost and shell-shocked and aching, Oskar often wondered if his horse hadn't been the luckier after all.

He must not think of the horse. He had cared for her too little. Had cared for her just enough to destroy her . . . *Liebchen.* Oskar stared at the summerhouse window. Beyond the gauzy glass the sound of rain like a mountain stream overbrim with April snowmelt. He remembered Mürren's midsummer air, thin and cold as a spinster aunt's kiss.

Had he only painted the roses yesterday.

A CANVAS OF EXCELLENT QUALITY, 80 BY 120 CENTIMETERS. HE HAD stretched it himself.

He'd been saving it. The canvas was made to fit a marvelous carved frame he'd been hoarding. He'd come upon the frame in the dusty labyrinth of a Stockholm shop on a cold morning when he was still trying to decide upon the best method of killing himself. The price quoted by the shopkeeper had suggested the press of gun barrel to temple. Prosaic? Perhaps. But virtually foolproof.

The frame had been one of Karin's many gifts to him. His lovely, lascivious Baroness von Fock-Kantzow, so recently widowed, was grief's intimate. And no stranger, God knew, to desire. As Oskar took the prescribed rest in her canopied bed that afternoon, Karin had returned to the shop, paying, Oskar was certain, every last larcenous krona the shopkeeper asked. Money could not, the Baroness allowed, buy happiness. Still, despair could be diverted, no? The marketplace depended upon brisk trade in diversionary goods.

The Baroness was not lacking in wisdom. Karin lacked, in fact, for little. It would have been ungracious to kill oneself while a guest in her villa, particularly in the immediate aftermath of such largesse. The price of the frame had been three times Oskar's monthly stipend now, at the Academy. And he'd left Sweden more than a year ago, before the war's inflation had fully set in.

Lovely Karin: hair pale and silky, more platinum by lamplight than gold, fine fair tufts under plump arms . . . the frontal pelvic arch downy as a newborn's fontanel.

Less easily aroused than Alma, and so more grateful. Karin's husband had been close to elderly when they married, ill shortly thereafter, and then so ill for so long. Oh, but he'd had gentle hands, Lars. Such understanding. And so much money! Loved him? Of course she had. He had been her tutor in love, her master, though certain lessons had perhaps been slighted.

Karin never made a sound when Oskar entered her. His deepest thrust could not coax from her a moan or a sigh. His mouth upon her

breast, however, quickened her breath and drew from her, finally, a helpless childlike sound. These small whimpers terrified Oskar, who heard
in them the pure desperation of her need for him.

She demanded of him nothing. There was nothing she thought he
might want that she would refuse. Karin kept her hopes to herself, except insofar as her eyes betrayed them. Karin wouldn't have blinked or
haggled over price. The frame, should it move Oskar to resume painting, would prove a bargain. And should hers happen to be the portrait
he . . .

It had seemed to Oskar one of suicide's most persuasive arguments,
the hope in Karin's blue-pearl eyes.

He could not paint. When he told her, three weeks later, that he must
leave, a soft whimper, not quite stifled, rose from the back of her throat.
Oskar wondered if sorrow aroused her, if, like Alma's, her lust was lu-
bricated by tears.

That night, alone in the guest quarters of Karin's estate, Oskar
wrapped the beautiful frame in flannel and placed it at the back of a
cupboard. Dovetailing so meticulous it seemed all of a piece . . . his chest
ached with the pain of leaving it behind. But to keep so costly a gift
would have been, under the circumstances, inexcusable.

Weeks later, a large flat parcel followed Oskar from Sweden to his
parents' home in Vienna. The frame was accompanied by a short, affec-
tionate note. A magnanimous soul, Karin. Much would have been
solved, actually, by marrying her. Not, however, the hope in her pale
steady gaze . . . nor the artist's inability to render cool northern perfection where he could envision only Alma's hectic beauty.

Mad inappropriate beauty, Oskar thought now, his turpentine-raw
fingers feeling their way along the frame's scrolled edge. Unusual, so formal a design having been spared stain and varnish and gilt. The wood,
ash rubbed to satin, bore the subtle anointment of human oils. He imagined rough fingers night after night caressing the wood, seeking in friction the warmth and light to survive the bottomless dark of a Swedish
winter.

For a moment he saw her there, Karin, saw clearly that the frame was
no proper venue for Alma's histrionics, her ripe and squalid beauty. A
voluptuary's face imposed upon the dogmatic purity of a Macedonian
icon? Sacrilege!

I should have painted her, he thought, even if I couldn't marry her.

Karin was about to marry again, an acquaintance reported . . . betrothed to a dashing and much decorated pilot named Göring, whose daring loop-de-loops had been the apogee of a German air show's Scandinavian tour.

Oskar hoped the pilot was in vigorous health, and that his heroics were not confined to thin air. He set the frame on a pillow, propped against the headboard of the bed. Stepping back, he could almost see . . .

When he stepped closer, the features of the fair face inside the frame began to fade. He withdrew, but too late. The frame remained empty. All he could see was how wrong, how *impossible,* Almi would have been there. While Karin . . .

Presented with the face, he could not paint. By the time the painter's prodigal gifts returned, passion had fled . . .

Mein Gott, *I believe in you,* Oskar thought. *I do. Pray forgive the puny and lackadaisical faith of my naive youth.* How could God's existence be in doubt? Who but an omniscient and omnipotent Deity could tailor such intricate tortures to fit each life?

I can't even kill myself, unless it pleases my bully God to allow it.

At the head of the bed, the frame, backed by golden pillows, gleamed like a vacant monstrance. *Lord, I am not worthy* . . .

A storm of rage tore through him, uprooting everything. Frail structures of hope and conviction toppled. Oskar turned and looked at the lumpish sprawl on the divan. His beloved. His ersatz mistress. Her painted lids were not quite closed. The glassy eyes peeked at him, their indolence coy, their blue too vivid. There is nothing true about her, Oskar thought. There never was.

This was the secret he'd been trying to keep from his soul, a soul still innocent and so inquisitive. How to keep that soul alive in the face of such ruinous clarity? How, without heaven's permission, could he destroy himself? My one recourse, Oskar thought, is madness.

A refuge of sorts, madness. But he could not, as a madman, paint. He knew this. Faith in madness was a luxury Oskar could not, as an artist, afford.

Nothing but truth could keep the painter alive.

17

Oil on canvas, 80 x 120 cm.
"Self-Portrait with Doll."
Inscribed "OK" b.l.

The painting, rather fittingly for a creation so . . . well, a bit sordid, no?
That the painting would wind up in Berlin seems fitting indeed. But
Oskar, waiting for the paint to dry, waiting to fit truth in its right and
proper frame, could not know the work's fate.

Oskar rarely thinks about what might become of his paintings once
he has finished with them . . . something of a shortcoming, perhaps, in
an artist with so little income, so much ambition. Portraits are especially
problematic. Oskar sets out with the best intentions, but hand and eye
rebel. His instinct for flattery, a sweet social grace, abandons him the
moment he picks up a brush. And palette knife? Disgruntled subjects,
reneging upon commissions, have sworn it was a weapon he turned on
them.

Occasionally he'll thrill his students with accounts of such setbacks.
They envy, he knows, each accusation and slight accorded him. Such
recognition of their work, from even the most vicious critic, would be
welcome. For is not the vigor of condemnation a reliable measure of
one's importance? How thrilling to be publicly castigated!

Oskar does not want his students' envy. He wants no one's. He merely wants his students to know what he knows:

"You carry weapons," he tells them, waving a palette knife. "But not this." He tosses the palette knife aside. It clatters to the studio floor. They've been under his tutelage for months now. Some of them manage not to look alarmed.

"*Sight,*" he says. "That is our weapon. All that is false must be destroyed by our eyes."

It amuses him to observe his students' reactions, or the studied lack thereof. It is clear that more than one of them think him mad.

But Oskar is never more sane than here, at the Academy, teaching. With the rest of his life forgotten, its truth is easy to see. Truth separates from lie and delusion the way an egg's bright yolk pulls from the white's viscous cling.

Fräulein,

The project of our mutual interest reached its destination here on the appointed day, somewhat after the appointed time, some weeks now past. I apologize if my delay in thus notifying you has been the cause of anxiety. The packing crate was unmolested. The mode of conveyance was, albeit crude, satisfactory. The delay of several hours (which at the time seemed interminable) was caused by an obstruction of the rails in the countryside near Crimmitschau and was, by all accounts, unavoidable. All costs of transport were, as you know, paid in advance and in full. With the enclosed draft to you, in the sum previously agreed upon, all debts I have incurred in connection with this project (working title: Die Schweigsame Frau*) are to the best of my knowledge hereby discharged in full and without further obligation. May I request written confirmation and receipt for the final payment enclosed at your earliest convenience?*

Regards.
Oskar Kokoschka

THE LETTER, LIKE THE DOZEN OTHERS WRITTEN SINCE THE SILENT WOMAN arrived, is sealed in a pale-blue envelope and addressed with a wide nub, in midnight-blue ink, to Stuttgart. It bears the same stamps as the others, two per letter, one faded red, the other watery green.

Unlike the other letters, however, this one is posted.

Finally, it is finished.

The letter is dispatched in the morning. That evening in the summer-house, despite August's sultriness, Oskar lights the stove. The nicked saucepan, beginning to corrode with rust, sits on top. He remembers a heady concoction of apricot nectar and beeswax flecked with gold. For a moment he forgets what he is doing and stands staring at the stove. Small tongues of flame lick the edges of its door.

Across the room, in the corner, the Silent Woman sits, atilt, on the bottle-green divan. She is wearing a mauve silk dress. The dress is severely tailored. Its sleeves, too tight, make her arms look like great sausages. Madame has been wearing the same dress since Sunday. It is now Wednesday evening.

Oskar stands beside the stove, engrossed in the fire. He does not look across the room toward the divan. What was it he'd been doing? The flames, small and agile, press their heat into his groin. He steps closer to the stove.

How, he wonders, would it feel, burning to death? He has often tried to imagine it. Pöchlarn, the Danube village where his parents lived when he was born, had erupted in flames not more than an hour after his birth. His poor mother, thighs still bloody and slick, had been yanked from childbed, her newborn son lashed to her belly with a bedsheet. They were spirited away from the advancing flames on the back of a hay cart that, later, simply vanished. Just who had rescued them was never known . . . certainly not the hapless new father who, chasing rumors of employment in Vienna's jewelry trade, missed everything.

Romana's own birth, she would later tell her boy, was accompanied by a similar inferno. Flames raged up one side of the mountain and down the other, miraculously sparing the nameless hamlet that harbored her family. Her father kept watch on the Emperor's forests, Romana said, a quiet and beautiful wealth of trees and game. "On the night I was born the sky was pierced with spears of flame. My mother heard, through the roar and smoke, the screams of falcons and wild boar.

"The Gypsies' doing." Her voice was smoky and dark. "They were starving. Once they found their curses could not evict us, they thought they would smoke us out."

As a child, Oskar both dreaded and craved the tale. His mother related it often. But always and only to Oskar, when his brother and sister could not hear.

"It marks us," she'd whisper, "the fire. But it means we must be brave. For its light reveals terrible things, things known only to us."

Romana would fix deep and fast on her boy's silver eyes then, extracting an exorbitant ransom of belief and terror and awe.

Oskar, as a man, was tickled by his mother's theatrics. Her blame upon the Gypsies, four-square and bitter, particularly amused him. For what blood was in Romana Loidl Kokoschka's veins, with her black eyes and conjurings, if not that of Gypsies? She told anyone who'd listen that she received regular messages from her first child, the son who died as an infant. Could babies talk, then, in heaven? he'd wondered as a child. Oskar wished his brother would tell *him* something.

Yes, even as a little boy, Oskar had known to take his mother's claims with more than a grain of salt. Still, her insistence that he'd inherited her gift of second sight could not, he felt, be discounted. Oskar saw too much, saw *through* too much. And yes, what he saw could be terrible. The fire's curse . . . the fire's gift. There was no escape from it.

Oskar leaned down close to the fire, plunging his face into the heat. He felt its scald on his forehead, the skin tightening on his chin and cheeks. His eyes seemed to sizzle.

He'd just been about to . . .

Inside the stove something popped. He heard a hiss then and smelled scorching. He had singed his eyelashes.

Oskar straightened and drew back from the stove. He stared for another moment at the fire. The flames, lithe and limber, seemed to be vying for his attention.

He went to the desk and took a stack of neat pale-blue envelopes from the top drawer.

He fed them, one at a time, to the fire. A shame to waste the stamps. But it was finished.

THE CALENDAR HAD VANISHED FROM ABOVE HIS BED. RESERL WONDERED if he had burned it.

A few nights before, hot as it was, there had been a fire in the summerhouse. The scent of smoke had sent her running into the garden after midnight. The air was damp and thick with insects. Reserl stood outside the kitchen door for a long time, watching smoke flow from the pipe in the summerhouse's furrowed roof, marveling at how quickly the milky moonlit sky swallowed it.

Were there only still a calendar to consult. Reserl had lost track of the days. The Direktor should be returning soon, she thought.

The Captain probably knew. The Captain had engagements. He'd played cards two evenings at Dr. Neuberger's and last week his friend Herr Loos had visited. Some days he even went out to buy the newspaper. He was vague, yes, dreamy and remote. Still, the Captain had ties to the world. He must know what day it was. But Reserl could not bring herself to ask.

For several nights he had not cried out in his sleep. Nor, since Sunday, escorted Madame into the dining room for dinner. Indeed, nothing was heard now from Madame. Reserl tried to imagine her content, or dead, or huffily departed, but no such occurrence seemed likely without a summons to the kitchen. Surely Reserl's help would have been required, if not for solace or sustenance, at least to help Madame pack.

The Captain had stopped speaking of her. On Monday afternoon, he asked Reserl to prepare a simple supper, cold sausage and bread and fruit, to bring to the summerhouse on a tray. He'd made the request as if it were quite usual. But then wasn't the Captain always adding to the elaborations of their charade?

"Around seven," he said. "Would that be all right? I don't sleep well after a late dinner." Playacting, surely . . .

"Madame." Reserl kept her expression neutral. "She is unwell?"

He did not look at her. "Oh, Madame," he said, as if the subject were tedious. "I'm afraid Madame is not quite herself."

"Perhaps she would like—"

"I haven't time," he said, turning away.

He stepped out into the glare of another hot, hazy afternoon, the door left ajar behind him.

Not once had he looked at her.

But at least he had not closed the door.

Madame must be having one of her tantrums.

It seemed to Reserl a hopeful thought.

OIL ON CANVAS . . . 80 BY 120 CENTIMETERS. "SELF-PORTRAIT WITH DOLL."
It is finished.

Finished. The word etches his thin lips into an acidic smile. A painting is never finished. There is only a moment (the best one can hope for, a matter of false bravado perhaps?) when the artist steps back from his work, looks it in the eye, so to speak, and says:

Here it is.

Enough.

I am done with you.

Some actually claim this moment can disclose the enigmatic smile of true genius . . .

A skittish matter, genius! The instinct for the single best instant to stop, neither cutting too soon vision's losses, nor too long dallying over attempts to conceal them . . . and knowing all the while, accepting with good grace, the truth: No moment could be *perfect.* The vision is always in some part lost . . .

Well might there be genius, yes, in the timing of such acquiescence.

Oskar cannot make up his mind whether such a thing as genius exists, though he does keep an eye out for it in himself.

Genius has by now been claimed for him a number of times by others. Such claims are, for the time being, extravagant, Oskar knows.

He has also been hailed as "an Old Master born late." And:

"A terrible wonder."

"A clumsy purveyor of decay."

Curious, how insult can suggest greater regard than any plaudit. He is especially proud of one early tribute:

Kokoschka brews up his paints from poisonous putrescence . . . smears them on like salve and allows them to crust scabrously, to form scars.

Ah, Roessler! The Viennese critic could sting like a wasp, but he is neither stupid nor blind. Despising Oskar's work, Roessler came closer than most to understanding it.

Genius or not, Oskar knows he is getting better at sensing it—the single best instant to let a painting go. If such a thing as genius exists, he suspects it belongs more to a moment than a man.

He moves back from his easel, pausing with each slow step. He studies the painting he has made. He tries to look it in the eye.

Eye. A foolish, sentimental metaphor, not one he'd care to defend, or even be caught entertaining. Still, the notion both beguiles and persuades: At a certain point, his paintings look back at him.

Could this, he wonders, be "the second sight" Romana prophesied? Oskar imagines reporting the phenomenon to his Gypsy mother and laughs aloud at the picture of her forked fingers, her spittle warding off the evil eye.

The eye of this painting, where is it—her belly, his hand? The divan is draped in deep red. Upon it lies the Silent Woman, lewd in her posture of lassitude. Or what would, in a woman, be lewd. But the painting makes clear that this splay-legged female can neither breathe nor see.

And clearest of all, that she cannot feel. She cannot be blamed for it. Feeling is simply beyond her.

While the shadowed presence behind her . . . what does he feel? It would be difficult to say just what, but something. His gaze suggests a soul stunned and mesmerized by grief.

Was that what I meant? Oskar wonders. I'd be last and least likely to know. Let Roessler and his tribe tell me what I was trying to say.

He is not, when he paints, trying to *say* anything.

He is trying to *see.*

Self-portrait with . . .

With the self incidental, mere backdrop.

Well, that would seem to be saying something, wouldn't it? But it matters little. To see is what matters. What Oskar sees now, studying this fresh painting, is *light,* the allocation of light.

Light does not so much relieve the darkness as stand up to it. The female figure's face, her thighs, raise massive objections to the darkness. Renegade patches of radiance break upon his chin, his throat. And behind him two small protests of gentian light, miraculous chinks in the heavy carapace of gloom.

What did he *mean* by those pittances of light? Someone is bound, eventually, to ask.

Mean?

Oskar will pretend to mull the question for a moment. The moment will elongate to the point where his interrogator—student, admirer, critic, biographer? It scarcely matters. Soon enough the sincere fool who asks the question, finding silence intolerable, will crowd it with some interpretation.

Then Oskar Kokoschka, latecomer Old Master and possible genius, will, after a suitable pause for thought, nod and smile and mutter something agreeable: "You very well may be right." Or: "A wonder I hadn't thought of that myself."

The eye of the painting is the light. He stares into it and sees it coalesce, conspire against the darkness.

He is finished with it.

He means nothing by it.

The meaning is the painting's to reveal.

It will, with patience and luck, come to him over many years.

All Oskar knows at this moment, as the paint undertakes the slow work of drying into some illusion of permanence, is that meaning begins with the light.

WHEN, SEVERAL DAYS LATER, HE LOOKS AT HER AGAIN, HE SEEMS TO DO SO with only one eye. He appears fevered and distracted. He stammers a bit as he tells Reserl he has decided . . . he feels the time has come . . .

Another party?

Reserl, supposing the occasion to be the Direktor's return, asks when.

Next Saturday evening, he says. A week from tomorrow. He hopes . . . will that be sufficient time to—

She tries to coax from him what she would not ask. "And the Direktor will be coming—"

He surrenders the precious fact as if it were worthless. "Sunday," he says. "The following day."

He seems not to notice her dismay.

Reserl tries not to think of the difficulties. Cleaning up after a party, making for the Direktor a proper *Willkommen* . . . perhaps that night she will not go to bed. Perhaps it will be nearly evening by the time the Direktor comes. The house will be filled with the fragrance of apples, spiced and buttery, the tabletops gleaming with oil . . .

She imagines the Direktor, white-lipped with anger at finding his dining room dismantled.

How many guests and what time and what does he wish her to prepare? She waits for the Captain to tell her.

"You will, of course, wear the uniform."

The uniform: its tiny black buttons, the apron's starched lisp their secret. Only he has ever seen . . .

Reserl nods. A week and a day. The weather by then will likely have cooled.

He gazes beyond her, looking out the kitchen window. The sky is cluttered with clouds. His attention wanders back to her, one eye still distant. "Just a few friends," he says, "after dinner. Little fuss, really. I'll see to wines this week and—"

"After dinner?" Reserl looks down. *Like an oaf,* she thinks. "Then shall I serve—"

"You shall serve Madame." Oskar tosses her a madman's smile. "Your simple duty, *mein Lamm . . .*" He smiles. "Is to *attend* her."

"You wish me to . . . be Madame's companion? While you are at the party with your guests?"

Oskar, looking out the window again, laughs softly. "To attend her needs *at* the party, Reserl. Madame is the guest of honor."

One of his eyes looks at her, one does not. One thing is true, the other pretend. Either the guests or Madame's presence cannot be true . . . one way or the other, he is joking. Reserl's smile does not commit itself.

"We'll receive our guests in the garden," Oskar says.

Summer has completed its ruin. An early spring lavish with rain, two months of moist heat followed by weeks of drought . . . everything in the garden overgrown now, and parched. Dry leaves, visited by a rare desultory breeze, collide and chafe, the sound of a dozen irked scribes crumpling spoiled papers. The summerhouse, in an ambush of ungainly brown shrubs, can barely be seen from the little slot of light in Reserl's room.

"But what if there is rain?" she says.

He shrugs. "A small table under the acacia . . ."

Die Akazie. Not knowing the word, she imagines some sort of umbrella or canopy.

"The round one in the corner of the parlor will do, I should think. I'll cover it with something . . . suitably opulent." He looks as if he wants to laugh, then sees Reserl is perplexed.

"The table, little one! Just for bottles and glasses and—"

"But where will they sit?"

Her worries amuse him. "The dining room chairs," he says. "Easily moved. Would you think me careless of my guests' comfort?"

At his laugh her eyes sting. She lowers her head.

"Reserl." His touch light and warm through the wool on her shoulder. Her dress is damp and smells of sweat.

"Reserl," he says again, "don't you know when I am joking?"

She nods but does not look up.

"You are so hot. Poor lamb! We should have seen to it that you had lighter clothes for summer."

Surprise raises her face in time to catch sight of his fleeting distress.

"I never once thought—" His large red hands twist and knot together.

"Summer is soon ending." Reserl smiles. "I could make at least, then, a cake?" *Brown sugar, the flush on golden-cheeked apples . . . some biscuits, a basket of black grapes . . .*

He shrugs. "I'm afraid I will need your help with the divan." Oskar smiles absently. "Madame, as you know, prefers to recline."

It takes her a moment to understand: he means to move the divan outdoors. Reserl sees it there, its velvet far greener than anything left in the garden. Its humped back is spattered with white bird droppings. Field mice and squirrels nest in its cushions.

"It may not fit through the door, I think." She sounds hopeful.

"Do you suppose they built the summerhouse around it?" He pats her on the head.

"For the other ladies perhaps—"

"Other ladies!" His laugh is like a dog's bark. "*Mais non, mein Lamm!* There will be no other ladies. Only Madame," he says. "And yourself, of course."

A little plate of rich cheeses, the kind the Direktor sometimes wishes for dessert . . . Appenzeller, Greyerzer, Topfen . . . and the cheese of goat's milk he has such fondness for . . . Altenburger? The farmer's wife from out near Gompitz makes the best, but she comes only once to the market each month . . .

Reserl tries to recall when she last saw the sour old woman in her straw hat and hairy gray shawl. Her cheeses are like no other, the Direktor says.

"There will be, I should guess, eight of us," says the Captain.

Does the number, Reserl wonders, take Madame and herself into account?

"No more than ten," he says.

After he has gone, she wishes he'd thought to tell her what time.

Another place must be found for the rose glass lamp, before he makes off with the table . . .

A shower of glass splinters rains down around Reserl, livid pink, sharp as darts.

THE FRAME IS ALL WRONG. HE SEES THAT THE MOMENT HE HOLDS IT UP TO the painting. *All wrong.* Then, as if hearing his own voice, he smiles. Not that *the painting* was wrong. No, of course not. What is at fault must be the frame.

The air is hot and greasy and thick. Like his mother's unfortunate gravies, Oskar thinks. Summer is taking its time with its death throes. He thought the paint would never dry.

But it seems to have done so, finally. He touches the painting once more to make sure. His fingertips caress the shadow that seems to sever the woman's thigh from her trunk . . . one of a number of places where once he might have lost himself. Now he imagines not a woman's skin but a beast's coarse nap. He withdraws his hand and examines it. No trace of black paint to mark the whorls on his fingertips.

So now at last the painting is ready, but he has for it no proper frame . . . 80 by 120 centimeters. Oskar holds the frame once more to the painting. An outlandish coupling. The Swedish frame, so refined and pure . . . had he actually expected it to confine such power, such rawness? Forcing them together demeans both. The frame looks prissy, the picture crude. The clash is offensive, disturbing, almost . . .

Die Obszönität.

An obscenity. Exactly. The pairing is wayward and smutty, bound to shock. At least one thing, then, to favor the union. Oskar smiles.

As is often the case, the improper liaison will be short-lived, a moment's heady temptation. The painting slips easily into the frame's hold, he has already seen to that.

Its spot has been selected and measured and prepared. Reserl, bless her tidy little heart, looked appalled at what she found in the space the divan has so long occupied. The wall's recess, vacated, forms a little alcove. A whole generation of insects bred and fed, wove shrouds and died there quite unnoticed. A gray heather of hair and lint and dust bloomed lush among the mummified. A few mouse (or, God forbid, *rat*) droppings also appeared. But these, Oskar pointed out, meaning to reassure the girl, were clearly quite old.

Reserl, her face pale, left the summerhouse so abruptly that he thought her ill. She returned in a moment with a whisk broom and dustpan. Kneeling in the alcove, doubled over to gather up the filth, she looked like a penitent crushed by the weight of her sins.

Which was perhaps what suggested the notion in the first place: turning the alcove into a kind of altar, a devotional space.

The moment it came to him, Oskar remembered the prie-dieu. He'd seen it in the attic, among the dubious treasures and antiquities Hans Posse had shown him one idle afternoon. Oskar, newly in Dresden, withdrawn and lethargic, had been both moved and irritated by his host's all too obvious attempt to pique his interest.

Recalling his irritation, Oskar feels shame. The poor Direktor must have felt as if he'd invited an ill-tempered ghost to share his home. Oskar wishes the man he is now could apologize, could somehow make amends, for the man he was last year.

Spring it would have been. He remembered the weather was still cool but the attic was hot. It was early afternoon, the extension of conversation over lunch. The Direktor had a weakness, he said, for . . .

Discarded things with a history of cherishing. Oskar recalls how the phrase had pierced his implacable ennui. Hans Posse frequently found himself at the mercy of orphaned treasures with questionable pedigrees. His attic had become a make-do purgatory, crowded with the imperfect, things too nearly ordinary for the museum, too odd or beautiful to let go.

"Or occasionally too hallowed." The Direktor had laughed like a man who did not mind being slightly ridiculous. "The possibility that something is sacred," he said, "is one I find hard to dismiss."

But how, Oskar wanted to know, did the possibility of sacredness occur to him?

"To me?" Hans Posse looked taken aback. "I'm no man for religion," he said. "A devout agnostic, at best."

"Then how—"

The Direktor held out his hands, as if to prove their emptiness. "If there have been those who have sincerely deemed something holy, have in some way pinned their souls on it . . ." Oskar saw deep humility in the way the older man's fine hands fell to his sides. "I am hardly one to refute faith," Hans Posse said. "I lack experience."

An arresting conversation, Oskar realizes now. He wonders how it could have lain so long fallow in memory's recesses. So much had been lost on him then . . .

What more Posse may have said about his custody of others' venerations, Oskar does not remember. He recalls the heat and dust of the attic, and topaz light falling through a dusty round window. And he remembers at least a few of the possibly hallowed objects: a sixteenth-century Koran unearthed in ruins outside Tabriz, a sharp-nippled fertility goddess spirited from the Ivory Coast, a thin-lipped golden chalice set with semiprecious stones.

The prie-dieu was olive wood, intricately carved. A stern nameless saint upheld at each side the padded and tapestried kneeler, the slanted shelf for prayerbook and folded hands. The matter of provenance was ticklish, the Direktor said. Sold under duress by an emaciated cloister somewhere near Radeburg, the prie-dieu was believed (at least by the nuns) to have been a wealthy bishop's gift to Christiane Eberhardine, Augustus the Strong's famously pious and double-chinned wife. This illustrious connection, regrettably, could not be documented. Which purported to explain how a wildly successful hotelier, in momentary straits, came to offer the piece to the museum at a price that . . . well, more philanthropy than a strict business transaction, the hotelier said.

The prie-dieu was not in fact old enough to have been familiar with the devout Christiane's dimpled knees. To point this out, however, would have been rude. Nor did it seem necessary to say the piece would reside not in a public museum but a private attic. Hans Posse offered half the asking price. If the hotelier found payment in cash curious, it was remarkably convenient and nothing he cared to question.

OSKAR TACTFULLY WAITED UNTIL RESERL WAS ABSENT FROM THE HOUSE before wrestling the prie-dieu down two flights of stairs and out the back door. The oatmeal-faced countrywoman had not been available at the market. Oskar directed Reserl to a cheese merchant Katja favored. The shop could be found in the Schiessgasse. Shooting Street. "Look in the police towers' shadow," he'd told her, grinning at her look of alarm.

The remnants of red and gold cloth find new purpose, deep folds

arching over the painting in the alcove. Oskar faces and centers the prie-
dieu before it, stands back to look.

Too close. He shifts it back an arm's length. Yes, delightful. The brass
wall sconces are perfectly spaced to accommodate the frame. Fresh tapers, pure beeswax and slightly squat . . . proper not to an ornate church
but a private chapel.

Below, on the floor, smaller candles occupy the Direktor's wealth of
ruby cordial glasses. Could they ever, all two dozen, have been needed
at once? He tries to imagine Frau Posse, the pretty but rather mousy
woman whose framed image hangs about the house, presiding over large
candlelit soirees . . .

The candles' white wicks crook above the red glasses like beckoning
fingers. Hans Posse seems like a man who has always been alone. When
Oskar tries to picture him with a wife, the Direktor looks gullible and
gaunt, like the nuns.

Two tall brass urns, etched in designs vaguely Arabic, look better here
than in their accustomed place on the library hearth. Weighted already with
water, they seem to kneel below the painting in stolid worship, awaiting the
fierce fresh red daggers they will hold tomorrow. Gladiolas, a rather charm-
less flower, generally, stiff-spined and too tall. *Gemein,* Almi would say. Vulgar. One of the more damning terms in his darling's lethal vocabulary. Yet
they will be just right here . . . dignified, ecclesiastical. I must not enfeeble
them, Oskar thinks, with greenery . . . unless perhaps blades of palm . . .

He sinks, without will, to his knees. The padded kneeler deflates,
sighing at his weight.

His gaze is borne, without will, to his painting.

The profane painting looks back at him from within a sacred light.

THE GIRL DRESSED AS A BOY IS THERE. FRÄULEIN KALLIN. MALINA, HE CALLS
her. And Niuta. *Niuta his little singing bird.* The others call her Anna.
Anna is, someone says to someone, a mad Russian. Reserl wonders if all
Russian girls bear three names and wear snug breeches.

Malina arrives with a slight officer who wears the sky-blue tunic,
the red breeches and brass helmet of an officer in the Emperor's
army. The Captain worms his way between the pair, entangling himself in their arms, peppering the air around their cheeks with little

kisses. The officer and the boy both wear lip rouge. Reserl is shocked.

"Welcome to Eden, my adorable chaps!" The Captain pulls the two closer to his sides. The one in fawn breeches snuggles against him. The officer, staring at Madame, pulls away. "This is what you've been keeping to yourself?"

When Reserl hears the voice she recognizes the officer: Käthe Richter. *Katja.*

No other women, Reserl, he said . . . only you and Madame . . .

A double row of gleaming buttons marches over the summit of Fräulein Richter's chest. The red breeches are perfectly molded to her slightly plump thighs. Both she and Fräulein Kallin wear riding boots of beautifully burnished leather. Their feet are, even in stout boots, dainty.

Fräulein Richter's eyes leave Madame with difficulty.

"I am very put out with you, Oskar."

"I cannot imagine why, my dove."

She looks down at her uniform. "You place poor Malina and me at a disadvantage." She casts a resentful glance toward the divan, then looks at her friend. "We're quite humiliated, Malina, aren't we?"

Anna Kallin, still nestled under the Captain's arm, shrugs.

Fräulein Richter's shame is badly feigned. Playacting. His pretending, his secrets and jokes, are shared with others. Reserl imagines his fingers slipping morsels of rich food between Fräulein Richter's pursed lips. For a moment she feels dizzy and sick.

"You look irresistible, Katja, as you very well know." As the Captain kisses Fräulein Kallin's ear, his arms let her go. "You both do. The tailoring . . ." He turns Fräulein Richter by the shoulders. "Superb!" He smiles. "What sorcerer's thread produced this miracle?"

"You, wicked boy, are no longer my confidant." Under the helmet she pouts and preens. "This is what comes of my telling you of the new dress I've been dying to wear."

"He is beastly," one of the actors agrees. "Come, *Liebchen,* let me console you properly."

But Fräulein Richter has succumbed to Madame's spell. She steps closer to the divan and stares down at the reclining figure. *"Mein Gott!"* she whispers after a moment. Then she looks up and notices Reserl. "You have enlisted a collaborator, I see."

Her voice is cold. The Captain does not hear it. "Schoenberg?" he is saying to Dr. Neuberger. "I did invite him, yes . . . and most properly, black ink on a fine heavy stock. Foil-lined envelope and all. Yet he has not seen fit to reply."

"Arnold is in Berlin," someone says. "Or Prague, is it?"

"A busy boy, our Arnold," Fritz Neuberger says.

"'Boy'?" Oskar scoffs. "Fifty in a few more years and still the wunderkind?"

The doctor smiles. "Still the enfant terrible, in any case."

"The Maestro's bastard son," Oskar mutters, "no matter how he grizzles and stoops."

"I thought you were fond of Arnold."

"I am." The skittish silver-blue eyes light on the figure on the divan. "We've nothing but affection for yon Schoenberg, have we, *Liebchen*? His lean and hungry look rather becomes him. We'd simply have thought he might make some effort to—"

The Hofkirche's chimes distract him. Can it be already ten o'clock? His uplifted face is a low wan moon against the thick dark sky. *"O Verklärte Nacht!"* he says.

O Radiant Night . . . O night Transfigured . . .

Dr. Neuberger lifts his wineglass. "To Schoenberg," he says, "wherever he may be."

Reserl does not know of this Herr Schoenberg, wherever he may be. The Captain's odd, beautiful words keep singing in her head like a holy chant escaping the windows of an alien church. *O Verklärte Nacht.*

Everyone seems to be watching the Captain now, while trying to pretend they aren't. The Hofkirche bell has done its duty. The garden falls quiet. The corners of the guests' eyes sharpen with vigilance.

He stands beside the divan, gazing down at the coarse painted face that, in the garden, looks even less human, all the more like an exotic animal. Reserl wants to reach across the curved boundary of green velvet and carved wood to touch his arm, to wake him before he cries out.

But he is, in the end, able to rouse himself. He smiles sadly at Dr. Neuberger. "My darling is disappointed," he says. "But yes—" He lifts his glass. "To our dear Arnold!"

Then the guests are again talking all at once, laughing, and flush blooms like a flower on the Captain's ivory face, and Reserl hears over and over, like the old widows in Roman churches mumbling over their beads: *O Verklärte Nacht . . . O Verklärte Nacht . . .*

Everything after this night will be different, Reserl thinks. But how? She wonders why she is afraid.

IN THE GARDEN HE HAD POSED HER LIKE A STATUE, MOMENTS BEFORE HIS first guest, Professor Löwenblatt, arrived. Reserl, placed just so, behind one end of the divan, the end where Madame's head occupied a crush of gold pillows. The Captain stepped back and looked. Then, taking Reserl by the shoulders, he shifted her slightly to the left.

Again he stepped back to study the arrangement. He stared at her intently. But he was not seeing her.

His eyes looked like that when he painted. One day he would paint her, Reserl thought, looking deeply to see . . . beyond her. She must not mind. She hoped he would allow her to wear the dress of the Direktor's dead wife.

Madame was, for the first time in several weeks, beautifully dressed. Her low-cut black velvet frock was free of lint and creases. An elaboration of curls coiled above her smooth brow. Pearls bound her wrists and delved into her bosom's cleft, ropes of pearls disappearing into the darkness of her gown.

She was waiting there, dressed and coiffed and perfumed, when the Captain called Reserl to the garden. The sight of Madame so perfectly turned out scored Reserl's heart. It could all be done without her . . . even the hair. Reserl saw a marzipan nipple vanishing between wet lips, heard the midnight cries of wolves. A tired breath of wind made a papery rustle through the leaves. In the branches of a half-clad tree, a lantern flickered. No longer does he need me for so much, Reserl thought.

EVERYONE IS HERE NOW, IT SEEMS, MORE THAN HE SAID . . . RESERL HOPES there will be enough cheese. Even without herself and Madame, and the Captain also uncounted, there are nine: the two not-women and Professor Löwenblatt, Dr. Neuberger and the two actors who board at his house, and . . .

The three men last to arrive are introduced to Madame in a formal manner. Herr Hasenclever is to be a famous playwright, the Captain says, then pauses, nodding. "Ah!" He smiles mischievously. "'We should all live so long,' she says."

Herr Hasenclever removes a round black hat. His nearly bald head is rather a shock above his big-eyed boy's face. "*Meine gnädige Frau* is most astute!"

The Captain chuckles. "And these two reprobates, my darling, Iwär and Paul—"

Two hungry-looking young men, both wearing dingy white shirts with extravagant sleeves, step forward and bow as one.

"These two are our esteemed holy fools. Which is to say, of course, poets."

Everyone laughs. Everyone but Reserl and Madame.

The two young men straighten their backs and stare at Madame, their eyes stunned and excited.

"She has a soft spot for poets . . . I trust you won't try to take advantage? She can be a bit fickle."

The Captain's whisper could, Reserl thinks, be heard across the park.

"A little . . . inert for my taste," the taller one says.

"She's not," his friend agrees, "the sparkling conversationalist of legend."

This time when everyone seems to laugh, Reserl notices Professor Löwenblatt does not. He looks embarrassed. Dr. Neuberger's smile stretches his face tight.

Fräulein Richter, having decreed she shall be addressed as *Captain* Richter, drops to one knee before the divan. The gesture is made difficult by the snugness of her red breeches. Nor are Madame's upper parts easily gathered to one's bosom. The resulting embrace looks comfortable for neither.

Reserl imagines Madame's face, fallen behind gold epaulets and a stiff sky-blue shoulder, wrenched into fury's shape.

The moment is like a nightmare. In the face of terrible danger Reserl cannot move. Nothing makes sense. Her sole duty is to attend Madame, but what—

The Captain needs to tell her . . .

He will not look at her.

If we wake her, she will kill us.

Fräulein Richter is, of course, an actress. What she says and does is not meant to be real. Reserl understands this. She watches events unfold before her, bathed in light, surrounded by darkness. Just as it is, the Captain has told her, in theaters where actors perform his plays about burning bushes and murdered women. Reserl would be afraid to see such plays, she thinks. But she wishes she could look inside a theater. The Opera House is grander than a church and the people who go there—the women's jeweled gowns are wider than doorways, Valda says. The men's chests stick out, bright with silk sashes, with medals of silver and gold.

"Conversationalist?"

Fräulein Richter makes now the voice of an angry man. Reserl trembles. *A voice like Hulda's father naked among muscled trees when* . . .

"*Conversationalist,* you say?" Pointing her chin at the light, the actress drops her voice to a whisper. "My dear man, is *wit* what one desires of a *voluptuary?*"

The word seems to uncoil like a serpent from Fräulein Richter's tongue. *Voluptuary.* Reserl does not know its meaning. She imagines it slithering through dark dry grasses, sliding between the shutter slats into the vacant palace.

"Here, here!" and "Brava!" the young men cry.

"Amen." Dr. Neuberger looks sheepish.

Reserl watches the Captain. Everyone is watching him, watching the helpless silver eyes that dote on the form upon the divan.

"Actually," he says softly, "she is a goddess."

The holy fools cheer again, but feebly. Herr Löwenblatt and Dr. Neuberger exchange a nervous glance.

"A *goddess,* of course. Need it be said? Surely we all recognize her divine antecedents?" Fräulein Richter releases her risky hold on Madame. "Aphrodite's modest twin, no?"

Her small quick hands pounce on the neckline of the black velvet gown and give it a yank.

The furred white breasts, exposed, huddle like scared animals on the snowy slope of Madame's chest.

"*Mein Gott!*" someone whispers.

"*Meine Göttin,*" says the actress. "A goddess, yes. And a little bit of a whore, too. Aren't you, darling?" She pinches one bright grainy nipple and laughs.

"*Prosit!*" says the girl in fawn breeches. *His Niuta.*

The Captain stares at her, Fräulein Kallin . . . his little singing bird. There is a small gasp of wind. "Amen," he says. Reserl imagines the breeze carrying the word out into the world like a message.

Amen. Käthe Richter, still on her knees, looks up, smiling. She plucks a long-stemmed goblet from a nearby tray and drains it. Then, leaning over the divan in a mockery of devotion, she releases a stream of red wine from her mouth, filling the bowl of the Silent Woman's navel.

There is a shocked silence. Reserl's low moan is like a spark in darkness. The pale wings of her hands fly to fold over her mouth, but too late.

The Captain's eyes roll back, dull white marbles in the bruised hollows of his face.

The Doctor moves toward him in alarm. Herr Löwenblatt, reaching him first, puts an arm around his shoulders. "Steady," he says.

The Captain closes his eyes and sags against his friend.

"Oskar?" The Doctor's voice is gentle.

Fräulein Richter looks afraid.

Reserl stands very still, the thin heels of her boots imbedded in the clotted dirt.

The Captain slowly opens his eyes.

"You are all right, Oskar?"

He looks at Dr. Neuberger.

"Are you going to be all right?"

The Captain throws back his head and howls at the starless sky.

18

He loiters, still awake, in the garden. Soon it will be dawn. He wonders if Reserl is sleeping. Much must be remedied before the Direktor's return.

Two crystal wineglasses have been crushed: Paul demonstrating something about Hebraic wedding ritual, Oskar seems to recall; *Die Schweigsame Frau* hoisted aloft, a canopy over Katja and . . . was it Iwär? Some inebriated youth using the soiled lace tablecloth as a bridal veil. Can that possibly have . . .

Yes. It is simply too asinine, Oskar thinks, to be a dream.

Heavy casualties, too, among the red cordials. The heat, when the candles burned low, was too much for the delicate little glasses. Five or six had shattered before the damage was noticed. *You might have burned down the house,* Fritz Neuberger said. The Doctor had looked, Oskar thought, a bit disgusted.

Otherwise no one seemed much unsettled by the rowdy and ridiculous evening. Except *der Blätterteig,* perhaps. Oskar should have realized that Karl would not belong. But his friend's tolerance did not depend on wine's fumes. Forgiveness seemed, along with innocence, his natural state. Nor was Fritz Neuberger likely to hold a grudge, not when he'd played host to so many drunken revels himself in the Felsenberg's heyday. Still, the ribald physician had looked . . . less than amused at a few points in the evening. We are all getting on, Oskar thought.

Around the garden, crumpled napkins lay like miraculous white blooms sprung from dead foliage. The very notion of bending to gather them was exhausting. Oskar sank down on the divan, neither concerned nor curious at finding it unoccupied and damp.

He lay back, sighing. When he closed his eyes, Malina's deliciously round little rump strutted by, then Katja's. Fawn broadcloth . . . red wool . . . swirling, intertwining . . .

Countless changeling colors rushed past, fading before they could be given names.

IT WAS RAINING AGAIN WHEN HE AWOKE. NOT HARD. JUST ENOUGH OF A drizzle to glaze his face. Dawn had silver-plated the city's eastern edge. He heard a rooster's distant crow. The rustic sound seemed outlandish as daylight fell upon Dresden's self-important cupolas and spires.

Oskar rose slowly, steadying himself on the divan's curved arm. The velvet would soon be drenched. If only the day would bring sun, the upholstery might dry some before the Direktor . . .

It was entirely too much to think about. Oskar slanted his face away from the dilemma.

"Oh, there you are," he said.

She lay, facedown, toward the back of the garden. The remains of her gown dangled above her, dark goblin impaled on a gnarled dwarf tree. A thick seam bisected her bald head. A noose of pearls, the keen upturned heels of dainty boots . . . he might not, but for those, have known her.

Oskar cut an oblique line through the garden and stopped shy of her, a bed's length away. Shivering, he buried his hands in his pockets, but they refused to stay. Lowering his head, he clasped them together in front of him, fingers intertwining to seek warmth.

Her limbs, swelled with rain, had lost all pretense of shapeliness. The body's position, lent the least likelihood of having, ever, been human, would be an obscenity: the splay of thigh, the outstretch of arms as if in crucifixion . . .

For a moment Oskar saw himself rushing to overturn and close her upon herself like a night-shy moonflower. He would wind her in a rich ruby shroud, lay her to rest on a bier cushioned with gold . . .

He imagined building a funeral pyre, reducing her to a purity of smoke and ash.

He longed to claim for her a kind of decency, and so to make some small claim on decency for himself.

But he could not touch her.

The hem of light was widening in the east. It rose above the highest tower, shone on casements and roof tiles rinsed with rain.

Oskar made his way to the sickly pear tree and unsnagged the black gown from its branches. The velvet, soaked and reeking of wine, dropped heavily into his hands. He shook the gown out and examined it. Nothing to salvage, he thought, and why would he? His eyes were averted as he laid the heap of dark wet cloth beside her on the ground.

He did not hear the cart approach. When it came to a stop in the alley, the solid planks of the garden gate blocked it from view. Then a horse snorted softly. Scuffing hooves quibbled with the stillness. Boots landed hard on the cinders.

"What is it?" Oskar, imagining a band of thieves, forced himself to stand his ground. "Who's there?"

A shadow passed through the gate. "Good Sabbath, mein Herr."

The dustman.

"Guten Morgen."

"Is it?" Everything about the old man was gray. His grin made much of Oskar's shabbiness and the signs of debauchment around him.

"I regret you did not see the Garden before the Serpent's visit," Oskar said.

The frank ancient eyes implied he'd run into more than a few lunatics loitering in the crack of dawn.

Something in the old man's face made Oskar want to redeem himself. "I'm surprised you work on Sundays."

"It is only a day." The dustman shrugged. "No Sabbath to me. Any of this you want hauled away?" He glanced around the garden.

His gaze found her then, asprawl in the mud. The dustman drew back. One hand groped behind him for the gate.

"It's all right—"

The old face had lost its equanimity.

Instinctively Oskar moved toward him.

A bolt of dull light shot from a gloved hand.

Oskar froze.

The dustman was holding a knife. *"Der Mörder."* His voice was soft and sounded sad.

"I did not do this," Oskar said stupidly.

"Ah." The long silver beard swayed back and forth in sympathy. "But I must go, you understand, to the police?"

"You don't understand," Oskar said.

The moment he moved, the knife came up. It had a bone handle, a broad short blade with a fierce tip.

Like the old man, Oskar thought, small and homely and unassailable. He raised his hands above his head. "I am nothing to fear," he said.

The old man slowly lowered the knife, but his grip on it did not loosen.

After a minute Oskar, keeping his eyes on the dustman, began to move toward the back of the garden. The sun slipped over the top of the garden wall. Oskar thought he saw a wisp of steam begin to rise from the figure on the ground.

His diagonal journey over the wet brown grass seemed to take forever. When he stubbed his toe on a hard green pear, he stopped. Close enough. Extending one leg, he overturned her with the toe of his boot.

"Die Puppe," he said softly. "You see? Only a . . . toy. And yes, I wish her taken away."

The old man, without haste or apology, returned the knife to his belt. His eyes, avoiding Oskar, no longer looked kindly as he went about his task.

She had never been light . . . and heavier now, sodden. Oskar wanted to help carry her through the ruined garden and lift her up onto the cart. But he could not touch her. And the old man, without a word or glance, made plain that help would be unwelcome.

Oskar turned and went inside.

In the summerhouse, his back to the half-clad altar, he waited for the sound of the latching gate. When he heard it, he looked down. Splinters of garnet glass lay at his feet.

The horse whinnied softly. The wheels of the cart groaned.

Oskar turned around, sank to his knees on the prie-dieu, and gazed up at the painting.

So altered was the work from his memory of it that for an instant he wondered if one of his guests might have tampered with it. Discounting Fritz's occasional amateur dabblings, however, Löwenblatt was the only other painter at the party. Karl would not think of such a prank.

Oskar stared at the painting.

In the foreground a face, white and womanly, vivified with suffering . . . eyes pools of pain above a wanton inconvenient body. She was nothing like what he remembered, a picture of martyred virginity as it might have appeared to Caravaggio's late indecorous eye . . .

While lying in shadows of culpability behind her, he . . .

But no, he was being maudlin. Without the initials in the lower left corner, who on earth would have recognized him there?

Self-portrait with Doll. Oil on canvas, 80 by 120 centimeters. Perhaps in time to be allotted its meager portion of condescending regard:

A rather early work, lacking mastery, *of course. Nonetheless some suggestion of the startling originality that would later come to characterize* . . .

A last caper of the artist's protracted adolescence?

Hardly a major *work in the painter's oeuvre.* Yet clearly a work of art . . . inevitably less than it might have been.

But *done,* Oskar thought. As finished as it can be.

He got up and took the painting down from the wall.

It pulled easily from the frame. He found a sheepskin in the back of the wardrobe. He wrapped the frame and shoved it under the bed.

A stack of canvases leaned in a corner next to the water closet. He added the painting, keeping its face turned to the wall.

SHE LEANED OVER THE BED. THE CAPTAIN HAD BEEN SICK. SHE KNEW THIS. She touched his shoulder lightly. "I must wake you," she said. "I am sorry."

Rolling toward her, he sighed, breathing the odor of illness on her.

"What is it?" His eyes opened slowly.

"The divan must be moved," she said, "before the Direktor comes."

Weak midday sunlight barged in through the windows and the open door. The air was hot and thick and still. Oskar, squinting, sat up and looked around the room. The red glasses and candles . . . even the prie-dieu was gone. But for the divan's empty place, the summerhouse looked just as it should.

Nor would the garden, Oskar knew, betray the night's secrets. He imagined the girl, her back aching with fatigue, stooping to gather a bouquet of crumpled white napkins from the mist.

"I'm sorry," he murmured. He pushed off his blanket and stood up. He had not removed his clothes. Red wine stained his chest like seepage from a wound.

Reserl shook her head. "There is something else," she said.

For the first time he looked at her. Her face was drawn. She was trembling.

"Madame is gone," she whispered.

"Yes," said Oskar. "I know."

She stared at him.

He turned away.

"It's all right," he said. "Never mind."

He would have spoken with greater care but for the awful pain in his head. He could not think. He turned around. He saw that she was crying.

"Reserl," he said.

She covered her face with her hands and whispered through her fingers. "I did not know what to do. I did not know what you wanted."

"Listen," he said, then fell into silence. She was a simple girl, an ignorant servant. How was she to make sense of what he himself did not understand?

"I wish you wouldn't cry," he said. "Everything is all right."

"The glasses." She could not seem to stop weeping.

Oskar's temples throbbed. "You had nothing to do with that, Reserl. You had nothing to do with any of it."

She came out from behind her hands and regarded him with wet, sharp eyes.

"I will tell the Direktor," Oskar said. "He will know you are not at fault."

Reserl, abruptly, turned away, turned as if to leave.

But she did not leave.

"Reserl?" His hand ventured toward the small of her back, then retreated. "The divan must be carried in," he said. "Will you help me?"

She nodded without looking at him.

"Thank you," Oskar said.

She preceded him, by several paces, into the glare of noon.

ODD HOW SMALL DRESDEN LOOKS, HANS POSSE THOUGHT, TO AN EYE grown used to contending with mountains.

The Wall Pavilion's elaborations appeared precious. The Grosser

Garten's trees were a sallow disappointing hue. For an instant the Di-rektor's eye wandered back not to the spas and peaked jade vistas of his holiday, but to the bashful Anhalt village of his birth. *Now I must get used to everything all over again,* he thought.

The small white oval of her face floated in an upper window as the hired car pulled in before the house. Watching for him like a wife. And then, in a trice, there beside him on the cobblestones, her eyes soft at the sight of him, full of gladness and . . . relief?

What is wrong?

He forbade himself to say it.

The quick chapped hands wheedled a valise from his grip. Welcomes were murmured in a voice he could not hear.

The driver, showing off for the girl, hefted a brass-cornered locker to his shoulder and bore it, without invitation, inside.

Posse set down a portmanteau and fumbled in his vest for the tip he now feared inadequate.

When he stooped to reclaim his satchel, it was no longer beside him. He glanced up in time to see her, two bags in each hand, staggering through the front door. Nothing left to carry. Hans Posse paused on his home's first step and coaxed more currency from his billfold.

A warm cinnamon-and-apple scent hovered inside the door. Posse paid his respects to the driver and saw him out. Hulda had vanished. He felt oddly deflated. She was likely seeing to something on the stove. He resisted an impulse to go to the kitchen. He would not wish to embar-rass or addle her with distraction. He imagined returning to the street, gathering up the lost words she had murmured to him and carrying them inside.

There was a muffled thump from above. Light footsteps crossed the bare planks of his bedroom floor. She would be putting his things away. Of course. She should not trouble herself, not when he was perfectly ca-pable . . .

He'd managed in Rathen to find a laundress, a broad-hipped widow in a ramshackle cottage surrounded by ill-natured geese. Her starch was insipid, her iron a bit lax. Still, the Direktor was glad he hadn't six weeks' worth of soiled shirts to drop into the girl's sweet ruddy hands. She looked tired.

He recalled a family that had shared his hotel one week, two little girls in pinafores, one still too young to be in school. The father, a printer from Ravensbrück, wore thick spectacles and appeared nearly as old as Hans Posse . . . an affable fellow, if a tad self-important. The wife could not have been half her husband's age . . . no beauty surely. Yet her calm radiance as she watched her daughters in their white frocks parading hand in hand with their father beside a leek-green pond . . . the devotion with which her eyes replied to her husband's words . . .

The Direktor and the couple had been but briefly introduced. Perfunctory pleasantries supervised by the hotel's jolly chatelaine. Their surname started with *H,* he thought, a commonplace. Heinrich? Hesse? What Hans Posse recalled with disturbing clarity was Hulda, intruding on his mind whenever he saw the family's contentment, his suddenly poor appetite that week the H——s occupied a table near his in the drab little dining room.

Often, those nights, the girl found her way into his dreams.

The Direktor would wake expecting to find himself a younger man . . . a man whose life still had room for . . .

Hans Posse, daydreaming, did not hear her steps on the carpeted stair.

"It is so good that you have come home."

He started at the gentle voice.

She smiled, then said something else.

"I beg your pardon?"

"I said, you must be tired from your journey, I think."

"Oh, no," Posse said. "I find traveling quite restful." Why would he make a claim so far from the truth? "I would rather be here," he said, "than anywhere."

Her regard was grave, as if she could gauge his words' precise weight. She looked so young, hardly more than a child, yet worn.

"Professor Kokoschka," the Direktor said, "he is out?"

"No, sir, he is . . ." Flushed, she looked still younger. "He awoke with a headache. I believe he has gone to rest."

Carousing. Hans Posse smiled. The occasional spree was proper for an unmarried man scarcely past thirty.

The girl, hovering in the doorway, said something. His hearing was getting worse. *"Wie bitte?"*

"You will have dinner—"

"Yes, of course." The devotion in her gaze made his voice gruff.

She looked down.

"I suppose I am a little tired," Hans Posse said.

THE DIREKTOR IS HOME BARELY A WEEK BEFORE HE IS OFF AGAIN. BERLIN, he says. But for only a few days.

"I envy you," the Captain says. "I've had no taste of Berlin's sweet decadence since my Job's afflictions put the Kammerspieltheater to sleep."

"Such modesty!" Hans Posse smiles. "Max Reinhardt—did I tell you I met him? He says they are still talking about you."

"Local custom," Oskar observes. "Berlin talks about you after you've gone."

It is pleasant, Reserl thinks, hearing the men laugh at breakfast. She wishes the Direktor were not leaving.

The Captain, however, seems delighted. "You will be gone . . . ?"

"Just a day or two."

"You ought to stay longer. There is much in Berlin to fathom."

"This auction draws me only by a Bernini sketch. I assure you I shall otherwise suffer, forced to view vast treasure my little museum cannot afford!"

"Loos is there now," Oskar says. "He'd be honored by a visit. You could even see Katja's new play. It opens next week, you know."

"Are you trying to get me sacked? Dear boy, I'm just back from the mountains! The Museum—"

"I've seen its trustees nibbling from your palm, sir. If asked, they'd give you a year's sabbatical in Katmandu!"

The Direktor butters a second piece of toast. "How I envy your extravagance of mind."

He sets the toast, untasted, down on his plate.

Of course. It is no longer warm.

Reserl, unnoticed, hurries out to the kitchen.

KATJA'S CHEERFUL FAREWELL IS A BIT OF A LETDOWN. HE'D EXPECTED ONE of her scenes. At least a little one. She is to be gone several months . . . perhaps even longer if the new theater company's successes continue to mount as they lately have been.

"After Berlin," she says, "Vienna . . . then for a week Stuttgart . . . Munich . . ." She is incandescent with possibility.

"Why would anyone squander a week in Stuttgart?"

His coolness of tone briefly penetrates her self-absorption. "My, aren't we jaded," she says.

The party was only a few days ago, yet she has nothing to say about it? Oskar must admit to himself he is, yes, a little dejected.

"Can you imagine how lonely I shall be?" he says.

"Forgive me if I rather doubt it, my pet. Do you think me so obtuse I'd fail to notice the little bird newly nesting in your . . . branches?"

Of course Katja would notice. Everyone did. He and Malina have been . . . well, and why ever not, when Katja is so blithely abandoning him?

"You're not really in love with her?" She seems merely curious. How he'll miss her jealous rages.

"I am in love *mit dir*," Oskar says. "Darling, you know that."

The unladylike noun she hisses is fortuitously doused by the squealing brakes of her approaching train.

Katja stands on tiptoe and kisses his cheek. Rather perfunctorily, Oskar observes.

"You must always be in love," she says, "with someone."

There is no time to think about it, really. She is gathering up her astonishing retinue of baggage, summoning a porter, slinging various straps over his shoulder. Oskar hopes he will remember later to ponder Katja's theory. Who knows him better?

You must always be in love with someone. It is true. The artist's passion requires attachment to an earthy keepsake. Now that Katja will be gone, why not his little Malina? Yesterday, the morning after dining with her, staying out far too late, he painted from sunup to sundown.

Oskar is herded onto the train, wedged between an elderly porter weighted like a packhorse and Katja, the trailing skirts of her fetching violet travel costume bringing up the rear. Both her hands, in supple cream gloves, are ceremoniously occupied with a flowered hatbox in which, she's confided, she carries her secret diary, as well as her jewels. No thief, she claims, is apt to squander time on *hats*.

Oskar, recalling what Almi could spend on a hat, might differ, but he says nothing. Even I, he thinks, find the subject of her tedious. His goddess. Good thing Herr Gropius is prospering. He'd have hell to pay if he tried to put his Frau on a millinery budget.

Katja strides the length of a crowded passenger car, the hatbox held out in front of her like the Holy Book in the hands of a priest.

"Katja?" Oskar whispers loudly. *"Liebchen?"*

She stops and turns.

"Your ruse might be more effective if you acted as if there were . . . *hats* in there."

"Ssh!" She favors him with a mighty scowl.

"There," Oskar says. "That's better."

Turning, she grinds a heel into the carpeted aisle and plows ahead.

He really *is* going to miss her. He hopes little Malina won't go anywhere, not for a while at least.

AnnaMalinaNiuta . . . his little singing bird . . . a fey and flighty girl with an angel's voice and sweet devilish preoccupations . . .

Oskar, dreaming up diversions to enhance Dresden's appeal for her, licks his lips.

Katja, emerging from her compartment, snatches a bag from his hand.

"Sometimes you look," she says, "remarkably like a cat."

My precious snake-eyed Cossack bird-girl,

There you (presumably) are on your narrow cot in your pernicious little boardinghouse halfway across the city, while I, here in my drafty exile, languish and long and freeze. You might as well be on the other side of the world . . . singing lieder to Incas or Mandarins. How cruel of you, my Malina, to locate yourself anywhere but here beside me. You are a very wicked girl and I intend to see, most personally, to your punishment.

In the anguished interim, however, perhaps these chocolates will sweeten your disposition toward me . . . and maybe even add another delightful ounce to the plump little cushion on which you sit . . . and on which I often, in such wee hours as these, meditate.

Do you find me playful, Niuta? And for that believe me insincere? The first verdict is one I cannot refute . . . but the second? You wrong me, little bird, if you deem my affections inauthentic.

This is perhaps not good news for either of us, but I cannot conceal it: I fear I am falling in love with you.

Are you laughing, Fräulein Kallin? Does my misery merely tickle the rough casing of your hard Russian heart? Dare I trespass again those foreign regions where already I have known mortal wounding?

A temperate guide (our Dr. Neuberger, for instance, or Löwenblatt, my esteemed colleague and chum) might warn me from further intercourse with Mother Russia. Wise counsel, I suppose. Yet there are Russian delicacies my foolhardy cravings cannot resist:

Comrade Fabergé's extortionate eggs.

Incomparable varieties of caviar and sturgeon, sable and roulette.

And—God help me—you.

When will you come to me, Niuta? When will you teach me to sing in this desolate bed?

I must not, you say, "pester" you. Nor use "my wiles" to coerce a precocious union.

Of wiles, my love, you will find in me few. My passion burns pure, and with a steadfast flame no impatient urge can extinguish. You know where my bed may be found, myself within it dreaming of the night you will join me here.

For that bliss I have some patience, but not for this: When, my Malina, may I paint you? When shall I be permitted to try? Shall my simple palette prove equal to the green of your eyes? Their shade I have seen heretofore but once, in the emerald gaze of a bronze snake braceleting a harem woman's slender arm. (In no squalid seraglio, this woman, but a schoolroom. My first teacher, in fact. The salacious green so heedlessly displayed above her wrist has haunted me from the age of seven, yet eluded me until now. Perhaps still to elude me! But will you not allow me to try?)

Ah, is it a painting's duration you fear? The effects upon me of prolonged exposure to your nakedness . . . there might be, I agree, some risk! Condone, then, but a simple drawing. When, oh when, little bird? Please send your message of assent without delay, offering this poor stump of charcoal in my hand the hope of once more leaping to life at the incomparable sight of you.

I turn to you, my darling, to stroke your hair. But I have promised I'll not pester you!

My tongue's kiss is so quick upon you that you will scarcely heed . . .

Yet I taste my Niuta here . . . and here . . . and

Always.

Your Flèche d'Orient

SHE RETURNED IN LATE MORNING FROM THE MARKET, HER NET BAG HEAVY with autumn's fruits: freckled brown pears and flame-colored apples,

tender persimmons and dark grapes. A second bulging bag, rough
burlap, bumped against her shoulder. Two cabbages, each the size of a
man's head. One would have been more than enough . . . but so perfect
and at such a price . . .

Their flesh, below a leafy green casing, was close-woven and white.
Never had she seen such cabbage—almost beautiful, like something he
had transformed with his brush. For a moment she squeezed her eyes
shut, as if her eyelids could screen her thoughts. Then she opened them
and looked around the kitchen. She would scour the bricks. She would
polish the stove. She would make a great cauldron of *Bauernsuppe*. It
would keep well in this cool weather. And the perfect outer leaves saved
for stuffed cabbage. On Thursday, when the Direktor would come
home.

The Captain startled her, coming into the kitchen. She hoped he was
not looking already for lunch. Perhaps she'd dawdled longer than she'd
thought in the market.

"Ah, there you are!" His smile was distracted.

"You are hungry?"

"I wanted to ask you—"

*He would paint her. Today. If only she might wear Frau Posse's
dress . . .*

Reserl set the mesh bag on the table, left the heavier one on her
shoulder, insensible for the moment to its weight.

"Yes?"

*Her face, calm and grave, a perfect stillness framed in a filigree of
lace . . .*

The Captain cast a harried glance in the direction of the garden. "I
have company," he said.

Reserl nodded, careful to conceal her surprise. His clothing was
paint-spattered. He wore the threadbare carpet slippers she still waited
for him to discard. Soon again the mornings will be freezing, she
thought.

"Perhaps you might bring some tea," he said. "In a while. Would you?"

"Your guests will stay to lunch?"

The fine pumpernickel, baked yesterday, was still uncut. A goodly
length of the Direktor's cherished *Jagdwurst*. The cheeses a bit dry by
now, but perhaps if warmed in the sun . . . thank heaven the fruit was
fresh.

"Just bring the tea," the Captain said. "I'll let you know if we want anything more."

The burlap strap cut into her shoulder. Reserl slipped off the sack and lowered it to the floor.

How many guests were there? He hadn't said. It was too late to ask. He had gone out the door.

Probably two, she thought. Visitors most often came in pairs, it seemed. Except Fräulein Richter. But Fräulein Richter was in Berlin.

Reserl covered a silver tray with a round embroidered cloth and, after much thought, set four cups and saucers on it. Surely better to offer too much, she thought, than too little.

With the steeping pot placed in the middle, the tray still had room for a plate of biscuits, a small bowl of fruit. Droplets of water glistened on the grapes, but their midnight skins looked foggy. Grapes were mysterious. Beside them the pears looked plain.

He had left the summerhouse door slightly ajar, perhaps realizing both her hands would be occupied with a tray. Reserl's toe nudged the door open wider. Then she slipped inside.

"Ah, here is our tea."

The teacups rattled. Several biscuits slipped off the plate. The tray nearly fell from her hands.

He stood at his easel, his back to the door. "Just set it down . . . anywhere you find room." He did not turn around.

The room was a shambles, most of it created by the remains of Madame's wardrobe. Hats tilted rakishly atop lamps. Dresses trailed from the bed and chairs, their hems dragging on the floor. Wisps of silk stockings and lingerie lay everywhere. A flounced petticoat, flung over a defunct gaslight fixture, seemed to cling to the ceiling. Boots covered the tops of the bedposts, kicking up their dainty heels.

Fräulein Kallin, reclining on the green divan, wore only a rope of pearls. Niuta, his little singing bird . . .

Anna Kallin twisted her head slightly and looked at Reserl.

"Don't," said the Captain. "I forbid you to move."

"You don't mean I am actually to be allowed tea?" Fräulein Kallin sounded, as rich people often did, as if each word tired her. Was she rich? She stared at Reserl, her eyes sleepy and amused.

"He loves me, he says, yet he treats me like his slave. How am I to believe him?"

She looked at Reserl, but she was talking, of course, to him.

Reserl's face was on fire. She must leave. Where was she to set the tray?

An array of hair combs and gloves, brooches and fans cluttered his writing table. A nosegay of brittle brown flowers. An ivory-handled buttonhook. With a clumsy sweep of her elbow, Reserl swiped at the jumble. Setting down the tray, she heard the brittle sound of something crushed beneath it.

He did not, even then, turn around. His eyes remained faithful to the body on the divan.

Where Reserl's gaze, too, was held. How could this body so neatly have fit into a boy's clothing? Anna Kallin's buttocks and calves, even her arms, were round. Freckled breasts like overripe pears, their nipples the velvety brown of cattails. Her thighs, curving toward her body's center, met in a shock of coppery curls.

With only Madame's body and her own for experience, Reserl was stunned by this other woman's nakedness. She wondered for a moment if Anna Kallin might be one of those fabled creatures possessed of both sexes, if a man's organs lay hidden in that burrow of bright hair.

Fräulein Kallin sat up and stretched.

The Captain groaned, as if in pain. "No, Malina, not yet!"

"You might have informed me your maid was to be included." Her words now did not sound tired.

Reserl could not move.

The Captain hurled a paintbrush. It left an inflamed welt on the floor. He looked at Reserl with cold silver eyes.

Anna Kallin pulled a gold cushion to her chest. "Oskar, what are you up to? Why is she here? I didn't—"

"Hush, Malina, she isn't—"

"*You* hush! I take off my clothes for you . . . no, *not* for you, for *your art.* Then this one appears, she stands staring at me as if . . . you think— what? That you find in me another doll, someone for you to dress and undress with your little helper here to watch?"

"She's a child, Niuta. She means nothing."

Fräulein Kallin covered her face and began to cry.

Reserl stood paralyzed beside the desk.

"Please go."

The Captain moved swiftly toward the woman on the divan. His eyes, already there with her, were anguished. His voice was distant and cold.

"Get out of here, Hulda," he said. "Go on."

A SHEER CURTAIN OF DUST LAY UPON EVERYTHING, AS IF NO ONE HAD come here in many years. But it wasn't true, of course. Here the Direktor had found table linens. And his wife's dress. The Captain had claimed and carried from here the odd and beautiful contraption for worship that she herself, surprised at its weight, had coaxed back up the steep stairs.

The carved wood, the plush padding did show signs of disturbance, yes. One had to look closely. Reserl wondered what name was used for such a thing and why it was in an attic, rather than a church. Surely its proper place was in a church?

The Direktor stored here a great many things, some of them odd, all of them old and beautiful. His wife was beautiful, though not yet, when she died, so old. Reserl had often studied pictures of Frau Posse: the painting over the parlor hearth, the photographs on the tea-colored walls of the Direktor's study. Her skin was very white. Her hands were very small. It had surprised Reserl that no pictures of the Direktor's wife were in his bedroom. He probably did not need pictures to see her there, Reserl thought.

She held the Direktor's wife's dress, carefully wrapped in a clean muslin cloth, out in front of her, as if the Direktor's wife were there to receive it. Reserl feared the dress smelled of her now. She'd been afraid to wash it. The dress was old, the lace collar especially delicate. She had hung it outdoors for hours to air in the shade. Before folding and wrapping the dress, she held it to her nose. It seemed to smell only of fresh air and . . . a faint scent of lilac, perhaps?

Still, one's own scent was too familiar. Reserl had been very nervous the night of the party. Being nervous made her sweat more than heat or hard work. The dress has spoiled a little, she thought, because I have worn it.

Reserl looked slowly around the attic. The Direktor had found the dress here, yes, but where? She studied the dust's patterns. After a while, with the moving of the sun, she noticed that one of two brass-hinged steamer trunks seemed less dusty than the other.

The trunk was not locked. She opened it cautiously. She should not be getting into the Direktor's things without permission, but she did not know how to ask for that. She wanted only to return the dress to its rightful place.

Rightful place . . . there must be a place where everything, where everyone, was meant to be. Kneeling beside the trunk, still holding the borrowed dress out in front of her like an offering, Reserl looked out the attic window. Dresden, too, in its haze of weak autumn sun, looked dusty. The palace was forlorn, the Hofkirche's steeple sooty and stern . . .

Stern and remote, like the Captain: *Please go. Get out of here. Go on.*

I have no place here, Reserl thought. No rightful place.

She was frozen inside.

She means nothing.

It should have been easy to weep.

Reserl sank back, setting the muslin-wrapped dress on her faded green hem, freeing her hands to open the trunk.

She knew as soon as she lifted the lid that she had found the right place. The trunk was filled with women's clothing, carefully folded between layers of the same yellowing tissue in which the Direktor had brought his wife's dress to her.

She placed the dress upon the starched pleats of a stiff-necked linen blouse. Linen the color of cream . . . surely once white, Reserl thought.

As a girl, she had imagined herself in such a blouse, standing in front of a cottage with Emil, her husband, a coddled bed of babies and flowers growing up around them. Each year in a new picture the hand-stitched tucks of her blouse would be beautifully ironed, perfectly white.

Her feet had gone to sleep beneath her. The numbness crept up her legs. Reserl stared sightlessly into the open trunk, without wondering what else it might hold.

THE DIREKTOR, IN HIS STUDY, WAS OUT OF SORTS. SINCE HIS HOLIDAY HE could not seem to concentrate. The trip to Berlin had not helped, of course. Too much rich food, too little money . . . the Bernini sketch was en route to America. Chicago, at that. New York might have been a bit easier to accept.

Hans Posse smiled wryly, catching himself at the snobbery of the thought. Chicago was probably a fine and cultured place. What did he know of America? It was vast, that he knew, its scale unimaginable to a European. Chicago probably had *hotels* larger than Dresden. Not to mention richer, more beautiful. He hoped Bernini would be suitably prized there.

He wrenched his unruly attentions back to the printer's proofs on his desk. The Friedrich monograph was finally to be published, albeit in a rather musty old journal in Berne that no one but musty old critics and curators read. Rereading this work of several months was less than gratifying. Only the printer's outlandish errors kept the article from putting him to sleep. I can probably retire, Posse thought, at least as a critic. I doubt I shall be missed.

The unexpected sound of footsteps above seemed a welcome distraction. It had to be Hulda, of course. Oskar was out for the afternoon, with the charming Fräulein Kallin. What on earth could the girl be doing up there in the attic? Not bothering herself about the dust, he hoped.

Because he was a quiet man, he climbed the stairs quietly, but not stealthily. Still, the girl seemed not to have heard him. She was slumped on her knees in front of one of the old trunks. The trunk was open. She would have seemed to be looking inside it, but for the vacancy of her eyes.

"I am sorry."

It was only when she softly spoke that the Direktor realized she'd become aware of his presence.

"I should ask permission," she said.

"What are you doing, Hulda?"

She bowed her head. "It is not my place," she said. "I know this."

He shook his head, but she was not looking at him. "My dear, you may go wherever you wish."

She raised her face and looked at him.

"I wished to return your wife's dress," she said. "It is here, you see." She gestured toward the trunk.

"I gave it to you," he said. "I meant you to have it."

The girl shook her head. "Thank you, but no."

"It does no good here."

She offered the Direktor a slight, crooked smile. "Nor on me," she said.

Hans Posse sighed.

After a moment, he crossed the attic and held out a hand to her. She hesitated, then took his hand and, wincing, got to her feet.

He looked concerned.

"Pins and needles," she said. Her face was awry with another small smile.

"I wish you would keep the dress," Hans Posse said. "It looks lovely on you."

Pain flickered in her eyes. She slanted her face away.

"You are kind to me," she said. "Always so kind."

"As you are to me. To *us*."

Hans Posse realized he was still holding the girl's hand. He let it go reluctantly. "The dress is here, Hulda." He leaned down to close and latch the trunk. "If ever you would care to have it, you needn't ask. Just come and take what is yours."

"Perhaps if there is another party," she said, still keeping her gaze from him.

Hans Posse's eyes followed hers to the window, an oval glimpse of red roof tiles and watered-silk sky. He wondered what the girl saw. A mere foot from him, yet from where she stood the angle of vision would be entirely different.

She seemed to have forgotten he was beside her.

For a brief moment the Direktor's eyes indulged themselves. Dust motes danced around her on planes of silvery light. The faded green of her dress turned to verdigris. Her face was a perfect stillness, pale as stone.

There is something ancient in her, Hans Posse thought. While I am merely old.

He turned and, without another word or glance, descended the stairs. Not because her sorrow was lost on him. On the contrary. Because he somehow understood at this moment that sorrow might be all the girl possessed.

And that he could offer her nothing.

Nothing at all.

OSKAR SPREADS THE DRAWINGS ACROSS THE RUMPLED BED. *MY LOVES,* HE thinks, then smiles. *A random sampling.*

A painting has been hung above the bed. He does not look at it. No need. It is always there, in the center of his vision, the light by which he sees. *My love.* Anchored by his arm, her face pale and peaceful as death, his own aged and gray with suffering . . . a suffering that he has begun to suspect is . . .

Extravagant.

He studies the drawings on the bed with a critical eye. A swirling sea, a tempest of moonlight, suspended above his head by only a snip of thin wire. He is of course aware of them. He does not glance up.

The drawings on the bed, gleaned from an accumulation of years, have been chosen with a cool and canny eye. He is capable of a rigorous objectivity, Professor Kokoschka, when such is required. He is, in some ways, still an apprentice. Yet already he must serve as his own master. No one else on earth is equal to the task.

All the drawings are nudes. The earliest, a Berlin prostitute, is dated 1911. The most recent, Anna Kallin, was sketched the previous day. Most of the models have long been forgotten. Alma Mahler makes no appearance among them. She is merely the light by which he sees, sees the drawings on the bed, sees everything.

I shall come in time to accept her as one accepts daylight, Oskar thinks. I shall not think of her when I look at the moon.

But there are for now the drawings to consider. He is looking for something.

That little tart of a model—Ulrike, was it?—comes closest, in a way, to what he seeks. It is really only a sketch, idly undertaken to allow his students a few moments' privacy from his scrutiny. He might have done better with her had she shown up the next day, the rest of the week, as she was supposed to. The girl could as easily be dead as unreliable.

Ulrike. Not her real name, surely. Strange he'd remember it. Her fate is beside the point. What matters is the drawing's intensity. A mere sketch, yes, quick and crude, yet somehow it does stand apart from the work that surrounds it.

Ruthlessly, Oskar pushes aside the others, clearing a space around the sketch. Several drawings slide, unnoticed, to the floor. He steps back, better to study the sketch in the middle of the bed. A drawing of Käthe Richter tears under his heel.

Eighteen, the girl said, and French. Her sneer is as false as her claims. Her pose, almost laughably awkward, betrays everything it means to conceal—her innocence, her hunger and cold, her desperation to be desired.

Oskar stares at the drawing for a long time.

Finally, he permits his gaze to rise to the painting. His *Windsbraut*. But he does not see her now, not his bride of the wind, not Alma. Nor does he see a tempest of love that might utterly have destroyed him. Oskar, studying the painting, does not even see himself in it.

After a few minutes, his gaze returns to the drawing. The girl is nothing to him. He does not know her name. He would not care to know her fate. He knows only that he has penetrated her. Nothing else really matters.

When lust stirs his body, Oskar is unsurprised. A natural part of the process, lust, and scarcely a distraction.

He raises his eyes again, deliberately, to *Die Windsbraut*.

Sehen . . . to look. To behold. To perceive. It is everything. To see.

He sees paint.

He sees light.

It is good.

For a moment, Oskar Kokoschka smiles.

His hands meet with a sound like a whip's crack.

"You know nothing," he says. "Can you try, please, to understand this?"

AUTHOR'S NOTE

I am in love with a hundred and one different things, fantasies and people, and finding no fixed point anywhere except in my pictures, at least one of which will, before the year is out, become as joyous and illuminating as almost anything one could imagine, unless one starts to use rockets to paint with.

KOKOSCHKA IN A LETTER TO HIS FAMILY, 1921

Oskar Kokoschka continued his association with the Dresden Academy until 1927. Both his work and his reputation as a painter flourished during this time. His paintings were widely exhibited throughout Europe. A selection of his letters to Hermine Moos was published in 1926 in Berlin.

A prolific writer, Kokoschka also became an influential activist on behalf of peace and human freedom. The artist's most "urgent task," he wrote, is "to make society conscious of the fact that culture affects the life, freedom and happiness of every individual. . . . Our duty is to be honestly critical of everybody and everything."

By the end of 1937, more than four hundred of Kokoschka's works had been confiscated from German museums and impounded by the Nazis. In 1938 the artist fled to London with Olda Palkovská, whom he had met in Prague. The two were married in a Hampstead air raid shelter on May 15, 1941. Kokoschka was fifty-five years old. The marriage lasted until his death.

Kokoschka remained passionately engaged with teaching through most of his life. In 1953 he established the Schule des Sehens, the School of Seeing, in Salzburg. "Let your eyes ring like a tuning fork," he advised his students. "Look suddenly at some object or form, quickly and full of surprise. Record the sight within you and close your eyes. Then you will never forget the colours. Remember, and refresh yourselves with the memory. Only then look at the object again. You will see so much in it that you did not notice the first time."

In 1922 Oskar Kokoschka had a chance encounter with Alma Mahler at the Venice Biennale. Alma divorced Walter Gropius in 1929 and married the writer Franz Werfel. She died in New York at the age of eighty-five. Shortly before her death in 1964, Alma is said to have remarked, "I never really liked Mahler's music, I was never really interested in what Werfel wrote, but Kokoschka, yes, Kokoschka always impressed me."

Oskar Kokoschka briefly returned to what was left of Dresden after the war. He tried to find Hulda but was unable to locate her. Someone had heard she died, but no one could provide details. A rumor, Reserl's death . . . it could not be confirmed.

It seems he did not paint her. But late in his life, Kokoschka would now and then reminisce about the young housemaid who offered him comfort and care in Dresden after the First World War.

It is not difficult to imagine him looking back across a lengthening span of years, catching sight of her. Closing his eyes. Remembering. Looking again.

And perhaps, in time, seeing what once escaped him.

Oskar Kokoschka died on February 22, 1980, just before his ninety-fourth birthday.

ACKNOWLEDGMENTS

This book is a work of imagination, an imagination given license to play fast and loose with historical fact. The essential facts were generously provided, first and foremost and all along, by Frank Whitford's captivating biography, *Oskar Kokoschka: A Life* (Atheneum, 1986).

Other works I have shamelessly ransacked are: *Alma Mahler, or The Art of Being Loved* by Françoise Giroud (Oxford University Press, 1991); *The Bride of the Wind: The Life of Alma Mahler* by Susanne Keegan (Viking, 1992); *Oskar Kokoschka Letters 1905–1976,* selected by Olda Kokoschka and Alfred Marnau (Thames and Hudson, 1992); and the Solomon R. Guggenheim Museum's centenary catalog, *Oskar Kokoschka, 1886–1980* (texts by Richard Calvocoressi and Katharina Schulz, 1986).

Deepest gratitude also to Lotte Povar of Bristol, Rhode Island, for translating Oskar Kokoschka's letters to Hermine Moos into English for me. A true mitzvah: Only under their spell could I make them, at last, my own.

My editor at Morrow, Patricia Lande Grader, has been lavish with her kindly, insightful, meticulous attentions on these pages. She also, at a difficult time, restored my confidence in them. My gratitude to her is beyond expressing.

Esther Newberg is an incomparable literary agent. When my father first met her, he said it eased his mind to know she'd be there to look out for me. I remember this because he hardly ever gave me advice without being asked: "You listen to her," he said. "This is someone who will never let you down." I have, and she hasn't. Mark Mooney was a man of unerring instincts. How lucky can a person get, having a father like that and a friend like Esther besides?

Finally and with all my heart, I thank my sister, Gael. It was she who first told me about Oskar Kokoschka and the doll from Stuttgart. Then she let me borrow her copy of the Whitford biography. That was nearly ten years ago. I still have not returned the book. I offer her this one instead, in the hope she may see in it some reflection of all I have learned from her about patience and courage, about how the eye is meant to be used, and how the soul's sense of direction is to be trusted.